J. J. Connington and The Murder Room

>>> This title is part of The Murder Room, our series dedicated to making available out-of-print or hard-to-find titles by classic crime writers.

Crime fiction has always held up a mirror to society. The Victorians were fascinated by sensational murder and the emerging science of detection; now we are obsessed with the forensic detail of violent death. And no other genre has so captivated and enthralled readers.

Vast troves of classic crime writing have for a long time been unavailable to all but the most dedicated frequenters of second-hand bookshops. The advent of digital publishing means that we are now able to bring you the backlists of a huge range of titles by classic and contemporary crime writers, some of which have been out of print for decades.

From the genteel amateur private eyes of the Golden Age and the femmes fatales of pulp fiction, to the morally ambiguous hard-boiled detectives of mid twentieth-century America and their descendants who walk our twenty-first century streets, The Murder Room has it all. **>>>**

The Murder Room
Where Criminal Minds Meet

themurderroom.com

J. J. Connington (1880–1947)

Alfred Walter Stewart, who wrote under the pen name J. J. Connington, was born in Glasgow, the youngest of three sons of Reverend Dr Stewart. He graduated from Glasgow University and pursued an academic career as a chemistry professor, working for the Admiralty during the First World War. Known for his ingenious and carefully worked-out puzzles and in-depth character development, he was admired by a host of his better-known contemporaries, including Dorothy L. Sayers and John Dickson Carr, who both paid tribute to his influence on their work. He married Jessie Lily Courts in 1916 and they had one daughter.

By J. J. Connington

Sir Clinton Driffield Mysteries
Murder in the Maze (1927)
Tragedy at Ravensthorpe
  (1927)
The Case with Nine Solutions
  (1928)
Mystery at Lynden Sands
  (1928)
Nemesis at Raynham Parva
  (1929)
  (a.k.a. *Grim Vengenace*)
The Boathouse Riddle (1931)
The Sweepstake Murders
  (1931)
The Castleford Conundrum
  (1932)
The Ha-Ha Case (1934)
  (a.k.a. *The Brandon Case*)
In Whose Dim Shadow (1935)
  (a.k.a. *The Tau Cross Mystery*)
A Minor Operation (1937)

Murder Will Speak (1938)
Truth Comes Limping (1938)
The Twenty-One Clues (1941)
No Past is Dead (1942)
Jack-in-the-Box (1944)
Common Sense Is All You
  Need (1947)

Supt Ross Mysteries
The Eye in the Museum (1929)
The Two Tickets Puzzle (1930)

Novels
Death at Swaythling Court
  (1926)
The Dangerfield Talisman
  (1926)
Tom Tiddler's Island (1933)
  (a.k.a. *Gold Brick Island*)
The Counsellor (1939)
The Four Defences (1940)

The Castleford Conundrum

J. J. Connington

An Orion book

Copyright © The Professor A. W. Stewart Deceased Trust 1932, 2014

The right of J. J. Connington to be identified as the author of this work has been asserted in accordance with the Copyright, Designs and Patents Act 1988.

This edition published by
The Orion Publishing Group Ltd
Orion House
5 Upper St Martin's Lane
London WC2H 9EA

An Hachette UK company
A CIP catalogue record for this book is available from the British Library

ISBN 978 1 4719 0607 7

www.orionbooks.co.uk

CONTENTS

Introduction
by
Curtis Evans

During the Golden Age of the detective novel, in the 1920s and 1930s, J. J. Connington stood with fellow crime writers R. Austin Freeman, Cecil John Charles Street and Freeman Wills Crofts as the foremost practitioner in British mystery fiction of the science of pure detection. I use the word 'science' advisedly, for the man behind J. J. Connington, Alfred Walter Stewart, was an esteemed Scottish-born scientist. A 'small, unassuming, moustached polymath', Stewart was 'a strikingly effective lecturer with an excellent sense of humor, fertile imagination and fantastically retentive memory', qualities that also served him well in his fiction. He held the Chair of Chemistry at Queens University, Belfast for twenty-five years, from 1919 until his retirement in 1944.

During roughly this period, the busy Professor Stewart found time to author a remarkable apocalyptic science fiction tale, *Nordenholt's Million* (1923), a mainstream novel, *Almighty Gold* (1924), a collection of essays, *Alias J. J. Connington* (1947), and, between 1926 and 1947, twenty-four mysteries (all but one tales of detection), many of them sterling examples of the Golden Age puzzle-oriented detective novel at its considerable best. 'For those who ask first of all in a detective story for exact and mathematical accuracy in the construction of the plot', avowed a contemporary *London Daily Mail* reviewer, 'there is no author to equal the distinguished scientist who writes under the name of J. J. Connington.'[1]

Alfred Stewart's background as a man of science is reflected in his fiction, not only in the impressive puzzle plot mechanics he devised for his mysteries but in his choices of themes and depictions of characters. Along with Stanley Nordenholt of *Nordenholt's Million*, a novel about a plutocrat's pitiless efforts to preserve a ruthlessly remolded remnant of human life after a global environmental calamity, Stewart's most notable character is Chief Constable Sir Clinton Driffield, the detective in seventeen of the twenty-four Connington crime novels. Driffield is one of crime fiction's most highhanded investigators, occasionally taking on the functions of judge and jury as well as chief of police.

Absent from Stewart's fiction is the hail-fellow-well-met quality found in John Street's works or the religious ethos suffusing those of Freeman Wills Crofts, not to mention the effervescent novel-of-manners style of the British Golden Age Crime Queens Dorothy L. Sayers, Margery Allingham and Ngaio Marsh. Instead we see an often disdainful cynicism about the human animal and a marked admiration for detached supermen with superior intellects. For this reason, reading a Connington novel can be a challenging experience for modern readers inculcated in gentler social beliefs. Yet Alfred Stewart produced a classic apocalyptic science fiction tale in *Nordenholt's Million* (justly dubbed 'exciting and terrifying reading' by the *Spectator*) as well as superb detective novels boasting well-wrought puzzles, bracing characterization and an occasional leavening of dry humor. Not long after Stewart's death in 1947, the Connington novels fell entirely out of print. The recent embrace of Stewart's fiction by Orion's Murder Room imprint is a welcome event indeed, correcting as it does over sixty years of underserved neglect of an accomplished genre writer.

Born in Glasgow on 5 September 1880, Alfred Stewart had significant exposure to religion in his earlier life. His father was William Stewart, longtime Professor of Divinity and Biblical Criticism at Glasgow University, and he married Lily Coats, a daughter of the Reverend Jervis Coats and member of one of

Scotland's preeminent Baptist families. Religious sensibility is entirely absent from the Connington corpus, however. A confirmed secularist, Stewart once referred to one of his wife's brothers, the Reverend William Holms Coats (1881–1954), principal of the Scottish Baptist College, as his 'mental and spiritual antithesis', bemusedly adding: 'It's quite an education to see what one would look like if one were turned into one's mirror-image.'

Stewart's J. J. Connington pseudonym was derived from a nineteenth-century Oxford Professor of Latin and translator of Horace, indicating that Stewart's literary interests lay not in pietistic writing but rather in the pre-Christian classics ('I prefer the *Odyssey* to *Paradise Lost*,' the author once avowed). Possessing an inquisitive and expansive mind, Stewart was in fact an uncommonly well-read individual, freely ranging over a variety of literary genres. His deep immersion in French literature and supernatural horror fiction, for example, is documented in his lively correspondence with the noted horologist Rupert Thomas Gould.[2]

It thus is not surprising that in the 1920s the intellectually restless Stewart, having achieved a distinguished middle age as a highly regarded man of science, decided to apply his creative energy to a new endeavor, the writing of fiction. After several years he settled, like other gifted men and women of his generation, on the wildly popular mystery genre. Stewart was modest about his accomplishments in this particular field of light fiction, telling Rupert Gould later in life that 'I write these things [what Stewart called tec yarns] because they amuse me in parts when I am putting them together and because they are the only writings of mine that the public will look at. Also, in a minor degree, because I like to think some people get pleasure out of them.' No doubt Stewart's single most impressive literary accomplishment is *Nordenholt's Million*, yet in their time the two dozen J. J. Connington mysteries did indeed give readers in Great Britain, the United States and other countries much diversionary reading pleasure. Today these works constitute an estimable addition to British crime fiction.

After his 'prentice pastiche mystery, *Death at Swaythling Court* (1926), a rural English country-house tale set in the highly traditional village of Fernhurst Parva, Stewart published another, superior country-house affair, *The Dangerfield Talisman* (1926), a novel about the baffling theft of a precious family heirloom, an ancient, jewel-encrusted armlet. This clever, murderless tale, which likely is the one that the author told Rupert Gould he wrote in under six weeks, was praised in *The Bookman* as 'continuously exciting and interesting' and in the *New York Times Book Review* as 'ingeniously fitted together and, what is more, written with a deal of real literary charm'. Despite its virtues, however, *The Dangerfield Talisman* is not fully characteristic of mature Connington detective fiction. The author needed a memorable series sleuth, more representative of his own forceful personality.

It was the next year, 1927, that saw J. J. Connington make his break to the front of the murdermongerer's pack with a third country-house mystery, *Murder in the Maze*, wherein debuted as the author's great series detective the assertive and acerbic Sir Clinton Driffield, along with Sir Clinton's neighbor and 'Watson', the more genial (if much less astute) Squire Wendover. In this much-praised novel, Stewart's detective duo confronts some truly diabolical doings, including slayings by means of curare-tipped darts in the double-centered hedge maze at a country estate, Whistlefield. No less a fan of the genre than T. S. Eliot praised *Murder in the Maze* for its construction ('we are provided early in the story with all the clues which guide the detective') and its liveliness ('The very idea of murder in a box-hedge labyrinth does the author great credit, and he makes full use of its possibilities'). The delighted Eliot concluded that

Murder in the Maze was 'a really first-rate detective story'. For his part, the critic H. C. Harwood declared in *The Outlook* that with the publication of *Murder in the Maze* Connington demanded and deserved 'comparison with the masters'. 'Buy, borrow, or – anyhow – get hold of it', he amusingly advised. Two decades later, in his 1946 critical essay 'The Grandest Game in the World', the great locked-room detective novelist John Dickson Carr echoed Eliot's assessment of the novel's virtuoso setting, writing: 'These 1920s [. . .] thronged with sheer brains. What would be one of the best possible settings for violent death? J. J. Connington found the answer, with *Murder in the Maze*.' Certainly in retrospect *Murder in the Maze* stands as one of the finest English country-house mysteries of the 1920s, cleverly yet fairly clued, imaginatively detailed and often grimly suspenseful. As the great American true-crime writer Edmund Lester Pearson noted in his review of *Murder in the Maze* in *The Outlook*, this Connington novel had everything that one could desire in a detective story: 'A shrubbery maze, a hot day, and somebody potting at you with an air gun loaded with darts covered with a deadly South-American arrow-poison – *there* is a situation to wheedle two dollars out of anybody's pocket.'[3]

Staying with what had worked so well for him to date, Stewart the same year produced yet another country-house mystery, *Tragedy at Ravensthorpe*, an ingenious tale of murders and thefts at the ancestral home of the Chacewaters, old family friends of Sir Clinton Driffield. There is much clever matter in *Ravensthorpe*. Especially fascinating is the author's inspired integration of faerie folklore into his plot. Stewart, who had a lifelong – though skeptical – interest in paranormal phenomena, probably was inspired in this instance by the recent hubbub over the Cottingly Faeries photographs that in the early 1920s had famously duped, among other individuals, Arthur Conan Doyle.[4] As with *Murder in the Maze*, critics raved about this new Connington mystery. In the *Spectator*, for example, a reviewer hailed *Tragedy at Ravensthorpe* in the strongest terms, declaring of the novel: 'This is more than a good detective tale. Alike in plot, characterization, and literary style, it is a work of art.'

In 1928 there appeared two additional Sir Clinton Driffield detective novels, *Mystery at Lynden Sands* and *The Case with Nine Solutions*. Once again there was great praise for the latest Conningtons. H. C. Harwood, the critic who had so much admired *Murder in the Maze*, opined of *Mystery at Lynden Sands* that it 'may just fail of being the detective story of the century', while in the United States author and book reviewer Frederic F. Van de Water expressed nearly as high an opinion of *The Case with Nine Solutions*. 'This book is a thoroughbred of a distinguished lineage that runs back to "The Gold Bug" of [Edgar Allan] Poe,' he avowed. 'It represents the highest type of detective fiction.' In both of these Connington novels, Stewart moved away from his customary country-house milieu, setting *Lynden Sands* at a fashionable beach resort and *Nine Solutions* at a scientific research institute. *Nine Solutions* is of particular interest today, I think, for its relatively frank sexual subject matter and its modern urban setting among science professionals, which rather resembles the locales found in P. D. James' classic detective novels *A Mind to Murder* (1963) and *Shroud for a Nightingale* (1971).

By the end of the 1920s, J. J. Connington's critical reputation had achieved enviable heights indeed. At this time Stewart became one of the charter members of the Detection Club, an assemblage of the finest writers of British detective fiction that included, among other distinguished individuals, Agatha Christie, Dorothy L. Sayers and G. K. Chesterton. Certainly Victor Gollancz, the British publisher of the J. J. Connington mysteries, did not stint praise for the author, informing readers that 'J. J. Connington is now established as, in the opinion of many, the greatest living master of the story of pure detection. He is one of those who, discarding all the superfluities, has made of deductive fiction a genuine minor art, with its own laws and its own conventions.'

Such warm praise for J. J. Connington makes it all the more surprising that at this juncture the esteemed author tinkered with his successful formula by dispensing with his original series detective. In the fifth Clinton Driffield detective novel, *Nemesis at Raynham Parva* (1929), Alfred Walter Stewart, rather like Arthur Conan Doyle before him, seemed with a dramatic dénouement to have devised his popular series detective's permanent exit from the fictional stage (read it and see for yourself). The next two Connington detective novels, *The Eye in the Museum* (1929) and *The Two Tickets Puzzle* (1930), have a different series detective, Superintendent Ross, a rather dull dog of a policeman. While both these mysteries are competently done – the railway material in *The Two Tickets Puzzle* is particularly effective and should have appeal today – the presence of Sir Clinton Driffield (no superfluity he!) is missed.

Probably Stewart detected that the public minded the absence of the brilliant and biting Sir Clinton, for the Chief Constable – accompanied, naturally, by his friend Squire Wendover – triumphantly returned in 1931 in *The Boathouse Riddle*, another well-constructed criminous country-house affair. Later in the year came *The Sweepstake Murders*, which boasts the perennially popular tontine multiple-murder plot, in this case a rapid succession of puzzling suspicious deaths afflicting the members of a sweepstake syndicate that has just won nearly £250,000.[5] Adding piquancy to this plot is the fact that Wendover is one of the imperiled syndicate members. Altogether the novel is, as the late Jacques Barzun and his colleague Wendell Hertig Taylor put it in *A Catalogue of Crime* (1971, 1989), their magisterial survey of detective fiction, 'one of Connington's best conceptions'.

Stewart's productivity as a fiction writer slowed in the 1930s, so that, barring the year 1938, at most only one new Connington appeared annually. However, in 1932 Stewart produced one of the best Connington mysteries, *The Castleford Conundrum*. A classic country-house detective novel, Castleford introduces to readers Stewart's most delightfully unpleasant set of greedy relations and one of his most deserving murderees, Winifred Castleford. Stewart also fashions a wonderfully rich puzzle plot, full of meaty material clues for the reader's delectation. *Castleford* presented critics with no conundrum over its quality. 'In *The Castleford Conundrum* Mr Connington goes to work like an accomplished chess player. The moves in the games his detectives are called on to play are a delight to watch,' raved the reviewer for the *Sunday Times*, adding that 'the clues would have rejoiced Mr. Holmes' heart.' For its part, the *Spectator* concurred in the *Sunday Times*' assessment of the novel's masterfully constructed plot: 'Few detective stories show such sound reasoning as that by which the Chief Constable brings the crime home to the culprit.' Additionally, E. C. Bentley, much admired himself as the author of the landmark detective novel *Trent's Last Case*, took time to praise Connington's purely literary virtues, noting: 'Mr Connington has never written better, or drawn characters more full of life.'

With *Tom Tiddler's Island* in 1933 Stewart produced a different sort of Connington, a criminal-gang mystery in the rather more breathless style of such hugely popular English thriller writers as Sapper, Sax Rohmer, John Buchan and Edgar Wallace (in violation of the strict detective fiction rules of Ronald Knox, there is even a secret passage in the novel). Detailing the startling discoveries made by a newlywed couple honeymooning on a remote Scottish island, *Tom Tiddler's Island* is an atmospheric and entertaining tale, though it is not as mentally stimulating for armchair sleuths as Stewart's true detective novels. The title, incidentally, refers to an ancient British children's game, 'Tom Tiddler's Ground', in which one child tries to hold a height against other children.

After his fictional Scottish excursion into thrillerdom, Stewart returned the next year to his English country-house roots with *The Ha-Ha Case* (1934), his last masterwork in this classic mystery setting (for elucidation of non-British readers, a ha-ha is a sunken wall, placed so as to delineate property boundaries while not obstructing views). Although *The Ha-Ha Case* is not set in Scotland, Stewart drew inspiration for the novel from a notorious Scottish true crime, the 1893 Ardlamont murder case. From the facts of the Ardlamont affair Stewart drew several of the key characters in *The Ha-Ha Case*, as well as the circumstances of the novel's murder (a shooting 'accident' while hunting), though he added complications that take the tale in a new direction.[6]

In newspaper reviews both Dorothy L. Sayers and 'Francis Iles' (crime novelist Anthony Berkeley Cox) highly praised this latest mystery by 'The Clever Mr Connington', as he was now dubbed on book jackets by his new English publisher, Hodder & Stoughton. Sayers particularly noted the effective characterisation in *The Ha-Ha Case*: 'There is no need to say that Mr Connington has given us a sound and interesting plot, very carefully and ingeniously worked out. In addition, there are the three portraits of the three brothers, cleverly and rather subtly characterised, of the [governess], and of Inspector Hinton, whose admirable qualities are counteracted by that besetting sin of the man who has made his own way: a jealousy of delegating responsibility.' The reviewer for the *Times Literary Supplement* detected signs that the sardonic Sir Clinton Driffield had begun mellowing with age: 'Those who have never really liked Sir Clinton's perhaps excessively soldierly manner will be surprised to find that he makes his discovery not only by the pure light of intelligence, but partly as a reward for amiability and tact, qualities in which the Inspector [Hinton] was strikingly deficient.' This is true enough, although the classic Sir Clinton emerges a number of times in the novel, as in his subtly sarcastic recurrent backhanded praise of Inspector Hinton: 'He writes a first class report.'

Clinton Driffield returned the next year in the detective novel *In Whose Dim Shadow* (1935), a tale set in a recently erected English suburb, the denizens of which seem to have committed an impressive number of indiscretions, including sexual ones. The intriguing title of the British edition of the novel is drawn from a poem by the British historian Thomas Babington Macaulay: 'Those trees in whose dim shadow/The ghastly priest doth reign/The priest who slew the slayer/And shall himself be slain.' Stewart's puzzle plot in *In Whose Dim Shadow* is well clued and compelling, the kicker of a closing paragraph is a classic of its kind and, additionally, the author paints some excellent character portraits. I fully concur with the *Sunday Times*' assessment of the tale: 'Quiet domestic murder, full of the neatest detective points [. . .] These are not the detective's stock figures, but fully realised human beings.'[7]

Uncharacteristically for Stewart, nearly twenty months elapsed between the publication of *In Whose Dim Shadow* and his next book, *A Minor Operation* (1937). The reason for the author's delay in production was the onset in 1935–36 of the afflictions of cataracts and heart disease (Stewart ultimately succumbed to heart disease in 1947). Despite these grave health complications, Stewart in late 1936 was able to complete *A Minor Operation*, a first-rate Clinton Driffield story of murder and a most baffling disappearance. A *Times Literary Supplement* reviewer found that *A Minor Operation* treated the reader 'to exactly the right mixture of mystification and clue' and that, in addition to its impressive construction, the novel boasted 'character-drawing above the average' for a detective novel.

Alfred Stewart's final eight mysteries, which appeared between 1938 and 1947, the year of the author's death, are, on the whole, a somewhat weaker group of tales than the sixteen that appeared between 1926 and 1937, yet they are not without interest. In 1938 Stewart for the last time managed to publish two detective novels, *Truth Comes Limping* and *For Murder Will Speak* (also published as *Murder Will Speak*). The latter tale is much the superior of the two, having an interesting suburban setting and a bevy of female characters found to have motives when a contemptible philandering businessman meets with foul play. Sexual neurosis plays a major role in *For Murder Will Speak*, the ever-thorough Stewart obviously having made a study of the subject when writing the novel. The somewhat squeamish reviewer for *Scribner's Magazine* considered the subject matter of *For Murder Will Speak* 'rather unsavory at times', yet this individual conceded that the novel nevertheless made 'first-class reading for those who enjoy a good puzzle intricately worked out'. 'Judge Lynch' in the *Saturday Review* apparently had no such moral reservations about the latest Clinton Driffield murder case, avowing simply of the novel: 'They don't come any better'.

Over the next couple of years Stewart again sent Sir Clinton Driffield temporarily packing, replacing him with a new series detective, a brash radio personality named Mark Brand, in *The Counsellor* (1939) and *The Four Defences* (1940). The better of these two novels is *The Four Defences*, which Stewart based on another notorious British true-crime case, the Alfred Rouse blazing-car murder. (Rouse is believed to have fabricated his death by murdering an unknown man, placing the dead man's body in his car and setting the car on fire, in the hope that the murdered man's body would be taken for his.) Though admittedly a thinly characterised academic exercise in ratiocination, Stewart's *Four Defences* surely is also one of the most complexly plotted Golden Age detective novels and should delight devotees of classical detection. Taking the Rouse blazing-car affair as his theme, Stewart composes from it a stunning set of diabolically ingenious criminal variations. 'This is in the cold-blooded category which [. . .] excites a crossword puzzle kind of interest,' the reviewer for the *Times Literary Supplement* acutely noted of the novel. 'Nothing in the Rouse case would prepare you for these complications upon complications [. . .] What they prove is that Mr Connington has the power of penetrating into the puzzle-corner of the brain. He leaves it dazedly wondering whether in the records of actual crime there can be any dark deed to equal this in its planned convolutions.'

Sir Clinton Driffield returned to action in the remaining four detective novels in the Connington oeuvre, *The Twenty-One Clues* (1941), *No Past is Dead* (1942), *Jack-in-the-Box* (1944) and *Commonsense is All You Need* (1947), all of which were written as Stewart's heart disease steadily worsened and reflect to some extent his diminishing physical and mental energy. Although *The Twenty-One Clues* was inspired by the notorious Hall-Mills double murder case – probably the most publicised murder case in the United States in the 1920s – and the American critic and novelist Anthony Boucher commended *Jack-in-the-Box*, I believe the best of these later mysteries is *No Past Is Dead*, which Stewart partly based on a bizarre French true-crime affair, the 1891 Achet-Lepine murder case.[8] Besides providing an interesting background for the tale, the ailing author managed some virtuoso plot twists, of the sort most associated today with that ingenious Golden Age Queen of Crime, Agatha Christie.

What Stewart with characteristic bluntness referred to as 'my complete crack-up' forced his retirement from Queen's University in 1944. 'I am afraid,' Stewart wrote a friend, the chemist and forensic scientist F. Gerald Tryhorn, in August 1946, eleven months before his death, 'that I shall never be much use again. Very stupidly, I tried for a session to combine a full course of lecturing with angina pectoris; and ended up by establishing that the two are immiscible.' He added that since retiring in 1944, he had been physically 'limited to my house, since even a fifty-yard crawl brings on the usual cramps'. Stewart completed his essay collection and a final novel before he died at his study desk in his Belfast home on 1 July 1947, at the age of sixty-six. When death came to the author he was busy at work, writing.

More than six decades after Alfred Walter Stewart's death, his J. J. Connington fiction is again available to a wider audience of classic-mystery fans, rather than strictly limited to a select company of rare-book collectors with deep pockets. This is fitting for an individual who was one of the finest writers of British genre fiction between the two world wars. 'Heaven forfend that you should imagine I take myself for anything out of the common in the tec yarn stuff,' Stewart once self-deprecatingly declared in a letter to Rupert Gould. Yet, as contemporary critics recognised, as a writer of detective and science fiction Stewart indeed was something out of the common. Now more modern readers can find this out for themselves. They have much good sleuthing in store.

1. For more on Street, Crofts and particularly Stewart, see Curtis Evans, *Masters of the 'Humdrum' Mystery: Cecil John Charles Street, Freeman Wills Crofts, Alfred Walter Stewart and the British Detective Novel, 1920–1961* (Jefferson, NC: McFarland, 2012). On the academic career of Alfred Walter Stewart, see his entry in *Oxford Dictionary of National Biography* (London and New York: Oxford University Press, 2004), vol. 52, 627–628.
2. The Gould-Stewart correspondence is discussed in considerable detail in *Masters of the 'Humdrum' Mystery*. For more on the life of the fascinating Rupert Thomas Gould, see Jonathan Betts, *Time Restored: The Harrison Timekeepers and R. T. Gould, the*

Man Who Knew (Almost) Everything (London and New York: Oxford University Press, 2006) and *Longitude,* the 2000 British film adaptation of Dava Sobel's book *Longitude: The True Story of a Lone Genius Who Solved the Greatest Scientific Problem of His Time* (London: Harper Collins, 1995), which details Gould's restoration of the marine chronometers built by in the eighteenth century by the clockmaker John Harrison.

3. Potential purchasers of *Murder in the Maze* should keep in mind that $2 in 1927 is worth over $26 today.

4. In a 1920 article in *The Strand Magazine,* Arthur Conan Doyle endorsed as real prank photographs of purported fairies taken by two English girls in the garden of a house in the village of Cottingley. In the aftermath of the Great War Doyle had become a fervent believer in Spiritualism and other paranormal phenomena. Especially embarrassing to Doyle's admirers today, he also published *The Coming of the Faeries* (1922), wherein he argued that these mystical creatures genuinely existed. 'When the spirits came in, the common sense oozed out,' Stewart once wrote bluntly to his friend Rupert Gould of the creator of Sherlock Holmes. Like Gould, however, Stewart had an intense interest in the subject of the Loch Ness Monster, believing that he, his wife and daughter had sighted a large marine creature of some sort in Loch Ness in 1935. A year earlier Gould had authored *The Loch Ness Monster and Others,* and it was this book that led Stewart, after he made his 'Nessie' sighting, to initiate correspondence with Gould.

5. A tontine is a financial arrangement wherein shareowners in a common fund receive annuities that increase in value with the death of each participant, with the entire amount of the fund going to the last survivor. The impetus that the tontine provided to the deadly creative imaginations of Golden Age mystery writers should be sufficiently obvious.

6. At Ardlamont, a large country estate in Argyll, Cecil Hambrough died from a gunshot wound while hunting. Cecil's tutor, Alfred John Monson, and another man, both of whom were out hunting with Cecil, claimed that Cecil had accidentally shot himself, but Monson was arrested and tried for Cecil's murder. The verdict delivered was 'not proven', but Monson was then – and is today – considered almost certain to have been guilty of the murder. On the Ardlamont case, see William Roughead, *Classic Crimes* (1951; repr., New York: New York Review Books Classics, 2000), 378–464.

7. For the genesis of the title, see Macaulay's 'The Battle of the Lake

Regillus', from his narrative poem collection *Lays of Ancient Rome.* In this poem Macaulay alludes to the ancient cult of Diana Nemorensis, which elevated its priests through trial by combat. Study of the practices of the Diana Nemorensis cult influenced Sir James George Frazer's cultural interpretation of religion in his most renowned work, *The Golden Bough: A Study in Magic and Religion.* As with *Tom Tiddler's Island* and *The Ha-Ha Case* the title *In Whose Dim Shadow* proved too esoteric for Connington's American publishers, Little, Brown and Co., who altered it to the more prosaic *The Tau Cross Mystery.*

8. Stewart analysed the Achet-Lepine case in detail in 'The Mystery of Chantelle', one of the best essays in his 1947 collection *Alias J. J. Connington.*

1
THE FIRST CAMP

As Philip Castleford came down the broad stairs, a faint burst of laughter reached him through the closed door of the drawing room. At the sound of his wife's shrill titter rising above the bass of the two men's voices, he winced and gave vent to his spleen in an ejaculation, all the more vehement because it was uttered under his breath.

"Damn those people!"

In that concise imprecation he included his wife, the two brothers of her first husband, and her companion, Constance Lindfield. He hesitated for a moment at the foot of the stair, trying to brace himself to face that hostile group; but his mental conflict was a pure make-believe, like a stage-fight with its foregone conclusion. In a weak attempt to keep up his self-respect he pretended that he was considering whether to join the others or not, though all the while he knew that he could not force himself to enter the drawing-room that night.

The Glencaple brothers' visits were never pleasant to him, but that night's dinner had been even worse than usual. He had sat at the head of the table, nominally the master of the house but almost totally ignored by everybody. When he tried to join in the general talk, a cool glance and a monosyllabic reply was the best he got; someone else cut in with a fresh topic; and he was left out in the cold. Without being definitely offensive, they had made it quite plain that they weren't interested in anything he had to say. A child forcing itself into a conversation between adults might have

1

been disposed of in much the same manner. It wasn't exactly snubbing, but it came to much the same thing in its results.

His daughter had come off rather better, which was always something to be thankful for. Kenneth Glencaple, turning his red face and stolid eyes upon her from time to time, had flung isolated sentences across the table, enough to recognise Hilary's existence without encouraging her to talk freely. Laurence Glencaple had been a shade more considerate. In his faintly cynical way he had made some attempt to draw her out; but whenever she spoke more than a sentence or two, her stepmother or Constance Lindfield had skilfully edged her out of the talk and turned the current into some fresh channel.

Most galling of all to Castleford, during that dinner, was the knowledge that the very bread he ate was paid for with Glencaple money and that the two brothers never forgot the fact. His wife had been the widow of the third Glencaple, the rich one, and now enjoyed his whole fortune. Naturally enough, a country doctor like Laurence or a struggling business man like Kenneth would be jealous of a stranger—"and one of these damned out-at-elbows artists, too, of all things"—established in their brother's stead and sharing in the income which he had left.

He might have got over that, if there had been any common ground between him and them; but they seemed to take pains to prove that there was none. Over their coffee that night, after the women had left the room, the two brothers had discussed bridge (which he detested), stock exchange quotations (in which he took no interest), and some acquaintances of theirs (whom he had never met). Tacitly he was shut out from their confabulation. In their eyes he was not the host, though he sat at the head of the table; and they took no pains to hide their view of his position.

When they rose to pass into the drawing-room, he had left them and gone upstairs, making the feeble excuse that he had forgotten something or other that he needed. They hadn't waited for him—just as he expected. He could take refuge in his study, if he chose, for no one would miss him.

2

While he was still hesitating over that foregone conclusion, with his eyes fixed on the closed door of the drawing-room, he heard a light step on the stairs above. A graceful, fair-haired girl came down, carrying some sewing in her hands. Castleford moved aside to let her pass.

"Are you going into the drawing-room, Hilary?" he asked as she reached his side.

His daughter's tone, in her reply, was that of one discussing a purely impersonal question.

"I don't think I'm wanted there."

Castleford could well believe that. Hilary, at twenty, was apt to draw men's attention away from her stepmother. On her side, the rivalry was quite unconscious; but Winifred, fifteen years older, preferred not to risk comparisons when they could be avoided. Nothing definite was ever said, but Hilary knew very well that her stepmother was best pleased if she slipped away on some pretext when male visitors were about. Winifred wanted men to talk to her, not to waste time on her stepdaughter.

The interruption had given Castleford time to find the excuse which was to salve his self-esteem. After all, his wife and the Glencaples were a sort of family party. It was reasonable enough to leave them to themselves, in case they might want to discuss any Glencaple affairs.

In turning towards the study, Hilary caught sight of something lying on the hall table.

"That's Dr. Glencaple's bag, isn't it?" she asked carelessly as she passed. "He might have taken it with him to the cloak-room when he came in."

"I suppose he wanted to have it handy," her father suggested. "I expect he's brought a fresh supply of insulin tonight. The last lot's almost exhausted."

Laurence Glencaple had certainly made a success of Winifred's case with that stuff, he reflected. He had got her practically back to normal, apparently, barring the strict dieting and the substitution of saccharin for sugar in her tea and coffee. It was hardly surprising

3

that she swore by him. That gave him a pull with her. Castleford made a wry face as he thought of it. He could guess well enough how that pull was being exerted, just then. His wife had no knack of concealing her thoughts; and from remarks which she dropped now and again, it was easy to divine the sapping and mining which the Glencaple brothers were doing in order to induce her to alter her will.

Castleford wondered how much his daughter saw of these things. There was nothing of the sphinx about Hilary; and yet he could never be sure what she was thinking about or how much she noticed. She had an air of watchful reserve, always, when her stepmother was present. He had shirked telling his daughter what his exact position was. Occasionally she rebelled against some edict of her stepmother's, and for the sake of peace he had to make an appeal to her on personal grounds. "Do it on my account, please. I don't want a row." Hilary was fond of him and had hitherto given in without difficulty; but sooner or later, now she was grown up, that explanation would have to come.

Hilary led the way into the study, placed a reading-lamp beside her chair, and prepared to begin her sewing. Her father, when she had settled herself, chose a deep armchair near hers and dropped into it with a faint sigh of satisfaction. Here at least he was free from all the little pin-pricks and petty discomforts which made up the background of his life.

For some minutes Hilary busied herself with her work. Then, without looking up, she made an apparently casual observation:

"I didn't know the Glencaples were coming to dinner tonight."

"Neither did I, till the dressing-gong rang," Castleford admitted. "She only told me as I was going upstairs."

Between father and daughter, the stepmother was never given a name. Winifred was always "She" or "Her" to them. When she married Castleford, eight years back, she had suggested that her stepdaughter should call her "Mother"; but Hilary, without a direct refusal, evaded the point by omitting any form of address when she spoke to Winifred. To third parties she spoke of "Mrs. Castleford."

She made no comment on her father's last remark. As she sat intent upon her sewing, Castleford watched her for a moment or two with quiet satisfaction. They might despise him, in that house, but they could find no fault with Hilary's appearance, at any rate. The reading-lamp showed up her profile, clean-cut as a cameo, and he studied it, feature by feature, with regret that his days of miniature painting were over. She would have made a better model than most of those he had used in the old days. No wonder Winifred kept Hilary out of the way when men were about, he mused with a certain grim satisfaction. A girl like this was hardly the foil for his wife, who looked her full thirty-five years. And Winifred had no intellectual gifts to throw into the scale. All her talk, in that affected drawl of hers, was the merest chatter about trifles; her knowledge of current events was drawn entirely from the pictures in the illustrated papers; her enthusiasms were all for shams of one sort or another—anything that seemed "out of the common." Her one engrossing topic was dress; and yet, though she spent a small fortune on her wardrobe, she never seemed to get a result which Hilary achieved on her tiny allowance.

Castleford pulled his pouch from his pocket and began to fill his pipe. He paid for his own tobacco. It, at any rate, was not bought with Glencaple money, and could therefore be enjoyed without afterthoughts. He stuffed the bowl left-handedly, for his right hand lacked the index and the top joint of the middle finger; but the injury was evidently of long standing, since he showed no awkwardness in his manipulation.

"She allowed that cub to stay up for dinner tonight," he observed when he had got his pipe well alight. "I suppose that was because his father was here. His manners don't improve."

The "cub" was Kenneth Glencaple's boy. Kenneth lived in a town some fifty miles away and the child had been sent to stay with the Castlefords during his school holidays to give him a chance to get over a recent illness. He was a flabby, pasty-faced youngster; but Winifred, who had no children of her own, had taken a fancy to him; and Castleford had a suspicion that young Francis might be a pawn in the game the Glencaples were playing.

5

"Connie Lindfield's given him a present—a rook-rifle," Hilary explained briefly. "It came by the late parcel post, and I expect he was burning to get dinner over so that he could get back to it."

"I'm not sure it's quite the toy for him," her father said doubtfully. "See that you keep out of his neighbourhood if he starts shooting round about here. He's a thoroughly careless little brute. He might easily do a lot of harm."

"He's a horrible little creature!" Hilary broke in. "I caught him this morning, round by the garage, when I went to get out the car. Guess what he was doing. He'd got hold of a wretched little black kitten. He was drowning it in a bucket of water, holding it under with a mop. Then, when it was at the last gasp, the little fiend took it out and let it revive again before he put it back. 'Making the fun last longer,' he said quite seriously when I caught him at it. I'm in his black books because I stopped him."

"I hope you didn't make a fuss with her about it," Castleford muttered, avoiding her eyes.

Hilary caught the note of apprehension in his voice and bent over her work again as she answered.

"Not I. What good would it do? Of course she'd have backed up her little Frankie. It would just have been raising trouble for nothing. He'd lie his way out of any scrape. He doesn't know what truth is, that child."

"He's not exactly straight, I know," her father admitted. "But after all . . ."

Now that Hilary had had her say, it was safer to change the subject. One never knew who might happen to overhear an incautious remark in that house. The less said, the better.

"Making a new evening frock?" he asked, leaning forward to examine her work.

Hilary saw that he wanted to change the subject. She lifted the fabric from her knee and held it out for inspection. But though Castleford looked it over with apparent interest, his thoughts were elsewhere. Hilary had clever hands. If he had been able to give her some proper training and set her up with capital, she might have

6

made herself independent. But things had turned out very differently from what he had hoped.

He came back with a start to the present, to find Hilary's big hazel eyes fixed upon him. She was hesitating over something she wanted to say, and wondering if this was the best moment to approach the subject. Her father looked more than usually worried tonight. Perhaps she had better postpone things. But then, nowadays, he never seemed to be anything but worried, though he tried to put a good face on it. Apparently something encouraged her, for after a second or two she decided to risk it.

"I suppose you couldn't increase that allowance of mine, Father?"

Then, at the involuntary blink which he gave as he heard her request, she hurried on to tone down her demand.

"Oh, I don't mean double it, or anything like that. But just a little more, if you can spare it. I'm frightfully hard up."

The change in his expression showed her that she had embarked on a forlorn hope.

"It's no odds, really," she assured him, without waiting for the verbal confirmation of his decision. "I just thought I'd ask, in case . . ."

She began fervently to wish that she hadn't broached the subject. She hated to add another worry to those he had already. And he would worry at having to refuse, she knew quite well. After all, it would just be possible to scrape along on her present allowance, though it meant using the same frock a good deal oftener than she cared about. The pin-money that had served for a girl of sixteen or seventeen didn't seem to go far when you added four or five years to her age. It was a very tight squeeze, nowadays, even if she could make some things for herself to save expense. And she was fond of clothes. Some girls dress to attract men; others like to outdo other women. Hilary dressed to please herself first and foremost; and in doing so, she managed to achieve in a great measure the other two aims. Still, if her allowance couldn't be increased, there was no good in whining. She suppressed a natural sigh of disappointment and bent over her work again.

Castleford was spared the awkwardness of an immediate reply. The study door opened, and they both glanced up at the unexpected intruder: Winifred's half-sister.

Constance Lindfield was one of the powers behind the throne in that divided house. She was handsome, in a hard way, rather than pretty. Firm lips and a businesslike manner gave her an air of competence and decision. At thirty-three, she had lost the freshness of youth; but she did her best to replace it by scrupulous attention to her appearance. Her dark hair, in some mysterious manner, always seemed to have been freshly waved. Her lips and eyebrows were, if anything, a shade too carefully tended. The polish on her nails was almost obtrusively evident. Perhaps she overdid it a trifle. Her natural advantages seemed a little lost under that brilliant finish. Yet she did not spend undue time over the battery of toilette appliances which crowded her dressing-table. She had the knack of doing things quickly, systematically, and thoroughly.

Her women-friends did not deny her a certain degree of charm. Some men she attracted by her looks or by her quick intelligence. Others were repelled by a certain insensitiveness and by her obvious desire to exert what she termed "sex-attraction." But this desire she took care to curb when Mrs. Castleford was present. Then, quite naturally, she slipped into the background, leaving the field to her senior.

She did not come farther than the threshold of the room.

"Oh, Hillie, you're to bring the car round at half-past eleven tomorrow. Winnie wants you to drive her over to Sunnydale."

Hilary glanced up, evidently unpleasantly surprised.

"But she told me this afternoon that she didn't want the car tomorrow. I've fixed up a foursome for the morning."

Miss Lindfield shrugged her shoulders almost imperceptibly, as though to indicate that she cared nothing about the matter.

"Oh, of course, if you can't manage it . . ." she said. "I'll tell Winnie you can't go."

Her tone implied quite plainly: "Refuse if you like. You'll catch it; and I shan't care."

Hilary glanced across at her father and saw a mute appeal in his eyes. Mrs. Castleford was a fool in many ways, but in others she manifested a certain cunning. If Hilary displeased her, she left the girl alone but vented her spite on her husband, counting on the girl's affection for her father to bring her to heel rather than have him badgered on her account. It was a shrewd bit of tactics and almost invariably it proved successful.

On this occasion, however, Hilary set some store by her golf fixture. She made an effort to save it.

"I'm partnered with Dick Stevenage. Last week we'd arranged to play a single and I had to cancel it. I don't like to let him down twice running."

Miss Lindfield seemed to consider for a moment.

"I'll play instead of you, if you like," she suggested with the air of making a concession, though a faint undertone of eagerness was apparent in her voice.

Hilary did not seem to welcome the proposal.

"Wouldn't it do just as well if I ran her over to Sunnydale later on in the morning?" she asked.

Very occasionally Miss Lindfield would condescend to intervene on her behalf; but she could never count on it. It depended on Miss Lindfield's mood. She was sparing in her favours to Hilary and freakish in her choice of the occasions when she bestowed them. Tonight, evidently, she was not in a helpful frame of mind.

"You'd better go and ask Winnie herself," she suggested.

This time the shrug she gave was unconcealed. It meant: "Well, if you won't take my way out of the difficulty, find one of your own." The suggestion of a direct application to Winifred was obviously not meant seriously. Hilary knew quite well what would happen if she tried that. She would have to go, that very moment, into the hostile atmosphere of the drawing-room; and there her petition would be curtly refused under the cynical eyes of the two Glencaples. To take that course would be merely courting humiliation.

"It's hardly worth it," she said, ambiguously, concealing her chagrin as well as she could. "I'll ring up someone to take my place in the foursome."

If Miss Lindfield wouldn't help, Hilary decided, then she should not have the chance of replacing her as Dick Stevenage's partner. What a fool she had been to mention Dick's name at all! She ought to have remembered that Miss Lindfield might want to play with him and would seize the chance of keeping Hilary out of the way instead of helping her.

Miss Lindfield betrayed no disappointment at the sidetracking of her proposal. Her faint gesture said quite plainly: "Just as well you've caved in."

"I'll tell Winnie you'll be ready at half-past eleven, then," she rejoined, as she closed the door behind her.

Castleford had been a silent and embarrassed spectator of the scene. To intervene would merely have been to throw away the last chance that Constance Lindfield would take pity on Hilary. She had no love for him, and would have seized the occasion to strike at him through his daughter. As for persuading his wife to change her whim, he knew from experience how futile any attempt on his part would be. It would simply mean a peevish argument with a foregone conclusion. His convenience or Hilary's meant nothing to Winifred. In many ways she was more like a spoilt child than a grown woman. Opposition to even her lightest caprice was sure to rouse her obstinacy.

He hunched his shoulders into the yielding back of the deep armchair and pulled nervously at his pipe. It was mortifying to see this sort of thing going on, and yet be unable to lift a finger to stop it. He glanced covertly across at his daughter, whose eyes were fixed on her work. What could Hilary think of it all? She must look on him as a poor sort of father to have, a man who couldn't even assert himself in a case like this. He saw that long-postponed explanation would have to be made. Hilary was old enough to draw her own conclusions about the worst side of the position; and if she could do that, she might as well hear what could be said for the defence. After all, there was nothing actually discreditable in the affair.

Hilary looked up, caught his eye, and looked down again. When she spoke, it was characteristic of her that she left the major grievance unmentioned and concentrated on a minor point.

"I wish they wouldn't call me 'Hillie.' I hate the sound of it."

Castleford nodded a thoughtful agreement. He hated it too. Why should anyone want to corrupt "Hilary" into "Hillie" for the sake of saving a syllable? But in this house, no one ever seemed to be given their full name except by himself and his daughter. He lived in an atmosphere of diminutives. Constance Lindfield was "Connie"; Laurence Glencaple was "Laurie"; Kenneth was cut down to "Ken" or "Kennie" and his child was "Frankie" or "Frankie-boy." Winifred liked people to call her "Winnie," possibly because it sounded young. As for Castleford himself, he had never heard his own name since he came to Carron Hill. He was "Phil" to all of them, except when in moments of expansion—now grown rare—his wife addressed him as "Phillie." It was like going back to the nursery. Some unconscious pedantry in his nature rebelled against all that sort of thing. It was a trifle, of course, just like a crumb in a bed; but trifles grow to exasperation-point if one has to suffer them for long enough. One loses perspective under the continual irritation.

Hilary put aside her sewing and rose from her seat.

"I'll have to ring up somebody to take my place," she said rather ruefully. "I'll be back again in a minute or two."

Castleford turned slightly in his chair and watched her go out of the room. She seemed to have fought down her vexation, as she always did, nowadays. It wasn't because she had a yielding nature, he remembered. As a small child she had been rather a spitfire. But since she grew up she had controlled her temper, so far as outward signs went, though he sometimes wondered what was going on behind that calm exterior.

This business of the car was especially mean. Winifred could quite well afford to keep a chauffeur, but her spirit of petty economy had suggested to her that Hilary might serve instead. The girl was not asked to clean the car; the gardener had been taught to do that. But Hilary was expected to give up any of her own engagements if the car was needed. Winifred had always refused to learn to drive it herself; and though Constance Lindfield could drive when it suited her to do so, she generally left Hilary to take her

11

stepmother out. There would have been no harm in it, had there been any spirit of give-and-take in the matter. After all, Hilary lived in the house at her stepmother's expense and it was not unreasonable that she should do something to make herself useful. What made it hard was that Winifred cared for the convenience of no one but herself; and this car-driving demand was made without the slightest consideration for the girl's feelings or for her private engagements.

Castleford pulled moodily at his pipe and meditated, for the thousandth time, upon his situation. Only one thing could set them both free from this entanglement. Hilary might get married, and then the problem would almost solve itself. Winifred held him in her grip only because of Hilary. Once the girl was safely provided for, he could fend for himself.

"If I had my hands free," he assured himself bravely, "I'd bring that woman to her bearings—and double-quick, too."

What Castleford feared was that Hilary, exasperated by her position, might take the bit in her teeth and marry the first man who asked her, merely in order to escape from Carron Hill. That might be merely a jump from the frying-pan into the fire. At twenty, a girl may fall in love with a detrimental just as readily as with a decent man. Dick Stevenage, for instance. And at the thought of him Castleford's mouth twitched as though he had bitten on a sore tooth. Hilary seemed rather keen on that young scoundrel. He was always about Carron Hill, nowadays, hanging on to Winifred's skirts, giving Constance Lindfield the glad eye when Winifred was safely out of the way, and, lately, running after Hilary when both the others were off the map. Stevenage! Castleford cared little enough for Winifred, but still . . . nobody likes to see another man coming between him and his wife. And even at the worst, he supposed he'd have to put up with it. A divorce would throw Hilary and himself on the world.

"Damn the whole lot of them!" he cursed under his breath, with all the bitterness of a weak man who is denied any more direct outlet for his feelings.

2
A MARRIAGE OF CONVENIENCE

Hilary's return interrupted his train of thought.

"I've got someone to take my place," she explained as she gathered up her work and settled herself again in her chair.

She went on with her sewing in silence for a few minutes; but the quick, nervous movements of her needle betrayed her exasperation at this new display of her stepmother's wanton disregard for her arrangements. At last she put her work on the arm of her chair and looked across at Castleford.

"Why did you ever think of marrying her, Father?"

Castleford would have preferred her to couple the question with a recital of grievances. There was an ominous brevity about it which left him no loop-hole to escape into side-issues. He took his pipe from his mouth and made a helpless gesture with his mutilated hand.

"I did it for the best; really I did, Hilary."

Intent though she was upon her own grievances, his daughter was startled by the note in his voice. His disappointed hopes, his years of repression embittered by petty vexations, his exasperation at the fresh-scored humiliations of that evening, a certain shame at his position, and an appeal for sympathy from the only creature to whom he could turn: all were blended in that feeble justification. For once, that carefully-concealed misery had found expression.

It was not the tone that surprised Hilary; it was the intensity of it. She had not been so blind as Castleford had hoped. Where her father was concerned, she had sharp eyes and quick ears; and behind the screen of her reserve she had noted and remembered trifle after trifle, until she had built up a very fair structure of evidence. Had she chosen to do so, she could have given him a shrewd description of the lie of the land at Carron Hill. She had no illusions about the state of affairs. What she did not know was the chapter of accidents which led up to it.

Her father had married a second time when she was still a mere child. He had offered no explanations then; and in later years he seemed to shrink from giving any, even when she left him an opening. Now she had determined to force his confidence; and she had been aghast at the feeling which he betrayed in that single sentence. She had always looked on him as bent on quietness for the sake of quietness—"Don't let's have a fuss!"—and she had faintly resented his attitude, both on his own account and especially when she herself was sacrificed to maintain it. For the first time, she had got a glimpse of the misery which lay behind his patient manner.

When she spoke, her response was to his tone and not to his words.

"I'm sorry. I really didn't mean to hurt you. You know I didn't?"

Castleford's gesture acquitted her. Then he put his pipe back in his mouth, clenched his teeth on it, and stared before him for a moment or two. He was trying to find the best opening for the tale he had to tell, and it seemed a task of some difficulty.

"You don't remember your mother?" he began at length. "Not clearly, at any rate, I expect. She was something like you—the same eyes and hair, and about your height, too."

"I've seen your miniature of her," Hilary answered, mechanically picking up her work again. "I don't remember her very clearly, of course. I was only about eight when she died, wasn't I?"

Castleford nodded. That miniature was another of the things which he had to suppress. He kept it in a locked despatch-box upstairs, and looked at it only when he was alone. It was one of the best things he had ever achieved, vivid and subtle. More than mere craftsmanship had gone to the making of it; and now it was condemned to lie in the dark.

14

"If your mother had lived, things would have been different," he said in a tone which invested the truism with vitality. "She was like you; she didn't mind taking risks. I've always been too inclined to play for safety, myself, I'm afraid. She took a risk when she married me, for I was only twenty-two and I'd no reputation as a miniaturist, then, of course. She had some money—a hundred a year or so—and I had about the same. Just enough to live on, and no more, in these days. But she believed in me, you know; and she spurred me on. She took the risk."

He seemed to be speaking his thoughts aloud rather than addressing Hilary.

"She took the risk. I don't think I'd have done it if it had been left to me. But it turned out all right, as it happened. I got some sort of clientele together even quicker than we expected; I suppose my work must have been good enough to please people. Anyhow, we managed to do more than make ends meet. And then you were born, and that made more difference than you'd think."

He glanced across at his daughter with a faintly whimsical look which she was glad to see.

"So wonderful as all that?" she demanded, encouraging him.

"No, not so wonderful—rather an ugly baby, we had to admit. Disappointing in an artistic family, if anything. Still, we made the best of you, dreamed all sorts of dreams over your cradle, you know, just like any ordinary young couple, and made great plans for your future."

Hilary heard the sigh with which that sentence closed and hastened to force him on from something which had evidently cost a pang in the recollection.

"And then?"

"Oh, then, I worked twice as hard as before, and things turned out really very well for a time. In four years or so, I was quite on my feet—very lucky, really. And then came the war."

"The war?" Hilary queried.

Evidently she had been expected to understand that reference without explanation.

"Yes, the war," Castleford went on. "Of course there was a demand for miniatures; it didn't die out all at once. Here and there you'd find a girl wanting to give her officer sweetheart something to take with him; but not many of them came my way. I tried for a commission myself, but they turned me down on some point or other. They were more particular about small defects in those days than they were later, and they rejected me because one of my ears wasn't up to scratch—scarlet fever when I was a boy."

He got up, knocked out his pipe on an ashtray, and pulled out his pouch as he came back to his chair.

"The bottom seemed to fall out of things, just then. You're too young to remember anything about it. We were back where we started, you understand; no commissions came in and we'd have been on the rocks if we hadn't had that couple of hundred a year behind us. Your mother never seemed to lose heart over it, though; it was just one of the risks, I suppose; that was the way she looked at it. And then, quite unexpectedly, I got something steady—you'd never guess what."

"What was it?" Hilary asked, refusing to waste energy in guessing.

"There were all sorts of queer jobs in the war, you know," her father went on. "The rummest sort of things suddenly turned out to be essential, things one could never have imagined being useful at all in war-time. I got one of them: they wanted miniature painters at the Admiralty."

"Whatever for?" Hilary demanded in astonishment. Then a hazy recollection of something crossed her mind. "Oh, something to do with camouflaging ships, painting them so that the submarines were put off, was that it?"

"Dazzle-painting? No, it wasn't that. You don't need a miniature-painter to put weird streaks on a ship's sides. It was compass-card lettering."

"Compass-cards?" Hilary was evidently no wiser.

"For night compasses," Castleford explained. "Ships had to sail at night without a light showing even in the binnacle, so they put the lettering on the compass-cards with radium paint. That paint was worth a small fortune, you know—between £400 and £500 per ounce, someone told me once—so naturally they didn't want to waste it. And who could do fine work of that sort—the fine lettering on the cards—better than a miniature-painter who was trained in minute technique? And, of course, later on, they needed much the same kind of thing for the compasses of night-flying aeroplanes. There was plenty to keep the lot of us busy; and for the rest of the war I was painting nothing but the tiny lettering on these cards. It was trying to the eyes, after a while, but it wasn't heroic. Still, I suppose I did as much good there as I'd have done elsewhere. What they paid for the work was enough to keep us all afloat; and we were glad to see it coming in, your mother and I."

His voice trailed off into a silence for some seconds, as though he had forgotten Hilary was listening.

"Then came the Armistice," he continued, "and naturally they sacked the lot of us. Things were pretty black for a while, with no commissions coming in and prices up. How your mother managed it, I don't know, but we seemed to get along somehow or other. Then, in 1919, came that Spanish influenza epidemic; your mother went down with it . . ."

Again his voice dropped and halted for a time.

"I don't want to talk about it," he resumed, with an obvious effort. "It put the whole world out of joint for me; but you'd never understand how I felt, even if I tried to let you see it. I depended on her so much in ways I only realised after she was gone. You were what kept me straight; I had to pull through somehow on your account, you see? And still commissions didn't come in; and I had to begin nibbling at capital to keep afloat. It wasn't an easy time, round about then, anything but easy."

"And then?" Hilary interjected, lest he should add to his depression with these old griefs.

"Then? Well, it got worse, after that: prices up, cost of living rising, taxation enormous—not that I had much of an income to pay on—and our capital oozing away week by week. I had to keep up some sort of appearance, you know, with a view to commissions. Shabbiness wouldn't pay; clients didn't like it, naturally enough. And all the while, there was your future to think of, you see? That was at the back of my mind all the time; every cheque I drew on my capital account seemed a bit of safety whittled away from you."

With a quite unwonted demonstrativeness, Hilary slipped across and knelt down beside his chair. The gesture was enough; he needed no words to tell him that she understood what store he had set by her.

"You see the position, don't you?" he went on. "I—*we* were sliding downhill week by week and there seemed no way of pulling up again. I was nearly frantic with worry over it—not so much on my own account as yours, really. And then, unfortunately, I got a tip from a man who dabbled in shares. Dunlops were what he talked about. Sure to go up, he said; one could make three or four times one's capital easily. I hung back for a while. You see, I never took much interest in stocks and shares; they're out of my line and I don't understand speculation. Then, as I got more and more worried over our money affairs, I thought of your mother. I knew quite well what she would have said: 'Take a risk.'"

He stared in front of him for a moment, even lost in memories.

"Well, between one thing and another, I made up my mind at last to take a risk in Dunlops. I sold most of the investments I had— it was no time for half-measures, I felt—and I put the proceeds into Dunlops. You've no idea how I felt in the next few weeks; it was like a dream come true. Those shares went up and up; every day I used to read the quotations and they went higher and higher. I'd got over the safety-line and when I sold out we'd have enough money behind us to make you secure for life."

He made an inarticulate sound which was half groan, half sigh.

"If only I'd had any sense! But when I thought of selling, the man who had given me the tip cried out against it. Dunlops were going far higher yet, he knew; and I thought I might hold on for a week longer, just to snatch a little extra profit. And then the market broke. Of course I was a fool at that game; I thought it was just a temporary set-back and that it would be silly to sell. And I went on thinking that, knowing no better, until all the profit was gone, and most of my original capital had followed it. At the end of that speculation, I'd hardly anything left—a few hundred pounds, perhaps, which might bring in enough income to starve on, not more. That was a bad time.

"And then, after all, the tide turned again. Commissions started to flow in; I began to make a decent income; and bit by bit I was moving on the road towards a modest reputation in my own line. It was the big boom after the war; the profiteers were spending their money royally; and a good many of their wives wanted their faces painted on the flat as well as on the skin. Why most of them risked it is a mystery to me; but that didn't matter. I was making money again; that was all I cared about, even if it meant painting the portraits of human pug-dogs. And, after all, some of them weren't quite like that, you know. Things looked quite bright, then.

"And after that flash of sun, there came the slump. Everybody was hard up, or felt they were. Too hard up, at any rate, to want miniatures for family heirlooms, I expect. Before long, I was back where I'd been before. Like everyone else, I'd thought the boom would go on for ever; I hadn't bothered to be careful with money—I mean I hadn't saved every penny that I might have done. So when the boom collapsed, I wasn't much better off than I'd been at the start, after the Dunlop crash.

"I made just enough to let us keep afloat, but now, you see, Hilary, things were different altogether. My ideas had expanded a bit during that stretch when I had a big paper profit in Dunlops. I'd been planning all sorts of things for you: boarding-school, and after that Paris or Switzerland for a couple of years, and then a year abroad for the two of us. That had all been possible—on paper. After all that day-dreaming, poverty was a good deal harder than it had been before, somehow.

"And I'd got one idea ingrained into my mind by all that set of experiences—security for you. I didn't expect to get another chance; things looked too black for that; but I made up my mind that if any chance came my way, I'd take it, no matter what it was, so long as it meant that you'd be all right if anything happened to me. We've no relations, you know, and the idea of my dying and leaving you stranded in the world used to keep me awake at nights. I had some money invested; but the Dunlop affair had made me afraid even for the soundest investments. I'm a child in these things; I quite admit it; and the Dunlop business had turned me into a burned child.

"Then—and this was the last straw—something went wrong with my heart. I couldn't be sure how bad it was; I was afraid the doctors were lying to me and concealing the gravity of the case; and I had visions of a sudden collapse leaving you absolutely stranded. You were only eleven, then. The medicals told me I'd brought it on with anxiety; and that unless I stopped worrying, I'd go from bad to worse. Much good that advice did! I used to wake in the night with my heart beating sixteen to the dozen and a lump in my throat—*globus hystericus*, I think they call it and I'd lie there for hours, racked with anxiety on your account. Again and again I swore to myself that I'd take any chance that offered, anything, no matter what, so long as it meant that you'd be protected if anything happened to me."

He glanced down at Hilary with a mute question in his eyes.

"I really do understand," she reassured him. "Poor Father! I never guessed it was like that. She came along, wasn't that it?"

"That was it," Castleford went on. "I'm not trying to justify myself, even to you, Hilary. I'm simply explaining things. She came along. At first she was a client, merely. Some acquaintance had given her my name, and she wanted a miniature of herself. Then, during the sittings she gave me, we talked a good deal and I learned something about her. Her husband had been a war-profiteer in a small way—an ironmonger, or something, of that sort, who'd blossomed out a bit—and then when he'd made his pile, the 'flu epidemic took him off. She'd plenty of money to spend; and to judge from one thing and another, she seemed to spend it freely.

"I took care to make that miniature on the flattering side; you know it, in the drawing-room? It turned out that she painted in an amateurish way herself; and by-and-by she asked me to give her some lessons. I saw a good deal of her, on that excuse; and I had more than a suspicion that she had taken a fancy to me. I was better-looking then than I am now, you know. And I set myself to make that fancy stronger, not quite deliberately, in cold blood; but still with a feeling that I might as well see what came of it. It sounds beastly when one puts it into words, I know. I didn't want her at all, but I did want her money on your account; and between the two, I suppose I got into a sort of blow-hot, blow-cold attitude which, as it happened, was just the very one to goad her on. You know what she's like, Hilary; if she wants a thing, she must have it, and she must have it *now*, cost what it may. Well, before long, I was the thing she wanted. She wasn't in love with me—not in the way I understand falling in love, at any rate; but I was something she'd set her fancy on just then, and she meant to have me, even if she threw me aside again within a month, afterwards.

"And then, before I'd really made up my mind to it, a thing happened which forced the decision on me. It left me no way out. She used to hire cars, in those days; and now and again she'd take me away with her for the day in one. It was at the end of one of these days. She was dropping me on the way home; and I'd got out of the car. It was a touring car, and I stood on the pavement talking to her, with my hand on the car. I didn't notice what I was doing, and she didn't notice my hand, I suppose. Anyhow, she leaned over and slammed the door on my fingers."

He held up his mutilated hand.

"You see what that cost. By the time they'd operated, my livelihood was gone. You and I were done for. That decided me, you see. There was no way out, except the one. Of course she was in a great state over the accident and the result—or at least she seemed to be. I shouldn't like to say how much was pity and remorse in it and how much was just 'getting what she wanted.' She practically threw herself at my head while I was still an interesting invalid. I had no option that I could see. I let her have her way. I was desperate, you know.

"And she was so eager to do anything, anything whatever that I hinted at. She altered her will immediately after we were married, and made provision for both you and me, in case she died. I was devilish grateful; how could I have been anything else? You were sent to a decent school; I came to live here at Carron Hill. I still had some remnants of pride, and I paid my own way so far as my

21

little income ran to it—tailor's bills, tobacco, all that kind of thing; but of course she saw to the running of the place and all the household expenses. She could well afford that. And I never sponged on her for money."

His pipe had gone out, and he paused to relight it, possibly with the idea of giving Hilary time to consider what he had told her.

"Well, that's how it happened," he said at last. "I'm not trying to justify myself; but it means a good deal to me, how you look at it, Hilary. I've always shirked telling you the story, because I'm not proud of it; but there it is, anyhow," he ended, weakly.

Hilary reflected for a moment or two, while he waited in anxiety.

"I don't see anything to be ashamed of," she reassured him. "She crippled you, and she owed you a good deal more for that than she could pay any other way. Plenty of people get married without being in love. And you did it for me. I couldn't throw stones if I wanted to; and there's nothing to throw stones at, even if I wanted to. I'm glad you told me all about it. If you hadn't, I'd never have guessed how much you've done for me. I'll try to make up for it, now that I know."

Her tone said much more than her words. Castleford knew, with immense relief, that she thought the more of him now that his tale was told. He knew he had played an unheroic part, and it was a comfort to find that she had weighed his difficulties against his conduct.

"I may as well finish the story," he recommenced, in a less halting tone. "We were married at a registry office, quite quietly. She insisted on it; and it wasn't until afterwards that I understood why she wanted it. She had a pretty good idea what the two Glencaples would think of it; and she took the line of facing them with a *fait accompli*. They had no grounds for objecting, of course; she was her own mistress, even if she was their brother's widow. But she had more than a suspicion that if the thing came out beforehand, these two would do their best to dissuade her; and she didn't want to be dissuaded, since she'd set her mind on getting her own way.

"I met them first after the marriage. We didn't get on. I don't blame them, because in the meantime they'd discovered that she'd altered her will in my favour, and that cut them out of it. I expect

I'd have felt sore myself, if I'd been in their shoes; it's only human nature, after all.

"The Glencaples weren't the only surprise she sprang on me. Shortly after her husband died, she'd taken on that half-sister of hers as a companion. Just before she met me, the Lindfield woman's sister had to go to South Africa for her health—lungs gone wrong—and someone had to go with her to look after her. So that Lindfield woman went off there, and was away until after our marriage. Then when the sister died, Winifred brought Constance Lindfield back here again to her old post as companion, without saying a word to me about the matter. And, naturally, that trusted companion wasn't exactly pleased to find a husband installed here when she arrived at Carron Hill. Besides, I'd objected to her being taken on again, and that was a black mark against me from the start."

"I've never liked her," said Hilary, briefly.

"She's never liked us," Castleford returned. "And she's worse than the Glencaples, you know, for she's always on the premises. I get a rest from the Glencaples between times; but that Lindfield woman is always at one's elbow. She'd established a regular ascendancy here, before I appeared on the scene; she's in too strong a position to shake. And half the trouble about the place could be traced back to her, I'm pretty sure, if one could follow up the trail. She hates me. I suppose she counted on making a good thing out of her position here, one way and another; and no doubt she expected to come in for a good thing under the old will, if anything happened. I believe she was down for a fair sum in it. Now, she wouldn't get much."

Hilary thought for some moments in silence after he ceased speaking.

"Couldn't we get away from here?" she demanded at last. "I wouldn't mind pinching, not really, so long as we could get out of this house."

Castleford shook his head mournfully.

"Do you think we'd be here now, if it could be helped?" he asked. "It can't be done. I can't make money now that I've lost these fingers. I'm no good even as an untrained clerk. You've had no training in anything. I couldn't afford to give you any. And two of us couldn't manage to exist on about a hundred a year, which is all we've got now. No, it's out of the question; we've just got to face that."

He turned his pipe in his fingers, and added darkly:

"I'd be glad enough if that were the worst of it."

Hilary looked up sharply at his tone.

"What do you mean?"

"You may as well know the whole business, now I've gone so far," her father went on. "You know what I married her for—security, and security for you, mainly. I had all sorts of hopes about what she'd do for you, you see? She's got any amount of money, and I'd thought she'd send you to a good boarding-school, first of all, and then other things later on—a dress allowance, give you a good time, let you have your chance, and that sort of thing. She didn't. She'll spend money on herself freely; that Lindfield woman seems able to get a decent salary from her; but you . . . ? She's never spent a penny on you from first to last, except for the food you eat. She was jealous of you from the start, once we were married. I suppose she didn't like the idea of my having been married before, as soon as she had got her own way and grew tired of her new toy; and you were a constant reminder of that. Something of the sort, at any rate."

"Well, what does that matter?" Hilary pointed out. "She can't do less than she's doing, can she?"

"No," said Castleford, gloomily, "but she can do one thing that would knock the bottom out of our security: she can alter her will. Then, if she died—and she's got this diabetes, remember, even if Glencaple's treatment seems to be keeping her afloat—we'd be left stranded. And I'm not such a fool that I can't see the pressure that's being brought to bear on her to make a new will. The Glencaples are at her on the one side; they've never forgiven me for stepping into their brother's shoes and putting out my hand towards his money. They feel they ought to have it if anything happens—and I don't blame them much for that. And on the other side, that Lindfield woman is playing the same game, always trying to stir up petty trouble so as to drive a wedge in a little deeper. Between

24

them, I think they've come pretty near success now; and I shouldn't wonder if she alters her will. She'll cut you out of it, for certain; and likely enough I'll be scored out also. She wouldn't think twice about it, in spite of all her original promises; I know her well enough for that. And then, if she happened to die—where would our 'security' be? I've paid dearly enough for it all these years; and when I see it slipping away . . ."

He broke off, as though he had blurted out more than he had intended. After a moment, he resumed in a quieter tone.

"That's how things stand. She's written to her lawyers and got her will back this morning. I saw the letter on the breakfast-table. The Glencaples came over to dinner tonight. It's easy to put two and two together; they're talking the business over now, I expect, in the drawing-room. And what can I do? Nothing! She has no use for me; I've no hold over her now, not the slightest. If she alters that will and dies next week, the Glencaples will turn the two of us out onto the street without the slightest compunction."

Hilary's strong young face turned to confront him with an expression he had never seen before. He could not interpret it, but he knew he had drawn her closer to him by his revelations; and he was glad he had forced himself to speak so frankly.

"It's a damnable thing, to lose one's independence," he said with a bitterness that made his daughter's nerves twitch responsively.

"Don't worry too much," she answered, with a catch in her voice. "I know just how you feel; but perhaps there's a way out."

Castleford seemed to be reminded of something he had overlooked.

"I think I'd better get these bearer bonds into my own hands," he said, suddenly. "They're in the safe, here, along with her jewels and some other stuff of hers. They'd be safer in a bank, now I come to think of it. There would be less risk of them being mistaken for her property, then. They're all we have."

His pipe had gone out and he rose to knock it out on the ash-tray. Hilary took up her work again as he resettled himself in his chair. For a time he stared in front of him, occupied with his own thoughts. With all his frankness, he had kept one thing back from

Hilary, a thing he could hardly tell to his daughter: that damnable anonymous letter about his wife and Dick Stevenage. His teeth clenched on his pipestem as he thought of it. It had come by the post that afternoon; and the brutal terms of it were burned into his memory. It might be true; and under his quiet exterior he was blazing with anger at the mere possibility. That would be the last straw. And yet, what steps could he take? In that precarious position of his, one false move might precipitate a catastrophe in which Hilary would be involved as well as himself.

3
THE SECOND CAMP

"I could shoot you, Auntie Winnie. Look!"

Frankie brought his new toy to his shoulder and took deliberate aim at his aunt across the drawing-room.

"Put that thing down!" she exclaimed nervously, as she caught sight of the muzzle turned towards her. "Put it down, *at once*, there's a good boy. It might be loaded and go off. Accidents are always happening, just like that. I saw a case the other week in the *Daily Sketch*."

Frankie, with a sullen face, lowered his rook-rifle.

"It really isn't loaded," Connie Lindfield's cool voice reassured her. "I looked through the barrel before I let him bring it into the room."

"So there!" added the amiable child.

He took good care, however, to speak below his breath so that his aunt failed to catch the words. It had been impressed upon him by his father, in unmistakable terms, that he must never offend his aunt. Miss Lindfield may have overheard his remark, but if she did so, she made no sign. In Frankie's eyes, Miss Lindfield was "a good sport." She never gave him away; she listened to his frequent lies with a smile which he thought encouraging and credulous; she could be counted upon, at times, to give him the very present he coveted; and if she checked him—on rare occasions—she did so in the guise of a fellow-conspirator warning him against trouble from the adult world. A very different kind of person from Hillie, with her indignant eyes and stinging words. That incident of the kitten was still rankling in his mind as well as in Hilary's.

Winifred Castleford had already forgotten the rook-rifle. She returned to her fashion-paper through which she was skimming idly, for any prolonged study of print was too great a tax upon her faculty of attention.

"Skirts are to be longer, Connie," she reported, without raising her eyes from the page. "Do you think that's a good thing?"

"Perhaps."

In point of fact, Miss Lindfield did not think it would be a good thing. She had neat legs and ankles which could stand the test of golfing-shoes. Short skirts set them off to advantage. If skirts were lengthened by fashion, one of her undeniable assets would be concealed from appraising male eyes; and she was not anxious for the change. She was too tactful, however, to voice her views on the point. Winifred's ankles were slim enough, but above them she had calves like a sturdy dairy-maid's. A slightly longer skirt would make a considerable difference to her.

"I think it'll be a good idea. I do indeed, Connie," Mrs. Castleford went on. "If we take to longer skirts, these working girls won't be able to copy us. It'll make a difference. They've got to hop on to motor-busses and squeeze into Tubes. They need to have short skirts. Longer skirts would put us in a different class from them. Just now we're all alike. I think it's a really good idea, don't you?"

Miss Lindfield neither endorsed nor dissented from these assertions.

"It'll make a difference," she admitted, in a tone which allowed Winifred to assume that she agreed.

"These men are a long time over their coffee," Mrs. Castleford complained, throwing her fashion-paper aside. "I hope Phil isn't boring them. I hope he isn't."

Then, with a sudden burst of peevishness:

"I wish you wouldn't snap that gun like that, Frankie. It annoys me. It does, really."

Frankie, who had been taking imaginary pot-shots at various ornaments, put his gun down wearily. Could he never do anything without some grown-up making objections? Evidently not, he reflected crossly, and relapsed into a sort of fidgety quiet. Miss

Lindfield, apparently having nothing to occupy her, picked up the rook-rifle and examined it incuriously.

The door opened and the two Glencaples entered in turn. Confronted by them, a stranger would have inferred that each took after a different parent, for there was little family resemblance between them. Kenneth came in first, round-headed, round-faced, round-eyed, waddling slightly as he advanced into the room on his short legs. His red face and the suspicion of a crumple in his shirt-front gave him the air of having done himself well at the dinner-table. There was a touch of commonness about him from which his brother was free. Laurence was taller, with a long thin face which looked hard in repose but could assume an expression of grave solicitude when a patient's case demanded that. A sound doctor, people declared: quiet, confident, and resourceful. He had the neatness of a surgeon, though he did no surgical practice.

Kenneth waddled across to the hearth-rug and took up his position with his back to the empty fire-place, his legs well apart. Laurence closed the door behind him, glanced speculatively at the various chairs before seating himself in the one which took his fancy, and then inquired lazily:

"Where's Hillie?"

"She's gone off somewhere, I suppose. I expect she's got something or other to do. She may have letters to write. I don't know. You don't want her, do you, Laurie?" Winifred ended with a faint note of discontent in her voice.

"Not I. Mere curiosity."

"Where's Phil?" Mrs. Castleford demanded.

"Gone off somewhere, I expect," Laurence answered with a vague parody of her own explanation, though his tone varied from hers enough to prevent her noticing that.

Kenneth, from the hearth-rug, contributed a grunt which suggested that he was not ill-pleased at his host's absence. Then, as an after-thought, he became articulate:

"We can spare him, hey? Never has anything to say for himself that anyone would want to listen to. Better without him, eh?"

29

His round eyes glanced from face to face, seeking endorsement of his views.

"Tried to draw him out tonight," he grumbled. "No good. Cliquey lot, these artists. Jealous. I asked him what he thought of that fellow Kirchner's drawings. You remember them, Laurie? Pretty girls. Came out in *La Vie Parisienne* during the War, didn't they? He didn't think much of them, I could see. Sort of shut up like a spider when you poke it."

Winifred broke into a shrill titter at his description. Miss Lindfield showed her admirable teeth in an encouraging smile. Laurence laughed, but with an air of being amused by something other than his brother's remark. Frankie laughed loudly. He knew exactly how spiders behaved when you tormented them, and he supposed that this was the point of his father's joke.

Kenneth made an automatic movement to straighten his tie, which had slipped to one side a little. His eye fell upon his brother.

"Nearly late for dinner tonight, Laurie. How's that? Not like you."

Laurence pulled out his cigar-case and picked out a cigar after a glance which asked permission from the two women.

"I had to pay a visit on the way over—Heckford. He detained me a minute or two longer than I expected."

Heckford's case was public property. He was a morpho-maniac. The police had been called in when he took to shamming fits on doctors' doorsteps in the hope of getting a hypodermic injection. He had been released under promise to put himself into Laurence's hands for treatment.

"Heckford? H'm!" Kenneth's tone expressed the contempt of a full-blooded man for a weaker type. "Rotter, that fellow. No good. You'll never make anything of him, Laurie. Giving him diminishing doses, hey? Cut him off entirely—snick!—that's what I say."

Laurence lighted his cigar carefully before answering. "That only works if you have 'em under restraint, and I'm not sure about it even then."

He pitched his extinguished match inside the fender adroitly.

"Curious creatures, these drug-fiends," he went on, as though discussing generalities. "One symptom turns up quite often. They

30

try to spread the drug-habit among their friends. They seem to want to get other people into the same boat. 'Just try it!' You can't trust 'em with the stuff, of course. If you handed 'em over three days' supply on their word of honour to take it in proper doses, they'd burst the lot in one orgy as soon as your back was turned. You have to keep a sharp eye on 'em when you visit 'em to give 'em their daily jag. They'd pick your pocket for the drug if they could. Why, tonight, as I packed the stuff back into my bag . . ."

He suddenly realised that he was mentioning a concrete case and broke off.

Miss Lindfield had been giving him polite attention, but Winifred obviously had not been listening to a word. She waited impatiently until he had finished speaking and then immediately rushed in.

"Connie!"

Miss Lindfield turned her head.

"Oh, Connie! I've forgotten something. Such a nuisance! Isn't it today I take flowers to that Hospital? I knew there was something I ought to do, and I couldn't think what it was. It's most provoking, that, isn't it, Connie?"

Winifred had the greatest difficulty in recalling her appointments. True enough, she had an engagement-book. But the chances were that she forgot to keep the book posted up and still relied on it, which did not help matters much. Constance Lindfield knew quite well that now she was being blamed, tacitly, for not reminding Winifred about the visit to the Hospital at Sunnyside. Winifred cared nothing for the patients; but she liked to pose as Lady Bountiful and drive over once a week in a car laden with flowers from the Carron Hill gardens.

Miss Lindfield hastened to put the matter right before she was openly arraigned for forgetfulness.

"It'll do just as well tomorrow, won't it?" she suggested quietly. "You're not doing anything special in the morning. Hillie can drive you over."

"Yes, I suppose so," Winifred conceded in a grudging tone. "That'll have to do. Just tell Hillie, will you, Connie? Say I want her to have the car ready at half-past eleven. Tell her to be there, sharp. I hate having to wait about."

Miss Lindfield rose at once and left the room without replying except by a nod of cheerful acquiescence. By the time she got back, she reflected, Winnie would be talking about something else, and the fancied grievance would be forgotten. These affairs could always be handled simply enough, if one knew when to hold one's tongue.

The door had hardly closed behind her when Frankie in his turn got up and slipped quietly from the room. The moment he was gone, Kenneth shot a glance of inquiry at his brother. A slight contraction of Laurence's brows warned him that the time was hardly ripe for the subject they meant to introduce.

"Nice girl, Hillie," Laurence said, reflectively.

He settled himself lower in his armchair as he spoke, and seemed to interest himself in keeping the ash on his cigar. Winifred did not notice the close observation he was keeping on her under his slightly lowered lids. That remark had been carefully calculated, in spite of its apparent casualness.

"Grown up quite good-looking," Kenneth chimed in, with the air of a man making a discovery. "Surprising how they shoot up, isn't it? Seems only the other day since she was a kid. In the marriage-market now. Well, well! Any applicants, Winnie? Any men coming about the house after her, hey?"

This suggestion quite evidently annoyed Winifred. "Don't be silly, Kennie," she chided, shrugging her shoulders as she spoke. "She's only twenty."

"Twenty, hey? '*Come and kiss me, sweet and twenty.*' Shakespeare. Needn't tell me Shakespeare didn't know what he was talking about. Surprising she hasn't got a string of them after her already. Young, fresh, on the quiet side, perhaps, but some like 'em so. You'll soon see, Winnie."

He nodded his head with an air of wisdom.

"Oh, well, the sooner she gets married, the better I'll be pleased," Winifred assured him, rather pettishly.

Laurence lifted his eyes from his cigar and threw a silent message across to his brother: "That'll do. You'll make a mess of things if you go on."

It was quite enough for Kenneth to remind Winifred of her stepdaughter. The last few sentences had blown up the flame of a jealousy which was never quite extinct. Beyond that, it was needless to labour the point and perhaps, in doing so, make her hostile to themselves. Laurence, the psychologist of the pair, was satisfied with the result so far.

As Kenneth was casting about in his mind for a fresh subject, his son and Miss Lindfield came back into the room together. Frankie had a cardboard box in his hands.

"I say, Daddy, I found this up in the attic today. Auntie Connie said I'd better let you see it. She wouldn't let me use them until I asked you about them."

Kenneth took the box from him, cut it on a table, and lifted the lid. A pair of old automatic pistols belonging to his dead brother met his eyes, as well as some packets of ammunition.

"Ronnie's old pistols!" he exclaimed in surprise. "Well! Well! That brings things back, doesn't it, Laurie? Remember how he got the wind up at the start of the war? Revolution, starvation, looting, God knows what! And he bought these things to be on the safe side. A worrying sort, poor old Ronnie! Always was."

He picked up one of the automatics and examined it with a faint touch of sentiment.

"A .32 by the look of it," he commented idly.

Miss Lindfield came forward and lifted its companion from the box, rather gingerly on account of the dust which had accumulated on the weapon during its long storage.

"Let's have a look at it, Kennie," Laurence demanded as his brother replaced his one in the box.

Kenneth passed it to Frankie, who reluctantly handed it over to his uncle. Connie Lindfield was still examining the other pistol.

"I don't quite see how it works," she said, after puzzling over it for some moments. "How do you open it up to load it?"

"I'll show you," Laurence volunteered.

Miss Lindfield moved across to his chair and watched him manoeuvre the breech-mechanism.

"I see now—like this?"

She repeated the action with the pistol in her hand.

"Here! Let me try, Auntie Connie," Frankie broke in, pulling the revolver away from her.

He snapped the jacket back once or twice, then pointed the pistol at a picture, and pulled the trigger.

"Can't I have a cartridge to put into it, Daddy?"

Winifred had been watching the scene with apprehensive eyes.

"Frankie! I forbid you to load that beastly thing in my drawing-room. I won't have it loaded, do you hear?"

"Oh, all *right!*" Frankie surrendered ungraciously.

His father saved the situation by holding out his hand for the weapon which, after a pretence of further examination, he dropped casually back into the box. Laurence handed the other to Miss Lindfield, whence it in turn passed to Kenneth who placed it with its companion. Frankie watched them covetously.

"I can have them, can't I, Daddy? I won't use them in the house, if Auntie doesn't like it," he added as an inducement.

Kenneth shook his head decisively.

"No. Not for you. Dangerous."

"But, Daddy . . ."

"You heard what your Daddy said?" Winifred broke in. "I won't have these horrid things used anywhere here. You'd be sure to hit somebody, Frankie."

Frankie, defeated, was about to make an angry retort when he caught his father's eye fixed meaningly upon him.

"Oh, all right, Auntie, if you don't like it."

Miss Lindfield apparently was touched by his disconsolate air, for she made a suggestion to divert him.

"I'd like to see what your rook-rifle can do, Frankie. You haven't fired it yet. Suppose we go over to the old harness-room and try it there? We can fix up a target on the wall. It'll be quite safe," she added for Winifred's benefit. "I'll see that there's no damage done."

Connie Lindfield's proposal was not put forward altogether on Frankie's account. She had a shrewd idea that the Glencaples wanted Winifred to themselves. Laurence had dropped a hint to her about "some business to be talked over after dinner"; and she needed no help in guessing what that business was. The Glencaple faction was in the ascendant now, and Connie Lindfield meant to stand well with the brothers. By taking both Frankie and herself off the scene at this juncture, she would score a good mark.

Frankie fell in with her suggestion at once, though he still cast longing glances at the forbidden brace of pistols on the table. He picked up his rook-rifle and followed Miss Lindfield out of the room. As soon as the door closed behind them, Kenneth straightened his tie mechanically, established himself firmly on the hearthrug, and emitted a slightly explosive puff of breath which was his habitual preliminary to discussing serious business.

"Now we've got rid of the rest of them for a while. No interruptions likely. Can talk business quietly, hey? Right! Well, did you ring up your lawyer?"

Winifred, with business men, adopted either of two poses. She might flatter them by displaying incompetence and admiring their ability to manage the simplest matters efficiently; or she might pose as a kindred spirit who liked to have everything ship-shape. She chose the second affectation on this occasion.

"I rang up Mr. Wadhurst yesterday," she explained. "I told him just what you told me to say. I said I'd changed my mind altogether about my will. I was going to alter it all, I said, and I wanted him to send it to me so that I could see what was in it. I hadn't made up my mind exactly, I said, what changes I was going to make. The main things in it were going to be changed; but some of the smaller bequests would most likely remain as they were. That was why I wanted the document, I said, to see what was what. And when I'd made up my mind, I told him, I'd see him or send him a draught so that he could make a new will for me. Was that right?"

"That's O.K.," Kenneth acquiesced with a nod of his bullet-head. "You've got the will here, eh? Let's have a look over it together. See things better with it before us, perhaps."

"It's in the right-hand drawer of the escritoire over there," Winifred indicated it with a gesture. "Get it, will you, Kennie?"

Kenneth waddled across the room, searched for a moment in the drawer, and produced the bulky document. He unfolded it as he returned to the hearth-rug; and began to glance through its provisions, making a running commentary in an undertone as he went along.

"H'm! 'I, Winifred Lindfield or Castleford, wife of Philip Castleford, residing at Carron Hill' and so forth. Trustees: Philip Castleford, old Wingham—dead now—and Young Hillie, when she gets to twenty-one. Very nice! H'm! Now we come to business. 'First, for the payment of all my just and lawful debts, sickbed and funeral expenses . . .' and so on. Then five thousand to me—thanks! And five thousand to Laurie, too. And a couple of hundred to Doris Lindfield or Seldon. That drops out; she's dead. And five thousand to Connie. I don't grudge that. And some odds and ends of jewellery to her, too. And another hundred or two in minor things to different people. And"—his voice choked very slightly at the next item— "the residue of my estate to my husband, Philip Castleford, or, if he predecease me, to his daughter Hilary Castleford."

He paused for a moment or two, involved in mental calculation.

"Let's see. Ronnie left you just over £46,000. Just about that. Death duties came off that, though. Wait a sec."

"The death duty was fourteen per cent, I remember," Laurence supplied as his brother hesitated.

"Fourteen per cent? Right. That's about a seventh chopped off. Say £6,500 went to the Government. That left you with round about £40,000 somewhere for yourself, Winnie. Now let's see. Five thousand each for Laurie, Connie, and me: £15,000. Death duties and odds and ends, say about £6,000—really less than that. And that gives you a residue of just about £20,000 which goes into Master Phil's pocket. Seems a lot."

He paused and glanced across at his brother. It was Laurence's turn now to throw his weight into the scale. Winifred liked Laurence the better of the two. He was a bachelor, for one thing;

36

and Winifred preferred single men. One could imagine things about them. Nobody could imagine anything romantic about Kenneth, with his stout, middle-aged wife.

Laurence sat up in his chair and leaned forward confidentially.

"This is the way I look at it, Winnie," he began, with an air of giving disinterested advice. "Neither Kennie or I have anything personally at stake in the affair. You're younger than either of us and you'll see us both out, now that I've got the upper hand of that trouble of yours with the insulin treatment."

He paused almost imperceptibly to let this sink in. Winifred had a horror of death; she could hardly bear to let the thought of it cross her mind; and when she had turned diabetic she had seen herself in fancy at the very edge of the grave. Laurence's phrases reminded her—as they were carefully calculated to do—that his skill had set her up again and that she might put away all immediate fear of decease. Any gratitude of which she was capable was due to her doctor.

"But if we're out of it," Laurence went on, "still there's young Frankie. You like him. Neither his father nor I can leave him much. And, after all, Ronnie was his uncle. It would look a bit queer, wouldn't it, if Ronnie's money went to Hillie, and Frankie got left out in the cold?"

Laurence had no need to scan his sister-in-law's face closely to see the effect of this last shot. The ever-present jealousy woke at once in response. When that will was made, Hilary had been a child. Now she was a rival, even if an unconscious one. Let her have the money? Winifred, now that she saw the possibilities, was in little need of spurring on to alter the will. It would be changed now, in any case, if merely to cut that girl out of it. And in her eagerness to set that matter right, Winifred was ready to take any suggestions which the brothers cared to offer her.

"Of course," Laurence went on casually, "merely for the sake of appearances, it might be as well to put Kennie's name and mine into the new draught. I've left everything to Frankie myself; and Kennie, of course, has done the same."

"Naturally," Kenneth jerked out in confirmation.

"So if you care to put our names in, it'll do no harm," Laurence pointed out. "We shan't be there to hear your will read, but still I'd like to feel I was in it. You too Kennie?"

"Same here. Sentiment, hey? Just for the look of the thing. After all, we've been good friends, eh, Winnie?"

Winifred was listening with only half her attention. The rest of her mind was filled with a malicious delight at the thought of being able to damage Hilary at no cost to herself. What an escape that had been! When the will was made, she had paid little attention to its details, her mind being filled with other things; and she had been too stupid to follow out the implications of the testament until Laurence had put them bluntly before her that night. Now that she knew where she stood, she would take good care that no money of hers went in that direction. She had a vision of Hilary surviving her, still young and fresh, and rich as well. Not that!

"Yes, yes," she said, absently, in response to Kenneth's half-heard remark. "Of course, Kennie. I quite agree with you. I do indeed."

Laurence struck while the iron was hot. In her present mood she would agree to anything; and once it was down in black and white, she would stick to it, merely to avoid trouble. He pulled out a notebook, rested it on his knee, and began to jot down items.

"Just let me have that will, Kennie. Thanks. Now how would something like this do? I'll dot down the points. Then Wadhurst can turn the draught into legal form."

Winifred nodded absent-mindedly in response.

"First, then," Laurence went on, "All just and lawful debts, etc. That's usual. Second . . . let's see." He consulted the will. "The two legacies to Kennie and myself come later, so they drop out at this point. Your half-sister Doris drops out also. Connie's the next. What about Connie?"

"Connie's down for £5,000 in that will," Kenneth put in nervously.

"I know that," Laurence retorted rather impatiently. "But do you think five thousand's enough for her, Winnie? She's no relation of ours; but she's your half-sister. Relationship ought to count.

I'd be inclined, in your shoes, to give Connie more than that. Say £7,500. How would that do?"

Kenneth's mouth opened to protest, but closed abruptly as Laurence's brows contracted sharply. Kenneth could not see the point of this generosity—which would be at their expense—but Laurence was the chief tactician of the pair and Kenneth was accustomed to follow blindly on the lines laid down by the mastermind.

"Yes, let Connie have it. I think she ought to have it. I do indeed," Winifred hastened to agree.

"And the same jewellery?" Laurence pursued. "Or perhaps you'd like Hillie to have some of that?"

"No! I don't want that. She's to get none of it. Put it down that Connie's to get all my jewellery. Not just those things you have there in the will. I've bought a lot of things since then, and Connie's to have everything. Make that clear, Laurie."

"Very good, then. And now there are one or two odd legacies. They can stand, I suppose? You agree? Then that's that. And the next item's Phil. H'm! A man ought to be able to look after himself in this world. Say a couple of thousand for Phil? How would that do? That'll give Hillie a hundred a year after Phil dies. Let it go at that?"

A hundred a year to that little upstart! Winifred was driven to protest.

"A. hundred a year seems an awful lot for that girl, Laurie. She ought to be able to earn her own living, at her age really. She's no relation of mine. She's no claim on me, not the slightest. Connie's different altogether."

Laurence's face admirably concealed his enjoyment at the success of his tactics. He had steered very neatly round the rock of Castleford himself.

"It might look shabby, if you didn't do something," he pointed out in a convincing tone. "We want to be fair, don't we? And that seems fair enough—generous, if anything, but still fair. It might cause talk if you didn't do something on that side, and for the sake of Ronnie's memory I think any talk of that sort would be a pity. You agree, Kennie?"

"Oh, all right," Kenneth acquiesced sulkily.

Then a jest in his own peculiar line of humour occurred to him.

"You can always marry the wench yourself, Laurie. Keep it all in the family, hey? Ha! Ha! That's a good notion, eh?"

Laurence shot an angry glance at him under frowning brows.

"Sometimes I feel like Queen Victoria, Kennie. 'We are not amused.' If I thought of marrying, I'd want somebody ten or fifteen years older than Hillie—somebody with experience of life."

At this sentiment, Winnie gave an unconscious nod of approval. Laurence was a man of discrimination, she reflected. He had the good sense to see how little real attraction there was in an empty-headed chit, compared with a woman of her own age.

Kenneth opened his mouth and closed it again abruptly. He had meant to say: "Like Connie, eh?" but his brother's face warned him that further personalities had best be left alone.

"That's about all," Laurence pointed out, returning to the problem of bequests. "I take it that your wishes would be met by this arrangement for the residue of the estate: Kennie and I are to be put down for the life-rent of it, divided equally between us. After we're gone, Frankie comes into the capital sum. That makes sure he gets it eventually and it puts Kennie and me nominally into the will for sentiment's sake. Executors: say Connie, Kennie, and I, with a Bank or the Public Trustee to come if Kennie and I die first. That's what you wanted, I think, Winnie?"

"Yes, yes, that's just what I wanted. That'll do very nicely, Laurie. Thanks so much for putting it all so clearly. You think it's all right too, Kennie?"

Kenneth nodded sagaciously.

"Seems to me you've made a very sound disposition, Winnie. You've got a good business head on you."

The phrase seemed to recall something to Winifred's mind.

"Oh, now I come to think of it," she exclaimed, "I got a letter from some company the other day. Something about reconstruction or a word of that sort. I'd like to show it to you. It's upstairs. I'll go and fetch it."

She left the room in search of the document, and Kenneth seized the chance which her absence gave him.

"You're too deep for me, Laurie. What d'you want to give Connie that extra twenty-five hundred for, hey? Seems to me she was damn well off with her five thousand. I followed your lead, of course. Stuck in my throat a bit, though. Chucks away £125 a year, bang!"

Laurence repressed a contemptuous smile as he answered.

"Look at it this way, Kennie. We've pulled the thing off easier than I expected. I knew she was a bit jealous of Hillie, but I hadn't seen how deep it went till I began to lead her on. We've won this round, hands down. But if we did the trick so easily, somebody else might manage to play the same game later on. And not in our interest. And anybody who gets Connie on their side stands to score heavily. She's always on the spot, ready to put in a word. I don't think she'd help Castleford. There's no love lost there. Still, it's as well to be on the safe side. I'll see that Connie knows we've looked after her. She may not be grateful—not the grateful kind, I guess—but she's got a sound appreciation of which side her bread's buttered on. She'll back us, after this, if there's any occasion for it."

Kenneth reflected owlishly for some seconds.

"Something in that," he admitted. "Connie's worth enlisting. It was the price I was kicking at. But p'raps you're right. If we need her, we may need her badly, eh? All right. Let it go."

"So long as this lasts, we've spiked Master Phil's guns," said Laurence, grimly. "And if Hillie gets £100 a year she won't starve. That clears my conscience."

"She could starve for all I'd care," Kenneth commented lightly. "She's nothing in my young life. And that's *our* money; Ronnie made every stiver of it. I'd have cut the pair of them clean out."

"Public opinion counts for something, even in these days," Laurence pointed out. "When this will comes out, we don't want any talk about undue influence. That hundred a year will gag a lot of gossip."

"No 'hard case,' you mean? Something in that," Kenneth confessed.

Winifred's return put an end to further discussion. She submitted the document to Kenneth who, after a brief struggle to make her understand the course she should take, volunteered to look after the business himself and clear it up.

By the time this had been settled, Frankie and Miss Lindfield came back from the improvised shooting-gallery.

"I got six bull's eyes in ten shots, once, Daddy," he shouted as he burst into the room. "Didn't I, Auntie Connie?"

Miss Lindfield corroborated this, but she was tactful enough to make no mention of the range at which the bulls had been scored.

"Auntie Connie tried, too; but she's no good," Frankie went on eagerly. "She shuts her eyes when she pulls the trigger."

"A haystack would be safe from me at twenty yards," Miss Lindfield admitted frankly.

Frankie suddenly remembered something which he had not mentioned to his father before.

"Daddy! I've been making fireworks. Good ones, really. Squibs, starlights, golden rain, Bengal lights. Would you look at some of them before I go to bed? You mayn't be here again at night before I have to go home."

"Firework-making, hey?" his father broke in, apparently not well pleased. "Blow your head off, if you don't look out. Lose a finger or two, with carelessness."

"It's really all right," Miss Lindfield pointed out.

"I'm helping him to make them, and we're very careful."

"Oh, so long as you're superintending, Connie," Kenneth gave way. "Don't mind that. You're not likely to risk your looks in a blow-up, hey? Safe enough with you there."

"Look, Daddy!" Frankie interrupted, pulling something from his pocket. "Here's some slow match we made. Put your cigar to it, Uncle Laurie, and you'll see how well it burns."

"And stinks, too, no doubt," his uncle commented. "I think we'll take your word for it, Frankie."

"It's just twine soaked in potash nitrate and dried," Frankie explained, rather disgusted at his uncle's lack of enthusiasm.

"And where did you get the recipes for your starlights and all the other gauds?" Laurence inquired.

"Auntie Connie took me over to the Free Library in the car and we hunted up some books on fireworks there. She copied out the recipes we wanted and bought the stuffs we needed at the druggist's. *Please* come out, Daddy, and see me set some of them off. I'd like you to see them, Daddy."

"You're not to set off any banging things in front of the house, Frankie," Winifred ordered. "My nerves are like fiddlestrings just now, and I can't stand noises."

Miss Lindfield saw the mutinous look on Frankie's face and intervened swiftly.

"Bangs sound just as well in the day-time as at night, you know, Frankie; but it's only at night you can show off Bengal lights and so forth to any advantage. Your Daddy can hear the squibs some other time, if he's over in daylight. We'll let him see coloured fires and starlights while we've got a good chance, shall we?"

Frankie suffered himself to be persuaded; and after a few minutes of firework display, he was packed off to bed, while his elders returned to the drawing-room.

"Ring the bell, Kennie. You're nearest to it," Winifred said as Kenneth took up his favourite post on the hearth-rug. "You'll want whiskey-and-soda? You too, Laurie? They'll bring some tea for me, along with it."

"Regular tea-jenny, you are, Winnie," Kenneth commented. "How many times a day do you swallow the stuff, hey?"

"I like tea," Winnie answered, evading the point.

"Still the same?" Kenneth persisted. "Pour out a cup; let it go tepid; gulp it at a draught; then pour out more to cool?"

"I don't like scalding tea," Winifred admitted. "My throat's sensitive. I hate drinking anything very hot. That's why I let it cool down first. It seems to me the sensible way of drinking tea."

Laurence recalled something which he had overlooked.

"I've brought you a new supply of insulin, Winnie. You said the last lot's nearly finished. I'll get it now, in case I forget. It's in my bag out in the hall."

He rose, left the room, and returned almost immediately with a neat little parcel.

"Here you are," he said, putting the packet on the mantelpiece. "Same dose as before. By the way, you're keeping your hypodermic syringe sterilised, and all that?"

43

"Phil looks after that," Winnie explained. "I tried injecting the stuff myself, you know, but I simply couldn't bear to push the needle through my skin. It's not so bad when someone else makes the prick. I never could bear to do it myself. Knowing exactly when the jab was coming, somehow, always made it seem worse. So I made Phil do it for me. He manages it all. He cleans and sterilises the syringe and everything."

"I expect you can trust him to do it properly," Laurence conceded. "It's not likely he could go wrong. There's no skill required."

Tea was brought in, along with the whiskey decanter and soda. Winifred poured out a cup for herself. Miss Lindfield preferred not to join her.

"Kennie! Just look behind you on the mantelpiece—there, on the right—and hand me down that little bottle with the saccharin tablets in it, please," Winifred directed.

Kenneth searched obediently and turned with the phial in his hand before handing it over.

"'Each tablet is equal in sweetening power to one of sugar,'" he read from the label. "D'you believe that?" he added sceptically as he noted the minuteness of the tabloids.

"It's found to be three hundred times as sweet as sugar," Laurence pronounced shortly.

"Is that so?"

Kenneth seemed unconvinced. He opened the phial, extracted a tablet, and put it on his tongue.

"Doesn't seem very sweet to me," he grumbled, making a wry face. "Bitter, I'd call it."

"People vary," Laurence said, crossly. "Besides, it's meant to be used in very dilute solution, not solid. You won't get the taste of it out of your mouth for hours, Kennie."

Kenneth hastily got rid of the tablet and handed the phial to Winifred.

"I wish you hadn't wasted that tablet, Kennie," she complained, as she noticed how few were left in the phial.

"It's all right. I'll get some more for you before they run out," Miss Lindfield reassured her.

Under Kenneth's amazed eyes, Winifred counted out three tablets and dropped them into her tea-cup.

"Three? Beats me how you can stand one, let alone three."

"I used to take three lumps of sugar in my tea always. I had a sweet tooth. And now I can't use sugar at all; Laurie says I'd better not. So I take this stuff instead; one tablet for each lump of sugar, just as it says on the label. It's not really the same, though. It clings about one's mouth, just as Laurie says. Still, it's all I've got nowadays," Winifred explained, with a certain self-pity in her tone.

Her tea had by this time cooled sufficiently for her taste and she put her cup to her lips and drank the major part of the liquid at a gulp. It was a habit of which she had never been able to break herself. When strangers were present, she was on her guard and sipped her tea in what she regarded as a genteel fashion; but normally she swallowed most of the cupful at a single draught, as though she were over-thirsty.

After half-an-hour's desultory conversation, the Glencaple brothers exchanged glances. Kenneth put down his tumbler on the mantelpiece, straightened his tie, and prepared to take his leave.

"Must be going, Winnie. Getting late, hey? Had a very pleasant evening. Good dinner, too. Wish I had a cook like yours. Glad to see young Frankie picking up so well here. Looks a different boy. Good of you to take him, very good of you."

Laurence also rose and took his leave. Winifred went out of the room with Kenneth, leaving his brother with Miss Lindfield.

"I shouldn't mention it, Connie," Laurence explained in a low voice which would not carry beyond the door, "but Winnie's going to alter her will again. We advised her to do a bit more for you— say £7,500 instead of the £5,000 you were to get under the last will. I think she'll rise to it."

The glance which accompanied the news said quite plainly to Miss Lindfield: "Don't have friction of any sort with her just now. You know how things are now I've told you."

Connie Lindfield's smile was both grateful and subtle. She needed no underlining to make her understand the situation. Then, as a thought occurred to her, she gave an almost imperceptible nod towards the study.

"And . . . ?" she said, without voicing the question. Laurence made an expressive gesture.

"Down and out!" he said. "He's not likely to grow fat on his share of Ronnie's money, now."

Miss Lindfield made no comment. She did not believe in unnecessary chatter about confidential matters, once she had secured the essential information. With a nod of understanding, she accompanied Laurence into the hall to rejoin the others.

"No use knocking those two up to say goodnight, hey?" Kenneth inquired, with a gesture in the direction of the study. "No point in it. Well, then, I must be off. Long drive. G'dnight, Connie. 'Night, Winnie. See you soon again."

With a nod of farewell to his brother, he waddled off into the darkness; and in a second or two they saw his headlights flash up and heard the whirr of his self-starter. Laurence, after a slightly less cavalier leave-taking, went out in his turn just as Kenneth drove off. Winifred retired indoors at once, but Miss Lindfield stood watching the lights of the two cars until they disappeared round a turn in the drive.

"I'm going to bed now, Connie," Winifred informed her from half-way up the stair. "I've got a headache, I think. I don't want to sit up. You can switch off the lights any time you like."

"Very well," Miss Lindfield called after her as she busied herself in making the door fast for the night.

4
A BOLT FROM THE BLUE

In passing the hall-table, Miss Lindfield picked up a letter which had come by the late post, went back into the drawing-room, and switched off most of the lamps. Then, choosing a favourite chair, she sat down and fell to reconsidering the position in the light of the news which Laurence had given her.

A faintly sardonic smile passed over her lips from time to time as though she found the subject amusing. Despite their success that night, it was plain that the brothers were not entirely easy in their minds. Winnie might change her will again, if the idea came into her head. And it was evidently in view of this possibility that they had arranged for the increase in Constance's share. She recognised, quite coldly, the object of their move. She was worth conciliating, since she was always at Winnie's elbow, well-placed to intervene unobtrusively. She would never have favoured the other side; but she might have remained neutral. If the Glencaples wanted her help in future, it was only fair that she should have some reward. The tacit suggestion did not ruffle her in the least.

She had the less objection owing to the episode of the golf-match. As that business had sharply reminded her, Dick Stevenage was becoming a problem. It was all very well for him to play tame cat to Winnie. Miss Lindfield herself had suggested that role to him when he first attracted her; and she had taken a certain amusement in helping him to elaborate it. It gave him a sure footing in the house, and allowed him and Constance plenty of opportunities which could have been bought in no other way. If Winnie had supposed that Dick came there on Constance's account alone, she would soon have found ways of making his visits impossible. Miss Lindfield, secure in her hold over Dick, could look on with ironical eyes when he played up to Winnie and could coach him in the best methods of making himself indispensable.

But it was a different matter if he was beginning to hang round Hilary's skirts. Miss Lindfield seldom took the trouble to tell herself lies; and she knew Hilary had something which she herself no longer possessed: youth, freshness, natural charm, all of them went to the making of it. Winnie was just part of the game, where Dick was concerned; but Hilary might be dangerous. Dick was weak, unreliable, erratic, and eager to snatch at what he could get. All this she saw clearly. And yet she meant to have him for herself, for all that. She could have forced him into marriage at once; but unfortunately he was hard up. He was, as Constance recognised in her cooler moments, nothing more than a physically attractive loafer with a good turn for love-making; but though she admitted this frankly to herself, it had no influence on her desires. These stolen interviews, when Winnie could be got out of the way on some pretext, had become something to which she looked forward with ever-increasing intoxication and from which she came away only to long for the next one.

And though Dick seemed fast enough in her toils, her sober moments let her recognise that she could not trust him. At any moment he might go off in chase of some fresh light o' love. Hilary was practically penniless. There was nothing to be feared from marriage in that direction. But the mere thought of Dickie alone with Hilary was enough to flick Constance Lindfield on the raw.

Even at the suggestion of it, her hand clenched involuntarily; and that drew her attention back to the letter she was holding. It was addressed in a sprawling, illiterate hand, quite unknown to her. With her mind still dwelling on Hilary and Dickie, she tore open the envelope and extracted a dirty, ill-written note which she unfolded with more than a touch of fastidiousness.

Dere miss Linfield,

I write to tell you that *youre Young man* and missis Casselford are *laffing at You* behind youre back, as you coud see for yourself if you Go to the Shally when they are their and Peep in at the window, fine Goings-on, I must say, that's what you *High and mighty* Carron Hill people are Like, for all youre Fine airs. *What woud Connie say*, says he, and they both Laffed. Dere miss Linfield, I laffed to myself. *it was so Funny*. Have a Peep yourself, dere miss Linfield. it Costs nothing and *they say youre mean*. I think Ill write a Note to Casselford as Well, the more the merrier.

One who knows More than you Think

Miss Lindfield was one of those people who grow pale with anger instead of flushing. She sat now, white-faced and tense, reading and re-reading the venomously-phrased scrawl in her hand.

No need to ask if it were true. Now that she had been given the clue, her mind suddenly recalled and collocated memories which up till that moment had been isolated and unsuspicious. Winnie's sudden resumption of her hobby of painting, after a long discontinuance; her choice of the landscape view from the Chalet as a subject; her complaints of unsuccess with it and her quite surprising pertinacity in an attempt to "get it right"; her desire to be left alone to do her work uninterrupted; Dickie's "engagements" which often hindered his stolen meetings with Connie when Winnie's visits to the Chalet left the coast clear; Winnie's strange blindness on an occasion when Miss Lindfield had been less cautious than usual: these recollections and many others thronged into the field of her consciousness and settled down into a definite pattern.

"Laughing at you behind your back"! She had laughed at Winnie; Winnie had laughed at her; and Dickie, most likely, had been laughing in his sleeve at both of them, all the while. He had played the same game with each, evidently. When he and Winnie were together, it was Connie who was to be deceived; when he and Connie met, then Winnie was the person to be kept in the dark. Miss Lindfield knew how that had heightened the zest in her own case. She could guess that Winnie was in the same boat. And Winnie had a double thrill. Castleford had to be kept in ignorance as well, in her case.

But was he likely to be hoodwinked much longer? Suddenly Constance Lindfield remembered that he had received a letter by that morning's post. She had not seen the address on it; but she recalled now that from a distance it looked very much like the one in her hand. The yellowish cheap envelope, slightly crumpled, might have been the twin of her own. That anonymous writer, bursting with malice as he obviously was, would hardly have attacked her and left Philip Castleford untouched.

But Philip Castleford's troubles were no concern of hers, just then. She had her own affairs to brood over. Dickie she meant to have for herself. She was not shocked by the situation which the anonymous letter had unveiled; it took a good deal to shock Miss Lindfield. But her cool mind perceived quite clearly the main factors in the affair. The strength of Winnie's position lay in the Glencaple money. That made her entirely independent of all the rest of them. At the worst, she could well afford to let Castleford divorce her and then—well Dickie was not the sort of person who would refuse to marry for money if he got the chance. Constance Lindfield had no illusions about that side of his character. And if things did not get to that pitch, the money would enable Winnie to keep her present husband under her thumb up to a point, perhaps. Up to a point? Yes, but what point? Just how much would Castleford stand?

Her ear caught the faint sound of voices. Evidently Castleford and his daughter were coming out of the study and going upstairs to bed. Miss Lindfield's mind went back to an earlier matter. She picked up the box of pistols and ammunition, switched out the lights, and went out into the hall in time to intercept Castleford.

"Oh, wait a moment," she began, as she came up to the two in the hall. "Frankie's unearthed these things, Phil. Do you think they're safe?"

She put down the box on the hall-table, picked out the two pistols, and passed them to Castleford.

"I shouldn't think so," Castleford said, as he examined them.

He could not make out, from Constance's tone, exactly what her position in the matter was; and he preferred to be non-committal until she showed her hand.

Hilary took one of the weapons from her father and looked at it curiously.

"I hope he won't get his hands on these things," she said, briefly. "A rook-rifle's dangerous enough."

Quite obviously she was not yet ready to forgive Miss Lindfield in the matter of the golf-match.

Miss Lindfield took the weapon out of Castleford's hands.

"I think you're right," she admitted pleasantly. "At least, so far as these pistols go. The bother is, I don't know where to put them, so that he won't find them. Would you mind if I hid them in the study—in that cupboard where you keep some of your things? He's not likely to look for them there."

Castleford nodded assent, though with signs of doubt.

"That cupboard has no key," he pointed out,

"That doesn't matter. He's not likely to look into it," Miss Lindfield assured him, with a smile. "Hillie, would you mind putting them in there, now? I want to get to bed."

She handed the pistols to Hilary, wished them goodnight, and went up the stair, leaving them in the hall. Philip Castleford was ruffled by the incident. It was like that woman to use Hilary to save herself trouble; and it was just that attitude which he hated. It seemed to put his daughter into the position of an underling who had to fetch and carry for everyone in the house.

"Put them in the box with the ammunition, Hilary," he said. "I'll stow them in the cupboard myself. Off you go to bed, dear. It's later than I thought it was."

Hilary kissed him goodnight with more than her usual affection. He watched her go up the stairs; then, with the box in his hand, he made his way back to his study. The envenomed phrases of that anonymous letter recurred to his mind and he put his hand into his pocket in search of it; but he had left it in the pocket of his other jacket when he changed for dinner. He hardly needed it. Those malignant sentences were burned into his memory. Hilary thought she had heard the worst of the story; but this was far beyond anything that had gone before.

He opened the cupboard, picked up the box of weapons, and stood looking at them absentmindedly for a few moments before he put them away. If it were France, now, with the unwritten law in force . . .

A faint sound made him turn hastily. Miss Lindfield had come downstairs again and now stood confronting him with an expression which puzzled him.

"I didn't want to speak in front of Hillie," she said, hurriedly. "I think you ought to know, though. You won't tell anyone I said anything? Very well. Winnie's cancelled her will. She's going to make a fresh one, cutting you out."

"Cutting me out?" Castleford echoed, dully, as if he had not quite understood.

The blow, though he had long expected it, stunned him. Hilary would get nothing. These years of petty martyrdom were to go unpaid-for. And, as a final thrust, he learned it from this woman who, he well knew, hated him and his daughter. Winnie hadn't even had the decency to tell him outright herself.

"I'm sorry," Miss Lindfield said, though her tone showed plainly enough that the phrase was merely formal.

"She hasn't actually made this new will yet?" Castleford asked, as though to fill an awkward pause with a commonplace query.

"Not yet."

"H'm! Well, I can do nothing, obviously."

"No, I suppose you can't."

Somehow Miss Lindfield's voice suggested that something might be done, even at that stage. But Castleford had a shrewd suspicion that her motive was a mere desire to see him wince.

"Thanks for letting me know," he said, in as formal a tone as he could command. "She's written to Wadhurst about it, has she?"

"Yes." Miss Lindfield added a nod of confirmation. "She wrote to Wadhurst saying she'd changed her mind; and she asked for the will they had, because she wanted to destroy it. She told them she'd send them fresh instructions, by-and-by, so that they could draw up a new will in proper form. She hadn't quite decided, then, what she was going to do."

"I suppose she's destroyed it. Not that it matters much, now." Miss Lindfield's gesture disclaimed any knowledge.

"It was in the drawer of the escritoire when I saw it last," she volunteered. "It should be there now, if she hasn't burned it."

"It doesn't matter," Castleford said heavily. "Goodnight."

Miss Lindfield showed no surprise at this cavalier dismissal. She wished him goodnight in her turn and left the room. She had shot her bolt and saw no reason for lingering.

Castleford, as the door closed behind her, seated himself in his armchair and turned the affair over in his mind. The will—the actual document—was of no importance now. Wadhurst would testify that she had revoked it, even if she had not fulfilled all the legal niceties. And, in a day or two, she would give fresh instructions on the lines laid down for her by the Glencaples. He and Hilary were out of it.

He found he could not occupy his mind with the will. His thoughts went back to the anonymous letter, and at the remembrance of one phrase in it, he flushed and something seemed to swell in his throat till he could hardly draw breath. In his mind's eye he saw a picture of his wife, asleep upstairs, quite indifferent to the shame and disaster which she spread around her, untroubled by the faintest compunction for her doings. Fresh from Dick Stevenage, she had come in all carelessness to give her husband the final stroke in the matter of her will. Common decency might have saved her from that, he reflected, bitterly.

Castleford leaned back in his chair and indulged himself in the weak man's luxury of imaginary revenge. Suppose he loaded one of these pistols now and went up to her room? How would she look, and what would she say, when he showed her that anonymous letter? A faint sadistic smile twisted his lips as he pictured the scene to himself. *That* would make her pay something in exchange for what she had made him suffer. He could see her startled eyes and terrified face when she woke up to find him beside her, weapon in hand. It would almost be worth it!

Then, a fresh thought shot through his mind. If his wife died now, she was intestate. Where would her money go?

To satisfy a somewhat morbid curiosity, he got up and walked across to where an Encyclopaedia stood on the bookshelves. Intestacy. Inheritance. He consulted the articles, listlessly at first, then with a keener interest. So far as he could make out, if Winnie died before she had time to make a fresh will, he himself would be the person to inherit all her property. The Glencaples would be out of it completely. If anything happened to her, all his difficulties would be solved.

His mind began to range over the possibilities. A gun-accident, for instance: these things happened often enough, to judge by the newspapers. Some fool or other seemed to crop up who "didn't know it was loaded." That little brute Frankie, for instance, might easily shoot somebody—why not Winnie? Or she might come by a motor-accident; there were plenty of them, nowadays. Or there might be a mishap on the links; people had been killed by golf-balls hitting them on the head, though that rarely happened. Or, again, there might be a bungle with the hypodermic syringe, the kind of thing he'd read about somewhere . . . in Dorothy Sayers's *Unnatural Death*, that was it, of course. And who could swear that she hadn't tried to give herself an insulin injection and made a fatal botch of the business?

He became gruesomely entranced in following up some of these suggestions. The more he thought over them, the more they fascinated him. He pulled his pipe from his pocket, filled it, and settled down to think. Suppose one tried to "contrive an accident," how would one set about it? A gun-accident, for instance. Would it be better to have witnesses and chance deceiving them, or no witnesses and an unmistakable "accident," or a complete alibi?

He grew more and more engrossed in these problems, and time passed unnoticed as he smoked pipe after pipe. It was like a cricket-match, with questions for the bowling, the criminal batting, and the police organisation in place of the field, alert to pounce on any careless answer. The first ball would be the announcement of the discovery of the death. How should a murderer take that? Should he be cool, or should he pretend to lose his nerve, or should he be apparently deeply affected by the news? A slip there might lead suspicion straight upon him. And if he becomes obviously suspect, what should his pose be? Indignation? Refusal to take the thing seriously? An attitude of frank admission that the facts might be construed in that manner?

At last, in the early hours of the morning, he knocked out his pipe and got to his feet. As he switched out the lights he made a movement towards the room containing the house safe. His bearer bonds were stored in the safe, and he had decided to leave them no longer mixed up with his wife's property. If anything happened, it would be better that no mistakes could arise. He felt too sleepy to trouble about the matter, just then, however. After all, he could get the bonds any time he wanted them. And, as he reminded himself with a grim smile, if she died before changing her will, he would get the lot, so that no dispute could arise about the ownership of the scrip. Any time within the next day or two would be soon enough. He yawned sleepily and went up to his room.

5
THE TRAGEDY AT THE CHALET

Mrs. Haddon glanced from the paper jam-pot cover in her hand to the splintered pane of her cottage window and reflected once again that life was a worrying business. When Jack came home in the evening, he'd see that broken pane, and most likely he'd be angry about it. If he was in one of his bad moods, he might take it into his head to go up to Carron Hill and make a row; and if he did that, then she would probably lose her little job as caretaker to the Chalet.

Jack had been a changed man when he came back from the West Front, she ruminated dejectedly. He'd got among a bad set in the Army and picked up all sorts of notions about Bolshevism and the class-war. Nowadays he spent most of his time in grousing against anyone better off than himself, sneering at the local bigwigs in the taproom of the Pheasant Inn until the landlord—a staunch Conservative—grew restive. He was getting himself disliked by everybody; and steady work was hard enough to find, nowadays, without setting employers against you with that sort of talk.

She licked the gum of the jam-pot cover thoroughly, and then pasted the disc neatly over the starred glass. Next time Jack spotted a winner, they could get a new pane put in. The sooner the better, she reflected, as she inspected the ugly repair. She had still some pride left; and she felt that this makeshift advertised their poverty to anyone who passed the cottage. Wondering how it looked from the outside, she went to the door to examine it.

The cottage looked northward over some rolling pasture-land dotted with feeding sheep. Farther in the distance, the grounds of Carron Hill began, but they were hidden by the nearer undulations of grassland. Immediately behind the cottage rose a belt of plantation netted with intricate foot-paths threading its undergrowth; and on the south face of this strip of woodland the Chalet had been built. Beyond that again, at some distance, ran the nearest road fit for wheeled traffic. Mrs. Haddon had no neighbours; and the only passers-by, in the ordinary course, were lovers seeking the seclusion of the plantation glades. Mrs. Haddon used to watch them pass her gate in the summer evenings with feelings which were half-envious and half-pitying. Sometimes one of them would ask for a drink from the well in the garden and give her a chance of talking for a minute or two. Apart from that, she had to depend for conversation on Jack and the people she met when she went out with her basket to buy supplies from time to time.

As she inspected the patch on her window, the tail of her eye caught a spruce figure in a brown golfing-skirt emerging from one of the paths which led into the labyrinth of the plantation; and, turning to face it, she recognised Miss Lindfield. Probably on her way home from the Chalet, Mrs. Haddon guessed, since there was a short cut to Carron Hill across the pastures. A thought crossed her mind, and she hurried down the little nasturtium-bordered path to the gate. If she could get the damaged window paid for now, it would lessen the risk of Jack making trouble when he came to hear of it.

She was glad that it was Miss Lindfield who had chanced to pass and not Mrs. Castleford. Mrs. Castleford either ignored her completely or else found fault with her over the cleaning of the Chalet; but Miss Lindfield was more approachable and would sometimes do her a favour in an offhand sort of way. By Mrs. Haddon's humble standard, Miss Lindfield was "a real lady" who knew her own place and your proper place, too; whereas Mrs. Castleford "thought a bit too much of herself and treated you as if you were just dirt." Besides, if the cottage needed a bit of repairs done, Miss Lindfield was the one to go to. You couldn't impose on her; but she'd listen to you; and if she said she'd mention the matter to Mrs. Castleford, then you knew the thing was as good as done. If you went to Mrs. Castleford direct, nothing ever came of it. She forgot all about the business at once, and got cross if you ventured to remind her.

Miss Lindfield had seen Mrs. Haddon's dash to the gate. She turned away from the short cut and came towards the cottage, an alert brown figure, bare-headed, and carrying a light cardigan over one arm.

"Good afternoon, miss," began Mrs. Haddon, who was a stickler for the minor ceremonies of social intercourse.

"Good afternoon, Mrs. Haddon."

Mrs. Haddon was not quite sure, from the tone, whether she had caught Miss Lindfield in one of her best moods. However, it was too late to draw back now.

"I just wanted to show you this, miss," she explained, retreating up the path towards the cottage. "If you'll be so good as to step this way for a moment, miss, you'll see it for yourself."

Miss Lindfield, brought up to the window, showed no desire to be helpful. She merely waited in silence for enlightenment.

"It was Master Frankie did that, miss," Mrs. Haddon explained hopefully. "He's shooting with that new gun of his over in the wood and I think one of his shots must have got through the trees somehow."

She pointed to where the plantation pushed out a narrow belt of trees to the west of the cottage.

"Anyhow, it *was* one of his shots did it, miss, for I've found the bullet in the room. Very dangerous, really, miss. It might have hit me when it came through the window. I don't really think he ought to be shooting off his gun so near here, without taking more care, miss. It might have put my eye out quite easily if it had hit me there. It makes me a bit nervous, miss, for . . . there! he's at it still, you hear?"

Miss Lindfield heard the snap of the report.

"I didn't pay much attention at first," Mrs. Haddon went on. "I never thought a shot would get this length, miss. And then he was quiet for a while and I thought he'd gone away. Then it began again, miss, and the first thing I knew was the window going smash and something hitting the wall at the back of the room. It gave me such a start, miss."

"So I can well understand," said Miss Lindfield with a touch of unwonted grimness in her tone. "You see, you're not the only sufferer."

She spread out part of her cardigan, and Mrs. Haddon perceived a small hole in the fabric.

"What! Did he hit *you*, miss?" Mrs. Haddon demanded in a horrified tone.

Miss Lindfield shook her head.

"No, I was carrying it over my arm, as you saw. But a shot went through it, as I was coming along."

"Well, miss, that was a narrow shave, that really was," Mrs. Haddon declared. "What a bit of luck it didn't hit you. Really, he didn't ought to be allowed to have that gun, when he's so careless."

"I don't think you need worry any more about that," Miss Lindfield said, in a tone which betrayed an anger only half-suppressed. "I'll see that he gives up that rook-rifle tonight."

Miss Lindfield glanced at her watch.

"It might be as well to take it away from him now," she said aloud.

Then her instinct for thoroughness betrayed itself.

"I'd like to see that bullet you said you'd found," she explained. "I prefer to have something definite to go on, even when I'm dealing with a child."

Mrs. Haddon hurried into the cottage and came out with a tiny misshapen mass of lead in her palm. "That's it, miss."

"That's certainly one of his bullets," Miss Lindfield confirmed. "Well, I'll see that he pays for the damage to your window. Let me have a note of what it costs to put in a new pane. That's only fair, and it may teach . . ."

Another report from the plantation broke into her sentence, and she stopped abruptly.

"Did you hear that?" she demanded anxiously.

"What, miss? The shot? Yes, I heard that all right."

"No, something just after the shot—like a faint cry, I thought it was."

"Perhaps he's hit a rabbit, miss. There are a few rabbits in the plantation. Sometimes they give a squeal when they're hit, you know."

Miss Lindfield shook her head impatiently.

"I know a rabbit's squeal well enough. It wasn't that."

She bit her lip as though she were trying to identify the sound she had heard. Mrs. Haddon, faintly perceiving something sinister in the atmosphere, strained her ears in vain to catch any further noise.

"Do you think, miss . . . ?"

"Sh!"

They listened intently for some moments, but nothing came to them except the whistle of a bird in the plantation.

"There!"

Miss Lindfield unconsciously lifted her hand.

"I didn't catch it, miss," Mrs. Haddon confessed. "My ears aren't just what they used to be, somehow. I'm not deaf, really, or anything like that; but Jack often hears things when I can't."

Miss Lindfield paid no attention to the explanation. Another gesture demanded silence; and again they pricked up their ears. In vain, however, for only the ordinary wood-sounds came to them.

"I don't like that," Miss Lindfield said at last. An idea seemed to strike her. "Was Mrs. Castleford at the Chalet this afternoon?"

"I don't know, miss. She didn't come this way, if she is."

Miss Lindfield paused irresolutely before speaking again.

"I don't like this. We'd better go over to the Chalet, I think. There may have been an accident and . . ."

She took Mrs. Haddon's acquiescence for granted and led the way out of the tiny garden. Once on the edge of the plantation, Mrs. Haddon asserted herself.

"This is the shortest way, miss," she explained, diving into one of the numerous paths which opened before them. "This is the way I always go myself, when I'm going to the Chalet to wash up."

Miss Lindfield surrendered the leadership and allowed herself to be conducted through the labyrinth. There was a thick undergrowth which prevented them from seeing any distance ahead, and the path wound in and out, avoiding the clumps of bushes.

"You don't think, miss . . ." Mrs. Haddon panted apprehensively as she hurried along.

"I may have been mistaken," Miss Lindfield admitted.

Her tone betrayed both doubt and misgiving, as though she had begun to regret her impetuousness.

"I thought I heard something after the shot," she continued in a still more dubious tone, "but it may have been just imagination. We may as well go on, now we've come this length."

They emerged from the spinney immediately behind the Chalet. It was a one-storeyed erection, about thirty feet in length; and the style of its architecture was just sufficiently Swiss to justify the name which had been given to it. Its single floor was divided unequally into a large lounge or sitting-room and a tiny scullery with a sink fed from a rain-water tank on the roof. There were no windows in the wall facing the spinney. On the south side, fronting the view, was a concrete-floored verandah, hardly elaborate enough to be described as a loggia; and onto this opened the single door of the summerhouse. From the verandah, the ground sloped gently away for a hundred yards or so; then came a sudden dip, at the bottom of which wound the road, so that the Chalet itself was invisible to passers-by on that route.

Mrs. Haddon, still leading, rounded the corner of the building, and as she did so, Miss Lindfield heard her exclaim sharply. A moment later, Miss Lindfield herself turned the corner of the house and came in sight of the verandah. With its back to them stood a rustic armchair with a woman's figure in it; and a trickle of blood descended to a pool on the concrete floor.

Urged by that curiosity which the refined deem morbid, but which is more probably merely animal, Mrs. Haddon scuttled forward and gazed eagerly at what she saw.

"It's Mrs. Castleford, miss," she exclaimed, mingling awe and excitement in her tone. "She's been shot, miss. Look, she's been

61

shot in the back. Oh, dear, miss, this is a dreadful business. What ought we to do? She'll be dying under our eyes, miss, unless we do something, quick."

She looked up at her companion, as though demanding instructions; but for once Miss Lindfield's efficiency had met a situation beyond its scope. The fallen jaw of the body, the dreadful transmutation of the complexion, the lack-lustre eyes, all told their story beyond misapprehension. Constance Lindfield need have no fear that Winnie would ever again come between her and Dick Stevenage.

Mrs. Haddon, her world already shaken by the discovery of the body, was flabbergasted to find that she was relying on a broken reed. Instead of issuing orders, Miss Lindfield broke into an hysterical laugh; and then, seeing Mrs. Haddon's thunder-struck expression, she hurried into the Chalet and slammed the door behind her. Through the window, Mrs. Haddon heard sounds of conflicting emotions which she was hard put to it to interpret. She herself was excitable but not hysterically-inclined; and the idea that Miss Lindfield's nerves had given way was almost as disturbing to her as the body in the chair before her.

"Lord! If she's cracked up like that, what'll *I* do?" was her unspoken and terror-shot comment.

Utterly incapable of initiative in the circumstances, she stood on the verandah waiting for something to happen. She averted her eyes from the body and gazed round her in an attempt to put herself again in touch with a familiar world. There was the easel, with its half-finished picture. On the ground beside it lay the wooden sketching-box with its array of squeezed and distorted oil-colour tubes. The palette had been propped against one of the legs of the easel, and the open japanned tin brush-case had been put down close at hand.

Mrs. Haddon stared at the uncompleted sketch on the canvas. When she took up her old fad once more, Winnie had enlisted in the non-representational school of artists; and Mrs. Haddon's artistic education had not advanced sufficiently to let her appreciate this style of painting.

"I could draw about as well as that myself, I'm sure," was her uncultured mental criticism.

Her eye passed from the artist's materials to something which she understood better: the little square cane table which carried the tea things. That, at any rate, had a homely, normal appearance. There had been a visitor, evidently, for there were two used teacups and plates with biscuit-crumbs on them. Opposite one place, a cane armchair had been pushed back a little when its occupant rose from the table. That would be where the stranger sat, Mrs. Haddon surmised; for the teapot, spirit kettle, and slop-basin were beside the other cup and plate. There was no chair opposite them. Mrs. Castleford had apparently shifted her chair when she had finished her tea. Mrs. Haddon observed a fly gorging itself in the sugar-basin and with a mechanical movement of her hand she chased it away.

The sounds from within the Chalet had died down. She heard steps crossing the floor. The water-tap of the sink ran for a short time. A minute or two later, Miss Lindfield reappeared at the door, her eyes slightly reddened in spite of bathing, but apparently her own cool, collected self again.

"I'm sorry, Mrs. Haddon. I couldn't help it, you understand?"

"Yes, miss, I'm sure . . ."

Miss Lindfield had evidently no desire to dwell upon her momentary weakness.

"One of us must stay here. The other will have to go for assistance at once."

Mrs. Haddon found no difficulty in making the implied choice. She was not afraid of staying alone with the body, of course—not in broad daylight, she assured herself She wasn't one of your superstitious ones. Still . . . it seemed "more like the thing" that Miss Lindfield should remain on guard over the Chalet. If anyone happened to come along, she could explain things better. And besides, at the back of Mrs. Haddon's mind was a vision of herself, a really important person for once, breaking the tragic news in Thunderbridge village.

"I'll go, miss," she volunteered.

Much to her relief, Miss Lindfield accepted the proposal without demur.

"Very well, then. You must hurry as fast as you can. Get hold of the constable in Thunderbridge. He's very stupid, but that can't be helped. Tell him to ring up the nearest inspector, or superintendent, or whoever it is he ought to notify. See that he does that immediately. And make him ring up Carron Hill, too, and tell the people there what's happened. And then bring him back here with you. Can you remember all that? Sure of it?"

Mrs. Haddon nodded, though her brain was rather in a whirl with all these instructions.

"I'll see to it, miss."

She turned away and moved along the verandah, repeating under her breath the list of things she had to do. As she walked, her foot encountered a tiny object lying on the concrete.

"Here's something, miss," she exclaimed excitedly as she glanced down and recognised what it was. "Here's the bullet, miss. Look!"

"Where? Don't touch it!"

Miss Lindfield came to her side, stooped down, and examined the tiny missile.

"That's just the very same as the one that came through my window, miss, just the very spit of it."

Miss Lindfield stared at the little bullet for a few seconds without replying, and Mrs. Haddon saw a puzzled frown on her face.

"Leave it there," she said at last. "You'd better tell the constable you found it. But if I were you, Mrs. Haddon, I'd say nothing about it to anyone else. You understand? Sometimes it suits the police to keep things to themselves for a while, and they might want to say nothing about this. So the less gossip, the better."

Mrs. Haddon, rather annoyed at having this titbit of her own discovery treated in this way, acquiesced reluctantly.

"Well, then, get away now. Be as quick as you can."

Mrs. Haddon retreated in the direction of the path which would take her down into Thunderbridge village. She looked back once, and found Miss Lindfield covering the face of the body with something white. Mrs. Haddon wondered why she had not thought of that herself, and then continued her walk, hurrying as best she could over the rough path.

CONSTABLE GUMLEY'S SUSPICIONS

Owing to certain well-marked personal peculiarities, Police Constable Christopher Ebenezer Gumley led a drab and isolated existence, disjoined from the normal social life of Thunderbridge. His openly-expressed misogyny deprived him at a single stroke of the sympathy and companionship of half the available adult population. A staunch teetotaller, with unconcealed leanings towards Prohibition, he had wholly alienated the convivial section of the community and had cut himself off from the informal club which met nightly in the bar of the Pheasant Inn to discuss local happenings and the way of the world generally. From the sporting set he had earned undying dislike by swooping down and impounding betting slips on the one occasion when practically every client had backed the winner. True enough, they had got their stakes returned eventually, on the basis that "if you can't win, you can't lose"; but the incident had left a grievance rankling in the mind of everyone concerned, except the bookmaker. His gratitude, though warmly expressed, was lost on the constable. As to the local farmers, P. C. Gumley's activities failed to give them satisfaction. They described him as "fussy" (qualified by an adjective or an adverb according to the state of education of the speaker) on account of his proceedings in connection with straying cattle, lights on farm-vehicles, barbed wire, the Diseases of Animals Act, and innumerable other matters in which he did not see eye to eye with them. Finally, he attended no church functions except when summoned to them in his official capacity; so that even the clergy looked askance at him.

It was symptomatic of his Ishmaelite condition that no one in the village ever called him Gumley. Even in plain clothes he was branded with official rank. "The policeman," or some handier synonym, was the only description employed.

Thus on the surface, P. C. Gumley's life seemed to exemplify Gilbert's dictum. In actual fact, however, this was not so. Under his drab exterior, P. C. Gumley nursed a passion which consoled him for his estrangement from social life. He was an enthusiast for literature.

Literature is an elastic term; but in the case of P. C. Gumley it meant two things, and two only: a manual of *Police Law* and the cheaper type of crime stories. From each of these he extracted peculiar delights and equally peculiar regrets. His *Police Law* had been conned until its binding showed signs of disintegration; but an acute observer would have noted that the finger-prints had accumulated to an abnormal extent on those pages which dealt with Treason, Treason Felony, Sedition, the Official Secrets Act, and Piracy. These were the special joys of P. C. Gumley. The accompanying sorrow arose from the facts that the inhabitants of Thunderbridge village knew Treason only in connection with Guy Fawkes, that Sedition was beyond their ken, that they had no opportunity of acquainting themselves with any Official Secrets, and that Piracy is a vain dream in an inland village. No scope here for a zealous but unpracticed detective.

What life failed to provide, he sought in print. His day's duty done, he retired to his bedroom at his lodgings and, after thumbing over the long row of tattered paper-bound volumes on his shelf, he plunged with zest into a re-perusal of the rounding-up of Thick-Eared Mike or the tracking-down of Slim Harry, the International Crook. From time to time he would pull out the stub of a pencil, thoughtfully moisten the lead with his tongue, and add yet another to the series of lines which called attention to exceptionally ingenious inferences drawn by the master-sleuths.

P. C. Gumley, in fact, was a typical specimen of the unoriginal romantic. Incapable of inventing dramas, he had just enough imagination to see himself in the shoes of the hero-detective. "*Give me a body," said Detective Sergeant Gumley, "and I'll know what to do."* Or, in a more dashing vein: *"Hands up!" ordered Inspector Gumley, whipping a stubby automatic from his pocket.* Or, again, in the role of controller of destinies: *"This is where we finish with Slim Harry," said Superintendent Gumley as he picked up the desk-telephone.* These vivid little episodes were just as much a part of P. C. Gumley's life as the weary hours spent in patrolling his beat.

And now, as he stood in the village street, ruminating disgustedly on the dullness of his lot, opportunity approached him in the guise of a flurried, hatless, and rather unattractive woman, wearing old slippers and a house-apron.

"Lost her wits, and expects me to find them for her," grumbled P. C. Gumley under his breath, as he caught sight of the untidy figure. "Ugh! These women!"

Mrs. Haddon, breathless with haste and excitement, fished up to him.

"Mrs. Castleford's been shot. You know, Carron Hill. At the Chalet. In the verandah on a chair, the body is. Miss Lindfield's there. She says you're to ring up and get an Inspector or somebody at once. You're to ring up Carron Hill and tell them about it, as quick as you can. And you're to come along with me this minute and take charge till someone comes who can do something."

Those dramas played out on his mental stage had fortunately fitted P. C. Gumley for just such a situation as this. By a great effort, he guarded himself against any outward display of surprise; for by the canons of his fiction the star detective was never surprised by anything. He nodded ponderously, as though he had expected news of this kind just about that time; and then he turned over in his mind the instructions which had been transmitted to him, in the hope of striking out a fresh line for himself. Unfortunately, he could think of nothing. Miss Lindfield had covered the ground.

"Just like that wench's nerve to give me orders," he reflected crossly, as he made his way to the post-office telephone box. "She takes a lot too much on herself."

He completed his telephoning and came out into the street again to find Mrs. Haddon broadcasting an account of the tragedy to a small but increasing crowd.

"Here! None o' that!" he commanded, scowling upon her. "You keep your mouth shut and come along o' me."

Mrs. Haddon, her brief spell of glory thus cut short, shrieked a few final details to the crowd and then followed him dejectedly up the street. When they were clear of the village, he turned to her.

"Now that you've had a good bit o' gossip with your friends," he said, severely, "p'raps you'll be so good as give the Authorities your tale, if you're not too tired. The Authorities is represented by me, at present," he added, lest there should be any misunderstanding. "And anything you say may be taken down in writing and given in evidence."

Mrs. Haddon, deprived of her larger audience, was eager enough to pour out her narrative into the only available ear; and in a short time P. C. Gumley had gathered all she had to tell. He listened in silence, interpreting the data according to the rules impressed upon him by his study of crime fiction.

"Humph!" he ejaculated at last, when he had weighed the evidence. "This Lindfield . . . What's her other name? Constance, you say? Well, this Constance Lindfield seems to have managed things very well, if you ask me. V-e-r-y well, indeed," he laid marked emphasis on the words, converting what seemed a tribute into an insinuation. "She lets you discover the body—you was on the spot first, eh? She leaves you outside and goes into the Chalet where you couldn't see her. And what was she doing in there, I ask you?"

"She was having hysterics," said Mrs. Haddon simply. "I told you that. I heard her having them, laughing and sobbing and carrying on."

"I'm trying to establish the facts," said P. C. Gumley vexedly. "And you keep butting in with silly talk like that. She had a fit of hysterics then—or so you say—and then she came out again onto the verandah. And what did she do then, tell me? She sent you to the rightabout, straight off, didn't she? She got you off the premises, didn't she? Leaving herself a free hand to do anything she liked: destroy evidence, or arrange things to suit herself, or cover her tracks. If she was the criminal, you couldn't have helped her better nor what you did."

Mrs. Haddon disdained to defend herself against this charge.

"Haven't I been telling you it was an accident?" she demanded in exasperated tones. "It was that young whelp with his rook-rifle. Didn't I tell you I found the bullet on the verandah, the very identical same as the one he put through my cottage window not long before? And besides that, wasn't Miss Lindfield standing right beside me in my own garden when the shot was fired?"

P. C. Gumley assumed the expression of weary superiority which he thought suitable to the occasion.

"Here am I trying to consider this affair from every side, and you start in to try to muddle me up with your notions. If you'd studied crime the way I have, you'd know that the first thing a murderer needs is a good alibi; and the better alibi a person's got, the more I'd suspect him. For why? An ordinary innocent person isn't thinking of getting up an alibi. He has to take his chance of one. But a murderer's planning for a good alibi all the time. It's plain enough. You're talking just like what one expects from the ignorant public; I'm telling you what experts think."

Mrs. Haddon was silenced, but not convinced. They hurried on, side by side; and P. C. Gumley, in his mental theatre, rehearsed the role which he meant to play when he reached the Chalet. His first speech, he decided, should be on the lines of: 'I am Hawkshaw, the Detective.'' That would give the criminal a jar, straight off; and one could then follow it up with something incisive, with a double meaning if possible, which would make the guilty party blench or wince or cower, as in the books. He was not quite sure how one blenched, but he expected to recognise the symptom when he saw it.

Despite his mental preparation, the scene shaped itself quite differently in reality. In the first place, as they hurried up the wood-path, they came suddenly upon Miss Lindfield walking to and fro among the trees with her eyes on the ground. P. C. Gumley's mental scene had been staged on the verandah itself, and this change of venue disconcerted him. Besides, he was taken unawares.

"I'm Police Constable Gumley."

Somehow, even to his own ears, it had hardly the same ring as: "I am Hawkshaw, the Detective."

Miss Lindfield appeared quite unimpressed. She did not cower or wince; nor could P. C. Gumley see anything which might have been blenching. She looked him up and down coolly; and P. C. Gumley felt that here was the very type of the ruthless women criminals whom he had met so often in his studies. Then she spoke, and his self-importance wilted while his suspicions and animosity increased.

"I know that. Have you done what Mrs. Haddon told you to do? Rung up someone in authority? Given the Carron Hill people the news? Very good. Then you can go over these"—she nodded towards the Chalet which was visible among the trees—"and sit down on the verandah till someone comes. Don't touch anything, you understand?"

P. C. Gumley did not cower, but he unmistakably winced under this treatment.

"I'm in charge here now," he pointed out in what was meant for the grand manner but which was not a markedly successful assumption. "I've got to get the evidence ready for the Inspector, when he comes."

He fished a battered notebook from his pocket and searched for his pencil. Miss Lindfield watched his efforts unsympathetically.

"I can lend you a pencil, if you've lost yours," she said impatiently. "If you want to do something, you'd better take down Mrs. Haddon's account of the affair. You can sit on the verandah steps, if you like. Don't sit on the chairs. They mustn't be shifted. And don't bother me. I'm worried. I'll see the Inspector when he comes."

Things had hardly worked out as P. C. Gumley had planned. He felt that he was losing his grip on the situation. All the woman-hater in him rose to his assistance. He gripped his notebook firmly, licked his pencil, and stood his ground.

"I'll just have to ask you a few questions," he said in what he hoped was a stern tone.

Miss Lindfield shrugged her shoulders and her eyes sparkled dangerously.

"You can't force me to answer questions. You ought to know that. I'm going to wait here until your Inspector comes. I'll give him all the necessary information, then."

She paused. Then an afterthought struck her, and she added:

"And don't go trampling about that verandah. Keep off it altogether. There's a bullet lying there. You might crush it with those boots of yours."

Without awaiting a response, she turned away from him and resumed her pacing among the trees.

P. C. Gumley watched her for a few moments, but for all the notice she took of him he might have been still in Thunderbridge village. His lips moved as he repeated under his breath: "Ugh! These women!" This time, however, his intonation betrayed less superiority and much more resentment than when he had used the phrase before. P. C. Gumley had been thoroughly snubbed; and not all the resources of his mental theatre could disguise the fact.

A half-turn brought Mrs. Haddon within range of his eye, and he found her staring at him curiously. He bethought himself of his dignity and resolved to assert himself in her case.

"I'll begin with you," he announced. "You come along o' me, and I'll take down your story. I've got to draw up my Report for the Authorities."

He led the way towards the verandah.

"Now you sit yourself down there"—he pointed to the bottom of the broad flight of steps leading from the verandah to the grass—"and I'll sit here"—choosing the top step—"and then we can talk."

P. C. Gumley was a tall man and had learned by experience what an advantage is gained in an interview by superior elevation. He opened his notebook again, sucked his pencil thoughtfully, and began his investigation.

"You was in your garden and you saw this Lindfield coming out of this spinney on the far side, alongside your cottage. Was she coming from this Chalet? Are there two 'l's' or only one in Chalet?"

"There's only one," Mrs. Haddon assured him. "It's a Swiss word."

"It don't look right, somehow," P. C. Gumley said doubtfully after writing it down. "However, be that as it may. Was this Lindfield coming from this Chalet, that's what I want to know."

"No, she wasn't," Mrs. Haddon said, positively.

P. C. Gumley made a movement to jot this down and then hesitated.

"How d'you know that?" he demanded,

"Because she told me so, herself," rejoined Mrs. Haddon, triumphantly.

P. C. Gumley was falling back into the Hawkshaw pose. He lifted his eyebrows slightly.

"She tells you that, and you tell me that again. That's hearsay, that is—like what the soldier said. It ain't evidence. Where would she have been coming from if it wasn't from this Chalet?"

Mrs. Haddon turned half-round and waved her hand towards an outlying spur of the plantation which ran down towards the sunken road.

"She was taking the short cut to Carron Hill when I called her: I told you that before. There's a path runs up from the road down there, through these trees into the spinney, and then it goes on over the fields in front of my cottage. That's where she was going."

P. C. Gumley shook his head, murmured "Hearsay" a contemptuous tone, and jotted down a note.

"Had this Lindfield a pistol in her hand, or a gun of any sort, when you saw her first?" he demanded.

"No, she hadn't. I've got eyes in my head, haven't I?"

"I suppose your eyes are the kind that can see into people's pockets?" he inquired with delicate irony. "She might have been carrying a dozen pistols, and you no wiser for it."

But here he was challenging an expert on her own ground.

"If you'd gone and got married, you'd have known more than to talk silly like that," Mrs. Haddon retorted. "She was wearing a golfing-skirt, as you can see for yourself if you cast your eyes over there. Ladies don't have pockets in their skirts. And there was nothing in the pockets of her cardigan either, for she spread it out to let me see the bullet-hole in it. So there!"

"I'll put it down that you saw no pistol in this Lindfield's possession at that time," said P. C. Gumley judicially. "That's all the evidence warrants. Now, what time was it when you saw her come out of the spinney?"

Mrs. Haddon made a gesture which suggested that the answer was beyond her.

"How do I know? The kitchen clock's the only one I've got, and it stopped last week."

P. C. Gumley nodded wearily. Just what one might have expected from an ill-trained mind, he reflected. No powers of observation, no accuracy. Hopeless. He sucked his pencil, seeking for inspiration but finding none. Then he glanced back at the verandah and noticed the tea table.

"This Mrs. Castleford, she had a visitor this afternoon."

Mrs. Haddon's nerves were beginning to weaken under the strain of the afternoon's events; and she had lost her awe of P. C. Gumley.

"I can see two teacups myself," she said, tartly.

"Then this Lindfield was having tea with her?"

"That she wasn't," said Mrs. Haddon, positively.

"Now, wait a bit," said P. C. Gumley with ponderous alertness. "You was at your cottage until this Lindfield came there, you say. You wasn't at this Chalet. And yet you say you're sure it wasn't this Lindfield that was having tea here. I warned you before about hearsay. How can you make out that you know whether she was or she wasn't having tea here?"

"Because I keep my eyes open, of course. I've washed up the cups here for years. Mrs. Castleford's dropped sugar; she takes some stuff called satsharin or something like that for her health. Miss Lindfield never touches sugar in her tea. One of those cups has sugar in it, 'cause I saw it myself when I looked at the tea table a while ago. That's how I know."

P. C. Gumley tried to find a flaw in this reasoning, but failed. He jotted down a fresh note, attributing the deduction to himself.

Then he cudgelled his brains for fresh questions which seemed hard to devise.

"This boy with the rook-rifle—has he a firearm certificate and a gun licence?"

Mrs. Haddon quite rightly regarded this as outside her scope.

"You'd better ask at Carron Hill about that. Miss Lindfield could say, maybe."

"This boy's been shooting off his gun round about here this afternoon you say. Has he been firing a lot?"

Mrs. Haddon seemed to regard this question as of greater importance than some of its predecessors, probably because it touched her more personally.

"I didn't pay much attention to him at first," she said carefully. "I heard him firing now and again, but that's about all I can remember. Then he was quiet for a bit, and I thought he'd gone away. And then a shot broke my window-pane, and I was just thinking about going out to check him when he stopped firing for a bit. Then there was another shot or two, and there was more while I was standing talking to Miss Lindfield. At least, that's how I seem to remember it."

P. C. Gumley laboriously noted down these statements and was about to carry his inquiries further when his eye caught two figures coming over the edge of the dip at the sunken road. He recognised them and rose to his feet.

"That's Inspector Westerham and Sergeant Ferryhill," he informed Mrs. Haddon. "They've come up in a car, I expect."

The two figures drew near to the Chalet. P. C. Gumley's hour of opportunity had run its course.

7
INSPECTOR WESTERHAM'S INQUIRY

Inspector Westerham, though a bachelor, had none of the morose misogyny which distinguished P. C. Gumley. As a private individual, he liked pretty girls better than the other kind, and never scrupled to tell them so. When acting in his official capacity, however, he pursued his inquiries with equal thoroughness, whether the witness was good-looking or ill-favoured. Or rather, to be more accurate, he suffered a mental dichotomy when dealing professionally with a pretty girl. One part of his mind registered and reviewed her physical attractions, whilst another part, wholly uninfluenced by these, stolidly devoted itself to the collection of the facts necessary for his case. Thus, at no cost to his efficiency, he managed to make the best of both worlds.

As he came up the grass slope from the road, followed by the sergeant, he took in the verandah with the still figure in the chair, the easel, the tea table, Mrs. Haddon on the steps, P. C. Gumley on his feet, ready to salute; and then his glance passed to Miss Lindfield who, at the sight of him, had come out from among the trees and was approaching him without haste.

"Fine girl, that," commented the unofficial half of his mind approvingly. The official part of his brain registered the fact that here was an educated witness who might, if she kept her head, be able to give him a plain story unencumbered by wholly irrelevant details.

Stuffing his notebook into his pocket, P. C. Gumley came forward hurriedly and saluted his superior.

"I've got the main facts ready for you, sir. Acting on information received, I . . ."

Inspector Westerham knew something about P. C. Gumley's exterior personality. In his opinion, P. C. Gumley was a dull fellow, thoroughly honest, but with an unfortunate way of handling affairs. The Inspector was wholly incognizant of the Hawkshaw side to the constable's character. If it had been revealed to him, he would have been excusably amused.

"I'll hear your report by-and-by," he said. "The surgeon will be here before very long. Go down to the road there and stop him if he doesn't know where we are."

P. C. Gumley, with an effort, concealed his annoyance at being temporarily shunted off the main scene and trudged away in the direction of the sunken road. The Inspector turned to meet Miss Lindfield, who had now come up to him.

"I'm Inspector Westerham," he introduced himself. Then after a slight and natural pause he added: "I'm new to the district, and I'm afraid I don't know your name."

"My name's Lindfield—Constance Lindfield. I live with Mrs. Castleford at Carron Hill, over yonder. This is a dreadful affair, Mr. Westerham. She's dead, you know."

She bit her lip and nodded in the direction of the verandah. The official section of Inspector Westerham made an entry in his mental ledger: "Had a bad shock, this girl. Plucky, though. Holding herself down well. Needs careful handling, or her nerves may go to bits all at once." He made an understanding sound helped out by a reassuring gesture, and waited for her to continue.

"It's a gun-accident," Miss Lindfield explained, in a voice which she had evidently some difficulty in mastering. "We found her here, dead—Mrs. Haddon and I—and I sent for you at once. I don't know whether that's right or not. It was the first thing that came into my mind after I pulled myself together."

"That was quite right," the Inspector reassured her. "Very wise of you to bring us in at once."

With a word of apology, he left her for a moment or two and made a brief examination of Mrs. Castleford's body. When he returned, he was still more doubtful about the state of Miss Lindfield's nerves. The sight of some rustic chairs at the nearer end of the verandah suggested his next move.

"It's been a bit of a shock to you," he said, kindly. "I think you'd better sit down, while you tell me about it. You're hardly fit to stand."

The sergeant, at his orders, brought down a couple of chairs, and Inspector Westerham unobtrusively manoeuvred Miss Lindfield into the one which had its back to the Chalet. She sank into it gratefully and rewarded his thoughtfulness with a rather pathetic smile.

"Now, Mr. Westerham, if you'll ask your questions . . ."

The Inspector gave a swift appraising glance at her face and concluded that over-much badgering might precipitate the nervous collapse which he feared. If that came, he would have to postpone his examination, lose time, and have the whole affair to go over again on some future occasion.

"I'd rather you told me in your own words what you know about it," he suggested. "If anything occurs to me as you go along, I'll ask a question or two."

Miss Lindfield nodded to show that she understood his point.

"I'm in a horrible position, Mr. Westerham," she said, frankly, leaning forward in her chair and looking him in the face. "I can't help feeling that I'm responsible for this dreadful affair, to some extent; and you can guess how that makes me feel. The fact is, some days ago I gave a boy who's staying with us at Carron Hill a rook-rifle as a present. Of course he was warned to be careful with it. I looked on it as a mere toy, myself. It never entered my head that it might be really dangerous, you understand?"

"A rook-rifle? That would be a .22?" interjected the Inspector.

"Yes, I think that's what it said in the advertisement when I ordered it."

"What about a firearms certificate and a gun licence?" Westerham inquired casually.

"That was all right," Miss Lindfield explained. "It said in the catalogue—I bought the thing by post—that a police permit was needed before I could buy the gun. So I got one and sent it on with

78

my order. Then it turned out that Frankie had to have one as well. I explained about that, and they made no difficulty. He's just over fourteen. And I got him a gun licence as well."

Inspector Westerham had no acute interest in these formal matters. His aim in asking the questions had been to set Miss Lindfield at her ease, if possible, before tackling the graver side of the affair.

"I understand," he said. "Everything's in order there."

Miss Lindfield did not immediately take advantage of the pause. She crossed one knee over the other, mechanically smoothed down her skirt, and seemed to be pondering for a moment or two.

"I hardly know where to begin," she admitted candidly, at last. "At lunch, I happened to ask Frankie—Frank Glencaple is the boy's name—I happened to ask him if his ammunition was running out. I knew he'd been firing it away pretty fast; and it turned out that he was very near the end of his supply. I'd made up my mind to go for a walk this afternoon; and I suggested that he might meet me as I was coming back and go with me into Thunderbridge to buy some more. The ironmonger in the village stocks cartridges, but it occurred to me that he might make difficulties about selling them to a boy like Frankie, who looks younger than his age. If I were there, it would be all right."

"A very sound precaution," said the Inspector, approvingly. "Of course, the police permit safeguards the seller from dealing with boys actually under age; but still, it's as well to have an adult as a sort of guarantee."

Miss Lindfield nodded slightly and then continued her story.

"While we were at lunch I gathered—I can't remember exactly how it came up—that Mrs. Castleford proposed to come here, to the Chalet, this afternoon and do some painting. It was probably mentioned in the general conversation. I paid no particular attention to it at the time, for she often comes here to paint. By the way, I don't think I told you that she is my half-sister? That's how I come to be at Carron Hill."

"I see," the Inspector interjected as she halted for a moment. "Do you mind telling me who else there is at Carron Hill?"

"Only Mr. Castleford and his daughter. Not a daughter of Mrs. Castleford—a stepdaughter."

"What age is she?" inquired the Inspector.

"Hillie? Her name's Hilary. She's about twenty."

"And Mrs. Castleford?"

"Thirty-five. Her husband's eight or nine years older."

"What's Mr. Castleford's profession?"

"None. Mrs. Castleford had money from her first husband—Mr. Donald Glencaple."

"Thanks," said the Inspector apologetically. "I'm supposed to collect facts like these. I'm sorry I had to interrupt you."

Miss Lindfield seemed to have lost the thread of her narrative.

"Where was I? Oh, yes, I remember now. At lunch, I arranged with Frankie that I'd meet him in the spinney here, on my way back from my walk. I didn't fix any particular time, because he could easily amuse himself with his rook-rifle until I turned up. I wish I'd never thought of that, and then this dreadful affair wouldn't have happened."

She turned her head and glanced away over the belt of wooded land which stretched out below them. Inspector Westerham, unwilling to embarrass her unnecessarily, looked down at her ankles, which the unofficial part of him found of interest. The official section, its scope of observation thus limited, took note of the fact that one shoe was tapping the ground mechanically. "Nerves still on the stretch," was his inference.

He lifted his eyes again to find her looking at him with a slightly ashamed expression.

"I'm sorry," she apologised in a dry voice. "I'll go on now. You see that arm of the spinney that stretches down towards the road there, on the right? I arranged to meet Frankie there. It's only a belt of trees about a hundred yards wide, so there didn't seem to be much chance of missing him in it. I came into it from the far side and followed a path that runs up the middle, so I didn't come in sight of the Chalet. Besides, I'd something else to think about. As I was coming through the wood, I heard the rook-rifle go off, and a bullet went clean through the cardigan I was carrying over my arm. It was the merest luck that I wasn't hit by it."

The Inspector made an inarticulate sound expressing sympathy.

"I was furious, of course," Miss Lindfield went on, "and I called to the boy. Probably he saw that I'd lost my temper, for he kept under cover and I didn't get hold of him. He's not altogether obedient at times. As I knew I was sure to see him later on, I didn't waste time over him then, but went straight on up the path to the back of the spinney—over yonder—where Mrs. Haddon's cottage is. She's a kind of caretaker for the Chalet—washes up tea things when necessary, and keeps the place tidy. She came out and told me a story about having her window smashed by a bullet from the rook-rifle; and I promised to confiscate it. I was angry with the boy for his carelessness, naturally."

She paused for a moment.

"I wish I'd never given him that beastly gun!" she broke out, vehemently.

After another pause, she continued her narrative.

"As Mrs. Haddon and I were standing at her cottage, I heard one or two more shots fired; and close on the last one I heard another noise, something that sounded like a cry. You can understand, Mr. Westerham, that I was naturally keyed up then for anything about shots; and when I heard that sound . . ."

"You thought something was wrong?"

"Well, I was nervous after being so nearly hit myself. I remembered that Mrs. Castleford said she was going to the Chalet to paint; and the sound seemed to come from the direction of the Chalet. I was very uneasy. I asked Mrs. Haddon if Mrs. Castleford was at the Chalet. She didn't know. I had a kind of feeling that something was far wrong—I can't explain it. So I got her to come with me. We found Mrs. Castleford lying in the chair, there, quite dead. What happened immediately after that, I can't tell you. I'm afraid I had a bad fit of hysterics. I simply couldn't keep control of myself. But as soon as I got a grip on my nerves again, I sent Mrs. Haddon off at once to bring assistance."

"You touched nothing, I hope?"

"No, I had enough sense left to see to that. The only thing I did was to cover her face. Oh, one thing more, Mrs. Haddon found the bullet lying on the verandah. I made her leave it exactly where it was. It looked to me very like the one she said had broken her cottage-window."

Inspector Westerham, seeing that she had finished her tale, allowed a few moments to elapse before putting a question.

"Times are important, often. Could you give me any help there?"

Miss Lindfield shook her head.

"That's difficult," she confessed. "You see, I'm like most people; I don't go about with my eye on my watch. The only definite time I've got is eighteen minutes past five; that was when Mrs. Haddon and I discovered Mrs. Castleford here. I had just enough coolness left to make a note of that before I broke down. But the rest's guesswork; you can work it out as well as I can. I walk about three and a half miles per hour usually. I spent perhaps a couple of minutes trying to get hold of that boy in the wood. Mrs. Haddon and I talked for a short time at her cottage—I'd put it at three minutes or so but you'd better confirm that by asking her too. From that you can work out roughly when I entered the spinney from the road down there, if you take the distances into account. I can't give you any other definite figure."

Inspector Westerham had not hoped for even so much as this. He seemed to muse for a moment or two, then he asked another question.

"You did not actually see this boy in the wood?"

Miss Lindfield shook her head decidedly.

"No, as I told you, I didn't trouble much about him then, for I knew I could get hold of him later. I merely called, once or twice, and when he didn't come, I let it go at that."

"You saw nobody else in the wood?"

"No, nobody. There's a lot of undergrowth in that spinney and one doesn't see far in it."

"May I look at your cardigan?"

"It's over yonder on the rail of the verandah," Miss Lindfield indicated. "Do you mind holding over your questions for a little while? I'm feeling rather sick. Nerves, I expect," she added, with a feeble attempt to smile.

"You've kept up wonderfully so far," said the Inspector encouragingly. "You'd best just sit here quietly now, and try not to dwell on the details too much. I'll not trouble you just now. There are other things I can do."

Leaving her, he stepped over to the verandah and lifted the cardigan from the rail. A swift, furtive examination of its pockets disclosed nothing but a pencil stub, a golf scoring-card, a matchbox and a tiny pocket handkerchief. He spread out the garment on the grass and examined it with care. Instead of a single bullet hole, he detected two minute punctures; and by bringing the two together while the cardigan was draped over his arm, he satisfied himself that the shot had traversed the jacket while the fabric was doubled in a natural fold. The shot-holes were ill-defined, owing to the nature of the material; but their size corresponded roughly to what he expected from a .22 bullet.

Miss Lindfield's vanity bag had been wrapped in the cardigan, and he took the opportunity to make a surreptitious inspection of its contents. Except for a Yale key, he found only the ordinary appliances which every girl carries with her: lipstick, comb, powder-puff, purse, mirror, and a second flimsy handkerchief.

A gesture brought the sergeant to his side and together, after uncovering themselves, they stepped gingerly on to the verandah and began a detailed examination. Inspector Westerham was the first to discover the bullet. He noted mentally the lie of the bit of metal and then picked it up for closer inspection, marking its situation on the concrete with a piece of chalk which he took from his pocket.

"A .22 bullet right enough," he commented as he showed it to the sergeant. "All lead, you see. Might have come from one of these bulleted breech caps they sell for saloon guns."

He took a miniature envelope from his pocket, stowed the projectile in it, and returned it to his pocket.

The tea table next attracted his attention and he walked across to it, followed by the sergeant. Westerham ran his eye over the assembled articles and catalogued them in an undertone:

"Teapot on its stand under the cosy." He lifted the cosy, opened the lid of the pot and peered inside. "Looks as if they'd had a cup apiece and then filled up the pot again with hot water. It's a smooth electroplate teapot. Sure to be some finger marks on it, though there may be nothing in that. Electroplate spirit kettle on stand"—he lifted it slightly—"with most of the water gone, as I expected. Spirit lamp's been turned out. Ordinary box of house-matches. Slop-basin unused. That means just one cup of tea apiece, they had. That electroplate does take fingerprints nicely. This cut glass biscuit-box would be no good for that kind of thing. Sugar basin's electroplate too. Very wise, that. If they'd kept solid silver here, this Chalet would have been worth breaking into, especially as it's lonely and unused, half the time. Cut lemon and fruit-knife on a plate."

"What's that for?" inquired the sergeant, who was a simple person.

"Russian tea. Try a slice of lemon in your cup instead of milk, if you want to know what it's like. See the slices in these cups. Very wise, that."

"Why?" asked the sergeant, who was rather out of his depth among these refinements.

"How would they get fresh cream up here, when they only use the place now and again? Probably they don't like condensed milk. There's no cream-jug, anyhow, as you can see."

He turned with more interest to the teacups, tilting the lemon slices aside so that he could examine the interior of the cups.

"Some sugar left in this cup, opposite the chair. Not a sign of any in the other cup. I'd have expected some."

His eye fell on a little phial lying beside the unsugared cup.

"This explains it. Saccharin. Diabetic people use it instead of sugar. I wonder if she was diabetic. The bottle's empty, anyhow."

From the expression on the sergeant's face, it seemed as though he judged that life must be very complex for some people when even so simple a thing as a cup of tea could introduce him to two novelties simultaneously.

The Inspector was examining the remains of two cigarettes which had been left in the saucers. One was a mere stub, the other had gone out when only half-smoked.

"Both of them are the same brand: Craven A, Virginia, cork-tipped," he reported for the sergeant's benefit. "Let's look into this and get done with it. Where's Mrs. Castleford's hand-bag? She must have had one with her."

They drew blank in their search until the Inspector bethought himself that Mrs. Castleford might have slipped her bag down beside her on her chair. He drew it out warily, handling it with caution so as not to leave his own traces on it. Inside it was the cigarette-case he was seeking; and on opening it he found it stocked with cork-tipped Craven A's.

"So they were both smoking her cigarettes. That doesn't help much towards the identity of this visitor, whoever it was," he admitted to himself. "What about the matches they used?"

Two used matches lay on the concrete beside the table; but they carried him no further, since they obviously came from the box on the tea table.

"One match used to light the spirit lamp and one to light the cigarettes," the Inspector surmised. "Not worth bothering to look for more just now."

He moved over to the easel and stood for a moment before the unfinished picture on it. Apparently it suggested nothing to him from the artistic point of view. He put out a fingertip and ascertained that while most of the paint was dry, a small portion was still moist.

"She didn't do much work today, by the look of things interrupted by her visitor, perhaps."

Then, as his eyes travelled down to the painting materials, he noted something which Mrs. Haddon had missed. One brush, loaded with paint, was splayed out against the concrete flooring as though someone had trodden it flat in passing.

Inspector Westerham was endowed with one gift which may be either a blessing or a curse, according to the way in which it is used. He had a well-balanced mind. When he had started his investigation, he had begun entirely without prepossessions of any sort. If he had been forced to put his views into words, he would probably have said: "Here's a woman dead. It doesn't matter a damn to me, personally, whether she died by accident, or was murdered, or committed suicide. My job's to find out which it was and how it happened. I'd be a fool to get preconceived notions into my head until I've got data enough to go on. My case grows out of the data. Some people make up their minds first and then collect data to fit the case they've chosen. I can't do things that way, somehow." There was, in fact, a total lack of those flashes of intuition which played so large a part in P. C. Gumley's methods of detection.

Even at this advanced stage of his investigation, Inspector Westerham had only reached the point of dismissing suicide from the problem; and he had done that on the prosaic grounds that he could find no weapon near the body and that suicides do not usually shoot themselves in the back. Beyond this, he retained a completely open mind.

He stared thoughtfully at the crushed paintbrush for a few moments; then, apparently dismissing it from his mind, he turned to examine the general lie of the objects on the verandah. One chair, slightly pushed back from the table, was plainly that which had been occupied by the unknown guest. Equally obviously, Mrs. Castleford had been sitting at the table when she smoked her cigarette after tea, since she had dropped the unfinished remains of it into her saucer. The table had been set up close to the Chalet wall. Now the chair with the body in it was stationed some ten feet from the table and midway between the house-wall and the verandah rail. At the table, its occupant would have been fairly screened against a high dropping shot from the wood; whereas in the new position the verandah roof offered hardly any protection. To get the chair into this final situation, it must have been pulled diagonally across the verandah for some ten feet. And in the end, it had obviously landed in a position which must have made conversation more difficult than before, if the guest remained at the table.

Somewhat perplexed by this curious state of things, Inspector Westerham went forward and examined the faint track left by the wooden feet of the chair as they grated on the concrete during the movement. Clearly enough, the chair had been dragged into its new position and not simply lifted up and transferred.

Apparently the Inspector was not satisfied. He went along to the far end of the verandah where a similar chair was standing, and with one hand on its back he pulled it across the concrete in imitation of the movement of the fatal chair. Then, going down on his knees, he examined the track left by his own operation. It was strikingly fainter than the other; but otherwise both were much alike—simply straight lines of uniform thickness.

Why had Mrs. Castleford's chair left a plainer mark than the other? That seemed easy enough to answer. Probably she was sitting in it while she manoeuvred it into a fresh position, and her weight had made the scrape plainer. The empty chair would not bear so heavily on the concrete.

But this merely opened up a fresh problem to the Inspector, and he went back to examine the track left by Mrs. Castleford's chair. When a person tries to move the chair in which he is sitting, he does it by a series of jerks, since he has to shift his feet between each effort. These jerks should produce a track which is uneven in intensity and which is made up of a series of short zigzags instead of a single straight line. But the track of Mrs. Castleford's chair, as he assured himself, was a straight one of uniform intensity along its course.

The inference seemed plain enough. Mrs. Castleford was in the chair when it was moved—the intensity of the marks showed that. But the uniform and undeviating track proved that she herself had not been the agent in the movement. Therefore the chair must have been pulled or pushed into its new position by a second person, while Mrs. Castleford sat in it, callous to the uncomfortable grating which its movement was bound to cause.

"That's a rum start," was Inspector Westerham's reflection, which he took care not to utter aloud. "Presumably this visitor, whoever it was, must have shifted the chair. But why didn't she get up while it was being shifted? That would have been easier on the visitor and a sight more comfortable for her, too."

A fresh interpretation occurred to him, and he examined the concrete round the original site of the chair, close to the table.

"No blood here," he reflected finally. "So she wasn't shot here and then shifted into the other position after that. And yet she didn't shift for the sake of looking at the view. She's still side-on to that, and must have been looking along the verandah just the same as if she'd stayed at the table."

Still puzzling over this problem, he walked over and tried to enter the Chalet. A Yale lock baulked him. He recollected that when he had looked into Mrs. Castleford's bag in search of the cigarette-case, he had noticed a Yale key there, to which he had paid no attention at the moment. He picked up the bag, extracted the key, tried it on the door and found that it turned the lock. Then he remembered the Yale key he had seen in Miss Lindfield's bag.

"Go and ask Miss Lindfield how many people have keys of this door," he ordered.

In a moment or two the sergeant returned.

"She says that Mr. Castleford, Mrs. Castleford, Miss Castleford, and Mrs. Haddon have keys, as well as herself. There may be more, she says; but that's all she knows of, definitely."

The Inspector nodded in answer, and then entered the Chalet, followed by the sergeant.

He found himself in a sitting room. The curtains were drawn close, and only a twilight pervaded the place. Cautiously the Inspector parted them and let in more light. One glance at the floor and rugs satisfied him that there was no need to spend time hunting for footprints, especially for the kind of footmark which interested him at the moment. The person who had stepped on the paintbrush had left no traces inside the Chalet.

A big comfortable settee filled one corner of the room, its cushions tumbled in disorder.

"That would be Miss Lindfield's doing," suggested the sergeant. "Miss Haddon, she says Miss Lindfield had a bad fit of hysterics after they found the body. I expect she tossed and tumbled about on that settee there while she was carrying on the way they do in hysterics."

"Very likely," Westerham agreed.

He turned to examine the contents of the room. Three chairs were placed carelessly about the floor, but these had obviously not been used, for their down cushions remained just as they were after Mrs. Haddon had given them a shake-up that morning. The ashtrays on the little table were clean, and there was no tang of tobacco in the air of the room. The grate contained some ashes of burnt paper; but the fragments were tiny; and although Westerham went down on his knees and examined them closely, he could see no trace of any writing on them. The waste-paper basket detained him longer; but even a zealous hunt through its contents yielded nothing which seemed likely to help him. A torn-up invoice from one of the village shops took some time to piece together, and then turned out to be a bill for tea and sugar. He identified, easily enough, the bits of two golf scoring-cards, similar to the one he had seen in Miss Lindfield's pocket. Another crumpled-up piece of paper had nothing on it except what seemed to be a series of games of Noughts and Crosses, apparently the last resource of someone detained at the Chalet on a rainy day. The final document was obviously a shopping-list, with the items erased as they were purchased.

"Nothing much here," he commented as he rose to his feet again and dusted his knees.

A tiny writing desk raised his hopes; but on examination it yielded nothing but a stock of unused writing paper and envelopes.

"We'll try the back premises—the scullery, or whatever it is."

Pushing open a door, he found himself in a tiny room, hardly bigger than a large cupboard, fitted with a sink and some shelves for tea things.

"They've filled the kettle here," said Sergeant Ferryhill, whose strong point was the detection of the obvious. "See the bit of water splashed on the edge of the dish-board?"

The Inspector ran his finger along the surface of the cake of soap in the dish beside the sink, and then felt the towel hanging from a hook.

"Somebody's been washing their hands here, not so long ago," he pointed out.

"That would be Miss Lindfield, I expect," volunteered the sergeant. "That Mrs. Haddon, she told me she'd heard her—Miss Lindfield I mean—at the sink after she'd had her hysterics."

"Bathing her face, perhaps," the Inspector hazarded. "I thought she looked pretty trim when we saw her first, considering what she'd gone through. Well, there's nothing more to look at, here."

As they re-entered the sitting-room, they caught sight of P. C. Gumley standing at the door of the Chalet.

"The surgeon's come, sir. He's outside looking at the body."

"Take that cap of yours off," snapped the Inspector. "Do you usually stump about with your hat on in presence of the dead?"

P. C. Gumley sullenly removed his headgear and stepped aside from the doorway to allow them to reach the verandah.

8

DR. RIPPONDEN'S CONTRIBUTION

The police surgeon was kneeling beside the chair, but he rose to his feet as the Inspector greeted him.

"I left the body just as it was when I came on the scene," Westerham explained. "It hasn't been moved."

The doctor made a faint gesture as though to indicate that he had expected these ordinary precautions.

"What do you make of it, doctor?" the Inspector inquired, as the surgeon remained silent.

Dr. Berkeley Ripponden shrugged his shoulders slightly. He disliked a general question of this sort. His Court experience had implanted in him a habit of saying as little as possible in answer to queries. He seldom volunteered information. "Yes," "No," and "I can't say," were his favourite responses. His manner had just a shade of touchiness in it, as though at the end of every reply he added mentally: "And if you don't like that, then go and find out for yourself."

"She's dead, of course," he said curtly.

"You've seen the two wounds, the entry one in her back and the exit one in front?"

"Yes."

"The bullet seems to have gone clean through her," Westerham pointed out. "I found it farther along the verandah."

He fished the envelope from his pocket and showed the projectile to the surgeon, who nodded without comment.

"She's shot through the heart, isn't she?" Westerham persisted.
"It looks like it."

"That would kill her almost at once?"

"I'll be able to say more when I've done a P.M."

Westerham tried again.

"Did you notice anything about her eyes? A lot of iris showing?"

Dr. Ripponden seemed to bestow some tacit commendation on the Inspector's observational powers.

"You noticed that, did you? The pupils are much contracted."

"Is that usual in deaths by violence?"

Dr. Ripponden shook his head.

"Can you suggest any cause for it, then?"

"Some miotic drug, perhaps. Pilocarpine, picrotoxine, morphine, physostigmine—any of them would produce the effect. What they call 'pin-point pupil' is a well-known symptom with morphine."

"You think she's been drugged?"

"It looks like it," Dr. Ripponden admitted, cautiously. "Would you like to have her shifted into the Chalet, so as to make a fuller examination?" the Inspector asked.

Dr. Ripponden nodded affirmatively.

"Well, just a moment before we alter anything," Westerham said.

He chalked round the four feet of the chair, to mark its position on the verandah. Then, taking a Coddington lens from his pocket, he went round to the back of the body and made a close study of the dress near the wound, continuing his exploration to include the hair about the nape of the neck.

"No sign of any singeing," he reported. "That's what one would expect, from a shot fired at a distance, obviously. Now I won't keep you waiting more than a minute or two."

From another pocket he extracted a small prismatic compass. Walking along the verandah and stationing himself at the point where the bullet had been found, he took the bearing of the body. Then, replacing the compass in his pocket, he summoned the sergeant and P. C. Gumley.

"We'd better carry chair and all, inside," he suggested to the surgeon. "It'll be easier, that way."

Dr. Ripponden offered no objection. As the Inspector was turning away, however, he stopped him.

"You'd better lend me that bullet for a minute or two," he said. "It's a bit battered; but the base is intact. I want to compare it with the entrance wound, once I can get at the skin."

The Inspector handed over the little missile. The body was transported into the Chalet, when Westerham dismissed his men and assisted the doctor to make the necessary preparations for his examination. That done, he left Dr. Ripponden to his task and went on to the verandah again.

Miss Lindfield was still sitting where he had left her; but she seemed to have recovered control of herself. She was leaning forward in her chair, elbow on knee and chin in hand, staring out at the scene in front of her, but obviously paying no heed to it whatever.

The Inspector left her alone for the moment and went over to Mrs. Haddon.

"I want you to show me the exact path you took when you came here from your cottage," he explained.

His real intention was to get her completely out of earshot of Miss Lindfield while he put one question to her; but he could kill two birds with a single stone by utilising this opportunity to see the cottage and learn the lie of the land in that direction.

Mrs. Haddon had no objection to showing him all she could. She led him along the path, exhibited her broken window, surrendered the bullet which had smashed the pane, and gave him a full account of the afternoon's events as seen by herself. Skilfully interleaved into her flood of information he managed to place his question in such a way that she would attach no particular importance to it.

"Miss Lindfield hadn't slipped in coming through the wood, had she? Her hands weren't soiled in any way?"

"Soiled? No, they weren't soiled, for I saw them when I was handing her that bullet to look at. Miss Lindfield keeps her hands just perfect, always—beautiful shiny nails, she's got. I wish I had hands like hers. But she hasn't my work to do. What made you think her hands would be soiled?"

The Inspector smiled broadly to intimate that a joke was coming.

"Well, if anyone put a shot through my coat, I guess I'd be down flat on the ground before he'd time to shoot again. She must be a well-plucked one," he added with a certain admiration in his tone.

"Trust her to keep her head," Mrs. Haddon advised. "She always keeps cool, never flies into a temper over anything—not so's you would notice, anyhow."

Westerham had got what he wanted and he let Mrs. Haddon continue the outpouring of her grievances.

"I'll take charge of that bullet," he suggested as he turned to leave her. "And I think I'd better have your key of the Chalet, too. You won't be allowed to go in there just at present, you know, and the key's safer with me."

When he had stowed the two articles in his pocket, a fresh idea seemed to strike him.

"By the way, Mrs. Haddon, just let's have a look at the soles of your slippers, if you don't mind."

Mrs. Haddon, after a slight hesitation, allowed him to do so. He seemed quite satisfied with his examination and took his leave of her. She watched him disappear into the wood and then in turn she removed her slippers and inspected each sole minutely without finding anything abnormal to reward her for her trouble. After staring at them for a considerable time, she came indignantly to the conclusion that the Inspector had "been having a game with her."

Meanwhile Westerham had made his way back to the Chalet with his eye on his watch. He hurried on his way, with the idea of getting a rough estimate of the time taken by Mrs. Haddon when she went through the spinney to the discovery of the body. Miss Lindfield was his next quarry.

"I hope you're feeling better now," he said sympathetically as he approached her chair. "No, don't get up, please!"

"I'm still a bit shaken," Miss Lindfield admitted. "But if you want to ask any more questions, I'm quite ready."

"I'm not going to worry you," Westerham assured her. "I'm really thinking of the risk to the carpets at Carron Hill," he added with a smile. "The fact is, someone's trodden on a paint brush on the verandah, and most likely some paint will have stuck to the sole of the shoe. I merely wanted to warn you, in case you walked into the house with paint on your shoes."

With a lithe movement which delighted the Inspector's aesthetic side, Miss Lindfield crossed her knees, removed one shoe, and held it up.

"Nothing here, apparently."

She removed the other shoe and held it up in its turn. "Or here, either. Still, I'm glad you mentioned it."

"I'm sorry I troubled you," Westerham apologised. "It was just in case you'd trodden on the paint while you were walking about up there."

As though to cover up his officiousness, he switched over to a fresh subject.

"We have to ask rude questions, at times, in a case of this sort," he said. "I'm going to ask one now. Do you know, or have you any reason to suppose that Mrs. Castleford took drugs?"

Miss Lindfield seemed markedly surprised by this inquiry.

"Drugs?" she echoed.

Then an interpretation seemed to occur to her.

"Oh, yes," she continued, "she did take drugs. She took aspirin whenever she felt she had a headache coming on . . ."

"What I meant was something more serious. She wasn't a drug-addict, was she?"

Miss Lindfield brushed the suggestion aside at once. "No, certainly not."

"Mrs. Castleford suffered from diabetes?" the Inspector inquired.

Miss Lindfield looked up sharply. Evidently she could not guess how he had inferred this.

"Oh, I'm not a Sherlock Holmes," he added, at the sight of her surprise. "I happened to notice a saccharin phial beside her cup, that's all."

Miss Lindfield's fine eyes betrayed her respect for his acuteness.

"Yes, she was diabetic. Her brother-in-law was treating her for it with insulin, and she had to keep off sugar."

"Her brother-in-law?"

"Dr. Glencaple—Dr. Laurence Glencaple. You must have heard of him. He practices in the neighborhood, here."

"Oh, yes, I've heard of him, of course. When you called him her 'brother-in-law' I was thinking of Castleford. I'd forgotten you told me she'd been married twice. He treated her?"

Miss Lindfield amplified her earlier statement.

"Well, he prescribed and looked after her generally. But usually Mr. Castleford injected the insulin. It's done with a hypodermic syringe, you know."

"I see," said the Inspector.

The tail of his eye caught a movement at the window of the Chalet. Dr. Ripponden was drawing the curtains together, and Westerham guessed that the surgeon had completed his preliminary examination. He excused himself, and went up to the verandah. Dr. Ripponden appeared on the threshold and closed the door behind him.

"Here's the bullet," he said, holding it out to the Inspector. "You'd better take charge of it. I may want it again, though I don't think I shall."

Westerham stowed it away in its proper envelope.

"Does it fit the entrance wound?" he asked.

"They're practically the same diameter. It's a very clean wound, and the base of the bullet almost covers it exactly."

"The exit wound's bigger, of course?"

"Yes. A good deal bigger, naturally, and nothing like so clean."

"The bullet didn't hit a rib, did it?"

The doctor made a cautious gesture.

"Not so far as I can see at present. We may know definitely when I've done a P.M."

"The bullet's not knocked out of shape much," the Inspector pointed out. "That's what I'm going on. There's another thing, but it's not very important, seeing the evidence we've got. She hasn't been dead long? Can you put an estimate on that?"

Dr. Ripponden shook his head decidedly.

"The skin-temperature's about 90° Fahrenheit on the abdomen. That might point to death any time up to three hours ago. One can't gauge these things closely."

"I suppose you examined the skin round about the wound?" Westerham asked. "Any singeing of the skin or frizzling of the fine hairs?"

"I could see no signs of powder-blackening, either on the dress or on the skin itself, around the wound," Dr. Ripponden admitted.

"There wouldn't be any, of course, in the case of a shot fired from a distance," the Inspector suggested.

Dr. Ripponden stared at Westerham as much as to say: "Do you think I'm such a fool that I don't know that?"

"What about this pin-point pupil business?" persisted Westerham. "Did you make out anything further about it?"

The doctor shook his head impatiently.

"You'll need to wait for the results of the P.M. These things take more than just guessing."

He paused for a moment, then added:

"You'll have the body taken down to the mortuary?"

"I'll let you know, as soon as that's been done," Westerham assured him.

"Then there's nothing more for me to do here," said Ripponden, with the air of a man who is anxious to get away.

He took leave of the Inspector and went off across the grass towards the point where he had left his car in the sunken road. As he disappeared, the Inspector pulled out his prismatic compass and walked across the verandah to the spot where the bullet had been picked up. He repeated his observation of the bearing of the chair from this point; and then he began carefully to pace along the line of the shot. This was easy enough until he got among the undergrowth; but then the bushes prevented him from following a bee-line, and he had to help himself out with his compass in order to be sure that he was really keeping the true course. The high shrubs concealed the verandah and made direct reference impossible.

Suddenly he pulled up sharp. Face-high before him in the air there hung a lamentable object; the draggled body of a dead cat, open-mouthed, its limbs stiffly extended as it swung. A noose of stout twine was round its neck and it was suspended from a tree-branch.

For a moment the Inspector stared at it in surprise, with which some anger was mingled, for he was fond of cats. Who could be responsible for a thing like that? Then a recollection crossed his mind, and the piteous little body became associated vaguely with the boy at Carron Hill. Only a cruel boy would play that sort of trick. Another gleam of intuition made Westerham step forward and examine the woebegone object more closely.

"Hung up, and then shot at," he muttered to himself as he discovered several bullet-wounds in the creature's skin. "That's a pretty trick!"

He looked round him and detected a second piece of twine dangling from another branch near at hand.

"He seems to have been at it there too," Westerham grumbled. "That must have been earlier, and he's cut the poor brute down and thrown it away, apparently. A nice young man, evidently."

Then a thought occurred to him and he went round to the farther side of the suspended cat.

"Suppose a boy of fourteen were firing at that poor brute," he reflected, "he'd have to elevate the barrel of his gun a bit above the horizontal. It's face-high for me; it would be higher than his head. Let's see roughly."

The bushes made a tiny glade at this spot, so that quite clearly the shooter must have been quite close to his victim. The Inspector retired as far as the undergrowth allowed, and then, crouching down to a boy's height, he went through the pantomime of taking aim at the carcase in the air. His imaginary line of fire, he noticed, was clear of the further undergrowth and might easily have carried a bullet undeviated onto the verandah of the Chalet.

"I'll have to give that young beggar a gruelling and get the truth out of him," was the Inspector's conclusion as he made his way back to the Chalet.

Still he was far from thinking the case sufficiently clear to make precautions unnecessary. When he reached the Chalet, he called up the sergeant and, with his assistance, shifted the tea table and all its paraphernalia into the sitting room, where they would be free from any tampering.

"Now, I'm going up to Carron Hill," he explained. "You, sergeant, will be in charge here until the ambulance comes up to remove the body. Here's a key of the Chalet. You'll have the constable with you in case anything happens and you need to send a message. I'll arrange later for the removal of that tea table and the things on it. Don't run any risks in shifting these cups and so forth; even the lees in them may have some importance, for all one can tell. I've labelled them, so there's no mistake as to which is which. And don't go finger-marking the silver. I may want to go over it for fingerprints later on. Oh, and another thing. There's a dead cat hung from a tree in the wood there. Come here and I'll point out the direction. See where I mean? Well, go in there and cut it down. Cut the twine well above the noose. And bring the body here to be collected with the rest of the exhibits. Do that yourself."

He made the sergeant repeat his orders; then he turned to P. C. Gumley and demanded his report, which he listened to without comment. It added little to his knowledge.

Finally, having settled everything so far as the Chalet was concerned, he went over to where Miss Lindfield was still sitting.

"I haven't come to bother you," he explained, as she looked up with a start. "I'm afraid I've kept you here a long time, and you've been very helpful to us indeed. Just now, I'm going up to Carron Hill, and I think you'd better come with me in my car. You're not really fit to walk any distance after all this strain. And besides, you may be able to help me in one or two things, up there," he added, to reinforce his invitation.

Miss Lindfield made no difficulties. In fact, she seemed relieved by his offer.

"That's very thoughtful of you. I don't believe I could have faced the walk in my present state. My nerves seem to have gone to pieces, and I'm like a limp rag after this strain."

As he accompanied her down to the sunken road, the Inspector remembered one thing he had overlooked.

"Do you mind giving me a key of the Chalet, if you have one? I've given Mrs. Haddon's to my sergeant."

"I have one in my bag."

The Inspector, feigning surprise, thanked her for the key.

P. C. Gumley, on the verandah, watched the two retreating figures morosely, and reflected on the ease with which "a brass-faced wench like that" could get round "a sap-headed softie like this Westerham."

"Ugh! These women! Delilahs, that's what they are. Just Delilahs," he commented to himself as he turned away.

9
THE CONSEQUENCES OF INTESTACY

When Miss Lindfield showed the Inspector into the drawing-room at Carron Hill, they found Frankie curled up on a chesterfield, engrossed in a twopenny boy's paper. Leaning against the chesterfield beside him was the rook-rifle. Frankie looked up crossly as they came into the room and was about to bury himself again in his paper, when Miss Lindfield addressed him sharply. She had been holding herself in for a long time, now; and here at last was a victim upon whom she could release the strain of her nerves. The Inspector was somewhat surprised by this new aspect of Miss Lindfield's character.

"Frankie! Put that paper down and attend to me. Were you in the spinney by the Chalet, this afternoon, shooting?"

Frankie turned round on the chesterfield and stared at Miss Lindfield in obvious surprise. He had never heard her speak to him in that tone before; and a glance at her face showed him an expression which was new in his experience. This wasn't the sympathetic Aunt Connie, the kindly auxiliary on whom one could rely to avert the worst consequences of one's little misdoings. This was a dangerous-looking Aunt Connie, with tight lips and frowning brows. At the sight of her, Frankie realised that something had gone far wrong. Reluctantly he twisted his feet off the chesterfield and faced her, cudgelling his brains to account for her anger.

"Well, what if I was?" he retorted with a defensive sulkiness. "You were going to meet me there, Aunt Connie, when you came back from your walk. And I had the gun with me 'cause you told

101

me to take it. You were going to buy me more cartridges. I don't see what you're rowing me for."

"Haven't you been warned to be careful with that gun of yours?"

Frankie's dull eyes grew even less expressive and more shifty than usual. Evidently, he saw, there were the makings of a bad row of some sort behind all this. Well, he would keep his mouth shut till he got his bearings, and then he could lie his way out of the business in some way or other. The least said the better, until he got his lie ready. He stole a sidelong glance at the stranger who had come into the room with Miss Lindfield, and, finding himself under scrutiny from that quarter, he hastily looked away again.

Miss Lindfield spread her cardigan across a chair-back. "This is what you call being careful? Do you see that?" She pointed to the two bullet-holes in the fabric. "You nearly shot me, you little wretch. Do you understand that? And why didn't you come when I called you, after you'd fired the shot?"

"I didn't hear you," Frankie mumbled in a surly tone.

"You must have heard me. I called more than once. Don't lie about it, now."

"I didn't hear you," Frankie repeated obstinately, with his eyes on the carpet.

"Didn't you see me?"

Frankie had discovered his line of defence. Deny everything and see what they made of that.

"No. You can't see anything in that wood. It's too thick," he protested doggedly.

"And yet you were firing your gun in it without caring where the shots went? You broke Mrs. Haddon's window, too."

"No, I didn't. I wasn't near her cottage," he muttered still staring at the carpet.

"Don't tell lies. I saw the bullet myself. What were you firing at?"

"Different things," said Frankie, desperately.

Much to his relief, Miss Lindfield switched off to a fresh line of inquiry.

"You were to meet me in the spinney. Why weren't you on the lookout for me?"

"I was. I waited ever so long. I thought you'd be there far sooner. Then I got tired of hanging about and I went off to meet you."

"Indeed!" said Miss Lindfield, making no effort to conceal her scepticism. "And which road did you take?"

Her tone made it plain that she expected him to fall into a trap.

Frankie reflected for a moment. Should he tell the truth now or . . . ?

"I took the short cut. I thought you'd be coming that way."

"Ah!" said Miss Lindfield, obviously disappointed by the answer.

She seemed about to put another question, then thought better of it, and washed her hands of the case.

"This is Inspector Westerham. He's going to ask you some questions. You needn't try to tell him any lies. You understand?"

"I'm not telling lies," Frankie protested mechanically; but his demeanour lent no support to his words.

To his rather limited intellect, the world seemed to have been turned upside down in the last few minutes. Auntie Connie, the friend in need who had helped him often in the past, had turned in a flash into an open enemy. She had always swallowed his fictions without comment; and now she had made it plain that she did not believe a word he said even if it was the truth. Worse than that, she had brought in the police. In his very early days, Frankie had fallen into the hands of a nurse whose ultimate threat—so awful that it was never executed—was: "I'll see the policeman gets you!" And round this menace, in Frankie's childish brain, there had accreted a throng of dim horrors, all the worse for being formless. As he grew older, experience modified his views. But still, far down in the depths of his consciousness, there lurked something of the early terror; and rumours of the Third Degree rekindled it at times.

Inspector Westerham looked him up and down, critically, before putting his questions. He was not altogether satisfied with the way Miss Lindfield had broken the ground for him. She had sense enough to withhold the real trouble; but she had obviously given the boy a bad jar and put him so much on the defensive that it might be hard to extract anything whatever from him now. As to

Frankie himself, the Inspector's shrewd mind classified him at once: "A rank bad witness at the best."

"Now, Frankie," he began pleasantly, "I want to ask you one or two questions, as Miss Lindfield said. Answer them if you can. If you can't answer, say you can't. If you aren't sure about anything, just say so. You understand?"

Frankie rubbed his toe into the pile of the carpet and muttered something in the affirmative. The Inspector's display of friendliness failed to elicit any response. "It's like his cheek, calling me 'Frankie,'" was the boy's mental comment.

"You took your rifle down to the spinney," continued Westerham, ignoring Frankie's hostility. "What time did you get there?"

"I dunno."

"Haven't you a watch?"

"It's broken."

"Was it long after lunch when you started?"

"A while."

Westerham tried the boy with one or two other questions, but failed to drive him into any admission. Frankie had made up his mind that if the time was important to the Inspector, it must be because it would tell against him, and he was determined to deny his questioner any information on the subject. Westerham gave it up at last and turned to a fresh subject.

"You were shooting in the wood. What were you firing at?"

"I don't remember."

"Come, come!" said Westerham, sharply, "this won't do. You must remember some things you shot at. Birds, for instance. Did you shoot at any birds? I saw a wood-pigeon there."

"I shot at some birds," Frankie admitted grudgingly.

The Inspector made a mental note that if that were so, Frankie's gun must have been lifted above the horizontal and that a dropping shot on to the verandah was now a proved possibility.

"Did you shoot a cat?"

Frankie's eyes slipped round momentarily to the Inspector's face and then slid away again. This was evidently the real thing, he thought. They'd found out about his hanging up that cat and shooting

104

the beastly thing to death while it choked at the end of the string. This was where he'd have to go warily.

"No, I didn't. I found a dead cat and hung it up to shoot at."

The Inspector, with a picture of the forlorn little corpse in his mind's eye, easily guessed that the boy was lying to save himself. Without ado, he accepted the last statement at its face value and brushed the cruelty question aside.

"Funny notion, that," he said, rather quizzically. "What made you think of hanging a dead cat up to shoot at?"

Frankie was obviously relieved to find that the deadness of the cat was accepted without question. Lest that matter should be reopened, he hastened to answer the Inspector's query at some length.

"I'd got tired of shooting at a fixed target. I wanted something stiffer to hit. So Auntie Connie suggested something hung up at the end of a string and we fixed up a tin can so that it swung about in the wind. Then when I . . . found the dead cat, I thought it'd be more fun to hang it up and shoot at it. So I took away the can and hung up the cat."

"I see. And you walked round it and shot at it, I suppose, just as it happened to swing, eh? By the way, that wasn't only today, was it? You've had it hung there for a day or two?"

Frankie paused for a moment before answering. Then, apparently, he decided that here the truth could do no harm.

"Yes."

"Well, that's that," said the Inspector cheerfully. "Now can you tell me what time it was when you left the wood to meet Miss Lindfield?"

Frankie's eyes went sidelong to the incriminating cardigan on the chair-back. Since the cat affair had been got over so easily, it was evident that the real trouble centred in this other business. He thought swiftly and decided to stick to what he had said before.

"I don't know. It was a good while after I got into the spinney. That's all I can tell you. You said I wasn't to say, unless I was sure. And I'm not sure."

"You're quite sure you're not sure?" demanded the Inspector, watching him keenly.

"I'm dead sure," Frankie returned firmly, guessing that here he was on absolutely safe ground.

Westerham realised that he had come up against a stone wall. The boy would never deviate from his denial.

"You've got some ammunition still left for this toy?"

He tapped the rook-rifle, as he spoke. Reluctantly, Frankie put his hand into his pocket and fished out a few cartridges.

"You may as well give me the lot," Westerham said, with a touch of grimness. "You won't be using this gun again. I shall have to confiscate it."

Frankie's face fell. He had been calculating that they would make him pay for the broken window; and he regarded that as quite sufficient punishment in the matter. He did not even know that he had broken the beastly thing; but one of his stray shots must have done it, somehow. He had an uneasy recollection that he had fired without thinking where his bullets might land. But to lose his gun was more than he had bargained for. In his strait, he turned for help to the old quarter.

"Auntie Connie! You won't let him take my gun? I haven't really done any harm with it."

But that appeal was the match which fired the mine of Miss Lindfield's pent-up emotions.

"You haven't done any harm, you miserable little beast! Do you know what you've done? You've shot your Auntie Winnie—killed her. That's one thing you've done. And you've robbed your father of £12,000. He'll have something to say to you about that. And you've taken seven or eight thousand pounds out of my pocket as well. That's what your shooting's cost us."

She pulled herself up suddenly with an obvious effort and turned to the Inspector.

"I'm sorry, Mr. Westerham," she said in a more restrained tone. "Have you done with this boy? You have? Then"—she turned on the cowering cause of her anger—"get out of my sight. Now! This moment I can't bear to look at you."

The Inspector raised no objection to this abrupt dismissal of Frankie. In the boy's present state of mind, there was nothing to be extracted from him; and at that moment Westerham had not enough information from other sources to be able to lay traps which would extort the facts from this confirmed young liar. Later on, there would be time enough for that, if it proved necessary.

Besides, Westerham had other things to think about at this juncture. Miss Lindfield's outburst had given him his first inkling of a new factor in his problem. Up to that time, he had been coming steadily to the conclusion that the death of Mrs. Castleford was purely accidental. All the evidence pointed to her having been hit by a stray bullet from the rook-rifle. But this sudden revelation of financial elements in the background shook his confidence more than a little. Evidently, in some way which Miss Lindfield's words had not made clear to him, she and the boy's father stood to lose heavily by Mrs. Castleford's death. A shooting accident is one thing; a death involving the transfer of thousands of pounds may be something quite different. This would have to be looked into at once.

With a question on his lips, he turned to Miss Lindfield; but at that moment the drawing-room door opened and a clean-shaven man in grey tweeds came in.

"Ah! You're here, Connie," he began. Then his glance caught the figure of the Inspector, and he stopped abruptly.

"This is Inspector Westerham," Miss Lindfield explained. "This is Dr. Glencaple. You've heard what's happened, Laurie?"

Laurence nodded.

"One of the maids rang up from here as soon as the news came through, and my girl has been chasing me on the 'phone from one patient's house to another till she ran me down. I came on here at once, of course. Well, this is a bad business."

To Westerham's ear the tone sounded much like that of a man commenting on a newspaper account of a railway accident. It seemed plain enough that Laurence Glencaple had not been deeply attached to his sister-in-law. But then, of course, doctors were inured to sudden death, and were bound to look at it from a standpoint of their own.

"How did it happen?" Laurence demanded, after a pause.

Constance Lindfield, after an exchange of glances with the Inspector, gave a concise account of the discovery of the body.

Laurence listened attentively to the details but made no comment. When she had finished, he turned to the Inspector.

"What do you make of it?"

Ten minutes earlier, Westerham would have been inclined to say: "An accident" without more ado; but with that new financial factor still obscure, he felt anything but cocksure. He contented himself with shrugging his shoulders as if to suggest that the matter was out of his province at present.

"Dr. Ripponden is going to make a P.M. examination," he explained. "Until that's finished, we know nothing definite, except what Miss Lindfield has given you."

"Just so," Laurence assented. "That reminds me, I'd better get in touch with Ripponden. She was a diabetic, you know; and he'd better know that. He'll find the needle-punctures of the hypodermic and they might mislead him unless he's told she was getting insulin."

Constance Lindfield seemed to be struck by an idea, as Laurence made this remark.

"I shall be back in a moment," she said to the Inspector, and she left the room.

Laurence turned to the Inspector.

"You think the shot came from young Frankie's rook-rifle? That's bound to come out before the coroner, I suppose. A bit awkward from some points of view, that. However, it can't be helped. Of course there's no idea of bringing a charge of manslaughter in the case of a kid of that age?"

"That's hardly my province," Westerham pointed out.

"No, I suppose it would be settled higher up," Laurence agreed. "Still, I hope nothing will come of it. There'll be enough talk in the neighbourhood without that; and it'll be rather unpleasant for the family."

The Inspector did not feel called upon to make any comment on this concern of the doctor about the public reactions of the case. He was saved from an awkward break in the conversation by the return of Constance Lindfield. She handed him a little, nickel-plated case.

"This is the hypodermic syringe that Mr. Castleford used for giving Mrs. Castleford the insulin injections," she explained. "Dr. Ripponden may want to have it, perhaps, so that he can see for himself that the needle is the one that made the marks on the skin."

"I hardly think he'll want it," the Inspector said indifferently. "However, since it's here, I'll see that he gets it."

Laurence glanced at Constance Lindfield, as though he thought she was showing herself over-zealous.

"I think I'd better mention, Mr. Westerham," he pointed out, "that Miss Lindfield, my brother, and I, are the trustees and executors for my sister-in-law's estate. That may . . ."

"We aren't, Laurie," Constance interrupted, with a catch in her voice.

"Of course we are," Laurence retorted sharply. "Didn't I tell you that was the arrangement in the will?"

Constance Lindfield gave a half-hysterical laugh.

"Yes, Laurie. But she didn't get that new will drawn up. She put it off. And now she's dead. And the old will's destroyed."

Laurence was manifestly thunderstruck by this news. "Didn't sign it? What do you mean? She was going to sign it. She told me so. Why didn't you . . ."

He pulled up quickly and glanced at the Inspector. As nearly as possible, he had let slip something—the suggestion of undue influence on the dead woman.

"Whether the old will's destroyed or not, isn't a matter of much consequence now. Her lawyers had her instructions that she meant to rescind it; and that makes it so much waste paper, I should think. Good Lord, Connie! This is the devil of a mess! I wonder what Kennie will say, when he hears about it."

He walked over to the window and looked out for a few moments.

"I wonder," he said doubtfully, when he came back again, "if the Court would take our word for her intentions. She explained them to us—fully. There's only the informality of the will not having been properly drawn up . . ."

Miss Lindfield had recovered her self-control, and now her usual efficiency came to the surface again.

"Nonsense!" she said decisively. "You and Kennie? The principal legatees under the new scheme? You don't imagine any Court would take your word for these intentions, now that she's died intestate? You don't imagine that Castleford would stand by and let that slip through his fingers without a struggle, especially as the costs would come out of the estate? No, Laurie. We've just got to put up with it."

"Damnation!" Laurence ejaculated bitterly. "I expect you're right. And does that beggar get the lot?"

"Every penny. It goes to 'the surviving spouse' before anyone else. I'm worse off than you. You've got your practice. But I'm penniless now. I won't even be allowed to stay on, at Carron Hill, if I know the Castlefords."

Laurence apparently had not seen this side of the problem.

"Hard lines on you, Connie," he said, rather indifferently.

They seemed to have forgotten the Inspector, forgotten the tragedy, forgotten even the dead woman, in their concentration upon this financial disaster which had befallen them.

Westerham had a skin sufficiently thick to prevent him from feeling *de trop* in the midst of this scene. He was there on business, and it appeared that there was something to be picked up by simply remaining where he was. These financial revelations threw a fresh light upon the whole tragedy. Obviously, if these people had lost something, then somebody else must have gained. That somebody, he gathered, was the deceased woman's husband, a character who had not yet appeared on the stage, so far as the Inspector was concerned. Evidently, Westerham reflected, he had better learn as much as he could while these two people were still perturbed by the shock.

"I'm afraid I must trouble you with some more questions," he said. "I don't suggest that these matters have any bearing on the death of Mrs. Castleford. But questions might be put to me, and I must have the materials for answers to these questions, if they are asked."

"Does that mean that the whole of our family affairs are to go into your report and be read by Tom, Dick, and Harry?" Laurence demanded.

"So far as I can see," Westerham returned, "they won't need to go into my report—that is, unless they turn out to be relevant to the case."

Laurence seemed disinclined to say anything, and Constance Lindfield threw herself into the breach instead.

"This is the state of affairs, Mr. Westerham. Mrs. Castleford's maiden name was Lindfield. She married Mr. Ronald Glencaple—Dr. Glencaple's brother. When he died—he was a rich man—he left everything to his wife. Later on, she married again. Her second husband was Mr. Castleford, a widower with one daughter."

"That's quite clear," the Inspector commented, as she paused.

"Very well," Miss Lindfield continued. "Mrs. Castleford made a will—I'll call it Will No. 1. to be clear—in which she left all her property to her husband, Mr. Castleford. You see what that meant? The money was originally Mr. Glencaple's money; but by this Will No. 1. it would pass into the hands of a complete stranger, while Dr. Glencaple and his brother, Mr. Kenneth Glencaple, would get nothing whatever. Under Will No. 1., I was to get £5,000, I ought to say, and my sister Doris was to get £200. My sister died some time ago, so her legacy doesn't come into the affair."

"I think you said you were a half-sister of Mrs. Castleford?" the Inspector inquired.

"Yes. Her mother died when she was a baby. Her father married again, and my sister Doris and I were the second family. Both my father and mother are dead, like my sister. Mrs. Castleford and I are the only survivors in the family. After Mr. Glencaple died, I became a sort of companion-secretary to my half-sister, which accounts for the difference in the legacies to myself and my sister. Besides that, my sister Doris had a pension. Her husband was killed in the War. But all this is rather beside the main point. I merely mention it so that you can see your way through the relationships in the family. They're more complicated than usual."

"You've made them perfectly clear," the Inspector assured her.

"For some time back," Constance Lindfield went on, "Mrs. Castleford has been a little troubled about having made Will No. 1. She began to see that it was hardly fair to Dr. Glencaple and his brother; and besides that, Dr. Glencaple earned her gratitude by taking her in hand when she fell ill with diabetes. A week or so ago, she decided to take action. She rang up her lawyers and told them she had changed her mind and wanted to cancel Will No. 1. She also brought Dr. Glencaple and his brother here and communicated to them the gist of the new will she proposed to draw up. I'll call it Will No. 2., though it was actually never put on paper so far as I know. My information about it comes from Dr. Glencaple."

She turned to Laurence, who gave a curt affirmative nod.

"By Will No. 2., she proposed to leave me £7,500. The rest of her property was to go back to the Glencaple family, where it came from originally."

"Some provision was made for Mr. Castleford and his daughter as well," Laurence pointed out.

"I didn't know what had been done about that," Miss Lindfield admitted. "Then I may have given Mr. Castleford a wrong impression. I thought it well to mention to him that a new will was going to be made . . ."

"Oh, you did, did you?" Laurence interrupted in a tone of disapproval. "You needn't have taken that on yourself, Connie."

"Well, it's done now and it didn't seem of much importance to keep him in the dark about it. What I want to make clear, Mr. Westerham, is the result of all this. Since Will No. 1. was cancelled and probably actually destroyed—cancelled, certainly, by her instructions to her lawyers; and since she did not draw up a new will before she died, she's intestate, and her estate will be fixed up under the Administration of Estates Act which was passed a few years ago. In that case, since there was no issue of the marriage, Mr. Castleford gets a life interest in the whole of her property. I get nothing. Dr. Glencaple and his brother get nothing. That is the state of affairs now, and you can guess what a shock it has been— to myself in particular."

Behind Miss Lindfield's bald recital of facts, the Inspector thought he detected something in the background.

"May I put one blunt question?" he asked. "Did Mr. Castleford hit it off well with his wife—and with the rest of the family?"

"That's a matter of opinion, isn't it?" Laurence suggested drily, as Miss Lindfield obviously hesitated.

Westerham refused to be content with this and turned to Miss Lindfield in obvious interrogation. She thought for a moment or two, as though choosing her words before she spoke.

"I should say that she wasn't as much in love with him as she used to be. But isn't that a fairly common result of marriage?" she added cynically.

"I'm not married myself," said the Inspector, hastily disclaiming any expert knowledge.

He did not need to force his inquiries further. If people are on good terms, it is not necessary to pick phrases carefully in order to describe their mutual relations. Quite obviously the Carron Hill group was not a harmonious one.

"Who administers this estate, if we don't?" asked Laurence, who had evidently been following a different line of thought.

"Oh, I suppose the Court appoints someone to carry on," Miss Lindfield suggested, carelessly. "That's what would happen, isn't it?" she asked the Inspector.

"I've no idea," he admitted. "That's hardly in my province."

Miss Lindfield crossed the room, sat down on a chesterfield, and dropped into her favourite attitude: chin in hand and elbow on her knee. She glanced incuriously round the room, as though it had suddenly grown strange to her. Laurence watched her in silence for a moment or two and then moved over to her side.

"A bit of a shock for you, Connie," he said, in a more sympathetic tone than he had hitherto used. "After running the whole place for years, and dashed efficiently, too, it's hard lines to be left stranded like this. I don't know what poor Winnie would have done without you. Well, I suppose this is the last of Carron Hill for us."

"I suppose so," Constance Lindfield acquiesced, dully.

Inspector Westerham thought he could understand their feelings. Dr. Glencaple did not interest him, as a personality; but Miss Lindfield did. It was seldom that one came across a woman with the triple advantage of looks, coolness, and brains. Good looks, she certainly had. Her coolness under strain he had seen for himself that afternoon. As for brains, the Inspector knew from personal experience the difficulty of telling a plain tale about a complicated subject; and her exposition of the relationships of the Carron Hill group had impressed him markedly. It had been concise and, rather surprisingly, almost impersonal. And not only that, but she had given them the law on the situation quite correctly, so far Westerham could check her statement. Not many women knew anything about the law. She must have been in her element as factotum at Carron Hill; and he could appreciate what a wrench it would be for her to hand over the reins to other people and go off to earn her own living somehow or other. He had no doubt that she'd get on all right. With her ability, she'd get a secretaryship or something like that. Still, that wouldn't be quite the same thing; for here, apparently, she had a very free hand.

His musings were interrupted by the opening of the drawing-room door; and he swung round to see a little man dressed in a dark lounge suit and a black tie. The Inspector's first impression was of a man wholly ill at ease, unsure of himself and of his reception. A closer scrutiny suggested something further.

"That fellow's in a quivering funk about something or other," was Westerham's expert diagnosis. "I wonder why."

"H'm! Turned up at last, Phil?" Laurence demanded. "I sent the maid to you with a message when I came in." The little man swallowed rather convulsively before replying.

"I was changing," he answered at last, with a glance down at his sombre suit.

Laurence obviously repressed some cutting remark. Instead he turned to Westerham.

"This is Mr. Philip Castleford," he explained abruptly. Then to Castleford: "This is Inspector Westerham. He's up here to find out what he can about this affair."

114

Castleford nodded mechanically, but did not open his mouth. Once again the Inspector got the impression that the loss of Mrs. Castleford in itself was not causing the kind of emotion which one would normally expect. He had no difficulty in amplifying Miss Lindfield's hint about the relations in the Castleford ménage.

"I'm trying to trace out Mrs. Castleford's movements this afternoon," he said briskly. "Perhaps you can help me?"

Castleford seemed to consider carefully before answering.

"She was going to the Chalet this afternoon, to paint," be said at last in a weak voice. "I was going over to the golf-course; so we started off together. That would be about three o'clock. It's about three-quarters of a mile to the turnoff where our roads parted. I think it would be about a quarter past three when I left her."

"And you went on to the club house?"

"Yes."

"And you didn't see her again?"

"No!"

The Inspector caught a change in the tone at that monosyllable. It was rather louder and more decided than the "Yes" which had preceded it. Natural enough, in a way. But only . . . only if Castleford had reason to suspect that his wife's death was not an accidental one. So evidently here was someone else beginning to think that there might be more in it than accident. Funny, that.

"You were playing golf?" he asked casually.

"No, I merely dropped in to read the papers. I always go over there on this day of the week to look at the weekly reviews."

"Meet anyone you knew?"

"One or two people," Castleford said, with an accentuation of the air of suspicion with which he had been regarding the Inspector.

Westerham rapidly considered his tactics. Quite obviously, if he pushed the matter further at this moment, it would be equivalent to a tacit accusation against Castleford; and he had not the faintest grounds for such a thing. It would be a better course to postpone an examination of Castleford until he himself had time to collect evidence by which he could check things independently.

"Did you meet anyone else on the road?"

"My daughter."

A thought crossed the Inspector's mind: "Now, why doesn't he resent my badgering him? Most people would have fired up at questions like that, and wanted to know what I was getting at." Then something in Castleford's attitude suggested a possible explanation. "He looks as if he'd no spunk left in him—as if he'd been browbeaten or henpecked, or something like that."

Then it occurred to Westerham that the hints he had gathered might point to that very state of affairs. A man married to a rich wife "who wasn't as much in love with him as she used to be," might quite likely become a cipher in the household, especially with a person like Miss Lindfield in the offing. A sideglance at the other two confirmed this idea. Laurence Glencaple was standing by the window, his hands in his jacket pockets, and on his face, as he watched Castleford, the Inspector saw a look in which enmity and contempt seemed to be blended. Miss Lindfield, still with her chin on her hand, had bent forward a little and was studying Castleford intently under knitted brows. There was no mistaking the hostility in the air. And if this was the sort of atmosphere in which Castleford spent his life, his demeanour was just what might be expected.

Still, the Inspector docketed in his mental pigeonholes the judgment that Castleford's initial nervousness hardly accounted for, even by these factors. "If he fell into a funk like that, every time he's had to meet those two, he'd have had a nervous break-down years ago."

Nothing further could be done, he decided, until he got the results of Dr. Ripponden's post-mortem examination. It was quite on the cards that all these suspicions of his might be entirely groundless; and it behooved him to go warily for the present.

At the earliest opportunity, however, he took the precaution of jotting down every detail of the conversations be had had—and his verbal memory was an extremely good one. He had an uneasy feeling that he had only touched the fringe of something and that he might yet need every scrap of evidence.

10
THE TELEGRAM

Relieved at last from his guard over the Chalet, P. C. Gumley returned to his lodgings and sat down to a belated supper. He had schooled his landlady to let him devour his meals without interruption; but on this evening he made no objection when she broke through the ordinary routine. She hovered about him, striving to elicit titbits of news which she could retail to her friends. P. C. Gumley was embarrassed by the fact that he had no fresh information to disclose; and he took refuge in an attitude which suggested that he knew a good deal more than he could impart. He met her inquiries by grunts and suggestive nods such as he supposed Hawkshaw the Detective would have found useful in this situation.

Failing to extract anything of interest from her lodger, his landlady fell back upon her own stores, and provided him with a full account of the reactions of the tragedy upon village gossip. P. C. Gumley listened without manifesting any concern until, while he was busy with his third cup of tea, she dropped a sentence which made him prick up his ears. With great restraint, he finished his meal while she babbled on. Then, putting on his cap, he sallied out into the street. This was something that would make that jack-in-office Inspector sit up, he reflected complacently. He'd find that all the brains and alertness weren't amongst the higher ranks.

As he passed along the village street, he saw a little knot of farm labourers congregated about a boy who was evidently a centre of interest. P. C. Gumley strode to the group with an official air and addressed the youngster, who was the local telegraph messenger.

"Here! You come along o' me!" he ordered gruffly.

By an adroit movement, he cut his prize out from under the guns of the company and carried him off up the street, followed by growls from those bystanders who had not yet secured all the information which they thought their right. When P. C. Gumley and his captive had reached a quiet spot, the constable condescended to open his mouth again.

"Acting on information received," he began impressively, "I've got to ask you a few questions. You got a telegram to deliver at the Chalet this afternoon?"

"Well, what if I did? What's it got to do with you? You attend to your job and I'll look after mine."

"You'll be getting yourself into trouble, bad trouble, if you go on like this," P. C. Gumley assured him. "This is a serious affair, this is; and anything you say may be taken down in writing and used in Court. So you'd better be a sight less cheeky and just tell the truth. See?"

"Well, I've nothing to be afraid about," the boy protested in a rather less cocky tone. "Delivering telegrams is my job, isn't it?"

"You got a telegram to hand in at the Chalet this afternoon," P. C. Gumley pursued. "When did you deliver it at the Chalet, eh?"

"About half-past four. I gave it to Mrs. Castleford herself."

"That telegram hasn't turned up," said P. C. Gumley, drawing a bow at a venture. "What have you got to say to that?"

"Well, I delivered it all right," the boy answered sulkily. "Mr. Stevenage could speak for that. He was there when I handed it over."

"Was he so," P. C. Gumley replied in a sceptical tone.

The information was both welcome and unwelcome to him. It was gratifying, because it meant that he had elicited a bit of information which the Inspector had not got. On the other hand, it seemed to tell against P. C. Gumley's firm conviction that "this over-bearing wench Lindfield" was responsible for the tragedy. With Stevenage hanging about the Chalet, her job would be a lot stiffer to pull off.

For a moment, P. C. Gumley wavered in his assurance. He tried to keep an open mind, and he could not quite dismiss the plain fact that Stevenage was actually in the dead woman's company immediately before her death whilst "that hoity-toity jade" was obviously elsewhere. Then in a flash of illumination he glimpsed a further possibility. Suppose Stevenage and that doxy were in it together?

He turned to the boy with a marked accentuation of the "official" demeanour which he assumed when engaged on investigations.

"Now, this may be highly important, see? Just you tell me exactly what happened up there. Where was they, when you arrived? What was they doing? What did they say to you? Things like that, you understand?"

The telegraph boy had no difficulty in setting out all the details. He had already told his story at least twenty times in the village, and it had settled down into a continuous narrative through frequent repetition. P. C. Gumley had only to interject a question here and there.

"I took the wire up on my bicycle and when I got to the road just below the Chalet I left my machine by the roadside and I climbed up the bank to go to the Chalet and when I got over the top of the bank I seen the two of them, her and him, sitting out on the verandah having their teas at a table there. Yes, she was sitting on my left and he was on the right of the table, just as you say, and they looked up when I came in sight and they didn't seem overpleased to see me, 's far as I made out, but that was no business of mine, so I just went forward and handed her the telegram."

He paused a moment for breath and then rattled on:

"She took the telegram and opened it and read it and she seemed struck all of a heap, like, and she looked at it again and then she crumpled it up in her hand and dropped it on the floor and she looked at him as if she was going to say something, but she didn't, and he seemed like as if he was going to ask a question, only she looked at me and then he looked at me and he shut up. So then she said: 'Give him sixpence' and he fished out a tanner and give it me and I came away."

"And you looked back, I bet," hazarded P. C. Gumley.

"What's the harm in that? I happened to look back when I was climbing down the bank to the road and I seen them with their heads together over the table, talking eager-like and looking this way and that, as if they expected someone; and that's all I know about it as you'll hear if you ask anyone I've told it to before."

"Just let's have one thing," P. C. Gumley demanded. "You say that they was both sitting at the table when you left them? Is that right?"

"Didn't I tell you about them talking to each other across the table when I looked back? Of course they were both at the table, sitting having their teas."

P. C. Gumley reflected deeply for a moment or two. It seemed very difficult to rake up further questions.

"Did you hear them say anything else at all, except what you've told me?"

The telegraph boy pondered for a short time; then in a tone of irony he amplified his evidence.

"Now you mention it, they did say something else. When I give her the telegram she said thank-you and just as I was coming up to them she put her hand on the teapot and asked: 'Will you have another cup, Dick?' and he said 'No, thanks; what about you?' And she shook her head and said something about liking her tea coldish; and I noticed, because of that, that she hadn't drunk any of hers at all although he'd finished his cup and I hope that's going to be important, 'cause I'd like my picture in the papers just like you."

P. C. Gumley, who was not wholly guiltless of such an aspiration, made a snarling sound expressive of indignation and contempt. He cudgelled his brains for other questions, but only one more occurred to him.

"By your say, the telegram produced some sensation?"

"Give you my word, it did. Fair took 'em in the dumpling-depot, I could see, with half an eye. Sensation, says you—and no lie, either. She was took aback rightly, at any rate."

P. C. Gumley made a prolonged effort to excogitate a few more questions, but he could think of nothing to the point.

"You run along, then," he said in dismissal. "And don't you go gabbing so free about these things. So far you've p'raps done no harm; but the less that's said, the better. Just you keep that jaw of yours shut for twenty-four hours. See?"

Twenty-four hours, P. C. Gumley reckoned, would give him time to complete his inquiries; and in the meanwhile the boy would not be likely to go to the Inspector with his news, after this warning.

P. C. Gumley retired to his bedroom, took down his well-thumbed manual of *Police Law* and plunged into study of the section dealing with telegraphs.

"It is an offence," he read, "for any person connected with the Post Office to disclose, contrary to his duty, the contents of any message entrusted to the Postmaster-General for transmission."

P. C. Gumley ran his fingers through his hair in a perplexed fashion, and re-read the passage. Then he sat for a while, deep in thought.

"'Contrary to his duty,'" he said at last in an undertone. "It ain't contrary to anyone's duty to assist the police. It's just the other way round, o' course. So that's that. An' if they raises any row afterwards, why, it's their own funeral. You can be dealt with summary for disclosing messages but it says nothing about there being any harm in having messages disclosed to you. There'd be no fault to find with me, over it, so far as that Act goes. Anyway, I'm going to get a look at that message somehow; and if I can't frighten that slip of a girl in the post-office into showing me it, I'll eat my hat."

He took this good resolution to bed with him; and next morning, as soon as the local post-office opened, he went in. Ten minutes later, P. C. Gumley was copying out a message, while a flurried and nervous girl watched him in obvious perturbation.

"You'd better say nothing about this," he cautioned her as he departed. "It might be serious for you, if it happened to come out. Just keep a still tongue, and I'll take the responsibility myself."

The slight grumpiness of his tone arose from disappointment. The telegram, when he had at last got his hands on it, conveyed nothing to him. He had hoped to find the key to the problem in it at the first glance, and it had turned out to be some silly message about a presentation to somebody or other. He pulled his notebook out of his pocket and read it over once again:

"Mrs. Castleford. The Chalet. Thunderbridge. Be punctual on Thursday. The presentation watch that Phyllis bought is not keeping time. A new watch needed on Thursday. You exchange this tomorrow afternoon. Dont send for your Welsh friend if away, but whenever convenient you should get together this party."

P. C. Gumley grunted in some vexation.

"If my handwriting was no better than what that was, I'd get back to school again. What a scrawl!" he commented contemptuously. "I'd have thought Miss Joan Heskett"—he had studied the name and address on the back of the form—"could have written better than that. And sending it by post, too, instead of handing it in at the office."

The telegram had not proved the talisman which he had expected; but at least it would serve to impress that jackanapes Westerham and show him that P. C. Gumley was a man of alertness and initiative. He decided to submit the matter to the Inspector.

The Inspector was a busy man that morning. He was throwing his net wide to sweep in all the information he could obtain with regard to the movements of the folk of Carron Hill on the fatal afternoon. And casting your net wide in a district where you have only a few scattered subordinates is equivalent to doing most of the work yourself. Thus when P. C. Gumley approached the Inspector, he was received rather cavalierly.

"Well, what is it you want?"

P. C. Gumley, with some pride, explained what he had done, and produced his copy of the telegram.

"Ah!" said the Inspector, sarcastically. "I haven't had time to read the newspaper today and see about the Cabinet crisis. So you're the new Home Secretary? You must be. He's the only person who can authorise post office officials to divulge the contents of telegrams. Or perhaps you've been made a Judge? Well, since you've put your foot in it, we may as well profit if we can. Let's see this telegram."

He took P. C. Gumley's notebook and studied the wording of the copied telegram.

"Miss Joan Heskett, Winterlea House. That was on the back of the form? Who's Miss Heskett?"

"She's a girl about twenty or so, a friend of young Miss Castleford," P. C. Gumley explained. "She's a sporting sort of piece, sir. Always has a dog or two at her heel when she goes for a walk."

"Fond of pets, evidently," the Inspector commented. "To judge by your description of her writing, she has a tame spider that she dips in the inkpot when she wants to write a letter and it crawls over the paper to her dictation. I don't, somehow, think that she's responsible for this telegram. You can ring up and ask if she sent a wire yesterday. But if I were you, I don't think I'd mention you've seen the contents of it."

He glanced at the wording of the telegram again.

"Know of any presentation that's due about now?" he demanded. "Anything in connection with a golf-club, or a tennis-club, or that sort of thing?"

P. C. Gumley shook his head.

"Ever hear of anyone called Phyllis in the neighbourhood among the Carron Hill grade of people, I mean?"

Again the constable had to admit ignorance.

The Inspector conned over the copied telegram once more, and as he did so, P. C. Gumley saw a fresh expression dawn on his face.

"I'll take a copy of this thing," he said, pulling out his notebook. "You needn't bother making inquiries about fêtes, or golf-clubs, or that kind of thing. I don't think that matters."

He copied out the telegram and returned P. C. Gumley's notebook.

"This telegram came to the post-office, ready stamped through the post?" he asked. "I suppose they didn't keep the envelope?"

"No, sir," P. C. Gumley assured him. "I asked about that, and they hadn't got it. Threw it in the wastepaper basket or into the fire this morning—their kitchen fire, I mean."

"Well, that can't be helped. Don't you bother further in the matter. I'll look after this part of the business, except that you can ring up Miss Heskett and ask if she sent any wire at all yesterday."

P. C. Gumley saluted and retired to ponder over the mysteries surrounding this incident of the telegram. When he had gone, the Inspector consulted his notebook once more, to satisfy himself of the exact tenor of the real message which he had unearthed by the simple process of omitting alternate words from the telegram:

> "Be on the watch. Phyllis is keeping a watch on
> you this afternoon. Send your friend away whenever
> you get this."

That certainly served to clear up some points in connection with the affair. It explained, for one thing, Mrs. Castleford's perturbation when the boy handed her the wire. Further, an innocent woman is not likely to be disturbed by a warning of that sort; so it was a fair inference that her meeting with Stevenage was not altogether above-board. Again, some well-informed person had her interests at heart and went out of the way to give warning; and yet that person had no desire to be traced by means of the telegram, since otherwise the wire would have been handed over the counter in the usual way. And that well-informed person was using a cipher which Mrs. Castleford could evidently read without difficulty, for it was absurd to suppose that the dead woman had instantaneously solved an unknown cryptogram.

Who was "Phyllis"? Stevenage, the Inspector had elicited from P. C. Gumley, was an unmarried man—not even engaged to anyone. "Phyllis" could hardly be a woman associated with him, so far as public knowledge went. Besides, the wire was to Mrs. Castleford, not to Stevenage. Who was the "Phyllis" who might have a grudge against Mrs. Castleford? The Inspector considered for a short time before a solution broke on his mind. "Phyllis"? Phil. Philip Castleford. That might be it. If there was any hanky-panky between Mrs. Castleford and Stevenage, Castleford was the very person against whom they might be warned. That fitted in quite neatly.

Whether Miss Joan Heskett was the sender of the wire, or whether her name had been borrowed by someone else, remained to be seen. Her connection with Carron Hill through Hilary Castleford was suggestive in some ways, though it did not lead very far.

11
PRELUDE TO TRAGEDY

Dick Stevenage lived in his mother's house and—it was generally believed—at her expense. In earlier days, an uncle had done his best to entice Dick into the ranks of the world's workers. A desk had been provided for him in a private room in the office, a clerk had been specially told off to instruct him in business methods, and from Olympian heights his uncle had kept a benevolent eye upon him. This lasted for a twelvemonth, during which the avuncular eye grew less and less benevolent. Finally, Dick returned home with a store of amusing anecdotes about commercial affairs. Retailed to his girl friends, these anecdotes had the effect of suggesting that Dick was too clever for a mere business career. To male acquaintances they were no less amusing since they artlessly revealed the frantic efforts made by the office staff to dislodge a wholly useless creature from the organisation, without giving offence to his patron.

Mrs. Stevenage seemed to have no objection to supporting her son out of her moderate income. She described herself in a hearty fashion as "a broad-minded old fool"; but she would have been much disgusted if she had heard this paraphrased into "a silly old ass," which was the version given by some people. Caught up in the swirl of new ideas which followed the War, she had assimilated everything without digesting anything, and she prided herself especially on her complete freedom from prejudices where the love affairs of the younger generation were concerned. Free love, unofficial honeymoons, trial unions, companionate marriages: all had her enthusiastic approval.

Only at one point did the rock of Victorianism show itself above the waves. "Of course, Dickie, I'd strongly object to anything of that sort under *my* roof." And Dickie, with that frank smile of his which women liked so much, reassured her at once. No girl would ever come into her house except at her own invitation; that was quite understood. In point of fact, this arrangement suited him admirably. "If a woman once gets her foot over your doorstep," he confided to a male friend, "it's deuced difficult, *deuced* difficult, to drop her when you want to. And one always wants to, sooner or later."

After his unfortunate incursion into commercial life, Dickie announced that he meant to devote himself to literature, an occupation which could obviously be conducted at odd moments without interfering with golf, tennis, badminton, or his other amusements. He said little about it himself; but in the early years his mother kept her friends posted on his progress. "Dickie is writing a play, and he's half-way through the first act already." That play never seemed to get any farther towards completion. Eventually it vanished from Mrs. Stevenage's bulletins and was replaced by a novel, which in its turn occupied many months without making any appreciable advance. Finally, even these vague details ceased to flow from Mrs. Stevenage, and the communiques to her friends took the form of: "My son Dickie's very busy just now—this literary work of his, you know, my dear." The public had to content itself with this, for nothing from Dickie's Workshop ever appeared in cold print. If any tactless person asked questions, Mrs. Stevenage smiled tolerantly and murmured that "Dickie is very thorough in his work, very thorough, not easily satisfied—like *some* writers."

Inspector Westerham, wasting no time after his interview with P. C. Gumley, went straight to the Stevenage villa; and, brushing aside all excuses that "Mr. Richard is busy just now," made his way into the author's study. He had never seen a writer's workroom before, and this one failed to impress him: an untidy flat desk littered with papers, an armchair at it for the author, a shelf of novels, a wireless set, one or two chairs, and a long comfortable settee on which a thinker might recline while he turned over in his mind the fate of his characters or on which he might even snatch forty winks when intellectual strain grew too acute.

When the Inspector was announced, Dickie was stretched out on the settee, a pipe held slackly in his mouth and an expression of unusual worry and gloom upon his face. At Westerham's name, he looked round with a smile which the Inspector judged to be mechanical. He sat up quickly, smoothed his hair with his hand, and eyed the newcomer for a moment before he rose to his feet.

"Well, what can I do for you?" he inquired, with a rather forced attempt at geniality and unconcern.

He motioned Westerham to a seat, while he himself dropped into the armchair behind the untidy desk. The Inspector ran a shrewd glance over his involuntary host. "The sort of fellow women would like better than men would," was his judgment, based on something slightly theatrical about his victim's air.

"I've come to ask a few questions with regard to the death of Mrs. Castleford," he began in a businesslike tone. "When did you see her last, Mr. Stevenage?"

Dick Stevenage appeared to be slightly shocked by the abrupt opening. He picked up a piece of india-rubber from the desk and toyed with it for a moment before answering.

"I don't know anything about it," he said at last. "When I heard the news of the accident, I was stunned. I was quite stunned by it. Dreadful, isn't it? A terrible affair."

"You were an intimate friend of hers, of course," the Inspector answered, infusing something of apology into his tone. "I quite understand *that*."

He contrived to invest this simple phrase with a peculiar significance.

"You saw her frequently, no doubt," he continued. "When did you see her last?"

Dickie hesitated for a moment, looking down at his india-rubber. Then, as he raised his eyes again, he found the Inspector consulting a notebook as though verifying some specific entry. How much did this damned policeman know? Westerham read the question in his face, just as easily as if it had been voiced. It did not surprise him; for even an innocent person is apt to be flustered in such a situation.

"I met her yesterday at half-past three—half-past three or thereabouts, I think," Stevenage admitted, hesitatingly.

"By appointment, perhaps?"

Stevenage pondered over this question for some seconds. Then with an air of a man trying to be perfectly exact, he explained:

"Well, yes, by appointment, if you like to put it so. Or rather, at any rate, I expected to see her round about then."

The Inspector jotted down a note.

"Half-past three. At the Chalet?"

"Yes, at the Chalet," Stevenage confirmed. "I want you to understand that I'll give you all the information that could help you, Inspector Westerham. You quite see that, don't you? I've nothing to conceal, nothing whatever. But I saw nothing of the accident, and I don't see how anything I say can be of use to you."

Westerham ignored this completely and stolidly continued his interrogatory.

"You reached the Chalet at 3.30 p.m., you say, Mr. Stevenage. Just tell me what happened next."

Stevenage was evidently far from anxious to go into details. He hesitated, boggled over his opening, and at last made a pretence of frankness:

"Oh, I met her on the verandah; you know the verandah? She was painting, out there, when I came up; had her easel set up and all her stuff scattered about. I sat down and talked while she painted; we just talked of this and that, you know, nothing of any importance."

"And she was painting all this time?"

"Oh, yes," Stevenage asserted, and then looked as though he wished he had not been so quick.

The Inspector turned over a leaf or two in his notebook and marked a certain place with his thumb.

"How long did this conversation last, between you?"

"I really don't know," Stevenage admitted, with obvious confusion in his voice. "It lasted a good while, I should say. Quite a long time, probably. You know how time passes when one's talking?"

The Inspector had a shrewd belief that this part of the story was untrue; but he had no desire to go too far. As the case stood, Stevenage was a witness like any other, and browbeating might raise trouble. He bethought himself of a side-issue which would disarm his witness's suspicions.

"You heard some shooting?" he asked.

"Yes, a few shots in the spinney. Young Frankie, it was."

"By the way," the Inspector asked, as though in curiosity, "what shoes were you wearing that afternoon?"

Stevenage, obviously, could see no point in this question.

"What shoes was I wearing?" he repeated. "A brown pair with crêpe-rubber soles."

"Do you mind if I have a look at them?" Westerham inquired. "Don't ring," he added, as Stevenage made a movement towards the bell. "If you don't mind, I'll go along with you and see them."

Stevenage was plainly at sea over this. He led the Inspector to a cloak-room where shoes were laid out on shelves.

"These are the ones," he pointed out.

The Inspector picked them up and turned them about in his hand as though gauging their size. Then, casually, he lifted one or two of the other shoes as if in search of something.

"They usually stamp the size on the sole," he explained, as if accounting for his proceedings. "Ah, here it is!"

He had ascertained that none of the shoes bore any trace of a paint-mark.

"That's all right, Mr. Stevenage. It's a matter of a foot-print; but it doesn't fit your shoes at all. Most likely it's of no importance; but with a coroner's jury . . . well, they might ask any absurd question, and we have to be ready to answer."

He put down the shoes, brushed his finger-tips to together, and led the way back to the study.

"Now, would you go on with your story, please? You talked for a time with Mrs. Castleford. Did you go into the Chalet with her?"

"No, I didn't!"

Stevenage's denial was over-prompt; and again he seemed to reconsider. This time he decided to retract what he had said.

"That's to say," he went on, "yes, I did. I went in to carry out the tea things."

Westerham could not resist the temptation to give Stevenage a jar; but he did it in so silky a tone that his statement sounded almost like a confirmation of the evidence.

"Quite so, Mr. Stevenage. And you drew the curtains of the Chalet sitting room so that you wouldn't be dazzled while you were carrying out the tea things. Very wise, no doubt. And when did you bring out the tea tray?"

Stevenage glanced sidelong at the Inspector, as though weighing whether or not he should take notice of the thrust. This damned policeman must have been primed, or else he was putting two and two together and coming near four in his answer. Better let sleeping dogs lie. No use saying anything which would throw him open to awkward questions.

"About half-past four, I think," he answered at length. "I'm almost sure it was about that time, because Mrs. Castleford suggested it was tea-time, and she'd looked at her watch. She liked her afternoon tea at half-past four. I didn't look at my own watch."

"You carried out the tea tray and so forth?"

"Yes, everything was set ready for carrying out. The caretaker looks after that. The kettle was boiling in the scullery-place. You know it: the little room off the sitting room."

"Was Mrs. Castleford on the verandah when you carried out the tea tray?"

Stevenage obviously hesitated here, and it was only after some seconds that he decided to take the plunge:

"No, she was inside the Chalet, in the sitting room. I remember that," he went on with an air of frankness, "because I called to her that everything was ready; and she told me to go ahead and pour out the tea. I remember that quite well, for she asked me to get her saccharin phial out of her vanity-bag and put three tabloids in her cup."

"And you did that for her? How many tabloids were in the phial when you picked it up?"

"Just three, as it happened," Stevenage replied quite promptly. "I remember I took out the three and thought how lucky it was that there were three left; for the bottle was empty then. I shook it to make sure there weren't any more."

"And you put sugar in your own cup at the same time?"

"Yes, I always take sugar in my tea. Two lumps, if it's of any interest to you," he added with a faint air of insolence.

"Everything's of interest if one looks at it the right way," said the Inspector, cryptically. "And now, what happened after that?"

Stevenage pondered for a moment as though joggling his memory.

"Mrs. Castleford came out of the Chalet and sat down at the table. Then . . . let's see . . . Oh, yes, she filled up the teapot from the kettle, to be ready for another cup or two if we wanted it. And she lighted the spirit lamp. I'd blown it out while I was carrying the tray from the scullery."

"I thought so," said the Inspector absently.

Stevenage glanced sharply at him. Evidently this damned fellow knew more than one bargained for.

"What happened next?" Westerham pursued.

"I don't know that anything happened, just then," Stevenage answered. "We talked over the tea table for a while, about one thing and another, you know: just casual conversation. I can't remember what we talked about. It wasn't anything special."

"Did she eat anything?" Westerham demanded suddenly, as though he attached importance to the point.

"No, nothing at all. She was diabetic, you know, and had to diet herself specially, on that account.

"She drank her tea, though?"

Something in the Inspector's tone seemed to put Stevenage on his guard. He reflected before he answered.

"No, she didn't drink her tea. She had a habit of leaving her tea to go tepid before she drank it—cold, almost. I finished my cup before she'd even tasted hers. In fact, now I come to think of it, she didn't drink any tea while I was there. A telegram came for her, just then, and interrupted us."

"Ah?" ejaculated the Inspector, as though this item was fresh to him. "A telegram? What was it about, do you know?"

"I don't know," Stevenage declared with an emphasis which went far to suggest that he had something to conceal. "I've no idea at all. She didn't show it to me."

The Inspector feigned a certain doubt.

"H'm!" he said. "A telegram, you say? Well, Mr. Stevenage, I found no trace of any telegram-form anywhere at the Chalet. How do you account for that?"

"I don't know; I can't account for it at all. Perhaps she threw it away or burned it, or something like that. I know nothing about it, I can assure you. She didn't show it to me. She didn't tell me who sent it, or anything."

"Well, that's as it may be," Westerham retorted in a sceptical tone.

Mrs. Castleford might, of course, have burned the telegram. But the ashes he had seen in the Chalet grate had no sign of writing or printing on them; and in quantity they equalled the remains of half a dozen telegram forms. Besides, from the evidence of the telegraph boy, Stevenage was obviously lying when he insisted that he had no idea of the wire's contents.

"What happened after that?" Westerham demanded.

"I came away shortly afterwards," Stevenage explained. "I left almost on the heels of the telegraph boy."

"You haven't told me why you left so quickly," the Inspector pointed out. "Is it usual, when you're having tea with a lady, to get up and go away before she's even begun to drink her tea?"

Stevenage was evidently unprepared with an answer. He played with his india-rubber, averting his face from the Inspector and obviously trying on the spur of the moment to concoct some fiction which would pass muster.

"She asked me to go," he said at last in a halting way. "She wanted to get on with her painting, I expect."

"Although she hadn't finished her tea? Curious, isn't it?"

132

"Oh, there's nothing in that," Stevenage hastened to explain. "She had a habit of drinking a whole cup of tea at a gulp. It wasn't as if she would have dallied over it after I was gone, you see?"

The Inspector pretended to be satisfied with this account. He felt himself in an awkward position. Except for the financial complications revealed to him at Carron Hill, he had no grounds for assuming that Mrs. Castleford's death was due to anything but accident; and on that basis his sole concern was with the immediate circumstances of her decease. He had no valid excuse for embarking on a roving commission and investigating collateral issues which might well turn out to be mere mare's nests.

Given a free hand, he would have probed further without hesitation; but, as it chanced, there had been an awkward case not long before which had filled the newspapers of the country and focused attention on the limits to which police questioning could reasonably be carried. With that in the background, Inspector Westerham had no desire to be held up as a busybody making impertinent and irrelevant inquiries into people's private lives.

He decided to steer a middle course, so far as it was possible; and to begin with, he made up his mind to trap Stevenage in some further lies in the hope that this would throw him off his balance.

"Let's see," he continued musingly. "You came to the Chalet at 3.30 p.m. and you had tea at 4.30 p.m. An hour, eh? And Mrs. Castleford was painting all that time, while you talked with her?"

The Inspector had a shrewd idea that Stevenage would endorse this in order to escape from more direct inquiries about the employment of that time.

"Yes, she painted and we talked while she was doing it."

Westerham knew that this was a lie. He had examined the canvas and made up his mind that ten minutes would have sufficed to put on all the fresh paint which it carried.

"She didn't say that she expected Miss Lindfield, or anyone else, to drop in at the Chalet during the afternoon?"

Stevenage shook his head.

"You know Miss Lindfield?" the Inspector went on "She's the main witness we have in this affair. What sort of person is she?"

Westerham's tactics bore the fruit he expected. Stevenage was only too glad to ride off on a side-issue.

"She practically runs Carron Hill," he explained. "She's Mrs. Castleford's half-sister, I think. I know Mrs. Castleford relied on her in everything. She's very efficient, you know; the sort of person who can run things without letting you think she's running them. She had a lot of influence with Mrs. Castleford."

"I see you know her intimately," commented Westerham, and he was surprised to catch a look of uneasiness on Stevenage's face as he spoke.

"Oh, well, I've been at Carron Hill a good deal, you know," Stevenage explained. "One picks up general notions of things from seeing people together."

"What about Mr. Castleford?"

Again Westerham saw that uneasy look on Stevenage's face; but this time he thought he was able to account for it.

"Castleford?" Stevenage repeated. "Oh, Castleford's just . . . well, to tell you the truth, I never had much to do with him. He seems a very quiet sort, rather under his wife's thumb, if you know what I mean. He was . . . as a matter of fact, he was pretty well negligible at Carron Hill. That's the impression I got."

"He has a daughter, hasn't he?"

"Miss Castleford? Yes. A pretty girl," Stevenage commented with an assumption of carelessness which did not quite deceive the Inspector.

"There were two brothers-in-law, I gathered?"

"The Glencaples?" Stevenage was evidently delighted to keep the talk in this channel lest it should veer back to his own doings. "I've met them from time to time. I couldn't stand Kenneth, myself. He's a thick-skinned type that says outrageous things to one without any care for one's feelings. Laurence, the doctor, is all right, although he's apt to pull one's leg and turn ironical at times. Of course they were both as mad as hornets at losing their brother's money and seeing it made over to Castleford, and they were doing their best to set that business right. So I gathered."

"From Mrs. Castleford?"

"From her, yes. She mentioned it casually. I wasn't prying into their family affairs, of course. But she happened to speak of it."

"At the Chalet?"

Stevenage thought for a moment. Evidently he did not want the Chalet to crop up if he could avoid it.

"Yes, at the Chalet yesterday, and once or twice before that. I think that in the last week or so the Glencaples have been doing all they could to get her to change her will."

"While you were with her, Mrs. Castleford was sitting beside the tea table? She didn't shift her chair?"

Stevenage seemed surprised by the suggestion.

"No, why should she? She was talking to me until I cleared out."

"That's all right," Westerham hastened to say. "You left her sitting at the table with her tea still untouched. I thought so."

Stevenage evidently wanted to hear more of this, but decided not to reopen the question of his own doings at that period.

"Did you meet anyone on your way home?" Westerham inquired in a casual tone.

Stevenage hesitated for a moment or two.

"I saw Mr. Castleford coming along one of the field-paths, but he didn't see me, I think. I didn't stop to speak to him."

"You can't give me the time when you saw him?"

"Well, as it happens, I can, roughly. It was about five to five. I was going to set my watch by the village chime, and I happened to look at it then, to see how time was getting on. He was coming up the field-path across Ringford's Meadow to the stile that lets you out onto the road—you know the place I mean."

"You were past that point before he came up onto the road? Is that what you mean?" the Inspector inquired.

"Yes, I must have passed the stile a minute or two before he came up to it."

"You met nobody else?"

"Not till I got to Thunderbridge."

Westerham rose, to Stevenage's relief.

"That's all you wish to say?" the Inspector asked, formally. "If you've anything to add . . ."

"No, that's all I can tell you," Stevenage hastened to assure him. "I've been perfectly frank with you; you quite understand that, don't you? And, by the way, you won't call me as a witness at the inquest, will you? I'd rather not."

"That's hardly my province," Westerham pointed out. "It's for the Coroner to decide what witnesses he'll call."

He closed the interview with one final question:

"Did Mrs. Castleford by any chance tell you exactly how her affairs stood yesterday—in the matter of her will, I mean?"

Stevenage seemed to consider for a few moments before he replied.

"She was never very clear in her explanations of things like that," he explained, slowly, "but I got the impression that she had cancelled one will and intended to make a fresh one. She kept putting that job off from day to day. She had a sort of morbid horror of anything connected with death, you know; and even making a will was a reminder that she might die sometime. She didn't like it, and so she put it off and off. She didn't say that to me in so many words, you understand? I'm simply giving you my interpretation of the thing. But I certainly got the idea that the new will hadn't been fully considered. She hadn't called in her lawyer about it, I know."

The Inspector took his leave; and, as he walked away from the villa, he began to collate the impressions left on his mind by that interview.

One side of Stevenage's character gave him little trouble. That sanctum of his might be anything else, but it was not a work-room. The Inspector knew enough recognise the signs of work, and there were none there, despite the warning that "Mr. Richard is busy." The whole of that side of the man's life was obviously mere camouflage to cover laziness. "That fellow would do almost anything for a living—except work," was Westerham's mental verdict.

Of more immediate importance were the symptoms of uneasiness displayed by Stevenage at various times during the interview. They fell into three groups. In the first place, he was obviously desperately eager to cover up the employment of his time between

3.30 and 4.30 p.m. Anyone could see through his lies about that. Secondly, he was almost equally desirous of pretending that he knew nothing about the contents of the telegram, though quite plainly he must have learned its purport. Thirdly, he was ill at ease when Castleford's name cropped up. The Inspector had no difficulty in finding the key to this minor problem. Stevenage, now that Mrs. Castleford was dead, had no desire to see his relations with her dug up and examined. He was cutting loose from that part of his past as quickly as he could. Once again, as at Carroll Hill, the Inspector got the impression that, as a human personality, Mrs. Castleford had counted for remarkably little with even her intimates. In the circumstances, Stevenage would naturally not advertise that he felt her loss keenly; but Westerham guessed that there had been little to suppress. This Romeo would not destroy himself on the tomb of his Juliet. Most likely he had somebody else in his eye already. Perhaps he'd grown weary of Mrs. Castleford long before the crash came.

And at this point there flitted across the Inspector's mind the recollection that Stevenage had jibbed slightly at the suggestion that he was intimate with Miss Lindfield. And the only other woman mentioned—Hilary Castleford—he had dismissed cavalierly from the conversation: "A pretty girl."

On two counts, the Inspector could give him a clean bill. Quite obviously, he had not been uneasy in the matter of the shoes; and his statements of the course of events at the tea table had been quite accurate, with the exception of the affair of the telegram.

Finally, he seemed to know as much as anyone else about the Castleford will problem.

12
THE CORONER

Mr. Oliver Renishaw, the local Coroner, was a dry, precise little man with a pair of alert eyes in an expressionless, leathery face. In private life, his talent was for monologue rather than for conversation; but his talk was objective and not subjective, so that even his longest speeches failed to reveal much of his intimate thoughts. In his official capacity, caution was his most salient characteristic. He confined himself to his allotted task—to ascertain the cause of death in the cases which came under his attention—and he had not the slightest desire to borrow the mantle of Sherlock Holmes and discover the identity of a criminal. That, in his view, was entirely a police affair; and his only duty in that connection was to do nothing which might make the task of the official detectives more difficult.

He had assembled a jury, taken the evidence of Stevenage, Mrs. Haddon, Miss Lindfield, P. C. Gumley, and Inspector Westerham, and had then adjourned his inquiry until a later date when the results of fuller expert investigations might be available. It was when he came into possession of these results that he decided to take Westerham into consultation.

The Inspector, calling one evening at Mr. Renishaw's house in response to a summons, was shown into a room where he found his host, apparently deep in thought, with a lighted cigar between his fingers. On a table beside his armchair lay a small pile of papers. Renishaw greeted his visitor with a certain dry courtesy and motioned him to take a seat.

"This conversation, you understand, Mr. Westerham, is to be regarded as hardly official. I have some information which may be of use to you. As against that, I look to you to tell me how much of that information—if any—can be made public without endangering the ultimate success of your investigations into this Castleford affair."

As though to mark the unofficial character of the interview, he solemnly drew the Inspector's attention to a box of cigars. Westerham helped himself. While he was lighting his cigar, Mr. Renishaw picked up the papers from the table at his side.

"I need not, I think, recapitulate the evidence given at the opening of the inquest, as that is already public property."

Westerham nodded in agreement. He knew the man he had to deal with, and he had resolved to interrupt as little as possible. It was quicker to give Renishaw his head and let him deal with matters in his own way, even if it meant listening to some things which the Inspector knew already from other sources.

"By my instructions," Renishaw went on, "Dr. Ripponden conducted a post-mortem examination of Mrs. Castleford's body. I have his written report here. He found, as you know, that a projectile had entered the skin at the back, had traversed her heart, and had emerged at the front of the body, inflicting in its passage a wound likely to be almost immediately fatal."

Again Westerham nodded. This was all familiar to him.

"Measurement of the diameter of the entrance wound suggested that it had been produced by a projectile of .22 calibre," Renishaw continued, "since the orifice was very slightly larger than the diameter of such a projectile and was less than that of a .32 projectile. Dr. Ripponden, in view of the fact that a .22 rook-rifle had been mentioned in connection with the case, was inclined to assume that a weapon of this calibre was actually responsible for the injury. He reported in that sense."

Mr. Renishaw tapped the bundle of papers on his knee.

"I was not, however," he continued, "entirely satisfied with this inference. Take a sheet of india-rubber; stretch it; punch a clean hole in it; and then allow it to contract to its normal dimensions.

You will find, as I did, that the diameter of the orifice in the rubber is less than the diameter of the punch which you used. Now the human skin is resilient like india-rubber, though of course not to so great a degree. In the case where the skin over a soft part of the body is struck by a high-velocity bullet, the skin first gives way before the bullet—stretches, in fact—and then, in that extended condition, it is pierced by the projectile; after which, when the bullet has passed through, it contracts again; with the result that the orifice is less in diameter than the bullet which has passed through it."

Mr. Renishaw's leathery face was hardly capable of beaming, but he nearly succeeded in doing so as he finished this part of his exposition.

"Very convincing, sir," Westerham admitted. "I was greatly struck by the force of the argument when Dr. Ripponden told me what you had said to him on the matter. In fact . . ."

A slight movement of Mr. Renishaw's hand arrested him.

"A further point is worth mentioning," the Coroner pursued without giving Westerham time to finish, "a further point is this. On looking up the matter in my reference books, I find that such behaviour is to be expected only from high-velocity weapons. It would not occur, apparently, in the case of revolver-shots. Thus as an alternative to the .22 rook-rifle, it is possible that the weapon used was an automatic pistol of slightly larger calibre—such as a .32, which seems to be the most likely."

"That's a wonderful bit of deduction, sir," Westerham broke in. "And it's right, too. Dr. Ripponden mentioned the point to me some time ago; and I've been on the hunt for a bullet of the sort ever since then. The line of fire was plain enough—I'd taken its bearing—and it was simply a question of making a thorough search. This afternoon Constable Gumley found the bullet embedded in a pile of old leaves and rubbish, just inside the boundary of the spinney, among the trees. It must have been fired into her at fairly close quarters"—he hesitated a moment, as though something had occurred to him—"and gone clean through her and then landed, nearly spent, in this mound of soft stuff. What's more, when the bullet turned up, I began to search for the cartridge case which must have been jerked out after the shot by the pistol's ejector. It's flung out to the right of the firing-position, and I found it among the grass below the verandah. The two of them prove your idea up to the hilt, sir, for they turn out to be .32 calibre."

Mr. Renishaw attempted to conceal his gratification with a dry little cough.

"That is very satisfactory, Mr. Westerham," he declared. "Now this brings me to my first question. Is it advisable that this matter should be referred to in any shape or form at present?"

Westerham's reply was immediate.

"No, sir. Certainly not. I'm glad you take this line, because with this card up our sleeve we've a better chance of finding the pistol than we should have if its owner were put on his guard. It's quite evidently a case of murder, now; and I'd rather not put more cards on the table than we're forced to do."

"I note what you say," Mr. Renishaw answered in a formal tone, "and I shall, of course, frame my proceedings in accordance with the public interest, which naturally comes first. I now come to another matter. As you know, the appearance of the body suggested the administration of some miotic drug. Dr. Ripponden, though an able man, is not versed in the technique of detecting and identifying such things; and I therefore, without in any way disparaging his ability, decided to exercise my powers under the Coroners (Amendment) Act of 1926, Section 22, by calling in an expert in such investigation, and submitting to him various organs of the body, for his examination. This has been done, and I have the report of the expert before me."

Mr. Renishaw turned over the papers on his knee and picked out one document to refresh his memory.

"From this report, it appears that morphine is present in the body. The stomach alone contained a fair quantity. The brain, and some other organs also, showed traces of the drug."

The Inspector was about to interrupt, but Mr. Renishaw restrained him with a gesture and proceeded with his exposé.

"I submitted to the expert not only the various organs of the body, but also the dregs of liquid left in the cups on the tea table, asking him to test these for morphia and for saccharin. Further, I provided him with the cigarette-stubs which you discovered and asked him to examine them for opium. He detected no opium in the tobacco. One teacup showed traces of saccharin; the second one yielded traces of cane-sugar. In neither cup did the expert succeed in identifying morphia."

"That's very funny!" ejaculated the Inspector mechanically, as he tried to harmonize these new facts the evidence he had already gleaned from other sources.

Mr. Renishaw suppressed any symptom of the elation which he no doubt felt.

"This is the second question on which I wished to have your opinion with regard to the public interest," he explained mildly. "Would it be undesirable that these facts should be divulged at present?"

"Most undesirable, I should say," the Inspector assured him. "I don't see my way through the tangle yet, but . . ."

The Coroner gave him no time to elaborate his ideas.

"I come now to yet another point," he went on. "If the morphia in the body did not come from the teacup, we may have to look elsewhere for an alternative source. Mrs. Castleford, as we know, was undergoing treatment with insulin, which was injected by means of a hypodermic syringe. That suggested—purely as an hypothesis—that possibly the syringe had been the channel for the introduction of the drug. I submitted the syringe you obtained at Carron Hill to the expert; and he reports that it shows traces of morphia."

"This gets worse and worse," the Inspector broke in. "If it was done with a syringe, then how did the morphia get into . . . ?"

Mr. Renishaw waved this aside rather peremptorily.

"These are the facts, whatever be the explanation," he said hastily. "I quite appreciate the objection which you were going to bring forward. I am not concerned with it at present, however. Public policy is the principal factor in my mind just now; and I merely wish to ask whether this evidence also should be held in abeyance for a time."

"There's no doubt about that, in my mind," Westerham. "These points which you've brought to light, sir, are far too important to the police to be broadcast just at present."

"That was my own impression," the Coroner admitted drily. "And as you have made it clear that none of them can be safely used in public, I think the best course will be to adjourn the inquest still further. I can hardly call the jury together to listen to Dr. Ripponden telling them that some fibres of cloth were embedded in the wound; and that appears to be the only remaining piece of evidence which we have to give them."

His leathery face creased in a faint smile and his eyes twinkled at the suggestion.

"It is outside my province to make suggestions, I think," he went on. "But these facts brought into my mind a rather amusing problem. Suppose that A administers to B a fatal dose of a drug; and that then, before the drug causes actual death, C shoots B and inflicts an immediately fatal wound. I put the conundrum to you; Mr. Westerham. How would you proceed to indict A and C respectively if you could prove the case against each of them?"

"Very neat," Westerham commented. "But the solution's plain enough to my mind. Indict A for administering poison with intent to commit murder; and indict C for murder. It would be hard lines on C, if A got off with penal servitude for life while C was hanged; but that's how I'd read the situation."

He suddenly recalled a question which he had meant to put earlier.

"By the way, have you the exact figure for the morphine which your expert found in the stomach of the body?"

Mr. Renishaw consulted his papers.

"He puts it down as seventy-five milligrammes—equivalent roughly to a grain and a quarter. The ordinary fatal dose, I understand, is three to six grains; but this varies considerably from person to person, and even half a grain has been cited as fatal in one case. One gram of morphine may be regarded as a dangerous dose; and in the case of this woman, with the complication of diabetes entering into the problem, it seems difficult to say what dose would actually have proved fatal. In her case, I should be inclined to think—though I am no expert—that a dose of a grain and a quarter was quite possibly near the fatal quantity."

13
THE ANONYMOUS LETTER WRITER

Despite the cautious attitude of the police, the general public had little hesitation in making up their minds about the affair at the Chalet. They spoke of it bluntly as "the Castleford murder," without troubling themselves greatly about the burden of proof. And, as a result of this, Inspector Westerham had not lacked unsolicited help. Letters flowed in to him: some well-meant, others mere vehicles of spiteful suggestion, yet more containing wildly improbable solutions of the problem. One man even surrendered himself and made a full confession. Unfortunately, he turned out to be an epileptic; and his friends had little difficulty in proving an unbreakable alibi for him. By that time, Westerham had grown weary of his self-constituted helpers; for even the wildest statements had to be sifted lest some truth should be missed, and this had added very considerably to his work.

It was therefore with a cynical eye that he observed on his desk a cheap yellowish envelope addressed in a sprawling hand to "Mister Westerham."

"Another of 'em!" he commented, as he slit open the cover and extracted the contents.

> Dere Mister Westeram,
> I write to tell you a Few things *you clever blokes* in the police Dont know for All youre smartness. You make me laff. You Dont know Casselford knew all About his wife and young Stephenage. *i Know he did*

becaus I took the Trubble to write and tell him About there goings-on Myself. thats Number I. and dere Westeram you dont Know Casselford was *in the spinnie* just before the Murder hapened and thats number 2. Youre *very clever* no dout but not so clever as i expec you think you Are. you Dont know that Casselford came back from the Shally *after the shot was fired* with a Face like a Sheet and made Off for all he was worth and thats number Three. Hurra for the *clever fellows* In the police i say dere mister Westeram. I dont blame Casselford for doing the piece in for she desdeserved to get it. he has my simpathy and Ill *Wear a black tie* the Day hes hanged altho he is a misrable little sqirt as we all know like all the rest of the boergoises. hang the lot dere mr Westeram.

One who Knows a thing or Two

Westerham leaned back in his chair and re-read this unsolicited contribution to the evidence in the case.

"It sounds more genuine than some of them," he conceded, rather against his inclination.

He examined the dirty envelope and found that it was postmarked in the village.

"Plenty of fingerprints to identify him by, at any rate, if we run him down," he mused disgustedly, as he took up the letter again with care. "Now, let's see. He's probably a local man, from the postmark. The notepaper's fairly distinctive, cheap yellow stuff with faint ridges on the surface to keep the writing straight: most likely bought at the village shop, and easy to identify. He leaves no margin on the left-hand side of the paper; writes up to the very edge of the sheet on that side. His spelling's got some consistent errors in it. And, from the whole tone of the stuff, he's a disgruntled devil with his knife in the police and the upper classes. With just a bit of luck, we might be able to lay our hands on him fairly easily. It's worth trying, if he knows as much as he pretends to do."

It turned out to be the Inspector's lucky day. On calling at the village shop, he learned that some packages of that peculiar paper had come into stock within the last month. Very little had been sold, and the shopkeeper remembered the names of most of the buyers.

"Mrs. Allgreave, Miss Kelbrook, old Mr. Hingham, Mrs. Haddon, and young Munslow?" the Inspector repeated, as he checked them off in his notebook. "Mrs. Allgreave? Who's she?"

"She's old Jim Allgreave's widow—three doors down the street," the shopkeeper explained. "You must have seen her, Mr. Westerham. She's very frail, nowadays, and hobbles about with a stick."

"What's young Munslow like? I seem to remember something about him," the Inspector lied blandly. The shopkeeper smiled knowingly.

"I know what *he* bought that paper for—he writes to his girl about twice a week. She's in service over in Bolsted Abbas. But she won't be there long. Young Munslow's a good lad, saves every penny towards the wedding. She's a lucky girl, she is, to get as nice a young chap as that."

"Miss Kelbrook, what's she like?"

"A parson's lamb—or mutton, more like. You'll see her any time you like to drop in at a service. Dresses always in black and white, she does, and won't see forty again. You'll recognise her easy enough if you want her. She lives in the little cottage with the creepers on it, along the road a bit in *that* direction."

"And this old man Hingham?"

"Holy Joe? Well, if you like to go to the 'Pheasant' at closing time any night, you'll see him being helped out, as like as not, in a manner of speaking. Not just drunk, you understand, but near enough it to make the landlord uneasy at times. He stays in bed on Sunday. It's a blank day for the likes of him, for the 'Pheasant' only got a six-day license. That's why they call him Holy Joe."

"H'm!" ejaculated the Inspector, as though this item had been what he was looking for. "A pub-crawler, is he?"

"Well," the shopkeeper said cautiously, "you can't exactly accuse him of crawling from pub to pub, seeing as there's only one pub in the village. But he does crawl to that one, as regular as clockwork, as one might say."

"I've got what I wanted," Westerham said disingenuously. "And of course," he added with a wink, "this is between the two of us, eh? We'll not go talking about it just yet?"

"Just as you say," the shopkeeper agreed, putting on his spectacles and taking up a newspaper which he had laid down when Westerham came into the shop.

The Inspector had a very fair idea of what that vow of secrecy was worth; but he felt pretty safe in the matter. Holy Joe did not seem a person likely to be injured by gossip.

His next victim was P. C. Gumley, whom he hunted down on his beat.

"I want to know something about Mrs. Haddon," he began. "What sort of person is she? Reliable, do you think?"

"I've never *known* her to tell me a lie," P. C. Gumley answered, grudgingly. "But I don't see her once in a blue moon, sir. She lives a very—a very secluded life, if you understand what I mean, sir."

"I can make a guess at it. Lives alone, does she?"

"No, sir, I didn't mean it in that way. She lives with that husband of hers—a rank bad lot, sir. What I meant was that she lives in a lonelyish sort of place and doesn't come much about the village."

"The husband's a bad lot, is he? Hard lines on her."

"He's a bad 'un, sir. Never a civil word out of him, and always sneering at us—at the Police, I mean, sir. One of these Red Raggers, sir: a red-hot Bolshie with a grouse against anyone better than what he is—and that's most of the human race, to my mind."

"Well, it takes all sorts to make a world," said the Inspector tolerantly. "Hasn't he got a human side—some hobby or other that would keep him busy in his spare time?"

Even this side of Mr. Haddon's character failed to please P. C. Gumley.

"He breeds and trains whippets, sir, if you can call that a hobby. Hares are getting scarce, hereabouts," he added, darkly.

"Educated man, is he?"

"Educated, is he?" P. C. Gumley took no pains to conceal his contempt. "Why, sir, that man's never opened a book since he left school. What he reads is the starting prices and the results in the newspaper, nothing else. Whippets and horses: that's all he cares for, sir."

"Hard lines on his wife," the Inspector repeated mechanically. "Well, it's no concern of ours unless he goes over the bounds. You think she's a reliable person, that's the main point."

After a few moments' further talk on other subjects, he left the constable to walk his beat while he himself busied himself with another matter. He had obtained the information he needed; and as it had come to him almost without exertion, he was correspondingly pleased. Quite evidently, Haddon was the most suspicious character connected with that particular brand of notepaper. It was worth while going further on the strength of what had come out.

The Inspector set himself to draught a letter dealing with whippets and their purchase, a letter which would demand a fairly full reply. When he had finished this task, he wrote out a fair copy and scribbled a covering note to an unofficial friend of his in a neighbouring town. Then, putting the documents into an envelope, he dropped them into the post-box.

Three days later, he got a reply from his correspondent; and when he opened the envelope an enclosure dropped out—a letter on the familiar cheap yellowish note paper.

"Got him, first shot!" the Inspector commented delightedly, as he examined this fresh document with its sprawling signature "J. Haddon."

"Same note paper, same writing, same habit of starting at the very left-hand edge, same blunder in spelling 'youre,' same sprinkling of capital letters at random, and same trick of underlining here and there. And enough fingerprints to amuse a dozen experts. There's going to be no difficulty about this bit, anyhow."

Examination of the fingerprints revealed a thumb-mark crossed by a scar, which occurred on both the anonymous letter and the letter from J. Haddon. The Inspector made no pretence of expertness in fingerprint identification; but this piece of evidence was enough to satisfy him. He made some inquiries as to Haddon's habits, and presented himself at the cottage when he knew the master of the house was sure to be at home.

When he knocked at the door, Haddon himself opened it: a tall, surly man with a slight cast in one eye. At the sight of the Inspector, he seemed taken aback for a moment, but soon recovered himself.

"Want to see my wife?" he demanded, gruffly.

Westerham shook his head.

"No, it's you I want to see. It's a matter of maliciously publishing a defamatory libel."

"What does that mean?" Haddon asked, in a rather shaken tone.

"Fine and imprisonment not exceeding one year," the Inspector answered, with wilful misunderstanding.

Haddon drew back a step and rubbed an unshaven chin with his hand.

"Oh. Indeed? And what's it got to do with me?"

"Come off the perch," Westerham suggested vulgarly. "It didn't take long for *clever blokes in the police* to run you down, did it?"

"D'you mean that letter?" Haddon asked, unguardedly.

"I do mean that letter," the Inspector assured him sardonically. Then he changed his tone to one of a man speaking in confidence.

"Come out into the spinney," he suggested. "We can talk easier there. You've got yourself into a bad hole, Haddon, and there's only one way out of it. I'm not going to be hard on you; I'll give you a chance."

Haddon, plainly thunderstruck at being detected so quickly, was evidently growing more amenable.

"All right," he agreed and followed the Inspector out of the garden where they were out of earshot of the cottage.

"Here's the way I look at it," Westerham explained in a less official tone. "You wrote me a letter making certain statements about Mr. Castleford. If I choose to take it as it stands, you've run yourself in for a charge of criminal libel; and you'll get it hot. I can prove it against you, up to the hilt. That's one way of looking at it;

and you can have it that way if you like. Here's another way. Well suppose that you're an honest witness, anxious to give evidence, and we'll overlook the slight informality of the way you've gone about it at the start. In that case, there's nothing against you. Now, which is it to be? It's all one to me. We'll put you in the witness-box and wring your evidence out of you, either way."

Haddon considered for a few moments, eyeing the Inspector with more respect than he had shown at the beginning of the interview.

"Well," he admitted at last, "you seem smarter than what I gave you credit for, and that's a fact. I don't see how you got on to me. And it looks, sure enough, as if you'd got me in a corner. But that don't matter to me. I'm no friend of Castleford's and there's no reason, that I can see, why I shouldn't give him away. What I wrote in that there letter was Gospel truth and I'm ready to take my oath on it any time you like. I was just having a game with you God-Almighty coppers for the fun of it."

"Very well," said Westerham, with a return to his official manner. "Now give us a plain story."

"The afternoon of that business," Haddon began, after a pause to gather up his recollections, "I was down at the east end of the spinney about five o'clock in the afternoon, on private business."

"What were you doing?" demanded the Inspector.

"Urgent private affairs," Haddon retorted with what was evidently meant to be an engaging leer. "Axe no questions and you'll get no lies: that's my motto."

"Setting snares for rabbits, eh?" the Inspector suggested. "They come out of the wood on that side at dusk to feed in the meadow beyond, don't they?"

"So you say," Haddon returned, with a gesture as though brushing the suggestion aside. "Urgent private business is what I'd call it. Anyhow, whatever it was, I wasn't exactly advertising myself, see?"

"You were hiding on the edge of the spinney," Westerham translated. "Very well. What next?"

"I seen Castleford come into the spinney just about then. I ought to have said I heard somebody shooting while I was working at my private affairs before that, somebody over in the other arm of the spinney. That didn't worry me. I guessed it was that young whelp from Carron Hill, for I'd seen him swelling around with his pop-gun before then. Well, as I was saying, I saw Castleford come into the spinney, and I lay low. For a man on his own ground, he seemed to be going mighty cautious, but I could give a guess at what he was after. No business of mine. I just wished him good luck to myself and hoped he'd like what he found up at the Chalet."

The Inspector seemed about to say something, but checked himself.

"I lay low, there," Haddon continued. "Some more shots went off, if I remember right. And then back comes Castleford—no caution about him this time. He passed quite close to me, and I could see his face—white as a sheet and his mouth working like as if he was going to cry, if you understand what I mean. He'd got a proper turn, I could see that with half an eye. Well, I supposed he'd been having a look in at the window of the Chalet and hadn't got as much amusement out of his peep as some people might. That was what I thought about it. And by that time I'd finished my little job, so I vamoosed myself, going down into Thunderbridge through the fields. Of course, when the whole yarn came out, I put two and two together, as one might say; and so I communicated with the police," he wound up impudently.

"What time did this happen? What's the nearest you can come to it?"

"It was just before the quarter past five, I'd say. I heard the church clock in Thunderbridge chime the quarter shortly after that."

"Did you see anyone else about there, round about that time?"

"Not a soul. Of course I couldn't see the Chalet. I was on the other side of the spinney."

"You said you could give a guess at what Castleford was after. What did you mean by that?"

"Spying on his wife and that Stevenage cove, of course."

"Ah, yes, I remember now. You 'took the trouble to write and tell him about their goings-on,' didn't you?"

Haddon was quite unashamed.

151

"What supposing I did, once or twice? Wouldn't you have done the same, in a friendly way, if you'd seen them at their capers, eh?"

Westerham did not seem quite so amused as he might have been. A thought crossed his mind, and when he spoke again the official tone of his voice was accentuated.

"You seem to have been pretty free with your modest information, Haddon. You wrote to Castleford. You wrote to me. Now, out with it and be done. Who else did you favour?"

Haddon hesitated for a moment, not from shame evidently, but merely on tactical grounds.

"This doesn't count against me? What I mean is, if I tell you, there'll be no more about it, eh?"

"I'm prepared to let it go at that if you make a clean breast of everything."

"Well, then, I dropped a note to Miss Lindfield, too."

"Why? What's she got to do with it?"

Haddon showed a set of yellow teeth in a malicious grin.

"Oh, I just thought I'd tip her off—let her know what her dear boy Stevenage was up to. She's a bit interested in him, you can take my word for that. You don't know what a rotten lot these bourgeoises is, Mr. Westerham, for all their fine airs and fine feathers. A rotten lot, and you can kiss the Book on that, any day. I know a thing or two about them, I do."

"Anybody else on your list of correspondents?"

"Well, I told Stevenage what I thought of him, too."

"That the lot now?"

"That's the lot."

"H'm! You seem to have been working on the mass-production basis."

Haddon, now that he felt his own skin safe, was cheerfully insolent.

"Oh, just holding up the mirror to Nature, as might say," he explained jauntily. "If they hadn't been playing around the way they was doing, I'd have had nothing to write about, would I? I was just letting 'em see they wasn't as smart as they thought they was. They'd be none the worse of a bit of a jar, none of them, to my mind."

14
THE BRACE OF PISTOLS

Inspector Westerham had not seen the study at Carron Hill before, and he let his glance run round it as he took his seat in response to Castleford's gesture. Then his eyes came back to the dark-clothed figure before him, and he plunged into his business.

"I'm sorry to trouble you again, Mr. Castleford," he said in a faintly apologetic tone, "but the fact is, some fresh information has come into my hands, and I'm trying to check it. You can help me there, if you don't mind."

"I'll give you any assistance I can," Castleford answered in a tone which mingled caution with reluctance, so far as the Inspector could interpret it. "It's a painful subject, as you can well understand, a subject that I'd rather keep my mind off, if I could. But I'm quite ready to tell you anything I can."

"Very well, then," said Westerham, a shade less sympathetically, "I'll come straight to the point. I've reason to believe that, not long before your wife's death, you received an anonymous letter from someone or other. That's correct?"

Castleford's reluctance became obvious. He hesitated quite perceptibly before he spoke, as though he were trying to gauge his best course.

"That's correct," he echoed at last. "I did get an anonymous letter. But how does that concern you? I've made no complaint on the subject, and I don't intend to bring any charge in the matter even if I could do so. It seems to me a private matter which concerns no one except myself."

"It's hardly that," the Inspector said bluffly, without deigning to explain. "What did you do with it?"

"What does anyone do with anonymous letters?" Castleford asked. "I burned it, naturally. One pays no attention to things like that."

"You can remember its contents, though, even if you burned it," the Inspector suggested in a tone that brooked no denial. "What did it contain?"

"It contained some vulgar abuse of myself, and I hardly see how that is a matter which concerns you."

"Was that all there was in it? There was no reference to Mrs. Castleford, for instance?"

Castleford made an obvious effort to appear annoyed at this suggestion, but his attempt failed completely to deceive Westerham.

"Really, this is disgraceful! You don't expect me to listen quietly to insinuations of that sort, do you, Mr. Westerham? What grounds have you for attacking my unhappy wife's character in this way?"

"Allow me to point this out, Mr. Castleford," said Westerham severely. "In the first place, I made no attack on Mrs. Castleford's character. I asked the plain question: Was there any reference to Mrs. Castleford in that letter? There's no insinuation of any kind in that. And, in the second place, I'll point out that you haven't answered that question yet."

"There was nothing about her in the letter," Castford said doggedly.

The Inspector mentally recorded the fact that Castleford was a very poor hand at lying. His manner gave him away completely, even if Westerham had not already known the truth about the contents of the anonymous letter.

"Very well, Mr. Castleford, I'll take a note of that," he said in a neutral tone. "Now, another point. Have you, recently, had any disagreement with Mrs. Castleford, any serious difference of opinion on any important matter?"

"What are you hinting at now?" Castleford demanded, in a voice which betrayed both nervousness and anger. "You seem to be taking a roving commission to pry into all sorts of affairs, and I can't see how they concern you in any way. No, I had no serious difference with my wife on any subject. Is that clear?"

"Quite clear," Westerham said, with a certain hint of triumph in his tone which made Castleford glance sharply at him. "You had no disagreement with Mrs. Castleford on the matter of her proposed alteration in her will, for instance?"

"None whatever," Castleford said boldly. "I knew that she had cancelled her will and that she proposed to make a fresh one. That was entirely her affair, since her money was her own. I had no right to dictate to her if she proposed to leave her money to her brothers-in-law. After all, as I knew well enough, it was originally Glencaple money; and I had no grievance if it went back to them."

"You didn't discuss the matter with her?"

Castleford obviously hesitated before answering.

"No," he said, uncertainly. Then in a firmer tone he added: "I certainly don't remember discussing it with her. It was a subject which, naturally, I would avoid."

"You had no other possible cause for disagreement?" the Inspector pursued.

"None whatever," Castleford declared emphatically. I can see what you're hinting at, and I may as well put a stop to this sort of thing. I had every confidence in Mrs. Castleford."

"I wasn't hinting at anything," the Inspector explained smoothly. "What did you imagine I meant?"

"Some scandal or other, I gathered from your tone; but if you say you meant nothing by it, then let it go at that, if you please. I had, as I say, perfect confidence in Mrs. Castleford. I hope that is sufficient."

"Quite sufficient," the Inspector acquiesced in a tone which suggested a double meaning. "And now I come to another matter. I'm looking for a firearm with a calibre about .32—an automatic pistol, I believe. Have you any knowledge of such a thing on the premises here?"

Westerham had merely been trying a long shot, and he was surprised to see a curious expression pass over Castleford's face at the question. There was a momentary pause before the answer came.

"Y-e-s," Castleford admitted reluctantly, "there's a brace of automatics here, though I know nothing about calibres and they may not be what you're looking for. But you don't imagine my wife was wounded by an automatic, do you? It was the rook-rifle that killed her, I understood."

"You might let me see them, please," Westerham requested, without taking any notice of Castleford's last sentences.

Castleford got up, went to the cupboard, and lifted down the box which he had placed there some time before. He brought it to a table and laid it down.

"Don't touch!" Westerham exclaimed, as Castleford put his hand into the box to pick out the pistols.

The Inspector went over and examined the two weapons, which he recognised as being of the calibre he wanted. Very gingerly, he shifted one of them, screwed up the corner of his handkerchief, and inserted it in the barrel. Then giving it a twist, he extracted it again and examined the dirt on the handkerchief. He repeated this in the case of the second pistol, and this time he recognised from the traces that the pistol had been discharged and had not been cleaned after firing. He sniffed the barrel of each pistol in turn: in the first case he detected a strong odour of cleaning-oil, whilst the second weapon had a peculiar smell of its own, due to the residue of the discharge, and there was little scent of oil.

"You have a firearms certificate for these?" he asked, as he put down the pistols again.

"I?" said Castleford, in some surprise. "No, I've got no certificate. They don't belong to me. They belonged to my wife's first husband. They've nothing to do with me."

"They're in your charge, apparently," the Inspector pointed out. "How did you get them?"

There was no hesitation in the reply this time.

"That young cub that was staying here unearthed them in the garret, where they must have been lying for years. Miss Lindfield was afraid he'd do some damage with them if they were left within

156

his reach, so she asked me to put them into that cupboard for safety. They've been there ever since then—that was a day or two before Mrs. Castleford's death, I remember."

"Well, I'll have to take charge of them for the present," the Inspector said casually.

He was considerably elated by his discovery, though no trace of this showed in his face. There was little doubt in his mind that he had come upon the very weapon with which the shooting had been done.

"Now there's another question I want to put," he went on, as he replaced the lid on the box. "Do you know if Mrs. Castleford had any access to morphia?"

Castleford shook his head.

"You mean, was she a drug-fiend?" he queried. "Not that I knew of, certainly. Besides, how could she get the stuff? No, I know nothing about that, whatever you're driving at."

"Can you suggest anyone connected with Carron who might have been able to procure morphia?"

Castleford reflected for a moment or two.

"Nobody that I can think of . . . unless . . . well, of course Dr. Glencaple could get morphia—as a doctor. In fact, I believe he's treating a man Heckford for the morphia-habit just now, so he's sure to have some of the drug. But he's the only person who could lay his hands on it easily. But what's morphia got to do with the case? There seem to be a lot of things I don't understand about this business, to judge by these questions of yours."

"We get bits of information here and there," Westerham said lightly, "and we've got to check them all up. Half of them lead to nothing, of course. Still, we have to go into them all. Now, there's another matter I want to ask you about. On the day of Mrs. Castleford's death, you and she left Carron Hill together at about three o'clock. You walked together to the point where the path to the Chalet turns off, I understand. What did you talk about while you were together?"

"Really, I don't quite see what business that is of yours, Mr. Westerham, if you don't mind my saying so," Castleford answered abruptly. "We discussed a number of matters, general topics of conversation which it would be hard to recall now: something about a new flower-bed, how she was getting on with her painting, the card she had put in for her golf-handicap, things like that. I don't really remember exactly."

"And her will wasn't mentioned at all?"

Castleford seemed annoyed by this persistent harping on the subject.

"No, nothing about her will. I've told you so already."

"Think again," Westerham advised.

"I don't remember anything of the sort."

The Inspector hesitated over the line which he should take. His industrious combing of the countryside had yielded several pieces of evidence which would enable him to check Castleford's story; and here, at the very start, he had come up against a flat lie. He made up his mind to show his teeth just once, even at the cost of disclosing part of the case which he was building up in his mind. Turning over the pages of his notebook, he came to a very rough diagram drawn to a time-scale instead of one of distance. It represented crudely the time which would be taken by a man walking at three miles per hour from point to point over the crucial routes.

"At 3.10 p.m., Mr. Castleford, you and Mrs. Castleford reached the little stone bridge over the stream to that road. You remember it? As it happened, just under that bridge a boy was busy netting minnows. He wasn't a child; he was getting the minnows for a young brother who happens to be ill and couldn't go and get them for himself. This boy, then, with his net and his pickle-bottle, was out of your sight as you crossed the bridge; but he had seen you as you came along the road up to the bridge. According to his account, you and Mrs. Castleford were talking rather heatedly then, and he caught one or two sentences. He remembers something about your saying, 'You've gone back on your promise' and 'You've made this new will?' and he heard Mrs. Castleford say, 'No, not yet. But after *this* I'll do it.' Is that story accurate, Mr. Castleford?"

Castleford seemed completely taken aback by the attack. He paused for some seconds before answering.

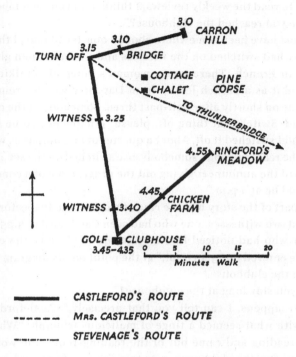

"If you're going to take that line, Mr. Westerham, I don't propose to follow you," he said at last, with a feeble attempt at dignity. "I've told you what happened, or rather what didn't happen. If my word isn't enough for you, I see no point in any further dealings."

The Inspector decided to leave the matter as it was, without comment.

"At 3.15 p.m., you reached the turn-off; and Mrs. Castleford parted from you, going along the path towards the Chalet. That's correct?"

"I told you that before."

"I'm not querying it," Westerham assured him soothingly. "I'm merely trying to get facts and figures down definitely. You went on to the clubhouse. You go there on that particular day each week,

159

you said, to read the weekly reviews, I think. Can you remember at what time you reached the clubhouse?"

"It must have been somewhere about a quarter to four, I think. Somebody had switched on the wireless and I heard a man giving a lesson in French. There was a woman's voice also talking. I recognised it as a French lesson from Daventry which I remembered came on shortly after half-past three. Somebody in the clubhouse said 'Switch that thing off, please.' I happened to be near the set and I switched it off. About a quarter of an hour later, when I was in the reading-room, somebody else switched on the set again and I heard the announcer giving out the programme of a concert. That would be at 4 p.m."

This part of the story had the ring of truth to the Inspector. He had found two witnesses: one who had seen Castleford at 3.25 and the other who had noticed him at 3.40, quite close to the clubhouse. He entered up "3.45 p.m.," at the point on his diagram representing the clubhouse.

"Did you stay long at the clubhouse?"

"As it happens, I can tell you that precisely," Castleford answered with what seemed a tinge of malicious triumph. "When I finished reading and came out of the reading-room, the woman who looks after the clubhouse, gets teas for members, and so on, was hanging about. I said good-afternoon to her as I passed; and she asked me if I'd seen my daughter. I said I hadn't. Then she told me Miss Castleford had left the place ten minutes ago and that I'd be able to catch her up without difficulty if I wanted to. That made us both look at the clock, and it was thirty-five minutes past four. I set out after her."

The Inspector nodded. This part of the tale was true enough, he knew, for he had already extracted all these facts from the woman at the golf clubhouse himself.

"Did you ask which way Miss Castleford had gone?" he asked.

"No, why should I? I took the usual road to Carroll Hill, the one that she was sure to take herself."

"Which is that?" the Inspector inquired doubtfully.

"Up by Peppercorn Ridge and along the right-of-way across the chicken farm and then by the field-path through Ringford's Meadows."

That sounded true enough, the Inspector had to confess to himself. One of the people on the chicken farm had noticed Castleford passing over the public right-of-way which cut across the grounds of the farm. He had been seen there at a quarter to five, just about the time that the three-quarters chimed from Thunderbridge. But the Inspector had not been able to discover the time when Miss Castleford passed the farm ahead of her father. No one had noticed her. Ten minutes would bring Castleford from the chicken farm to Ringford's Meadow; which meant that he would be there at 4.55 p.m.—and this tallied neatly with Stevenage's account of seeing him there at that time.

"And what did you do after that?" the Inspector demanded.

This was the crucial time—the quarter of an hour during which the murder had been committed.

"Very shortly after leaving Ringford's Meadow, I made up on my daughter."

"Where, exactly, did you make up on her?"

Castleford answered this question promptly.

"In a little pine copse about due east of the plantation round the Chalet. She had sat down there. She had nothing to do, and she thought there was a chance that I might make up on her. So she tells me."

"And what time would that be?"

"It would be just after five o'clock; I should say about five minutes past five, roughly, for I heard five o'clock chime in Thunderbridge shortly before I met my daughter."

The Inspector strove his hardest to show no particular interest in these statements. Here, for the second time, he had caught Castleford in a flat lie about the affairs of the afternoon. At ten past five, according to Haddon's evidence, Castleford was in the neighbourhood of the Chalet, behaving in a highly suspicious manner. Then a further thought struck Westerham. If the girl had been just ahead of her father, Stevenage might well have been expected to catch a glimpse of her as he came down from the Chalet. It was quite on the cards, of course, that she had crossed Stevenage's track and got up to the pine copse before his arrival. In that case, there was nothing in it. Or Stevenage might have seen her and left her name out of the business. The net result was that there was no confirmatory evidence bearing on her movements after she left the clubhouse.

"And what happened after that?"

Castleford at this point showed no hesitation.

"We sat in the copse together for quite a long time. We had a number of things to discuss, things which required a good deal of talking and which kept our attention entirely. I really can't say how long we stayed there. Afterwards, I went on to Carron Hill and reached there very shortly before you yourself arrived at the house."

"Didn't Miss Castleford come with you?"

"No," Castleford explained. "She had remembered something she wanted in Thunderbridge, and she went on into the village."

"I see," said the Inspector. "So she did not get back to Carron Hill till much later?"

"No."

The Inspector decided to open up a fresh line of inquiry.

"I remember," he said, "that when I came to Carron Hill on the day of Mrs. Castleford's death, you were changing your clothes, and you came down, rather later, in the dark suit you're wearing now, or one like it. What clothes had you been wearing just before that—during the afternoon?"

"A golfing suit—plus-fours," Castleford answered without hesitation. "There was just a chance that I might pick up a game when I got to the clubhouse, though I didn't set out with the idea of playing."

"You have that suit here, I suppose? Any objection to my seeing it? I have a reason for asking."

"I suppose you have," Castleford retorted, though without any marked signs of reluctance. "It's upstairs. I'll bring it down, if you wish."

"I'll go up with you," Westerham suggested. "There's no need to carry it up and down stairs."

Castleford agreed with a nod and led the way up to his room. Opening a wardrobe, he pointed to a jacket and waistcoat on a hanger, and then, going down on his knees, he opened a drawer and began to search for the corresponding plus-fours. The Inspector took the jacket from its hanger, spread it out on the bed, and made a rapid examination of it. Suddenly he suppressed an exclamation, as he turned over one of the sleeves. He then examined the waistcoat, without finding anything to interest him; and finally he scrutinised the plus-fours which Castleford was holding out to him with a slightly sardonic smile.

"Have you found anything to interest you?" he asked, hardly taking the trouble to repress a sneer.

"As it happens, I have," the Inspector returned blandly "You might take a look at this, Mr. Castleford."

He twisted the coat-sleeve over so as to disclose on its under surface—out of sight of the wearer—an ominous brown stain of considerable dimensions.

Castleford seemed to reflect for a moment before answering.

"I suppose I must have come up against some wet paint somehow or other, but I can't remember where it can have been. I leaned my arms on a stile that afternoon, to look at the view; and perhaps the wood may have been newly painted. That would have marked the sleeve just like that, wouldn't it? I certainly didn't notice that I'd got that smear on the cloth, and no one told me about it at the time."

"Most likely they'd other things to think about," the Inspector suggested drily. "Your house was rather badly upset when you came back to it that day, you remember. But take a good look at this mark, Mr. Castleford."

Castleford obeyed and the Inspector watched a look of consternation grow on his features as he stared, as if hypnotised, at the rusty brown stain on the cloth.

"I'll have to take this jacket away with me," Westerham said bluntly. "I'm not certain what this stain may be and I must find out. You don't object?"

Castleford evidently recognised that protest would be worse than acquiescence; and he gave a half-hearted permission with a nod.

"Then there's another point," Westerham pursued. "I suppose your stockings have gone to the wash—the ones you wore that day—but you might let me see the shoes you were wearing that afternoon."

Castleford led the way downstairs to a cloakroom and opened a boot-cupboard. The Inspector noticed that he seemed to have no objection to this part of the proceedings. He ran his eye along the shelves and picked out a pair of golfing-shoes which he handed to Westerham.

"These are the ones I was wearing. But I can't quite see what bearing they may have on my wife's death. Are you not taking rather much on yourself, with all this prying, if you don't mind my putting it in rather plain language?"

"Have you worn them since then?" asked Westerham disregarding the complaint.

Castleford shook his head. The Inspector, turning the shoes over in his hand in an apparently casual fashion, saw on the sole of one of them the thing he was looking for, but which he had not expected to find. Obscured by road-grit and worn away by friction, still the paint-mark was visible; and just under the instep, where the sole had been raised from the ground, it stood out almost as though fresh.

"I'll take these shoes as well; if you've no objection," the Inspector announced, with an effort to suppress all excitement from his tone.

Here it was plain that Castleford could make neither head nor tail of the proceedings. Westerham had continued to turn the shoes about in his hand as though examining the uppers, and Castleford had not noticed any special attention being given to the soles. He stared at the Inspector with unfeigned incomprehension written large on his face.

"I can't see what you want with them," he said, unsteadily, "but if you insist on taking them, I don't propose to object. I think I may ask, though, why you find them important."

"They may be of no importance whatever," Westerham answered disingenuously. "As I told you, I've got to check a lot of things, and these shoes may help me that. That's all I'm prepared to say at present."

Suddenly Castleford flashed up into the temper of a weak man.

"I'm not satisfied with this way of doing things," he exclaimed vehemently. "You come here; you suggest this and you hint at that; you pry into my affairs; you confiscate one thing and another without so much as by-your-leave. Are you suspecting me of being concerned in my wife's death? Is that what you're after? Is all this prying and spying . . . Are you going to charge me with causing her death? Is that what you have in view? Is that it?"

He stopped, apparently choked by his emotion.

"I'm not bringing any charge against you," Westerham retorted with more than his usual suavity. "My business is to collect all the evidence I can get which may bear even remotely on the case. There's no reason why any innocent person should object to that, is there? It isn't likely to do him any harm, if he's innocent, surely. This case, so far as I've gone, wouldn't justify my making a charge against anyone."

The moment his outburst was over, Castleford evidently realised what harm it might have done him. He calmed himself with an effort and made a half-apology.

"I quite understand, Mr. Westerham; but, as you can guess, this affair has given me a shock and I'm not quite so steady as I might be. My nerves are on edge, and perhaps I've been taking offence when there was no need for it. Although," he added, suspiciously, "you seem to be paying very special attention to me and my affairs."

The Inspector laughed a little at this criticism.

"That's only because you happen to be the first person whom I've questioned, here," he explained. "I shall have to do the same with the rest. Everybody has to go through it, you know, in the interests of justice; and there's no reflection on anyone until a charge is brought."

"Then you've reason to believe it's a case of murder, not accident?"

"All I can say is that suspicions have been aroused and we've got to allay them or confirm them. That's what I'm paid for, you know; it's part of my job. And I'll get on with it, now, if you don't mind. I understand that Miss Castleford is on the premises. I want to ask her a few questions. Perhaps you could send her to me?"

"I'll bring her," Castleford agreed, in a grudging tone

"I'd prefer to see her alone," the Inspector said, curtly, to make his position quite clear.

166

15
HILARY CASTLEFORD'S STATEMENTS

Inspector Westerham, connoisseur in feminine attractiveness, experienced a certain titillation when Hilary entered the study. He liked slim, straight-backed girls, especially when they looked as though butter wouldn't freeze in their mouths. A swift, appraising glance catalogued her hair, her features, her figure, and rested for a moment on her neatly-turned ankles—for ankles were to the Inspector one of the acid tests of a woman's appearance. The result of his survey satisfied him; and his human side pronounced the slangy verdict: "This is a bit of all right! She must have taken the shine out of the other women in the house."

The official half of the Inspector had been equally busy. This girl had hitherto been the single unknown factor among the personalities interwoven with the Carron Hill drama. He had been curious to meet her face to face and to gauge, if possible, the part she might have played in the events leading up to the tragedy. He was beginning to realise that the key to his problem might be found among the characters of the actors more readily than by a mere poring over material clues. From that standpoint, Hilary Castleford was already a suspect witness to some extent. Her interests were interlocked with those of her father; and since his evidence had been deliberately misleading, it might be expected that she would follow suit.

The detective half of Westerham noted that Hilary's dress showed no trace of mourning. Again he received the impression that no one at Carron Hill missed Mrs. Castleford as a human being. She seemed to have dropped like a stone into a pool; once the slight ripples died down no one would feel the worse for her loss.

Westerham's eyes returned to Hilary's face. He noted the set of the cleanly-chiselled lips, the firmness of the jaw under the softness of its curves, and the fully-lifted eyelids. "This girl can look after herself pretty well," was the official estimate. "She's as cool as a penny ice; and she's got sticking-power, unless her face lies."

"You want to see me?" Hilary demanded, as she came forward.

"Yes, Miss Castleford, I'd like you to help me with one or two little points, if you will," the Inspector explained in a tone which suggested that he attached no great importance to the questions he was going to put.

He felt sure that Castleford had given her a hint to be on her guard; and he made up his mind to approach the crucial subjects by degrees, so as to allay her suspicions if possible.

"Do you mind if I begin rather far back?" he asked. "I'd like to know what you remember about the party at the luncheon table on the day of Mrs. Castleford's death."

Hilary knitted her brows slightly, as though making an effort of memory.

"You mean, who was there? I can remember my father, Mrs. Castleford, Miss Lindfield, myself, and Frank Glencaple. That was all."

"Can you recall anything of the talk that went on at the table?" Westerham asked. Then, realising from the expression on Hilary's face that he had asked too wide a question, he limited his inquiry. "For instance, can you recall Miss Lindfield making any arrangements with the boy Glencaple for the afternoon?"

Hilary seemed in no haste to answer. She pondered for a time before making up her mind about her reply.

"If I'm not mistaken—and I may be, for I'd no reason to pay attention—she said she was going to take a walk round through Piney Holt, and that he could meet her on her way home in the spinney beside the Chalet. She said, if I remember, that she'd be starting from here at half-past two, and he could be waiting for her. Then they were going into Thunderbridge together."

She reflected for a moment and then added:

"Unless I'm mistaken, she warned him in an undertone to keep out of Mrs. Castleford's way if she was at the Chalet. He was taking his rook-rifle with him to pass the time, and Mrs. Castleford had a horror of guns. She was always afraid of an accident happening. I thought it was very sensible of Miss Lindfield to give him that warning."

"That reminds me," Westerham put in, "did the boy get on well with Mrs. Castleford?"

"He liked her for what he could get out of her," said Hilary, rather contemptuously. "He was fonder of Miss Lindfield, I think. I can't say he was a favourite of mine."

"He didn't strike me as being very obedient, from what I saw of him," the Inspector mused aloud.

"He isn't," Hilary confirmed. "He's been very badly brought up. You can't count on him to do anything he's told to do; and you can't believe much that he says. But I dislike him intensely and perhaps I'd better not say any more about him. I might give you a wrong impression of him, perhaps."

Westerham went back to his earlier line of inquiry. "Did you hear Miss Lindfield mention the exact time when she expected to meet the boy near the Chalet?"

Hilary shook her head decidedly.

"No, I don't think any time was mentioned. She told him she was going round by Piney Holt and back by Six Road Ends and the level crossing over the railway. He knows that walk well; and as he knew she was leaving here at half-past two, he'd guess that she'd be at the Chalet round about a quarter past four. He'd expect her then, I suppose, and make his arrangements accordingly."

Westerham noted that Hilary gave a fairly sound estimate of the time taken to complete that walk. It was evidently a favourite one for the Carron Hill people. Miss Lindfield had taken three-quarters of an hour longer over it than usual, since she only reached the spinney at five o'clock. But Westerham had unearthed some witnesses whose evidence accounted for this, easily enough. One man had seen her go into Piney bit at about a quarter past three. If she had walked straight through, she would have reached Six Road Ends at about twenty minutes to four. But the driver of a local grocer's delivery van had overtaken her at Six Road Ends at ten minutes past four, so that she had evidently loitered for half an hour in the cool of the pine wood; and the man in the signal box which controlled the level crossing had seen her walk over the line at a quarter past four.

"I'm not very sure of my ground," Westerham admitted, doubtfully. "On that route, there's a short cut to the Chalet, isn't there? Where does it start?"

"It branches off from the road in the middle of a thicket—they call it The Wilderness—about five minutes' walk from the level crossing," Hilary explained. "The short cut takes about a quarter of an hour off the walk to the Chalet. It's a full half-hour's walk if you follow the road instead of taking to the path."

"I see. Thanks very much."

The Inspector thought that he had managed to put the girl off her guard. She was answering quite frankly, without any apparent calculation, and he wanted to keep her in that form now that he was approaching the really dangerous part of the matter.

"Now, let's go back to that afternoon," he said casually. "Miss Lindfield went out for her walk; your father and Mrs. Castleford went out together about half an hour later. That left you alone in the house here?"

"No," Hilary explained, with no apparent change in her candour. "I'd gone out myself, immediately after lunch. Miss Heskett rang up and asked me to play nine holes with her. She called for me in her car, because I'd told the gardener to clean our own car that afternoon, and I didn't want to countermand the order. We didn't go straight to the course, though, I remember. Miss Heskett wanted to exchange some library books in Strickland Regis, so we drove there first, and she spent some time in the Library. After that, we played nine holes and came back to the clubhouse for tea. Miss Heskett had to go off to some engagement or other; and when she had gone, I set off home."

"When did you leave the clubhouse?" the Inspector asked, as if in casual curiosity.

Hilary looked at him sharply.

"Some time before half-past four, I should imagine—a few minutes before then, so far as I can remember. But I had no reason to look at the time. Is it of any special importance? Why?"

Westerham saw that her father had put her on her guard and that consequently it was useless to pretend that he was merely asking idle questions.

"It is important, perhaps," he admitted. "In cases of this sort it's difficult to say what's important and what isn't; so I've just got to collect all the information I can get and then sift out the chaff from the grain afterwards. You left the clubhouse shortly before half-past four? Which road did you take?"

Hilary's brows knitted for an instant, as though she were preparing to resent this examination. Then, apparently, the matter seemed to strike her in a fresh light and she became frankly communicative.

"I took the usual road—up through the chicken farm and by the field-path through Ringford's Meadow. Then I went and sat down in a copse which lies a bit to the east of the Chalet."

"About what time did you reach the copse?" the Inspector asked.

Hilary shook her head.

"I really don't know, Mr. Westerham. Remember, I don't go about with one eye on my wrist-watch. I walked at my usual pace—which is much the same as everybody else's—and I didn't loiter on the road. That's really all I can tell you."

Westerham had to admit to himself that there was nothing very suspicious in this vagueness. It was perfectly natural. And yet, he had the impression that something was wrong with the story. The girl was quite cool, but in some way which he could not define to himself she was betraying herself. It was a mere matter of trifles— the very faintest change in the set of her features, an almost imperceptible stiffening in her attitude, the very slightest change in the timbre of her voice: things which can be appreciated by the senses but which are almost beyond the range of verbal description.

"What made you sit down there?" he asked. "Had your golf tired you?"

Hilary rejected this suggestion with a very natural gesture of derision.

"Tired? Oh, no. But when I got up to the copse remembered—I'd forgotten it up till then—that this was the afternoon when my father always went over to the clubhouse to read the weekly reviews; and I thought that perhaps he might be coming along, later. If I waited, he might make up on me. That was all."

That, again, was unsuspicious enough. Westerham began to think that, so far, he had been told the truth and that the girl's nervousness was due to the anticipation of further questions in store rather than to those which he was actually putting.

"From the edge of the copse where you were sitting, could you see much of the path you had come along?"

Hilary seemed quite at ease as she answered this.

"I could see part of Ringford's Meadow and some of the nearer stretch. I remember that, because I was on the lookout to see if my father was coming."

"I suppose you could see the strip of road that runs from the Chalet down towards Ringford's Meadow?"

"Yes, I could see most of that," Hilary answered, after the very faintest hesitation.

"You were keeping a sharp lookout, of course, since you were expecting your father?"

Again Hilary seemed to hesitate for an instant as though she doubted what was the best answer to make.

"Yes, I was keeping a good lookout," she admitted finally, in a tone which the Inspector found much less frank than before.

Evidently, he surmised, he was "getting warm." They were coming to the "really sticky bit" as he phrased it to himself. It was here that he hoped to entrap her if she was lying, by fastening upon a piece of evidence for which she might be unprepared; but he had two points at which he wished to pin her down; and either of them might see her on the alert for the other. In his turn, he paused to consider, watching her face as he did so.

"You heard the Thunderbridge clock strike five, didn't you?" he asked at last, when he had made his decision. "Was that before or after you sat down, can you remember?"

"It was after I sat down," Hilary answered with a readiness which rather took the Inspector aback. "I'd been sitting there for some minutes—five minutes or more—when the chime sounded. I'm quite sure about that, because I glanced at my wrist-watch to check it. It runs a shade fast, and I like to know just how much ahead of time it is."

"You were looking out for your father. Did you catch sight of him before or after the chime struck?"

Here Hilary's hesitation was quite a couple of seconds long before she gave her reply.

"It was before I heard the chime . . . At least, I think so," she added hurriedly.

"Can't you be sure about it?"

Hilary seemed to have recovered from her tiny panic.

"Yes," she said definitely, "it was before the chime. I saw him in Ringford's Meadow just before the clock struck."

Now the Inspector decided to spring his mine. This girl and her father might have concocted their story very neatly, but perhaps they had left a loose end.

"Did you see anyone on the by-road leading towards the Chalet at that time?" he demanded sharply.

What he wished to do was to pin her down to saying whether her father crossed the by-road in advance of or behind Stevenage, since from Stevenage's evidence Castleford had been some distance from the road when he himself passed by. Quite obviously, the question took the girl aback. She had not been primed beforehand how to deal with it. She considered her reply for several seconds; but when it came, it eluded the whole point, much to the Inspector's vexation.

"I didn't notice anyone."

What annoyed Westerham was that this answer might quite well be dictated by any one of several factors. It might be the plain truth; for she might easily enough have missed seeing Stevenage as he passed. Or it might be a flat falsehood told to evade the very difficulty in which he was trying to involve her. Or, again, it might be an attempt to leave Stevenage out of the question, for some reason or other which had nothing to do with Castleford. Finally, there was the possibility that Stevenage's own evidence was inaccurate. If this last hypothesis were true then Stevenage must have had some cogent reason for mis-describing his movements.

Westerham saw that if she chose to stick to this statement he could get no further, so he switched off to a fresh line.

"When did your father meet you in the copse?"

"At five minutes past five, as near as I can guess it."

Westerham gave the girl an intentionally incredulous stare.

"Would you mind repeating that?" he asked.

Hilary looked him straight in the eye as she answered him.

"At five minutes past five. Certainly not later than that."

"Ah, indeed!"

Westerham made no effort to hide his disbelief. Haddon, a witness with nothing at stake, apparently, had seen Castleford in the spinney by the Chalet at ten or fifteen minutes past five. It was out of the question that he could have been in the copse at 5.5 p.m. and at the Chalet at 5.10 p.m. Here, on the face of it, this girl was lying; and was lying with coolness and calculation, since he had given her a chance to retract. Well, he would pin her down further by his next question.

"What happened after your father joined you?"

Here again there was no hesitation.

"We sat there and talked for a long time."

"H'm! What did you talk about?"

"Private matters. Nothing that would interest you I'm sure."

"I should know better about that if you'd tell me what you were discussing," the Inspector pointed out, "How can you say what would interest me and what wouldn't, Miss Castleford?"

"I'm quite sure about it," Hilary retorted icily.

The official side of the Inspector commented coarsely that Carron Hill seemed to produce a tough breed of women. Miss Lindfield had also been a cool card, he reflected; but what had most impressed him about her was a quality of detachment, as though she were a mere level-headed spectator. This girl's coolness was of a different sort. It suggested the poise of a fencer on guard with his whole attention alert to prevent an adversary pinking him.

It was clear to Westerham that this conversation between father and daughter must have had a close connection with the case. If it had been otherwise, Hilary would have made a parade of frankness and given him the facts in detail. Quite clearly, she and her father had not thought of concocting a spurious conversation; and she was afraid to launch out on her own for fear of putting her foot in it. But, as the Inspector realised, if she chose to stick to her guns, he had no means of forcing her to say anything.

Evidently she read something of his thoughts, for with a faint malicious smile she underlined her refusal.

"I certainly don't intend to discuss the matter with you. Have you any further questions to ask?"

"Yes, I have," the Inspector snapped. "Do you know anything about a pair of automatic pistols which have been unearthed here?"

If he expected to surprise her, he was disappointed.

"My father told me you had found them. Miss Lindfield produced them one evening and asked my father to put them away in his study cupboard for safety."

She paused for a moment as though undecided whether to say more or not. Then she added:

"My fingerprints are on them, I expect, and my father's, and Miss Lindfield's. We all handled them when she brought them out."

The Inspector had recovered from his discomfiture, and his voice showed no sign of it as he answered:

"Thanks. That may save me a lot of trouble. I'm glad you mentioned it, Miss Castleford. Now, I'd just like to put one or two more questions, if you don't mind. Dismiss the whole of this affair from your mind and go back to an earlier stage. You've lived here for years, and you must have kept your eyes open. Was there any friction here, at Carron Hill? Did you all get on well with each other?"

Hilary stared at the Inspector, a picture of astonishment.

"Friction here?" she asked in a tone of surprise. "What sort of friction would there be? One would think you imagined that my father and my stepmother didn't get on well together; that they'd led a cat-and-dog life. Nothing of the sort, really. My father's very easygoing and never interfered with his wife in the slightest. She had her own way in everything. As for me, I never had a quarrel with her in my life. Anyone will tell you that."

Then, after a moment's pause she added:

"But why are you asking me all this? I had nothing to do with Mrs. Castleford's movements that afternoon. I never even saw her after we left the table."

Westerham decided to leave this subject alone and to go on to a more delicate one. He ignored her question and put one of his own instead.

"I've heard some talk about Mrs. Castleford altering her will. Can you tell me anything about the matter?"

Hilary made a faint gesture as though to suggest that this was something beyond her purview.

"I know nothing directly—I mean, Mrs. Castleford never spoke to me about it. I learned from my father that there was some talk of her altering her will. And once, when I went into the drawing room unexpectedly, I heard a snatch of conversation between Mrs. Castleford and Miss Lindfield. Miss Lindfield, I gathered, was urging Mrs. Castleford not to be in a hurry and to think over the matter well before she actually did anything. 'I shouldn't hurry about it till you're quite sure what you want done,' she said, or some words like that. When they saw me come into the room, they began to talk about something else."

"You know, of course, the present position?" Westerham demanded.

Hilary's expression, for a fleeting instant, hinted at something which amused her in spite of the seriousness of the situation.

"You mean that she died intestate and that my father stands to gain by it? Yes, I know that. Miss Lindfield told me. Naturally, she wasn't altogether pleased. I can't blame her for that, can you?"

"Have you ever had any friction with Miss Lindfield?" he asked, evading her question.

Hilary shook her head decidedly.

"No, never. In fact, she's been rather decent to me at times. I had nothing to do with the running of Carron Hill. Miss Lindfield managed all that—entirely to Mrs. Castleford's satisfaction, I'm sure. I'd better be quite explicit while I'm at it. I never saw any friction between Miss Lindfield and Mrs. Castleford or between Miss Lindfield and my father. I don't remember a cross word spoken among us. Is that quite clear?"

"Perfectly clear," the Inspector acknowledged politely.

His mental comment was that it sounded almost too good to be true. And he noted also that Hilary had, apparently deliberately, refrained from saying a word in favour of her stepmother.

"I'd rather like to see Miss Lindfield for a moment or two," he said, after a pause. "I've one or two questions to ask her, if she's available just now."

Hilary looked at him with an air of speculation.

"You needn't trouble to get her to check what I've said," she declared coldly. "It's quite correct."

The Inspector sketched a gesture as though brushing the suggestion aside, but he made no verbal comment. Instead, he walked to the door and held it open for her to pass out.

Miss Lindfield did not keep him waiting long. She was in mourning, but she had the air of wearing black because it suited her, rather than as a matter of ceremonial. She greeted him with a friendly smile and made a gesture towards a chair. When he had seated himself, she sat down close at hand, crossed her legs, and gave him a lead with an interrogative monosyllable:

"Well?"

"I get rather tired of saying: 'I've got just a few questions to ask you,'" Westerham confessed. "But that's what it comes to. Now, first of all, Miss Lindfield, do you know anything of that brace of pistols in the box there?"

Miss Lindfield glanced over at the table on which he had placed them. She did not seem in the least surprised.

"These? Oh, yes, I can tell you about them. That boy whom you saw here the other day—Frankie Glencaple—unearthed them upstairs. His father forbade him to use them—reasonably enough, I think—and I handed them over to Mr. Castleford for safe keeping."

"I suppose the boy fingered them when he found them?"

Miss Lindfield showed her fine teeth in a faint smile.

"If you're looking for fingerprints on them," she said, "I'm afraid you'll find enough to stock a museum. Frankie handled them; so did I; so did Mr. Glencaple and Dr. Glencaple also, I think."

"You don't know of anyone having fired them, do you?" Westerham asked. "The boy didn't use them before they were taken away from him?"

Miss Lindfield shook her head decidedly.

"No," she said, confidently, "that's quite certain. He brought them straight to me as soon as he found them, and he had no opportunity of touching them again until his father forbade him to use them."

This evidence satisfied Westerham. Miss Lindfield obviously was sure of her ground in the matter.

"There's another question," he went on. "On the afternoon of Mrs. Castleford's death, you went for a walk through Piney Holt, didn't you?"

Miss Lindfield was quite clearly taken by surprise at this, but she nodded in confirmation, without comment.

"When you came to the thicket on this side of the level crossing—it's called The Wilderness, isn't it?—you had a choice between two routes up to the spinney by the Chalet. Which of them did you take, do you remember?"

"The long way round," said Miss Lindfield, apparently rather mystified by the question. "I missed Frankie in that way. He came by the short cut to meet me."

The Inspector remembered this quite well. He had merely been testing her. Already he had dealt with three distorts of the truth at Carron Hill: Frankie, Castleford and his daughter; and he had now fallen into a habit of setting traps for his witnesses merely as a matter of precaution.

"Another point," he went on. "I've come on the track of some anonymous letters which seem to have been flying about. Did you get one, by any chance?"

Miss Lindfield's lips curved in a contemptuous smile. "Yes, I was favoured with one."

"Did you keep it?"

"Keep it?" Miss Lindfield's expression showed what she thought of this suggestion. "Of course not! Would you keep a thing of that sort yourself?"

"What sort of notepaper was it on?" the Inspector inquired.

"Some cheap, yellowish stuff, I think. The writing was illiterate."

"You remember something about its contents, perhaps?"

"Need I go into details? I'd rather not . . . Well, if it's necessary, and if it's to be treated as confidential, I suppose I must tell you. It accused Mrs. Castleford of using the Chalet to carry on an intrigue with a man. And it said that the writer had sent word of this to Mr. Castleford, too. It was a thoroughly spiteful production, meant to hurt."

"The man's name was mentioned, was it?"

"Yes. Need I give it to you? Oh, well, then, it was Mr. Richard Stevenage."

"You didn't mention this to Mr. or Mrs. Castleford?"

Miss Lindfield's eyes opened wider at this suggestion.

"No, why should I? Mrs. Castleford would hardly have thanked me for the news, whether it was true or not. And the writer boasted that he'd told Mr. Castleford in another letter. I could have done nothing by interfering—except make people more uncomfortable. And an anonymous letter is not exactly proof, is it? I'm not eager to burn my fingers in affairs of that sort. I destroyed the thing and left it at that."

The Inspector felt that there was sound common sense in this attitude. It was one which he himself would have adopted in similar circumstances: let sleeping dogs lie. But as a sidelight on the state of things at Carron Hill, the incident seemed illuminating.

"Leaving that matter out of account," Westerham pursued, "can you tell me what were the relations between Mr. Castleford and his wife? Did they get on well together?—in the last year or two, I mean."

Miss Lindfield slipped into her favourite attitude with her elbow on her knee and her chin on her hand. She seemed to be considering how best to describe the state of affairs.

"Well," she said at last, "it's not easy to put these things into definite words; but my impression was something of this sort. Mrs. Castleford took a fancy to Mr. Castleford and married him on the strength of it. I mean that she was keener on him than he was on her, at that time. Then, before long, she grew tired of him. She felt she had made a mistake. And, of course, when a man marries for money he can hardly expect much deference from a wife whom he has ceased to attract, can he? A strong character might assert itself, but a weak man can do nothing but knuckle down. I've seen a good many incidents in which Mr. Castleford gave in, even when he was in the right. What else could he do? It wasn't a nice position for any man, I should imagine."

The Inspector nodded thoughtfully. This was the obvious truth of the business. Up to the very last there had been no open friction—just as Hilary had declared—but underneath the surface there had been contempt on one side and suppressed irritation on the other. And, finally, the anonymous letter might have come as a match to the mine. Or the suggested alteration in the will might have been enough to fire the train. Both together would be enough to throw a weak man off his balance and break the restraint he had hitherto imposed on himself.

"Had Mr. Castleford any friction with you, Miss Lindfield?" Westerham demanded bluntly.

Miss Lindfield's eyebrows arched slightly at the question.

"With me?" she asked in surprise. "No, none whatever. I don't suppose he liked me much. Probably I couldn't conceal that I hadn't much of an opinion of a man who married purely for money. He may have felt that. But certainly I never taunted him with it, even in the remotest fashion; and he didn't attempt to interfere with me in any way. I don't admire his type; but I've nothing to say against him personally."

"And his daughter, did she have any friction with the rest?"

Miss Lindfield lifted her chin, shook her head decidedly, and then returned to her former attitude.

"No, Hilary was in a very awkward position—a stepdaughter, you know, and dependent, like her father, on Mrs. Castleford's bounty—but she took it very well on the whole. She's had no disagreements with Mrs. Castleford for a couple of years, at least. She's done her best to fit into her place in the household. I don't know that I could have done as well myself, in her position; for, to be quite honest, Mrs. Castleford could be trying at times."

"I understand that you've lost to some extent by the present state of things, Miss Lindfield?"

Miss Lindfield's lips contracted momentarily at this home-thrust, but she recovered herself almost instantly.

"Yes," she admitted, in a level tone, "it's been rather a facer, as you can guess. I didn't expect to be left penniless; and that's the result as things have worked But I expect that it must have come as a worse shock to the Glencaple family; for they imagined that Mrs. Castleford had signed the new will and that therefore they would come into most of her money if anything happened to her."

She seemed to be taking the matter stoically, the Inspector reflected. Not at all a nice prospect to be pitched out into the world to pick up a living after years in charge of Carron Hill. He rather admired her for that. Most women would have been inclined to make a song about it. Or at the least, they would have shown some spite against the people who had come in front of her for the money.

"I'd like to put one or two more questions to Mr. Castleford," he explained, by way of showing that the interview was now ended. "Could you ask him to come here and see me?"

He opened the door for Miss Lindfield, and she passed out with a faint display of that efficient smile which had helped her to cover many difficulties.

"Keeps a very stiff upper lip," the Inspector commented to himself. "Well, if the worst comes to the worst, there's always the marriage market, open to her, with looks like hers. I wouldn't mind having her myself, if I could afford to keep her."

His unofficial reflections on this theme were interrupted by Castleford. Quite evidently, this fresh summons had perturbed him, and he faced the Inspector with an expression at once hang-dog and suspicious.

"Just one point," Westerham began briskly. "As you came up from Ringford's Meadow that afternoon, did you notice young Mr. Stevenage anywhere about?"

Castleford kept a fairly firm front; but the Inspector noted a blink when the name was mentioned.

"Stevenage? . . . No . . . I don't recall seeing him then."

Here again Westerham was left in doubt, just as he had been in Hilary's case. He could not be sure whether this assertion was true or not. Nothing was to be gained by persisting, he decided. Instead, he sprang a mine with his next question.

"You didn't tell me you received a letter at the clubhouse that afternoon."

Actually this discovery had been made by the indefatigable P. C. Gumley, who had elicited it by cross-questioning the woman who looked after the clubhouse. The Inspector had obtained it independently from her and had every reason to wish he had been first in the field; for P. C. Gumley had reduced the witness to a state of almost hopeless confusion of memory by his elaborate inquiries. Westerham had refrained from using this information in his earlier interview with Castleford. He calculated that it would catch Castleford in the reaction of relief, just when he imagined that the rain of questions was over and done with; and in these conditions he hoped to extract more from the incident.

"A letter?" Castleford repeated, with a very poor assumption of surprise. "I did get a letter, certainly. It was in the rack, waiting for me. But it had nothing to do with this case, so I didn't mention it, naturally."

All the same, as the Inspector knew, that letter had produced a marked effect on Castleford when he read it. "Seemed as if he'd got a bit of a shock, like," the woman had said, when she described the episode to Westerham.

"Come, come," said the Inspector impatiently. "You needn't try to fence with me. It was another of these anonymous letters, wasn't it?"

This was rather a risky shot, as the Inspector knew. The woman had described the envelope to him—an ordinary white one, which did not match the yellowish kind that Haddon used—but Westerham felt pretty sure in his own mind that such a disturbing document could only be of that type.

"It was another of the same sort," Castleford admitted after a pause of apparent desperation.

"Abusing you? Or accusing Mrs. Castleford of something?"

"I didn't read it through," Castleford explained lamely. "As soon as I saw what it was, I stuffed it into my pocket. Later on, I burned it without reading any more."

Again the Inspector was certain that this tale was false. The woman at the clubhouse had been quite definite in her evidence on this point. "He stood there and read it, going redder and redder in the face; and then he read it again right through; and then he went back to the front page and read it over, as if he couldn't stop. And it didn't do him any good, either time. I could see that by the look of him."

"Well, Mr. Castleford, I'm not going to conceal that I don't think you've been frank with me," Westerham said bluntly. "That's plain enough, and you must know it. And when people aren't frank in a case of murder . . . well, they've got themselves to blame for any opinion one may form about their motives. I'd strongly advise you, in your own interest, to go back on some things you've said. You can guess what I mean, easy enough. I'm giving you a fair chance. Of course, if you don't like to take it . . . I can form my own opinion without help from anyone. Now, what about it?"

Castleford stared at him with the expression of a wounded animal which sees no hope. He did not trust himself to make a verbal answer. He shook his head and made a gesture with his hands, as though to suggest that the Inspector was misjudging him.

"Very well," said Westerham curtly, as he began to collect his various prizes for removal. "We know where we stand. You may regret this, I warn you. I know a good deal more than you think."

And leaving this ancient barb to rankle in Castleford's mind, he took his departure with as much dignity as his laden condition allowed.

16
THE APPEAL TO WENDOVER

Mr. Wendover, squire of Talgarth Grange and Justice of the Peace for his district, had a character combining qualities which seemed in some ways antithetical. He prided himself on moving with the times; but in practice his outlook on life was tinged with a certain old-fashionedness. He liked to think the best of everybody; but nevertheless one of his chief interests centred in crime and its detection. On the Bench, he was always torn between the fulfilment of his oath and his desire to treat offenders as decent, though misguided, human beings. A confirmed bachelor, he had a soft spot for a pretty girl; and he was ever ready to extend a sort of chivalrous protection to any woman in difficulties. Women occasionally recognised this by describing him as "rather an old dear"; but it is doubtful if he would have been wholly gratified if he had overheard the comment.

Sitting at breakfast in a room overlooking the broad lawns of the Grange he was working his way through a pile of letters which had come by the morning post. When he had read them, and not before, he would turn to *The Times* which lay, warmed and aired for him, on the table—at his elbow.

He ran through a couple of letters from friends; then he turned over the remainder, seriatim, until among them he came across one addressed in a feminine hand which he failed to recall. With a faint curiosity, he opened the envelope, extracted the contents, and began to read:—

185

Carron Hill
Thunderbridge
Monday

Dear Mr. Wendover,

I'm afraid you won't remember me. I met you at
Lynden Sands Hotel three or four years ago, and we
played golf together more than once, but most likely
you have forgotten all about me. Perhaps the enclosed snapshot of the two of us on the last green
may help to recall me.

Wendover picked up the snapshot. It represented himself in
the act of taking the line of the hole, whilst beyond him, facing the
camera, a slim fair-haired girl stood in an easy attitude with her
putter in her hand. He remembered her quite well: a nice kiddie of
sixteen or seventeen. Sensible of her to send the snapshot, he reflected; for he had quite forgotten her name. He turned over the
pages, read "Hilary Castleford" at the end, and then went back to
where he had left off.

You may remember my father, Mr. Philip
Castleford. We are in dreadful trouble here. Someone has shot Mrs. Castleford, and the police have
practically accused my father of having done it. They
have made it quite plain that they don't believe a
word we say, and we don't know which way to turn.
It is a terrible position.

When we were at Lynden Sands, your friend, Sir
Clinton Driffield, cleared Mrs. Fleetwood of a charge
just like this, when things looked very black against
her. That's what makes me write to you. We did not
get to know Sir Clinton well; in fact I hardly spoke
to him, so it would be no good my going to him direct and asking him for his help. He wouldn't recall
us, I'm sure.

186

But if you remember us, and would persuade him to look into this terrible affair, I feel sure that things would come out all right in the end. And just now I am most horribly afraid of what may happen, for undoubtedly things do look very black indeed.

I know I've no claim whatever on your kindness, but I simply felt that I couldn't leave any stone unturned to help my father; and I made up my mind to write to you and beg you to do what you can for us. Please do help us.

Yours sincerely,
Hilary Castleford

The signature came at the foot of the page but Wendover mechanically turned the leaf and found in a postscript an even plainer indication of the writer's panic:

"P.S. Please, *please* help us if you can."

Wendover re-read the letter; then he picked up the snapshot and studied it for a moment or two. He remembered her well enough now: a cool, quiet little thing with a nice voice. He had played a round or two with her and rather liked her; but he admitted to himself that without the photograph he would have had difficulty in recalling her. Again he was favourably impressed by the common sense she had shown in enclosing the snapshot. That detail showed that she had kept her head even in the worst kind of trouble.

He put down the letter and snapshot and began to consider his best line of action. Already he had made up his mind to help. Wendover never mentioned the word chivalry and never thought of himself as a knight-errant; but his attitude towards people in distress had a generousness which verged at times on the quixotic.

He recognised, however, that there might be difficulties in the way. One cannot descend abruptly on a Chief Constable and expect him to put aside his normal routine merely because a pretty girl thinks she can whistle you in to help her. That kind of appeal would meet short shrift. Despite this, Wendover was not unhopeful. Sir Clinton liked to pit his wits directly against those of a criminal; and it was on this penchant that Wendover was counting for the achievement of his object. If the thing could be done without detriment to the public service, Sir Clinton would probably be quite glad to play detective once again.

After breakfast, Wendover put a trunk call through to the Chief Constable. He refrained from giving any details, but merely invited himself to lunch at Sir Clinton's house, as he had something which he wished to talk over in privacy. Later in the morning, he ordered his chauffeur to bring his car round.

During lunch, he kept to ordinary topics. It was not until they went into the Chief Constable's study that he broached the real subject of his visit.

"Do you remember our staying at Lynden Sands a year or two ago—the time you took a busman's holiday over the Foxhills case?"

Sir Clinton nodded without comment.

"Remember that girl, there?" Wendover asked, handing the snapshot across as he spoke.

The Chief Constable examined the photograph for a second or two, as though putting his recollections in order.

"Yes. Castleton or Castleford was her name, wasn't it? She was staying at the hotel with a father and a stepmother, if I'm not wrong. The father was a little shrimp of a man, the sort that apologises to you profusely if you tread on his toes. He'd lost a finger or two, and I used to wonder how he ever managed to play golf at all. The stepmother—let's see—she was a brainless creature with some pretensions to good looks of a sort and a perfect genius for vapid chatter. Still, she seemed to have the other two well under her thumb. Is that the crowd?"

"Those are the people," Wendover confirmed.

He was not surprised that Sir Clinton's memory proved better than his own, although Sir Clinton had come much less into direct touch with the Castlefords than he had. The Chief Constable had a knack of noticing the salient characteristics of even uninteresting people, so Wendover knew that this thumb-nail sketch did not prove any special interest in the Castlefords. To Sir Clinton they were merely specimens of humanity whom he had noted in passing.

"They seem to have got themselves into trouble," Wendover continued, passing Hilary's letter across in its turn.

Sir Clinton read it deliberately, but his face showed nothing of his impressions as he did so. He folded up the letter, replaced it in its envelope, and handed it back.

"Well?" Wendover inquired eagerly.

"Well?" Sir Clinton responded with a slight caricature of Wendover's tone.

"Can you do anything for them, Clinton? It seems a bad kind of position."

"What do you expect me to do, Squire? Call off the police, or what? There are limits, you know."

"Well, I think it's a pretty awkward position for them, Clinton; and . . . well, one doesn't like to think of it. I've enough imagination to understand how that girl's feeling . . ."

"That's where you get ahead of me, Squire. My imagination isn't strong enough. I've just got to go on my recollections. And what do they amount to? I remember this girl. She was good-looking, and she'd a nice, firm jaw. I remember her father. He was a miserable little worm with a few redeeming points. And I remember enough about the stepmother to save me any tears at the news of her demise. Is there anything there which ought to tempt me into interfering with the normal course of events?"

"Oh, if you're going to take that line . . ." said Wendover, rather hurt, "I suppose it's no good saying any more."

"I'm not taking any line, just yet," Sir Clinton pointed out, somewhat to Wendover's relief. "I'm merely stating a fact or two. I'm not going to set my imagination to work merely because somebody happens to get into a hole of some sort. I know nothing about these people. They may be guilty for all we know. Or they may be innocent. I'm certainly not going to put my normal work aside in order to act as their private defender. They seem dissatisfied with the local experts, and they propose to appeal over the local people's heads to Caesar—if you don't mind my putting it modestly like that. But suppose Caesar happens to be busy?"

"They wouldn't call you in unless they were innocent," Wendover declared, with the air of a man advancing an incontrovertible thesis.

"Why not?" Sir Clinton asked blandly. "They're suspected already. If they're guilty, they stand to lose little by dragging me in. From that girl's letter it's plain that she wants me only if I'm working to clear her father. I don't dance in leading-strings like that, Squire. If I go down there—I might manage a long weekend just now, as it happens—I go without any prejudices. I'm merely going to look into a case. Is that quite clear?"

"You'll come? That's the main thing."

"Oh, I suppose I may as well go down and see what the local people are making of it. That could be reckoned as a pursuit of one's duty. But if my interference makes things worse for friend Castleford, it's their own lookout, remember. This isn't a Rescue-of-Damsels-in-Distress Syndicate with you as Don Quixote and me as Sancho Panza. They've asked for it; and you're not to turn peevish if they get more than they asked for. That's understood, Squire?"

"Oh, of course that's quite understood," Wendover agreed gratefully.

He was still quite convinced by the force of his own argument. Hilary Castleford, as her letter showed, had vivid recollections of Sir Clinton's work in the case at Lynden Sands. She would never have dared to ask him to take up her father's affairs unless she had a clear conscience. Then a sudden thought made him uncomfortable. The girl hadn't said that her father backed her appeal. She hadn't even made clear whether he knew about it at all. And it was Castleford who was the suspect, not she.

17
MOTIVES

When the Chief Constable descended out of the blue, Inspector Westerham examined him covertly with curiosity and a faint touch of resentment. As was only natural, he chafed a little at this incursion from higher spheres. It suggested that his competence was being called in question.

At the first glance, he classified Sir Clinton as "a very ordinary-looking man"—a verdict which would have delighted his subject if it had been uttered aloud, for the Chief Constable took special pains to refrain from anything which would make his appearance notable. All that he offered to Westerham's cataloguing eye was a tanned face, a close-clipped moustache, fine teeth, and well-tended hands. His age the Inspector guessed to be in the early forties.

Sir Clinton sensed the faint but repressed vexation of the Inspector; and, by manner more than by words, he set himself to dispel it. Almost at once, Westerham began to feel that he was going to get fair treatment; and in a very short time he completely lost any suspicions which he harboured. Sir Clinton was so obviously a person who would "give a man a square deal," as the Inspector phrased it to himself.

Wendover, to whom Sir Clinton introduced him without explanation, was something of a puzzle to the Inspector. "Typical country gentleman of the good sort," he decided. "But what's he doing, mixed up in this business?"

"I've read these reports of yours," Sir Clinton explained, as though to set the Inspector more at ease. "Very clear and full. You must have had a busy time gathering your information."

"I can stand over every bit of them, sir. There's nothing there that I can't give you definite evidence for."

"So I gathered from reading them. Now let's have something else equally clear. I'm not taking this case out of your hands. You're responsible for it. If there's any credit at the end of it, that goes to you. If it's muddied . . . well, we'll not consider that possibility. You understand me? I'm interested in the case; I may want to poke about and look into things; but it's your case, not mine."

"I see, sir," Westerham concurred, in a tone of some relief.

"Very well. Now I want to see this Chalet where the affair happened. We can get up to it in my car, I believe? Come along with us and show us over the ground."

When they reached the Chalet, Sir Clinton listened while the Inspector described the position of things on the day of the tragedy. Westerham pointed out the spot where the rook-rifle bullet had lain, and showed the chalk-marks he had made to register the positions of the table and chairs. At the Chief Constable's request, he also led them to the pile of debris in the spinney where the automatic bullet had been discovered by P. C. Gumley. Sir Clinton listened in silence to the explanations.

"You had all that in your reports," he commented at last when they returned to the verandah. "Still, I wanted to see things with my own eyes. And now what about this dead cat you found? Where was it?"

The Inspector led them into the other arm of the spinney to the little glade where he had found the corpse.

"It was hung up here, sir, by that string. I've no doubt in my mind that the boy hung it up and shot it to death, although he made out to me that it was dead before he came on it. We found about a dozen rook-rifle bullets in the carcase of the thing when we came to open it up."

"I gathered that you didn't look on him as a reliable witness. By the way, Inspector, you gave me the impression in your reports that you were setting down most of that evidence verbatim. Did you take shorthand notes?"

"No, sir. But I've got a very good verbal memory."

"Have you?" Sir Clinton's tone was neutral. "Let's test it. What was the first thing I said to you after we met?"

Westerham was too sure of himself to take offence at the underlying suggestion.

"You said, sir: 'I've read your reports. Very clear and full. You must have had a busy time gathering your information.'"

"And what did you say yourself, before I put that question just now?"

"I said: 'I've got a very good verbal memory,' sir."

"You've proved it," Sir Clinton admitted. "Then I suppose I can take these reported conversations as almost textually accurate?"

"I think so, sir," Westerham declared, confidently.

"That may be useful," the Chief Constable said musingly.

He glanced round the little glade and his eye fell on the second piece of twine hanging from the tree-branch.

"This is the string young Glencaple said he'd hung a tin can on, I suppose?"

"Yes, sir."

Sir Clinton stepped over and examined the cord, incuriously at first, and then with more interest.

"Did you notice, Inspector, that the end of this has been burned? You can see the charring and the tiny point of blackened fibre, if you look closely."

Wendover and the Inspector came to his side and scrutinised the end of the twine.

"I see it's been burned," Westerham admitted, "but I don't quite see what bearing that has."

"Neither do I," Sir Clinton admitted blandly. "It strikes me as curious, that's all. Can you consult that memory of yours, Inspector, and tell us what the boy said about it?"

Westerham racked his brain for a few moments. Evidently he felt on trial and wanted to be sure that he made no mistake. Suddenly his face cleared.

"I remember now, sir. He said something very like this: 'Auntie Connie and I fixed up a tin can so that it swung about in the wind. Then I found a dead cat, and I thought it would be more fun to hang it up and shoot at it. So I took away the can and hung up the cat.' That was his account of it, sir."

Sir Clinton seemed to have lost interest in the matter.

"It's common enough twine—the ordinary three-strand stuff they sell in balls for household and office use," he said. "By the way, did you find the tin can hereabouts, just to check his tale?"

"No, sir, I didn't think of looking for it."

"I don't think I'd trouble, then. By the way, I suppose you have the two bullets: the rook-rifle one from the verandah and the .32 automatic one which killed her?"

"Yes, sir. I've kept them, of course. The .22 had been fired from the boy's rook-rifle, sure enough. I've fired a number of shots from that gun into water, myself, yesterday; and the markings that the rifling leaves on the bullet are quite clear. Three or four of my bullets are marked almost identically with the bullet I picked up on the verandah."

"You're lucky, then. Sometimes bullets from the same rifling are marked quite differently from others. And while we're on that subject, what did you make of the .32 pistol you secured? Did you try it for fingerprints?"

"I did, sir," the Inspector said, in a rather rueful tone, "but it was simply covered with them, all different. As you'd see from my reports, practically everybody in that household had handled the thing long before the shooting. The metal surface was a perfect mosaic of fingerprints with nothing much to pick and choose between them. But there was no doubt it was that pistol that did the trick, sir. Just yesterday I fired some shots from it and kept the empty cartridge-cases. You may remember that we found the empty shell in the grass in front of the verandah—the case of the cartridge that killed her? I've compared it with the others and there's no doubt the murderer used that particular pistol. The marks of the extractor hook on the rim of the cartridge case, and the indentation made by the striking-pin are identical all through the series."

"And you infer from that?" Sir Clinton asked.

"I infer, sir, that the murderer must be somebody who had access to that pistol, which narrows the circle very much; and it must be somebody who could replace the pistol afterwards—which limits the 'possibles' still further."

Sir Clinton nodded his agreement.

"Whom did you put into these two categories?" he inquired.

"Everybody at Carron Hill could have got at the pistol. That means Castleford, Miss Castleford, Miss Lindfield, the Glencaple boy, and the maids. In addition to them, sir, I'd include Dr. Glencaple and Mr. Glencaple, since they've been about the premises and could come and go as they pleased, being relations of Mrs. Castleford. And I'd add Stevenage, for he was always running in and out of the house and seemed pretty much at home."

"And then you begin to eliminate some from that list?"

"Yes, sir. The maids can be scored off. I've sound evidence that none of them left the house on the afternoon of the murder. Miss Lindfield, Miss Castleford, and her father, they—all knew exactly where the pistols were planted. The boy Frankie didn't know; but he was one of the ferreting kind—you remember he found them first of all in the garret, sir—and he might quite well have unearthed them in the cupboard after they were hidden there. Dr. Glencaple was at Carron Hill immediately after the murder; I saw him there. Mr. Glencaple wasn't at the house until a day later. Young Stevenage hasn't been near Carron Hill since the murder happened."

"But suppose he had an accomplice inside the house who could do the replacing of the pistol for him?" Sir Clinton inquired. "I don't say it's likely; but if you're going to eliminate on that basis you have to take every possibility into account, you know."

"Well, it's possible, sir," the Inspector admitted. "He was very friendly with both the girls, I find."

"It would take a lot of friendliness to make a girl into an accomplice of that brand," Wendover contributed in a rather grumpy tone which the Inspector did not like.

Sir Clinton seemed to think that question might be thrashed out further. He sat down in one of the rustic chairs on the verandah and with a gesture invited the other two to seat themselves also.

"That covers the matter of the pistol, we'll assume," he went on. "Now what about the other factor: the dose of morphia? That seems a rather weird addition to the case, doesn't it? Where do you think it came from, Inspector?"

"Well, sir, it obviously narrows things down very much further. Nowadays, morphia can't be got by the man in the street. Only a research chemist, or a medical man, or druggist could get it—I don't think dentists use it. And there's only one medical man in the Carron Hill circle—Dr. Glencaple."

"Perhaps he had an accomplice," Wendover interjected in a faintly ironic tone.

"What I'm concerned with now, sir, is the source of the stuff," the Inspector said, stiffly. "I'm not considering who actually used it."

"Then let's go on to that point," Sir Clinton suggested. "What's your view about it?"

"If Dr. Glencaple was the original source of the stuff, then he may have used it himself, or he may have handed it to an accomplice to use, or it may have been stolen from him, or he may have mislaid it and someone may have come across it and used it. That seems to cover all the ground," Wendover suggested.

"The way I look at it is this, sir," said the Inspector, ignoring Wendover. "I think there's only one source of morphia in the case: Dr. Glencaple. Now morphia appears twice in this affair: once in the body and once in that hypodermic syringe that was used for the insulin injections. Whoever it was that dosed Mrs. Castleford, that person had access to the hypodermic syringe and could use the syringe on Mrs. Castleford without exciting her suspicions about it. Who was that?"

Sir Clinton made a gesture to arrest the Inspector.

"Have you examined the remaining insulin, the unused stuff in the house? It might be worth analysing."

"That's been done, sir," the Inspector retorted triumphantly. "I got the bottle from one of the maids and got Miss Lindfield and Castleford to identify it after it was in my possession. It's been examined, and there's no trace of morphia in it. So she didn't get the dose out of that bottle."

"Very good, Inspector," Sir Clinton approved. "But to judge from my impression of her, Mrs. Castleford wasn't a very acute person. If an old bottle had been filled up with morphia solution, it might have been substituted for the proper stuff and she'd never have seen it."

"If that was how it was done, then the bottle was washed out afterwards. I got the maid to give me the emptied bottle as well," the Inspector explained with pardonable pride in his thoroughness.

"I'd have expected that from you, after your reports," Sir Clinton acknowledged with a smile. "Now let's take a third line. What about motive? We don't need to prove it, of course; but I'd like to hear your views."

"Well, sir, I don't think you need go far to look for that. The money question sticks out all over the case. Mrs. Castleford originally married a rich man with two none-too-well-off brothers. When he died, she got the estate—the Glencaple money. She married again, and made a will in favour of her new husband, Castleford. That cut out the two Glencaples; and they were as mad as hornets about it when they discovered the state of affairs. That's common talk about the neighbourhood, and I heard Dr. Glencaple himself say a few things that confirmed it. He and his brother persuaded Mrs. Castleford to tear up that will and she was going to make a new one in their favour. The new will, I understand, was going to put Miss Lindfield in a better position, too. The Glencaples assumed that the new will had been signed. I heard Miss Lindfield telling Dr. Glencaple that it hadn't been, and he was absolutely staggered—anyone could see that. Her death at that juncture upset everything. Instead of Miss Lindfield and the two brothers dividing the Glencaple money between them, the whole life-interest in it goes to Castleford."

"So that her death just at that stage made all the difference to him, obviously," Sir Clinton agreed. "But that's hardly news to me, after reading your reports."

"But wait a moment," Wendover interrupted, turning to the Inspector. "You're suggesting that Castleford wanted his wife's money. Well, then, if he was after her money and was ready to go the length of murder to get it, why didn't he kill her while the old will was in force—during the last five or ten years? Why did he wait until now?"

Westerham's smile was rather condescending. These amateurs, he reflected, were apt to be dense.

"Why should he do anything of the sort, so long as the old will was in force?" he demanded. "She was keeping him and his daughter. He was living in luxury, with nothing to do for it except loaf about and look pleasant. His wife was a diabetic; for all he could tell, she might die off comparatively young and leave him in possession. In these conditions, it wasn't worth running the risk of murder just to inherit a bit earlier. But when he got wind of this new will, why, then, things would look a bit different, I expect. It wasn't just going to be a case of waiting till the plum fell into his mouth sooner or later. It was a case of now-or-never, before the new will was signed. That's how I'd look at it."

Sir Clinton, at Wendover's rather crestfallen look, intervened by continuing the interrupted topic.

"Then I take it that you look at it rather in this way, Inspector. Miss Lindfield knew that Mrs. Castleford was intestate; and she knew also—I gather from your reports—that if Mrs. Castleford died, intestate, she would lose everything under the old will and would get nothing under the new will, since it wasn't executed. The Glencaples are in a different category. They imagined that the new will was completed and valid; so that if Mrs. Castleford died, they would scoop the pool. Philip Castleford was in a third class, along with his daughter. They knew that she was intestate and that on her death, before she signed the new will, her money reverted to her husband. That seems to be a fair statement of the case."

"It leaves one possibility out," Wendover commented. "Where does this man Stevenage come in? For all you know, he may have persuaded her to make a will in his favour—she seems to have been a very unstable-minded creature. Suppose he's sitting with that will in his pocket at this moment. He doesn't need to produce it instanter. He can wait till the clouds roll by, can't he, if he chooses to do so?"

"They'd roll up again pretty quick if he did that," said the Inspector, sourly.

"Yes," Wendover admitted, "but still, it's harder to get your evidence after months have elapsed. People forget things quickly."

"Well, it's an idea," Westerham said grudgingly.

Sir Clinton seemed anxious to keep along more orthodox lines.

"Is that all you have to suggest in the way of motive?" he asked the Inspector.

Westerham rubbed his nose doubtfully before answering.

"Well, there's no doubt in my mind that Mrs. Castleford and young Stevenage were a bit more intimate than they need have been. It sticks out all over the place—anonymous letters, his fencing with me about their doings at the Chalet, the way he hung about Carron Hill where Castleford, I gather, didn't want him. And Castleford knew all about it. The anonymous letters would tell him, if nothing else did. And yet he denied violently to me that there was anything wrong."

"Most men would do that, after she was dead," Wendover pointed out. "They'd want to bury the scandal in her grave if they could manage it."

"That I don't deny," said Westerham, "but it's beside the point. What I was demonstrating was that Castleford had another motive in addition to the money. By putting her out, he'd be squaring up his account with her for her little games with Stevenage, and he'd be filling his pocket as well."

Wendover had no answer to this.

"There seems to be just one possibility more which you haven't mentioned," Sir Clinton pointed out. "You've considered the matter of direct profit. What about contingent profit?"

"I don't quite follow you, sir," Westerham acknowledged after a moment's thought.

"Well, take Miss Castleford. Legally, she doesn't come into the limelight. But wouldn't she be—h'm!—rather better off, we'll say, if her father came into his wife's money? That's a contingency, isn't it?"

Wendover was displeased by this suggestion. He could see that the Inspector had caught at it as a confirmation of his own ideas on the case; and he was vexed with Sir Clinton for lending his weight to suspicions against the Castlefords. They were mere suspicions, after all; and he thought the Chief Constable might have held his tongue on the subject.

Sir Clinton rose and crossed the verandah to the Chalet door.

"I thought it just as well to make sure things weren't tampered with, sir," Westerham explained as he also went up to the door. "I've got all the keys of the place from the different people who had them; but just to make sure, I put seals on the door and windows."

"So things are just as they were?" Sir Clinton asked, as the Inspector broke the seals and opened the door.

"Exactly as they were, sir."

Sir Clinton stepped inside the Chalet and made a thorough inspection of it; but he seemed to find nothing fresh.

"Thanks for letting me have a sample of the paper-ash that you found in the grate," he said to Westerham as he paused in front of the hearth. "You made nothing out of it?"

"No," the Inspector admitted. "There was no writing of any sort on it. I'm sure of that."

"Then it obviously wasn't the ash of the telegram which Mrs. Castleford received just before her death."

"No, it wasn't that, sir, for certain. There was too much of it, for one thing. I'd guess it was from a quarto or a foolscap sheet of paper."

"I wonder what happened to that telegram," Sir Clinton mused. "Queer that it disappeared. If it hadn't been for the initiative of your constable—Gumley—we'd have had more trouble in getting the text of it."

"He'll be fortunate if he hears no more of *that*, sir." Westerham said with a wry smile. "The responsibility's his, in that affair."

"And the profit's yours, eh? Admirable arrangement," Sir Clinton admitted absently. "And now, by the way, what do you make of this point? Mrs. Castleford must have been shot at close range, if the shot went clean through her and landed away yonder in the spinney. Besides, she was shot clean through the heart, which only an expert could have managed from a distance. The pistol wasn't fired in actual contact with the skin, or the surgeon would have noticed the tearing due to the gas from the discharge. And both you and he observed that there was no singeing of the fine hairs about the wound. What do you make of all that?"

"Well, sir, I look at it this way. The thing was faked so as to look like an accident—a long-distance shot with the rook-rifle. It was very well-thought-out; and the murderer took care to avoid firing too close up, lest the hairs get singed and give him away. Also, as you say, he avoided too close a shot for fear of tearing the skin."

"There was no sign of burning the fabric of her blouse or of any tattooing of the skin by the powder? Smokeless powder leaves peculiar marks at close range, you know."

"There was nothing of that sort, sir. The shot must have been fired a good distance away."

"What do you call 'a good distance'?" Wendover demanded, suddenly. "Would you yourself guarantee to hit a person clean through the heart from three feet away? There's the kick of the pistol to be taken into account at that range."

"It's an interesting point," Sir Clinton commented. "By the way, have you that bullet from the rook-rifle? I'd like to see it."

"I've got it here, sir. I thought you might want to look at it."

Sir Clinton examined it minutely for a moment or two, and then held it tip uppermost so that the others could inspect it.

"I shouldn't think this shot came down on the concrete here," he suggested. "If it were a dropping shot, the bullet would have been flattened a bit on one side. Actually, as you see, the tip's been flattened as if it had struck something, dead on."

"Besides," Wendover pointed out, "the bullet would have been far more knocked out of shape if it had hit concrete. Barring the tip, it's much as it was originally."

"Look at the tip," Sir Clinton advised. "There seem to be some marks on it."

"There's a faint pattern, sir, I can see," the Inspector admitted. "Two sets of parallel lines crossing each other at right angles, it looks like."

Wendover held out his hand for the projectile and in his turn he examined the tiny indentations.

"Sometimes the threads on a victim's clothes leave their pattern on a soft lead bullet," he pointed out.

"Then the victim of this bullet must have been dressed in post-office mail-bags," said the Inspector sulkily. "Look at the coarseness of the pattern, sir. And besides, this shot didn't hit her at all, so how could it take the pattern of her dress?"

"I think that finishes our work here," Sir Clinton interposed before Wendover had time to retort. "Now what about this man Haddon? You have him waiting at his cottage, haven't you?"

"Yes, sir, I arranged that," Westerham confirmed. "It's only a few minutes' walk through the plantation. I'll show you the way."

"I only want to ask him a couple of questions," Sir Clinton volunteered as he followed the Inspector. "And I don't think I'll trouble Mrs. Haddon. I got the impression that she's extremely voluble and though that's some times valuable in a witness, it's always wearisome to a listener."

Haddon was lounging on the threshold of his cottage when they arrived; and he scanned the little procession with obvious disfavour as it trooped up to his door.

"Well, what d'you want?" he demanded rudely.

"Some information, and no insolence, Mr. Haddon," Sir Clinton answered explicitly.

Haddon evidently had not expected this opening. "Well, ask away and I'll see what I can do for you," he conceded ungraciously.

"Let's have things clear," Sir Clinton suggested. "You're in a bad position, Mr. Haddon, over these friendly little notes you've been sending round the countryside. You're not out of the wood yet. But if you give me the information I want, it'll do you no harm. It might even"—Sir Clinton took a note-case from his pocket and looked at it thoughtfully—"be slightly to your advantage."

Haddon's eyes fastened greedily on the notes.

"Well," he promised with a grin, "if it's a matter of ten bob or a quid into my pocket, I'll try to give satisfaction."

"I shouldn't expect a pound, if I were you," Sir Clinton suggested. "It would merely lead to disappointment, pitching your hopes as high as that; and that would be a pity, wouldn't it? Say five shillings and you might be surprised by ten. Or again you might not be surprised at all. It depends on what your news is worth.

Now what I want is a complete list of the people you sent anonymous letters to, about Mrs. Castleford."

Haddon took off his cap and scratched his head thoughtfully for a moment.

"Lemme see," he began. "I wrote a couple to Castleford himself. The second one was a snorter," he commented with a crude chuckle. "Then I wrote an amusin' one to Connie—to Miss Lindfield, I mean. I knew she'd be interested on account of young Stevenage."

"You sent these to Carron Hill, I suppose?"

"Yes."

"Why did you think Miss Lindfield would be interested?"

Haddon gave a coarse guffaw.

"Because Stevenage was running the two of them in double harness, didn't you know that?"

"Who else did you favour with your notes?"

"Lemme see. Dr. Glencaple got one. I thought he'd like to know how his brother's shoes was being well filled. I'd 'ave sent one to his brother too, only I didn't know his address."

"Dr. Glencaple's letter went to his house, I suppose?"

"It did. And that was all, so far's I remember, except one to Castleford's daughter . . ."

Wendover's toe was itching; and a glance at his face seemed to suggest a more prudent tone to Haddon. Sir Clinton merely put another question.

"You sent nothing to either Stevenage or Mrs. Castleford, then?"

"No," Haddon explained. "That 'd 'ave spoilt the fun, see?"

"I see," Sir Clinton acknowledged, gravely. "You left them in ignorance of the fact that anyone else knew about their doings."

"That's it. No good being a spoil-sport, is there?"

Sir Clinton abstained from criticising this sentiment.

"And now," he said, "if you'll hand over some samples of your notepaper and envelopes to Inspector Westerham, here, I think that closes our business, Mr. Haddon."

Haddon made no objection. He seemed more than a little relieved to get off so lightly. In a moment or two he procured some of the yellowish paper and envelopes, which he handed over to the Inspector.

Sir Clinton opened his note-case, leafed over the contents, extracted the dingiest ten-shilling note he could find, and passed it over to Haddon.

"Rather dirty money, I'm afraid, Mr. Haddon. But you're not the sort to object to that, I'm sure."

Haddon seized the note and stowed it away in his pocket. Then he seemed to catch the second meaning of the Chief Constable's remark.

"If people didn't do things, there'd be nothing for me to write about," he declared, impudently.

"If you ever put pen to paper in that way again," Sir Clinton said, incisively, "I'll see you gaoled for the full two years. You can count on that. In the meantime, if you breathe a word on this affair, we'll have to take up the case against you. So you're warned."

Haddon shrugged his shoulders as though making light of the threat; but his pretence was a feeble one. The Chief Constable's tone had carried conviction.

As they walked through the wood towards the Chalet, Sir Clinton turned to the Inspector.

"I'll take you down in the car, if you like, and drop you in Thunderbridge. After that, I've a call or two which I've got to make. Now there are just two or three things I want you to do for me. In the first place, I want you to clip a bit of the bloodstained cloth from Mrs. Castleford's dress. You have it still, I suppose?"

"Of course, sir. I'll do that for you at once."

"And another bit from the bloodstain on Mr. Castleford's coat."

"Very good, sir."

"Dr. Ripponden found some fibres in the wound, didn't he? I'd like some samples of them—as much of the stuff as you can spare. You'll not get them back, perhaps; but at any rate you'll get a report on them. I'm going to submit them to an expert."

"Very good, sir," the Inspector repeated.

"Another point," Sir Clinton pursued. "You examined the cups and saucers on the tea table for fingerprints. I don't suppose you found much?"

"No, sir. The cup Stevenage had been using had some blurred prints on the handle. I could see nothing at all on Mrs. Castleford's cup."

"When you say 'nothing at all,' do you mean it literally, or do you mean you could make nothing of the marks that were there?"

"I mean just what I said, sir. There were no marks of any sort that I could develop up. The marks on Stevenage's cup were just marks—nothing distinct. I didn't expect anything in either case, because you know how one picks up a teacup. You couldn't expect anything but a smudge, if even that."

Sir Clinton seemed to think of something fresh.

"Oh, by the way, I'd like to see the two rook-rifle bullets you got hold of—the one from the verandah and the one that broke Mrs. Haddon's window."

"Very good, sir. I'll see you get them this afternoon. If you want them sooner, you've only to say so."

"This afternoon will do," Sir Clinton said carelessly. "And now, just one more point. Can you show me exactly where the wound was, on Mrs. Castleford's back? Mr. Wendover here will do as a demonstration-ground. Turn round, Squire, will you? Now, Inspector, just put your finger on the corresponding spot, please."

Westerham did so at a point near the spine and almost level with the lower tip of the left shoulder-blade.

"There?" Sir Clinton verified. "It surprises me that the shot didn't hit a rib, either in entering or in passing out. The exit couldn't very well have been arranged; but the point of entry must have been carefully chosen to miss the bones, if that was intentional!"

"Dr. Ripponden would tell you I'm not far out in my estimate, sir," the Inspector affirmed. "He's got the exact measurements, of course; but I'm near enough in my guess, for all practical purposes."

"It's not very important, perhaps," Sir Clinton admitted. "It seems suggestive of something, that's all. And now I think we'll get down to Thunderbridge."

18
THE MORPHINE

When they had dropped Westerham in Thunderbridge, Wendover expected Sir Clinton to make for Carron Hill. He had difficulty in restraining himself during the interview with Haddon. He knew, of course, that in police work some dirty tools had to be used; but Haddon had made his gorge rise. The malice of the creature, coupled with that jovial assumption of jocosity, had made him regret that flogging was not a possible punishment in this case. His recollections of Hilary were vague but pleasant; and his face flushed as he thought of her reading one of Haddon's literary masterpieces dealing with her father's dishonour. The modern girl might be up-to-date and all that, he reflected impatiently, but a letter of that sort was trying her rather high.

"Carron Hill, next?" he asked.

"No, Squire, I've other fish to fry, first. Dr. Glencaple is the next on the list."

"But aren't you going to get the Castlefords' own story?"

"In its proper place," Sir Clinton said, curtly. "Don't forget that I'm not here on the Castlefords' behalf. I'll see them when I know exactly what I want to ask them."

Sir Clinton had evidently notified the doctor of the intended visit, for they were shown at once into his consulting room. In a few minutes Dr. Glencaple came in, Wendover examined him with some interest. He noted the long lean face, the thin and rather bloodless lips, the faintly cynical expression, and the reserved manner. Laurence Glencaple, he decided, was not a very approachable person; and this impression was deepened by the fact that, after a laconic greeting, the doctor made no effort to open a conversation. "I didn't ask you here. It's for you to state your business—" That was the suggestion in his attitude.

Sir Clinton, in an official tone, plunged straight into business.

"I've come to inspect your register under the Dangerous Drugs Regulations," he said.

Laurence Glencaple nodded in acquiescence, crossed over to a tier of drawers, extracted a manuscript book and placed it on the table before Sir Clinton.

The Chief Constable turned to the recent entries and conned them over for a moment or two before speaking.

"This patient Heckworth seems to represent most of your doses," he said, after a pause.

"He's a dope-fiend," Laurence explained shortly. "The police put him under my charge to cure him, if possible. He gets a regular series of jags."

Sir Clinton turned back in the register and examined the entries.

"Phew! He seems to have been taking a couple of grammes a day in the early stages. What's the fatal dose for a normal person?"

"What's a square meal for an ordinary man?" retorted the doctor. "It varies from individual to individual. It might be as low as a tenth of a gramme. I'm more accustomed to think of it in grains. Anything from a grain-and-a-half up to five grains might kill."

Sir Clinton turned over the leaves of the register.

"I see you put in a note when you open a fresh carton of tubes. Does that mean that at that point your previous box was completely exhausted?"

"My previous box of that particular dosage," Laurence pointed out. "For ordinary cases, I use one-sixth grain tablets. Heckworth needs heavier doses, as you see, so in his case I use half-grain tablets from another carton."

Sir Clinton took out a notebook and went through the register's later pages more carefully, jotting down figures as he went along. Finally he added up a couple of columns and wrote down the totals.

"I'd like to see your stock of morphine tablets," he said, when he had finished his examination.

Laurence Glencaple seemed to be taken aback by this suggestion. For a moment he seemed inclined to object. Then, taking out his keys, he unlocked a drawer in his desk and extracted two small brown cardboard boxes which he handed over to the Chief Constable.

"These are the cartons in use at present," he explained.

Sir Clinton examined the label on one of them.

"'This unopened package contains one dozen tubes of twenty. Morphine hydrocholoride. No. 66. One-sixth grain, 0.011 gramme,'" he read. "And the other packet's the same, except for the difference in dose."

He pushed open the slides, removed the glass tubes from their compartments, and proceeded to count the tablets of each type which remained unused. Laurence Glencaple watched him with an expression which Wendover thought was anxious. When Sir Clinton had finished, he looked up at the doctor with a grave look on his features.

"Your entries are quite correct?"

"Quite correct," Laurence Glencaple asserted, with a touch of annoyance in his tone.

"Then there's something which needs explanation," Sir Clinton said, with a marked return to his official tone. "Your entries don't tally with your stock of the drug. You're four tablets short—four half-grain tablets. The others are quite in order."

"You must have made a slip," Laurence Glencaple asserted.

"I don't make slips in a simple matter like this," Sit Clinton said coldly. "Check it yourself. It might be well that you should."

The doctor pulled the register across the table towards him and began to go through the entries. Wendover, watching him closely, could see that he was seriously perturbed. Quite obviously he had not expected to have his affairs investigated so thoroughly as this; and the detection of a discrepancy between his stock and his records had given him an uncomfortable jar.

"I can't account for it at the moment," he admitted at last, with an assumption of carelessness. "Perhaps I may have forgotten to enter up one of the doses I gave Heckford."

Sir Clinton shook his head decidedly.

"That won't fit the facts. I see you've been giving Heckford six-grain doses, according to your register. That's twelve half-grain tablets, not four. And all your other entries are in multiples of one-sixth-grain units obviously drawn from your second carton. No, it won't do."

Wendover noticed that Dr. Glencaple had lost a good deal of his initial assurance.

"Well, frankly, I can't account for it," he confessed, rather diffidently. "I'm quite sure I entered up all that I used in Heckford's case, because obviously I had to keep the run of my treatment of him. It's very strange."

He picked up the register and re-checked the entries, as though hoping to find some way out of his difficulty.

"Unless somebody's been getting at my supply . . ." he suggested at length in a tentative tone.

"Is it likely?" Sir Clinton demanded, incredulously. "That's a Yale lock on your drawer, isn't it? Do you leave your keys about?"

"No, my latch-key's on the same ring."

"H'm! Then how do you suggest the theft could have been made?"

Dr. Glencaple pondered for some moments before answering.

"Unless it was taken from my bag, I can't see how it could have happened," he said slowly. "I see Heckford every day, before dinner. He's the last patient I call on, unless I'm sent for specially."

Again he seemed to be considering. He took an engagement diary from his pocket and consulted it. Then for a few moments he seemed to be making up his mind on some point. Finally he handed the diary to Sir Clinton.

"I've only been out to dinner once in the last three weeks," he pointed out, deliberately. "On every other occasion, I've come straight back from Heckford and put the stuff back in the drawer there. But on that night, now I recall it, I went straight on to dinner at Carron Hill; and I left my bag on the hall table all through the evening."

"Unlocked?"

"Unlocked, of course. I didn't imagine anyone would tamper with it."

"So it practically comes to this," Sir Clinton suggested, "that the only chance of those four tablets going a-missing was at Carron Hill? You still hold to it that your register-entries are correct?"

Dr. Glencaple evaded the first question and answered the second.

"I'm quite prepared to swear that they are."

"So you suggest that someone at Carron Hill purloined these tablets from your bag. Can you make a guess at who did it?"

Dr. Glencaple seemed to have recovered his coolness.

"No," he said, bluntly, "I don't propose to insinuate anything that I can't prove. I haven't even said that the stuff was stolen by any of the Carron Hill people. I've given you facts, nothing more."

"You're aware, of course, that morphine was found Mrs. Castleford's body?"

"I'm quite aware of it. That's the very reason why I'm cautious in my statements."

"Very diplomatic," Sir Clinton commented, though his tone was not altogether that of admiration. "And now I'd like some more information which involves no insinuations. I understand that you and your brother were taken aback by the news that Mrs. Castleford hadn't signed this projected will?"

"Completely," Dr. Glencaple agreed, acidly. "Miss Lindfield took me entirely by surprise when she informed me of that."

"Where is Miss Lindfield at present? I understand that she has been left in a rather awkward position, financially, by this affair."

"She's still staying at Carron Hill. Between ourselves"—he glanced from Sir Clinton to Wendover as though assuring himself of confidence—"I'm tiding her over until she can look out for something to do. We're old friends, you understand, and naturally I could hardly see her stranded. I mention it lest you should find it out for yourself and put a wrong construction on it."

"Your brother is perhaps doing the same?" Sir Clinton asked.

Dr. Glencaple shook his head with a faintly sardonic smile.

"My brother's in a different position. He's married, you see."

"But surely the Castlefords would do something to help?" Sir Clinton persisted.

"The Castlefords?" Dr. Glencaple was obviously amused by the mere suggestion. "No, I don't see the Castlefords doing much for her. They've skinned her, financially. And you know the old saying: 'First injure, and then hate.' You never hate anyone so much as a person you've treated badly. That's the Castleford attitude towards Miss Lindfield. Rather hard lines on her."

Wendover had been watching the doctor closely, and so far as he could judge, this was the plain truth. He found his dislike for Dr. Glencaple lessening to some extent. After all, this was rather a nice thing that he had done, and he had confessed to it in rather a nice way, evidently without the slightest desire to boast of his generosity. Wendover had drawn his own conclusions from the house and its furnishings. Dr. Glencaple was not particularly affluent, he guessed; and that made his action rather finer. And, by a further reaction, he began to readjust his pre-conceptions on another subject. This unknown girl Lindfield seemed to have been rather badly treated. He knew that she had been provided for under the old will and under the new one; Sir Clinton had explained that to him. And on the face of things, the Castlefords had dealt rather ungraciously with her, according to Dr. Glencaple's account. Rough treatment, to turn a girl out into the world without any kind of help.

"Was that the only reason for treating her like that?" Sir Clinton asked casually.

"Well, I don't think Miss Lindfield and the Castlefords were exactly enamoured of each other at any time," Dr. Glencaple admitted, frankly. "She's an efficient person and Mrs. Castleford practically handed over the running of Carron Hill to her. That probably had something to do with it. And, of course, it's sometimes a difficult position When you get two good-looking girls, not related to each other, living under one roof . . . Well, I don't know, but women are curious creatures in some ways."

"Jealousy, do you mean?" Wendover interjected.

Dr. Glencaple seemed afraid that he had said too much.

"Well, I don't want to say anything against Hilary—Miss Castleford, I mean. I rather liked her, in fact, until this affair of Miss Lindfield. Still, as things were, one couldn't help feeling that there was some rivalry on the premises; and Miss Lindfield was made to suffer for it when the Castlefords got the upper hand. That's all the length I'd care to go."

Sir Clinton did not pursue the subject further. Instead, he turned to a fresh line.

"Inspector Westerham tells me you have your young nephew with you just now. He hasn't gone home?"

"No. He was sent here for a change of air, and there was no point in sending him home in the middle of it. At the same time, we could hardly leave him at Carron Hill. There's no relation of his there now, you see, apart from all other considerations. So I'm looking after him for the present."

"I'd like to see him," Sir Clinton explained.

"No objection to my being here while you question him?" Dr. Glencaple asked, with a quick glance at the Chief Constable.

"None whatever," Sir Clinton agreed, lightly. "I only want to ask him a question or two. We may need him as a witness, and I want to test his memory, just to see how far we could rely on him."

Dr. Glencaple did not appear to relish this idea, altogether. Wendover, who had learned something of the boy's mendacity, was not altogether surprised by the uncle's attitude.

Though a confirmed bachelor, Wendover liked children and had the gift of making himself liked by them in turn. But when Frankie Glencaple was ushered into the room by his uncle, the Squire decided at the first glance that this was not the kind of boy he cared for. Fat, flabby, with shifty eyes in a pasty face, Frankie made a very poor impression at first sight. Nor did Dr. Glencaple's caution: "Now, Frankie, tell the truth," help to mend matters. It was plain, from the glance which the boy threw at his uncle, that Dr. Glencaple did not stand any nonsense from his nephew and also that the boy resented this attitude. "A spoiled brat, if ever I saw one," was Wendover's disgusted verdict.

"I want to know something about this rook-rifle of yours," Sir Clinton began, pleasantly enough. "Miss Lindfield gave it to you, didn't she?"

Frankie acknowledged this by a rather discourteous nod.

"Nice of her," Sir Clinton commented. "I missed something in not having a generous aunt like her when I was your age, evidently. You've used it a good deal?"

"Yes."

"Birds, and so forth? Can you shoot decently? It sometimes comes in useful."

This was not precisely the kind of interview that Frankie had expected. His natural desire to brag overcame his suspicions.

"I can shoot sparrows on the wing."

"Pretty good," Sir Clinton admitted, with a complete acceptance of the story which gained him Frankie's liking and contempt at a single stroke. "Need to keep your eye in, though, for that sort of thing. What did you do on a wet day when there was nothing to shoot at out-of-doors?"

"I did target shooting in the old harness room. Auntie Connie fixed up an old archery target on the wall and I pinned cardboard targets on to it. But target shooting's no fun," Frankie confessed glumly. "I like to see things jump when I hit them. It doesn't hurt a target to shoot at it."

"I suppose you got some of the other people at Carron Hill to have shooting-matches with you?"

Frankie shook his head.

"No. I tried with Auntie Connie, but she just shuts her eyes when she fires. She's no good at all."

"And what about the others? Wouldn't they take you on?"

"Old Castleford and Hillie? Not much! He was always trying to pretend I wasn't there; and she was always finding fault with me. I'd no use for them. I'd never have thought of asking them."

"Your aunt seems to have been your stand-by. You and she got on better?"

For some reason which Wendover could not fathom, but which the Inspector would have guessed easily enough, Frankie seemed in two minds about the answer to this. He was about to say something;

213

then, after a swift glance at his uncle's face, he obviously changed his mind and his tone.

"Yes," he admitted reluctantly, "I liked her best."

"She helped you to make the time pass? Went walks with you, and that sort of thing?"

"Yes. She helped me with bird's-nesting, last time I was here. She's no good at climbing trees, but she knows about birds' eggs a lot. She took me over to the Public Library in the car and got out a lot of books with pictures of eggs in them when we didn't know some of the ones we picked up. I've got the best collection in school. And this time she helped me to make fireworks—better than the kind you buy."

"The Public Library again?" Sir Clinton suggested, "I suppose you got your recipes there?"

"Yes. I made some top-hole coloured fires and crackers out of a book they have in the Library."

"I suppose she bought the chemicals for you. You seem to have been in clover. Anything else she did for you?"

"Yes. She got me a fishing-rod and taught me to cast. I cast better than she did. I caught a lot of fish, more than she could. I caught a trout that length . . ."

"H'm! You and I must have a talk about the pools round here, sometime. I fish myself. Unfortunately I haven't got a rod with me. Do you play golf, by the way?"

Frankie shook his head.

"No, she tried to teach me, but I hate it. It's a girls' game. Hillie's good at it and she used to laugh at me when she saw me playing."

Sir Clinton looked at his watch.

"Time's getting on. I mustn't keep you any longer, Dr. Glencaple. If you can solve the mystery of these tablets—something may suggest itself if you think over the business—I'd be glad to know as soon as possible. Officially, I'm not inclined to make a fuss."

When they got back into the car, Wendover expected that Carron Hill would be their next halting-place; but Sir Clinton had other views.

"No, Squire. Curb your impatience. I've a call to make at the post-office."

Wendover had been putting two and two together during the interview with Dr. Glencaple, and now he thought he had fastened upon an important point.

"That man Glencaple didn't seem at all surprised when you mentioned that Mrs. Castleford had been dosed with morphine," he said thoughtfully. "I thought your people were keeping their thumb on that."

Sir Clinton grinned pleasantly.

"I hope you found a pedigree mare at home in that nest, Squire. Glencaple's a medico. He was called in to identify the body, formally. No medical man could help seeing the 'pin-point pupil' if the eye was open; and he'd draw his own conclusions. Besides, although you couldn't get a doctor to discuss his cases with you, he'll discuss them quick enough with a colleague. The medical profession's a sort of free-masonry. Ripponden wouldn't feel bound to secrecy with another doctor, though he'd never think of saying a word to an unofficial layman. I'd have been more surprised if Glencaple had pretended to know nothing about it."

"There's something in that, perhaps," Wendover admitted, rather against the grain.

At the post-office, Sir Clinton had little difficulty in inducing the girl to talk. P. C. Gumley's manoeuvres had raised many doubts in her mind with regard to her own position in the matter of the telegram which she had divulged; and she was so grateful to the Chief Constable for the reassurance he gave her that she was ready to help in any way she could. The envelope containing the telegram, she explained, had been collected from a pillar-box near Carron Hill. She knew that, because naturally she had been specially interested in the telegram and she had asked the postman about it. It was the only letter in the box, at that collection, and he had noticed the sprawling handwriting as he took it out of the pillar. There were only three collections a day from that box: one in the morning, one in the early afternoon, and one about six o'clock.

"When would letters lifted in the early afternoon collection reach this office?" Sir Clinton asked.

"About ten past four, or a shade earlier, sir."

"Has anyone else asked for this bit of information lately?" Sir Clinton inquired.

"It's funny you should ask that, sir," the girl replied promptly. "Somebody did ask. It was poor Mrs. Castleford herself. She asked me about all the collections from that box, just a few days before her death. No, I don't mean the times the letters are lifted from the box—they're marked on the box, of course. What she wanted was the times that letters collected from that pillar would be brought to the office here by the postman. Something about catching the London mail, I think, was why she asked."

"You're quite sure about this?" Sir Clinton asked, in a rather dubious tone.

"Yes, sir, quite sure. She asked me to write down the times for her on a sheet of paper."

"To write them down?" Sir Clinton was obviously surprised by this procedure.

"Yes, sir. That's why I'm so proof-positive about it. If it hadn't been for that, it'd most likely have slipped my memory. And of course, her dying like that, it made me think about her and kept it fresh in my mind. I'm quite sure about it."

"Don't forget it," Sir Clinton warned her with a smile. "And—if I were you—I think I'd forget about this interview for the present. You understand?"

The girl was only too glad to promise this. She wouldn't say a word to anyone, not she! She'd had one lesson from "that policeman"; and she'd take better care another time.

"This man Gumley seems an impressive character," the Chief Constable commented. "He's got some initiative and he evidently has a certain command of bluff, or he wouldn't have got a sight of that telegram."

Wendover was not to be diverted by laudations of P. C. Gumley.

"What do you make of that last piece of evidence?" he demanded.

"It's curious," Sir Clinton admitted. "It might even be highly suggestive to an ingenious mind. But then I never had that kind of mind. What does strike me as peculiar is that she wanted the times written down."

Wendover considered this dispassionately for some moments before answering.

"My recollection of her was that she was a feather-headed woman who couldn't concentrate on anything. Likely enough she didn't trust her memory."

"Very probably," Sir Clinton admitted. "And now, Squire, your patience will be rewarded. Carron Hill, next."

19
OPPORTUNITIES

Throughout the morning, Wendover had been chafing under Sir Clinton's procedure. In his opinion, the Chief Constable should have gone straight to Carron Hill and learned what the Castlefords had to tell. After that, there would be time enough to hunt up the minor characters in the drama and extract evidence from them. In his mind, he blamed his friend for putting the cart before the horse. Now, however, they had at last reached Carron Hill; and Wendover found himself looking forward—not altogether without apprehension—to hearing the Castleford side of the case.

On the very threshold, however, Sir Clinton disappointed him once more. Sending in his card, he asked if Miss Lindfield could spare him a few minutes; and a swift impish glance at Wendover showed quite plainly that he was amused at the Squire's baffled impatience in face of this unanticipated move.

Wendover had the knack of taking things philosophically, and he curbed his impatience with the reflection that Miss Lindfield promised to be an interesting personality. She was little more than a name to him. Sir Clinton had given him a *précis* of the evidence collected by the police; but this arid abstract dealt purely with events and interviews. Only by inference did it yield any indication of the actors' personalities. He had gathered vaguely that, under the old regime, Miss Lindfield had been virtual mistress of Carron Hill. The tragedy had dethroned her; and now, penniless and on sufferance, she was lingering upon the scene, dependent on Dr. Glencaple's charity until she found a fresh footing for herself.

For the first time, Wendover began to feel qualms about the Castlefords. Was it playing the game to turn this girl out, as they evidently meant to do? He had an uncomfortable feeling that there was more behind the business than appeared in the evidence—old scores being paid off, or something of that sort. The Carron Hill vice-regency might have led to friction; and now, with the tables turned, the Castlefords might be retaliating in kind.

While he was busy with these reflections, the door opened and Miss Lindfield came into the room. As she stood, glancing from one to the other, Sir Clinton saved her from awkwardness by taking the initiative.

"I hope we haven't interrupted you in anything," he said in a pleasantly apologetic tone. "I ought, perhaps, to have let you know beforehand of this visit."

Miss Lindfield made a gesture inviting them to sit down, and chose a chair for herself.

"You haven't interrupted me," she assured him. "I've nothing whatever to do, nowadays. Miss Castleford has taken the running of everything into her own hands—quite rightly, since things are different now."

If there was any tinge of bitterness in her tone, it was so faint as to be almost undetectable. Quite clearly, Miss Lindfield had no intention of making a song about her grievances. It would have been easy enough for her to angle for sympathy; but evidently she had no desire to do so. "Things are as they are" seemed to be the aphorism she had chosen as her guide; and she was doing her best to live up to it. Wendover, who had not expected such an effort at detachment, glanced at her with quickened interest.

Sir Clinton's opening scandalised Wendover by its tactlessness. He fished a cigarette-case from his pocket and offered it to Miss Lindfield.

"Would you care to smoke?" he suggested. "Interviews of this sort are always worrying, I know; and a cigarette sometimes helps to steady the nerves."

Miss Lindfield waved the case aside politely.

"I don't smoke, thanks," she explained. Then with a faint smile she added: "I don't think my nerves need bracing, though I suppose your Inspector told you I had hysterics at the Chalet, that afternoon. But perhaps you and Mr. . . . ."

"This is Mr. Wendover," Sir Clinton explained, briefly.

"You and Mr. Wendover would care to smoke yourselves?"

"No," Sir Clinton retorted, giving her smile for smile, "I think I can answer for our nerves."

He returned his cigarette-case to his pocket.

"You have a firearm certificate, I believe?" he asked in a perfunctory tone. "May I look at it, please? It's merely a formality."

Miss Lindfield crossed the room to an escritoire, turned over some papers in a drawer, and came back with the paper, which she handed over for inspection. Sir Clinton merely glanced at it and then returned it to her.

"Thanks. Now here's something which is rather more important," he continued, searching in his breast-pocket. "Ah, here it is."

He produced two slips of glass about the size of quarter-plate negatives, clipped together with passé-partout edging. Between the glass plates was held something which Wendover could not recognise at the first glance. Sir Clinton passed the specimen across to Miss Lindfield.

"This is a piece of cloth which might turn out to be of interest," he explained. "I want you to examine it carefully—both sides—and see if you can recognise pattern. Take a good look at it, please. There's no hurry."

Miss Lindfield bent over the little object, turning it this way and that with a faint puzzled frown as though she were striving to identify it. As she moved it to and fro, Wendover was able to see that the fragment was a piece of patterned silk of irregular shape.

"You don't recognise it?" Sir Clinton questioned, in a tone which betrayed that he had expected a different result.

Miss Lindfield shook her head as she handed the exhibit back to him.

"You haven't seen Miss Castleford wearing anything of the sort?" Sir Clinton persisted, anxiously.

"No," Miss Lindfield declared, in a decided tone. "So far as I know, she has no frock that's in the least like that."

Sir Clinton put his exhibit aside on a table near-by. From his manner it was plain enough that things had not gone as he had hoped. However, he dismissed the matter and turned to a fresh subject.

"I needn't make any mystery with you," he said. "We're very much interested in a brace of automatic pistols which seem to have played their part in this affair. Now can you tell me, to the best of your knowledge, what persons could have got access to these things between the time they were found by Frank Glencaple and the day of Mrs. Castleford's death? I don't want guesses, you understand. I want the names of the people whom you know *might* have been able to lay their hands on the pistols."

Miss Lindfield laid one hand on her knee and began to tick off the list on her fingers.

"I knew where the pistols were," she began, "because I asked Mr. Castleford to stow them away in his study cupboard. He knew, since I gave them into his charge. Miss Castleford must have known, because she was there when I spoke to him about them—in fact, I asked her to put them there. The three of us knew definitely about the cupboard. Then there's a possibility that Frankie might have rummaged round and discovered them. He was very angry when they were taken from him that night . . ."

"What night?" Sir Clinton asked.

"It was the night that his father and Dr. Glencaple were here to dinner."

She went again to the escritoire, picked up an engagement-diary, hunted through the pages, and finally showed Sir Clinton the entry of the dinner-engagement.

"I couldn't remember the day of the month," she explained. "I knew it was a Tuesday. But you can see the date's all right from the engagement-book."

Wendover began to understand why power had passed into Miss Lindfield's hands in the old days at Carron Hill. She was obviously so careful to think before she acted, and so decided in her action when once she had made up her mind. He had been impressed by her decisive denial in the case of the fragment of cloth, when Sir Clinton obviously wanted her to identify it if she could. Some women would have hemmed and hawed over it, trying to sit on the fence; but she had studied it minutely and had then come out bluntly with her statement.

"Frankie might have been hunting about and found the pistols again," Miss Lindfield continued, as she regained her seat. "His father told him not to touch them and so did Mrs. Castleford; but he wasn't a very obedient boy and the temptation may have been too strong for him. He didn't know they were in that cupboard; but he was very prying and inquisitive, and he might quite well have taken it into his head to rummage in the cupboard out of mere curiosity."

"I gather, from what you say, that his father knew of the existence of these pistols? And his uncle, Dr. Glencaple, too, perhaps?"

Miss Lindfield seemed very slightly taken aback by this suggestion. She paused for a moment before answering. Then, briefly, she gave a description of the scene in the drawing room when Frankie had produced the weapons.

"Of course, the maids had access to the cupboard," she added as an after-thought, "but I shouldn't think there's much in that."

"Then these are all the people you can think of?" Sir Clinton suggested. "Nobody else? What about Mr. Stevenage?" he added suddenly.

It needed no physiognomist to see that Miss Lindfield was startled by this allusion. Her self-control was not sufficient to conceal the suspicion in the look she shot at Sir Clinton as he brought out Stevenage's name. Then, with an effort, she repressed her surprise.

"Mr. Stevenage?" she said, after a marked pause. "What makes you think of him? He could know nothing about the pistols—unless somebody told him about them. I certainly didn't."

"Somebody else might have, though," Sir Clinton pointed out. "If he knew of the pistols' existence, could he have laid hands on them: that's the question. I understand that he was often on the premises here—a sort of chartered libertine."

"I beg your pardon?" said Miss Lindfield in a tone of offence.

Then she appeared to see that she had made a blunder. Wendover could not quite make out why she had objected to the phrase. Sir Clinton seemed taken by surprise by her interjection.

"Free as the air," he paraphrased. "I was thinking of Shakespeare's *Henry V*. He calls the air a chartered libertine somewhere in the first Act. What I meant was that Mr. Stevenage could go freely about the house—more freely than an ordinary visitor, perhaps?"

Miss Lindfield still seemed rather ruffled.

"Yes, he was very friendly with the family. That's true. He used the place as a sort of Liberty Hall."

"Friendly with all the family?" Sir Clinton asked specifically.

"I don't think that Mr. Castleford liked him very much."

It was quite plain that Miss Lindfield was not eager to volunteer any information in this field; and Sir Clinton made no attempt to press her. Instead, he reverted to an earlier line of inquiry.

"Since the night of that dinner party we spoke about, Dr. Glencaple has not been here to dinner?"

Miss Lindfield shook her head; then, picking up the engagement-book, she consulted it to verify her impression.

"No," she said definitely. "He hasn't been here to dinner. In fact, I don't think he's been here at all." Then, after a moment's pause she added, "I'm speaking of what I know, of course. He may have come to see Mrs. Castleford when I was out, and Mrs. Castleford might not have mentioned it to me."

"You've seen him, at times, elsewhere?"

"I've met him outside, once or twice."

"On the night of that dinner, he brought his doctor's bag with him, I believe?"

Miss Lindfield seemed to have no difficulty in recalling that.

"Yes, he left it on the hall table. I saw it there as we went in to dinner."

"Now this point is rather important," said Sir Clinton gravely. "Could anyone have tampered with that bag without being noticed?"

Miss Lindfield did not give an immediate answer. She looked down at the tip of her shoe, and her brows contracted slightly as if she were racking her memory so as to be sure of her ground when she spoke.

"Before dinner, I doubt if anyone could have touched it," she explained at last. "People were passing through the hall, the maids, and some of us, coming down from dressing. Then, during dinner, it was out of the question, of course, except for the maids. After dinner, Mrs. Castleford, Frankie, and I went into the drawing room, leaving the men over their coffee. Later on . . ."

"What about Miss Castleford, at that time? You didn't say what became of her after dinner."

"I don't know where she went. Upstairs, probably; or into the study," Miss Lindfield said, rather put out, apparently, that she had omitted the point. "Later on, Dr. Glencaple and Mr. Glencaple came into the drawing room. Mr. Castleford didn't join us. He went to his study. Miss Castleford went there also, for I saw her there later on."

She paused again, as though confirming her recollections in her mind.

"I'm trying to remember who left the drawing room. First of all, Mrs. Castleford asked me to give Miss Castleford a message. I went to the study and found her there with her father. After I gave her the message, she said she would telephone about something. I didn't see her telephoning; but I happen to know that she did telephone, a few minutes later. The telephone box is at the other end of the hall from the study. I went back to the drawing room and after a while Frankie and I went over to the harness room to try his rook-rifle on an old archery target which we fixed up. After we came back to the drawing room, Dr. Glencaple himself went out and got some insulin out of his bag. That was after Frankie had been packed off to bed. And after that, our party kept together until Dr. Glencaple went away, taking his bag with him."

Sir Clinton had listened intently to her account, and at the end of it he paid her a frank compliment.

"If only all witnesses could put things as clearly as you do, we should be saved a vast amount of time."

Wendover noticed something more than the explicitness of the narrative. Miss Lindfield had refused to answer Sir Clinton's actual inquiry. She had refrained from making even a tacit accusation but, instead, had given an objective account of the movements of the party, leaving the Chief Constable to put his own construction upon the facts.

"Now there's another point I'd like to clear up," Sir Clinton continued. "I don't want you to be offended, but we're handicapped by not knowing the relations between the members of the group at Carron Hill. If you don't mind, I'd like to put a question or two on that subject."

Miss Lindfield crossed her ankles, relaxed slightly in her chair, and then, as if thinking better of it, drew herself up again. She dropped her elbow on her knee, cupped her chin in her hand, and looked across at Sir Clinton.

"I don't mind what questions you ask," she said.

"You and Mrs. Castleford, of course, were likely to have a good deal in common. She relied on you more than on the others?"

Miss Lindfield admitted this with a nod.

"Naturally," she explained, "we'd grown up together; we were much of an age; and Miss Castleford was a good deal younger, with different interests."

"That's what I meant," Sir Clinton agreed. "You'd been school-girls together and naturally you had a good deal in common, things in which even Mr. Castleford couldn't share?"

"That was bound to be the case, wasn't it?" Miss Lindfield confirmed with just a hint of irony in her voice.

"I believe that the management of the place was left very much in your hands by Mrs. Castleford. You looked after everything, gave the orders, paid the bills, and so forth?"

"Yes. Mrs. Castleford had no head for business and was glad to hand all that kind of thing over to me. She hated to be troubled with the routine of things."

"She didn't think of letting her husband do it?"

"No," Miss Lindfield explained candidly. "The fact is, I doubt if Mr. Castleford could have satisfied her. He's rather dreamy—I suppose it's the artistic temperament or something," she added, as if in extenuation of her criticism.

"How did Miss Castleford stand with her stepmother?"

Miss Lindfield seemed to resent the question; then, thinking better of her first attitude, she answered reluctantly:

"I don't think Mrs. Castleford liked her."

"Mr. Stevenage came about the house. On whose account was that? Miss Castleford's?"

But this question evidently seemed to go over the score.

"I think you'd better ask Miss Castleford herself about that," said Miss Lindfield coldly. "Or Mr. Stevenage might be able to give you full details. It's hardly a matter that concerns me."

Wendover could see from her expression that she was displeased by Sir Clinton's line of attack.

"You're quite right," the Chief Constable agreed, apologetically. "We'll leave that aside. Now another question. Am I mistaken in supposing that Mrs. Castleford was not a very strong character—I mean that she was fairly easy to influence in some ways?"

"In some ways, yes," Miss Lindfield confirmed, with a faint but unmistakable accent on the "some." "But what makes you think that?"

"I was thinking of the history of her will-making," Sir Clinton explained. "I gather that her original will left a good deal to the Glencaple brothers. I'm correct there? Then she fell under Mr. Castleford's influence, and she made a new will under which he was the chief legatee. That's right, I think? And then, quite recently, it looks as if she had fallen under the Glencaple influence again and had made up her mind to change once more and to make the two brothers the principal heirs. She strikes me as a very amenable person, in that respect."

Miss Lindfield made no comment on this verdict. She shifted her elbow slightly into a more comfortable position and gazed across at Sir Clinton as though expecting him to say more.

"You had considerable influence with her yourself?" he asked in a neutral tone.

Miss Lindfield took up the implied challenge.

"You mean, I suppose," she said, frostily, "that I evidently wasted my opportunities, since I had more chance of influencing her than anyone else had? I didn't try. I knew that she meant to provide for me sufficiently. She did so in every will. If I had influenced her at all, it would have been in favour of Dr. Glencaple and his brother; for, after all, any money she had was Glencaple money. But as a matter of fact, the only advice I gave her was not to do anything in a hurry but to be sure that she had really made her mind up before she acted. She was too inclined to be impetuous in some things. I didn't want her to be acting rashly and then feeling that she'd been too hasty."

"I don't know that I'd have been able to show so much self-restraint myself, in your shoes," Sir Clinton confessed, frankly.

"Dr. Glencaple has always been very kind to me," Miss Lindfield said, rather irrelevantly.

Sir Clinton left this subject alone.

"You got an anonymous letter, I believe, making accusations against Mrs. Castleford and Mr. Stevenage?"

"I don't know how you got that information," Miss Lindfield said with some heat. "Is it necessary to go into it? I've burned the letter, of course."

"I merely wish to put a hypothetical case to you. Mrs. Castleford was easily influenced. Mr. Stevenage was in a position to influence her. Might he not have exerted his influence to get her to make a will in *his* favour? She seems to have chopped and changed a good deal in her intentions."

Miss Lindfield's hand tightened on her chin and she fixed her eyes on the floor. Wendover guessed that this suggestion had taken her completely aback and that she was thinking out its implications before replying.

"I hadn't thought of that possibility," she said slowly.

Then, after a further pause for thought, she seemed to dismiss the idea.

"No, I don't think there's anything in it. We'd have heard of such a will before now, if it existed."

"Not necessarily," Sir Clinton corrected her. "Wills often come to light long after the testator has died. Age doesn't invalidate them."

"That's true," Miss Lindfield acknowledged, rather reluctantly.

The introduction of Stevenage's name seemed to have disturbed her, and she knitted her brows in a very obvious effort of thought.

"Winnie would hardly have been such a little fool as *that*," was her final judgment, which she unconsciously uttered aloud.

Sir Clinton apparently paid no attention to her words. He allowed her to think in silence for a few moments; then, apparently growing impatient, he glanced at his watch.

"I wonder if you can tell me when the next post goes from the nearest pillar-box?" he asked. "I'd like to catch the London mail, there, if possible."

Miss Lindfield seemed to wake up with a start from her reflections.

"I really can't say," she confessed. "I just take my chance at the pillar."

"Then I suppose I had better follow your example," Sir Clinton said carelessly. "Now, there's just one further matter. You mentioned an old target that you had in the harness room—the one young Frank Glencaple was firing at with his rook-rifle. May I see it?"

"I'll send for it," Miss Lindfield suggested, rising to ring the bell.

"And if you could get your maid to bring some paper and twine," Sir Clinton added, "I may have to take it away. It might be required as an exhibit in the case, you see."

In a few minutes the maid had brought the target—a straw boss with a painted canvas face, evidently much the worse for use. She laid it on a table, along with a string-box and a large sheet of brown paper. Sir Clinton made a very cursory examination of the target and then set about the task of wrapping it up into a parcel. As he was just completing this task, he drew a folding knife from his pocket, one of those knives which take an old safety-razor blade instead of the usual cutting edge. With this open in his hand, the Chief Constable continued to tie up his parcel. As he drew the last knot, he turned to Miss Lindfield.

"Would you mind putting your finger on the string?" he asked. "I'd like to get this tight."

Miss Lindfield leaned over and put her finger on the half-completed knot. What happened next was hidden from Wendover, as they stood between him and the parcel. He saw the girl wince slightly and heard a muffled ejaculation and a quick apology from Sir Clinton. Then Miss Lindfield stepped back a pace and examined a cut in her forefinger, from which the blood was beginning to ooze. Manifestly the Chief Constable had been careless or clumsy with his pocket-knife.

Sir Clinton took a spotless handkerchief from his pocket and insisted on putting a temporary bandage on the wounded finger. Then he despatched Wendover to his car for a first-aid case; and, removing the handkerchief, he bound up the cut with proper dressings.

"I'm exceedingly sorry," he protested, when he had finished. "It was very stupid of me to try to tie that knot with a knife in my hand."

Miss Lindfield made no fuss over the incident; but by her manner she expressed plainly enough what she thought of the Chief Constable's clumsiness.

"Have you any more questions you'd like to ask?" she demanded with some asperity, when the bandaging was completed.

"One or two points about Mrs. Castleford's family I'd like to clear up," Sir Clinton explained. "Her parents are dead, are they?"

"Long ago," Miss Lindfield confirmed.

"She had no brothers or sisters?"

"No, none. She was my half-sister—my father and hers were the same, I mean. I had a sister younger than myself, but she's dead, now."

"Had she any other relations alive? Grandparents?"

"No, they died long ago. She had an uncle in America but she didn't correspond with him. He died three years ago."

After a pause, Miss Lindfield added:

"If you're thinking of the Administration of Estates Act, I'd better simplify things by saying that if she hadn't married and had died intestate, then I'd have been next in succession."

She glanced at Wendover with a smile which had just a touch of bitterness in it. Obviously there were limits to her power of hiding her hurts. The Squire sympathised with her.

"She's a plucky girl," was his unspoken verdict, and in giving it he was not thinking of her wounded hand.

Sir Clinton made no comment on Miss Lindfield's last remark.

"I don't think I need trouble you any further," he said. "If Miss Castleford's in, I'd like to see her. Perhaps you could ask her to give me a minute or two?"

"Certainly, I'll send her to you," Miss Lindfield assented briskly. "Then that's all?"

"That's all," Sir Clinton repeated, rising to open the door for her.

When she had gone, Wendover turned to his friend. "Awkward devil, you are, Clinton. You hurt that girl more than a bit, though she didn't show it."

Sir Clinton's defence took an unexpected line:

"'I must be cruel, only to be kind,'" he quoted. "'Thus bad begins, and worse remains behind.' Shakespeare, *The Tragedy of Hamlet*, Act Three, Scene Four," he added, blandly.

"You seem very strong on Shakespeare today," said Wendover testily. "That's the second time you've dragged him in."

"I always quote him on Tuesdays and Saturdays," the Chief Constable explained seriously. "After all, Squire, one must have some regular rules of life, or things would get into a dreadful state."

"Like that girl's finger, eh? H'm!" Wendover grunted. "So you did that intentionally?"

"What do you think?" was all Sir Clinton deigned to reply.

20
SIR CLINTON AND THE CASTLEFORDS

With Hilary Castleford's entrance into the room, Wendover discovered how far his preconceptions had led him astray. Instead of the "nice friendly little kiddie" whom he remembered, he found a slim, fair-haired girl with arresting hazel eyes and a determined chin. When he planned his "rescue expedition," he had pictured a helpless little creature caught by chance in the cruel machinery of the Law and crying in despair to him for deliverance. But the girl now before him did not suggest helplessness. At the very first glance, he got the impression that she was quite capable of looking after herself. There was nothing timid or shrinking about her, though she looked worried and anxious, certainly. But what struck Wendover most—in view of his preconceived ideas—was the very obvious fact that she did not seem altogether sure that she wanted him, now that he had actually arrived. There was a certain awkwardness for which he was wholly unprepared, an awkwardness of manner and not of manners. He felt suddenly discomfited. It almost looked as if she had appealed to him impulsively and regretted her move when too late to retract it.

"You remember Sir Clinton, don't you?" he asked, merely to break the very conspicuous ice.

"Oh, yes, of course," Hilary answered, without any enthusiasm in her tone. "I suppose you want to ask me some questions?" she added, turning to the Chief Constable. "Will that take long? I've just had a telephone message from the hospital to say they need me."

231

"At the Sunnyside hospital?"

"Yes. I'm on the list of donors there, for blood transfusion," Hilary explained. "There's been a bad motor-accident and they've rung me up. If you're going detain me long, I'll get my father to go instead. He volunteered too, and his blood's the same as mine. But it's the first time they've called on me for it, and I don't like to cry off unless it's necessary."

"I shan't keep you more than a few minutes," Sir Clinton reassured her.

"Very well, then," Hilary said, rather ungraciously. "You'd better begin."

Wendover was puzzled by her behaviour. Then his thoughts went back to the time he received her letter, and he began to see one possible explanation of her conduct. She had written to him spontaneously, without telling her father. Since then, she had consulted Castleford and he had persuaded her that she had made a blunder. That would explain the change in her attitude.

"Perhaps you won't see the point of some of my questions," Sir Clinton began, unperturbed by his witness's obvious lack of cordiality. "Don't mind that. I'm merely trying to get at the state of things at Carron Hill while Mrs. Castleford was alive. First of all, how did she treat you?"

"I was a poor relation with no claim on her and living at her expense. That was how she saw it and that was the way she treated me," said Hilary in a rather bitter tone.

"Ah, I think I understand. You mean that you had to work your passage?" Sir Clinton asked.

"Exactly," Hilary confirmed. "I drove her car and ran errands for her."

"And apart from that, how did you get on with her?"

"She snubbed me whenever she got a chance. Perhaps I shouldn't say that, but you asked the question, and I'm answering it. She disliked me and she behaved as if she grudged me my keep. I can't pretend that she was nice to me."

"No consideration?" Sir Clinton suggested.

"No consideration whatever," Hilary said bluntly. "If she wanted my services on the spur of the moment, then any arrangements I had made had to be cancelled for her benefit. It was very irksome."

"It must have been," Sir Clinton commented sympathetically. "What sort of errands did she send you on? Changing books at the local library and that sort of thing?"

"Yes. She never could understand the system there, though it's simple enough. When she wanted books, Miss Lindfield or I had to get them for her. I hardly got any use from my own ticket, for she always used it when she wanted an extra book. Father was in the same boat. If she wanted a book, we had to return the one we were reading so that she could use the ticket herself."

"I think I see. You had a ticket each, but one person could monopolise all four at times. And I suppose these tickets were kept in some place where anyone could get hold of them when they were needed?"

"Yes, they were kept in an open drawer. When I was sent for a book, I simply took the first ticket that came to hand in the drawer. They're not supposed to be transferable; but nobody minds about that rule."

Wendover found himself swinging round to Hilary's side again. Behind her brief phrases, he could glimpse a long vista of petty persecution which must have made a young girl's life anything but happy. With a history like that, she could hardly be expected to show conventional restraint in talking about her late stepmother.

"Here's something else I'd like you to do for me," Sir Clinton pursued.

He pulled from his pocket a pair of glasses with a piece of cloth clipped between them and handed them across to the girl; but to Wendover's surprise, the cloth-fragment in this case was a piece of tweed, evidently clipped from a man's suit.

"Can you identify that cloth?" Sir Clinton asked "Look at it well, so as to be sure about it. Have you ever seen anything like it?"

Here, evidently, Sir Clinton had sprung a nasty surprise on the girl. Wendover could see perfectly well that she did recognise the pattern of the cloth. She betrayed that in her face at the very first glance she took. But with an effort she restrained herself and made a pretence of a long and careful inspection. Then she lifted her head.

"I don't recognise it," she declared firmly.

Sir Clinton held out his hand for the exhibit and took it from her. He seemed to accept her statement without demur.

"Now there's another question," he went on. "Do you remember one night, not long ago, when the Glencaple brothers came here to dinner? Dr. Glencaple left his professional bag on the hall table. Did you see it there when you passed through the hall on your way to telephone, after dinner?"

"Yes . . . I think it was there then."

"You left your father in his study. Could he have come out of his study while you were telephoning and come into the hall without your knowledge?"

"He might," Hilary admitted.

She had evidently meant to add something—a denial of some sort, Wendover guessed—but pulled herself up. Then an idea seemed to occur to her.

"Miss Lindfield was in the hall before I was. She came to bring me a message from Mrs. Castleford about the car."

Sir Clinton ignored this side-issue and dropped the subject.

"Are you engaged to Mr. Stevenage?" he asked pointblank.

Hilary flushed.

"No," she said rather awkwardly.

"He proposed to you, perhaps?"

Hilary seemed to recover herself.

"I don't know what business you have to ask these questions," she said, with a nervous catch in her voice. "But I don't mind answering them, for fear you should go drawing all sorts of conclusions. Mr. Stevenage came very near proposing to me more than once. A girl can always tell. But I managed to put him off. I hadn't made up my mind about him."

"What came in the way? Was it because he paid too much attention to Mrs. Castleford?" Sir Clinton asked pointedly.

"I didn't feel very sure about him," said Hilary, guardedly.

Sir Clinton seemed to be considering this answer. For some moments he was silent. Then, looking the girl straight in the face, he spoke again.

"Just one final question, Miss Castleford. Why did you and your father tell Inspector Westerham a pack of lies?"

For one moment, Wendover saw a blaze of fury in the hazel eyes at this plain challenge. Then Hilary's expression changed; she made a very good pretence of astonishment.

"I don't know what you're talking about, Sir Clinton.

"Let it go at that, then," the Chief Constable said, icily. "I gave you your chance."

He crossed the room and rang the bell. When the maid appeared, he asked her to tell Mr. Castleford that he wished to see him. Wendover, who was wholly taken aback by the last turn of events, had no difficulty in seeing the meaning of this manoeuvre. Sir Clinton did not propose to allow father and daughter to consult together before had interviewed Castleford.

When Castleford came into the room, Sir Clinton, with a certain cold courtesy, showed Hilary out, without giving them a chance of exchanging more than a glance When he turned back to Castleford, his manner had resumed its earlier geniality.

"Miss Castleford tells me that she has been called up by the hospital for blood transfusion," he said, as he motioned Castleford to a seat. "You're on the list of donors also, I believe? Who does the blood-testing there, do you know?"

"Dr. Pendlebury, I believe," Castleford explained.

"I've heard his name," Sir Clinton said, musingly. "Quite a good man, I believe."

Wendover had nodded to Castleford as he came into the room, but now he had a better opportunity of studying him. Here again he was slightly disappointed. Castleford seemed subdued, furtive, and too obviously on his guard for Wendover's liking.

"I believe you have a good public library hereabouts," Sir Clinton remarked, as though merely making conversation before he began his real inquiry.

"Yes, there's one in Strickland Regis, quite a good one. They're very obliging, and they don't bother too much with red tape."

"You have a ticket, I suppose?"

Castleford was evidently glad to keep to such a safe subject as long as possible. He went over to a drawer and took out a little piece of pasteboard folded in half about the size of a visiting-card. He handed this over to Sir Clinton, who examined it with some curiosity.

"Thanks," the Chief Constable said, handing it back again. "Now you mustn't mind if I ask you a question or two which may seem futile. I'm trying to understand what sort of person Mrs. Castleford was. I gather that she was rather unstable in some ways. What sort of interests had she?"

Castleford reflected for a moment or two. Evidently he could not make out whither this was trending.

"Dress was one," he began. "She was very keen on clothes. And she was always very nervous about her health. The slightest thing going wrong with her always worried her. She was impulsive, at times; and she liked to have her own way."

He halted, as though unable to think of any other characteristics. To Wendover, it seemed a very brief and peculiar list, without a single engaging quality in it. Quite obviously Castleford had not been a doting husband.

"Generous? Frank? Open in her dealings?" Sir Clinton suggested in a perfectly neutral tone.

"No," said Castleford, evidently stung into plain speech.

"Secretive in some ways, perhaps?"

"Yes," Castleford blurted out, and then seemed immediately to regret what he had said.

"Can you give me an instance?" Sir Clinton persisted.

Castleford was no actor. His face betrayed him. Wendover could guess what was happening in his mind. He had been thinking of his wife and Stevenage; but that was the last instance he wanted to produce; so, instead, he paused while he cast about for something else.

"I can give you one example," he said, with a nervous laugh. "When we were engaged to be married, she was very worried lest her brothers-in-law should find it out. She made all sorts of silly arrangements for meeting me, lest they should get to know. She even used to wire to me in a childish kind of code—the sort of thing a couple of schoolgirls might devise—you read every second word to get the real message. She was immensely proud of it—thought no one could possibly fathom it. I don't know where she picked it up."

"Surely she might have invented it herself."

"She hadn't enough brains for that," said Castleford brutally. "No, she'd learned it from someone."

Wendover found that as the interview progressed he was liking Castleford less and less. There was a ring of dislike and contempt in the last two sentences which seemed . . . well, hardly the thing for the circumstances.

Sir Clinton appeared to have clarified his ideas about Mrs. Castleford, for he now produced the glass slips which had become familiar to Wendover, though yet again the cloth between them was different from the previous specimens.

"Have a look at that, Mr. Castleford, and see if you can identify it?"

Castleford examined it minutely. Wendover could just see that it seemed to be a fragment of some thin dress-material.

"No, I don't recognise it," Castleford said at last, with a faint hesitation which suggested to Wendover that he was lying.

"Look again," Sir Clinton suggested.

Castleford obeyed, then shook his head and passed the exhibit back.

"I don't remember it."

"Very well," Sir Clinton said stiffly. "I'll leave it at that. Now I come to an awkward subject. You said your wife was impulsive. Was she easily amenable to influence?"

Castleford evidently suspected some trap in this. He seemed to turn the question over in his mind before answering.

"Not to mine," he said, guardedly, at last.

"Do you know anyone who could influence her, then?"

"Miss Lindfield could generally manage her," Castleford admitted sulkily. "I think the Glencaples were able to get round her, too. She was easily flattered into doing things."

"Anybody else? Mr. Stevenage, for instance?" Sir Clinton demanded coolly. "Could he have influenced her enough to get her to make a will in his favour, do you think?"

This suggestion evidently came as a thunderbolt to Castleford.

"But there's no such will," he protested.

"No such will has been produced, so far, I grant you," Sir Clinton corrected. "I'm putting a purely hypothetical case."

"Well, I can't answer hypothetical questions," Castleford retorted. "I never dreamt of such a thing. You don't think it's likely, do you?" he demanded, anxiously.

"You ought to know more about it than I do," Sir Clinton said, meaningly.

Then he changed his tone sharply.

"I'll give you one plain piece of advice, Mr. Castleford. I'm quite certain that you've been lying, and lying hard, in this case. I'm not going to choose my words about it. You and your daughter have got up a cock-and-bull story between you. Each gives the other an alibi. For whose benefit was that double alibi put up? Either you *or your daughter* was intended to profit by it. If it was you, and you put that girl into the witness-box to repeat that tale, I warn you that perjury is a serious business. No matter what happens to you, she'll have to bear the brunt of it. You can take that as official. Think it over carefully."

He rose as he spoke.

"Come along, Wendover. I've other things to do."

They left Castleford staring after them with an expression on his face that suggested something very near panic.

As the car ran down the avenue to the Carron Hill gate, Sir Clinton was silent; but when they reached the open road he turned to Wendover.

"Not altogether the Don Quixote, Squire," he said sardonically. "A bit of a wash-out, in that role, I think, I never could stand liars."

"You think they're not straight?"

"Wait a bit."

Sir Clinton pulled up the car at a pillar-box, got out, and posted a letter after examining the time-plate.

"That's a note addressed to myself, Poste Restante, Thunderbridge," he explained. "We'll call for it at the post-office this afternoon and watch the postman bring it in. Nothing like checking up things when one can; and we may as well be certain about the reception of that posted telegram which disappeared at the Chalet. And that reminds me, I've to telephone to Headquarters to make some inquiry about that firearm certificate of Miss Lindfield's."

He got back into the driving-seat and started the car.

"You're sure those two weren't telling the truth?" Wendover persisted.

He had little doubt about it himself, but he wished to get Sir Clinton's reasons to compare with his own.

"Look at the evidence in the case, Squire. The thing stares you in the face. Besides that, I caught them both lying just a few minutes ago."

"Did you?" said Wendover, rather annoyed at not having seen this for himself. "How did you?"

"With these exhibits, the three bits of cloth. The one I showed to Miss Lindfield was nothing—a pattern I picked up in a shop. She didn't recognise it, of course; and she said so. Then I showed the Castleford girl a bit that had been snipped out of her father's coat—the one Westerham impounded. She recognised it all right. That was plain enough. But she denied quite flatly that she'd ever seen anything to match it. Then I showed Castleford a fragment of the dress his wife was wearing when she was killed—a thing with a quite distinctive pattern. He'd never seen it before, honest man. Do you expect me to fall on the necks of people like that, Squire?"

Wendover's simple code barred lying. He had no answer to Sir Clinton's sneer.

"So you arranged these things to trap them?" he asked.

"No," said Sir Clinton, with a faint grin, "it was a shade more subtle than that. I wanted their fingerprints, and I didn't want them to know I was taking them. So I gave them something else to think about while they were fingering the glasses, and they didn't tumble to what I was really after."

"That's neat enough," Wendover confessed. "You bamboozled me completely with it, and I expect you diddled them too. But why bother about fingerprints? There aren't any in this case, unless I've missed something."

"There aren't any, so far," Sir Clinton amended. "But there may be, before we're through. I'll be able to tell you when I've looked up the weather reports for the last few weeks at the Public Library. We'll go there this afternoon. I ought to pay a visit to the hospital, too."

Wendover knew that he would gain no further information by trying to cross-examine the Chief Constable, who was apparently in one of his impish moods. Instead he turned to another aspect of the matter.

"Why did you drag Stevenage's name in with all of them?"

"Well, see what I elicited," Sir Clinton explained. "First of all, Miss Lindfield was quite honestly anxious to keep Stevenage's name out of the business. In fact, she was more anxious than one would expect from a mere acquaintance, which confirms Haddon's story about them. Also, my suggestion about Stevenage's influence with Mrs. Castleford obviously disturbed her. There might be more than one way of interpreting that. As to the Castleford girl, she was as plain as print in that matter. She would have accepted Stevenage if it hadn't been that she felt there was something between him and Mrs. Castleford. As for Castleford himself, of course he knew all about his wife's game. What gave him a jar was the possibility of a will in favour of Stevenage, which would perhaps cut him out of his wife's fortune at this eleventh hour. These are interesting points, to my mind."

"So you think Stevenage . . . ?"

"Don't let us try to define things too closely," Sir Clinton begged, with a comic air of offended modesty. "Do you remember that German song about the fellow who knew three fair maidens?

"Die eine küss' i',
Die and're lieb' i',
Dritte heirath' i' einmal."

Friend Stevenage reminds me of him, somehow. Though which of the three he really wanted to marry is a problem beyond me, I admit. She'd have had to keep him, whoever she was."

21
THE PUBLIC LIBRARY

The Chief Librarian of the Strickland Regis public library was an alert little man, full of enthusiasm for his work. His tawny hair, bright eyes, and staccato movements, called up in Wendover's mind the comic simile of a squirrel in horn-rimmed spectacles. Sir Clinton could hardly have fallen upon a better man for his purpose; for Tenbury was immensely proud of the library under his charge and liked nothing better than to talk about it.

"Yes, Sir Clinton," he explained, "in theory, our readers' tickets are personal ones; but in practice we don't bother about that. If anyone brings a ticket to the counter and asks for a book that's available, we let them have the book whether it's their own ticket they show or not. We don't bother much about red tape. In my view, my job's to get books into the hands of the public. I want to encourage people to read as much as I can. I'm a librarian, not a bookkeeper. A little joke of mine, that; but it puts the thing in a nutshell. Books are no good to anyone if you keep them standing on the shelves here all the time."

"I quite agree," Sir Clinton said, heartily. "Now would you mind explaining your system? Suppose I were a local reader, how would I get a book out of the Library and how would I return it in proper form?"

"You'd have to apply for a ticket, first, and get two householders to sign your application. Then we'd supply you with the ticket. Here's one. It's got a number printed on the cover, you see, and a space inside for writing your name and address. You bring this ticket with you whether you want to take a book away or consult it in the library: the system's the same in both cases. You look up the book in the catalogue and find its shelf-number. Say it was H.144. You go to the indicator-board and look up H.144. If the figures are in red, the book's out. If H.144 appears on the indicator in black, you know the book's available. That saves needless trouble at the counter, you see? You go to the counter, if your book's indicated as available, and you give the number H.144 to the librarian there. You also hand in your ticket. He looks at the printed number on your ticket and jots that down, together with H.144 in our record-book. Then he goes to the indicator and twists a knob which reverses the H.144 plate so as to show its other side, with the figures printed in red. That shows the book's not available now. At the same time, he slips your ticket into a slit behind the H.144 plate in the indicator. Then he gets the book from the shelves and hands it over to you."

"And when I bring the book back again, the process is reversed, more or less?"

"Yes. You hand in the book at the counter. The librarian looks inside the cover and sees the press-mark H.144. He goes to the indicator, turns H.144 from red to black, and collects your ticket from the slit. He hands the ticket back to you at the counter and replaces the book on the shelves. The system's nearly automatic. Any untrained boy can learn it in a couple of minutes."

"And the only record made is the entering up of the two numbers: the ticket-number and the press-mark?"

"We don't need anything more," Tenbury pointed out—"We can find out from that list which books are most in demand and also what books have been drawn from the library with a particular card. We can't tell, of course, whether a book has been read on the premises or taken home by the reader."

"For my purposes, that doesn't matter," Sir Clinton explained. "Now, I'd like you to do this for me, if you will, Mr. Tenbury. Look up the ticket-numbers of the people at Carron Hill: Mr. Castleford, the late Mrs. Castleford, Miss Castleford, and Miss Lindfield. Then find out for me, please, what books have been read or consulted by means of these four tickets during the last six months. And jot down the date on which each book was called for. I know it will mean a good deal of work, but it's likely to be of importance."

"I'll do it myself," Tenbury volunteered without hesitation. "I'll have a list ready for you before we close the library tonight. There's really nothing in it, as you can see for yourself."

"Thanks," Sir Clinton said gratefully. "I don't think your time will be wasted. By the way," he added, "I noticed a Stevenson thermometer screen in the grounds outside. Do you do anything in the meteorological line?"

"We do what we can," Tenbury said modestly, but with some pride. "Mr. Saddell of Beechcroft generously presented us with a very good outfit: Jordan sunshine recorder, maximum and minimum thermometers, anemometer, barograph. I take the records myself."

"They may turn out to be very useful," Sir Clinton said, with unconcealed satisfaction. "Perhaps, later on, you'll go over them with me, Mr. Tenbury?"

"I'd be delighted," the librarian replied, though in a tone which showed that he could not see what Sir Clinton had in mind.

"Then that's that. Thanks very much. I'll come back again at your closing time and see what you've made of the list of books."

When they were back in the waiting car, Wendover turned to Sir Clinton.

"What's all that about?" he demanded. "You can't expect to infer much from the weather conditions on the day of the murder—and I suppose that's what you're going to look up."

"You suppose wrong," said the Chief Constable ungrammatically. "Exercise is good for the brain, Squire. Just puzzle away at it. I'll give you this hint. It's a damned long shot, which might just hit the mark. If it doesn't—well, I shan't record it in my memoirs. These things are all right if they come off. If they don't, they make one look silly."

"Where-away now?" Wendover inquired, as he recognised that he would learn nothing more about the visit to the Library.

"Sunnyside Hospital. I want to see this Dr. Pendlebury."

At the hospital, Sir Clinton's card brought the doctor with very little delay.

"I suppose it's this motor-smash?" he asked, as he came into the room. "I'm afraid you can't see the patient. He's pretty bad. We've had to resort to blood transfusion and I'm not sure if he'll pull through even with that help."

"You had Miss Castleford for that?" Sir Clinton asked. "Did she stand it all right?"

"She was very nervous; but everything went off quite well," Dr. Pendlebury explained. "She won't be any the worse for it."

"You're accustomed to the technique of this blood business?" Sir Clinton asked. "There's some way of detecting the difference between one blood and another, isn't there? You can't transfuse unless you're sure the new blood won't do some damage?"

Once again, it seemed, they had encountered an enthusiast. Dr. Pendlebury's face took on a less formal expression as he launched into what was evidently a pet subject.

"It's quite simple," he explained. "We can classify any individual, male or female, in one of four groups according to certain properties of his or her blood. The tests depend on two things. First, the manner in which the serum of his blood reacts with the red corpuscles of the blood of people belonging to the other three groups. Second, the way his red corpuscles react with the sera of the blood of people belonging to the other three groups. It's a question of agglutination of the corpuscles—whether they clump together or not, when the serum is added."

He picked up a piece of paper and jotted down a little table which he showed them:—

	Corpuscles of Group			
Serum of Group	I.	II.	III.	IV.
Group I.	—	—	—	—
Group II.	+	—	+	—
Group III.	+	+	—	—
Group IV.	+	+	+	+

"A cross shows agglutination, a dash shows there's no agglutination in that particular case," the doctor explained. "For example,
a Group II serum will agglutinate the corpuscles of blood drawn
from Groups I and III, but it won't agglutinate the corpuscles of a
Group IV blood. And naturally, it won't agglutinate the corpuscles
of its own type of blood, Group II. The technique's a bit tricky; but
the results are plain enough and perfectly sound."

"Let's take a concrete case," Sir Clinton proposed, with an air
of having not quite grasped the point. "Your motor-smash patient,
which group is his blood in?"

"Group III."

"Then I suppose Miss Castleford's blood belongs to Group III
also. Am I right?"

"Yes, she's in Group III too."

"How does this thing go in heredity?" Sir Clinton asked. "Is
her blood in the same group as her father's?"

"Her blood might belong to her mother's group or her father's
group—not to any other," Dr. Pendlebury explained.

"H'm!" said Sir Clinton, in a sceptical tone. "Is that just one of
your scientific assertions, or is it really proved?"

"It's proved in this case, anyhow," Dr. Pendlebury declared with
a slightly triumphant smile. "I've tested his blood too, and it belongs to Group III, like hers. She takes after him. Her mother may
have had Group III blood also, for all I know, of course."

Though Dr. Pendlebury had been deceived by Sir Clinton's profession of scepticism, Wendover saw that it—and probably a good
deal more—had been merely assumed. Sir Clinton had been fish-
ing for information and had obtained it without letting the doctor
realise that he was being pumped.

"You say there are four types of blood?" Sir Clinton went on. "I
suppose the numbers of people in each of the four Groups are about
equal?"

"No, no," Dr. Pendlebury corrected. "Some thousands of cases
have been examined, and the proportions work out something like
this: In Group I, you've got about 42% of the population; Group II

is almost as numerous—41%. In Group III, there's only 12%; and only .5% of people are in Group IV."

"Now I come to business," the Chief Constable explained, as though the previous talk had been on a side-issue. "I've brought three bits of blood-stained cloth with me." He took three envelopes from his pocket and showed that they were numbered. "Could you determine from these blood stains the character of the original blood in each case. I mean could you tell me to which Group each specimen belonged?"

"There's nothing against it," said Pendlebury, confidently. "The tests work perfectly well, even in the case of old, dried-up blood."

"This may mean your having to go into the witness-box, perhaps. Care to take it on?"

"I don't mind," said the doctor. "When do you want the results? I can give you them tomorrow, if it's an urgent business."

"That's very good of you. Tomorrow, then. Of course this is strictly confidential, doctor."

When they had left the hospital, Wendover turned to Sir Clinton.

"Three bits of blood-stained cloth? I can guess what some of them are. But what's it all about?"

"I'm not sure it will lead to anything," Sir Clinton admitted frankly, "but if it was worth doing at all, it was worth doing thoroughly. It might turn out useful to have a list of the blood-groups of the people at Carron Hill; but as nothing at all may come out of it, I didn't want to make too much of a fuss. Besides, if I'd asked openly for specimens, I might not have got them."

"I saw you manoeuvred the doctor into telling you that the two Castlefords are in Group III," Wendover commented.

"Yes, it was easy enough. I could have asked him a straight question about it; but the less dust raised, the better, I think. The specimens in the envelopes were a bit of Mrs. Castleford's blouse, a piece of Castleford's bloodstained sleeve, and a bit of the handkerchief I used to tie up Miss Lindfield's cut finger. If you really want to do a public service, Squire, you might get up a scrap with

Dr. Glencaple and tap his claret. Then we'd have a complete collection of the blood of everybody, bar that boy. We shan't need them all, though; it's merely that I'd like to have full data, even if we scrap part of it in the end."

He got into the car and started the engine before continuing.

"By the way, Squire, here's the Stop Press News, fresh off the 'phone after lunch. I rang up Headquarters; and I find that Miss Lindfield bought a Colt automatic pistol lately, which wasn't mentioned on her firearm certificate. She may have forgotten to notify it; but we'll need to pull her up about it."

"Good Lord!" ejaculated Wendover, as the implications of this flashed into his mind, "Do you mean to say . . ."

"Calm yourself, Squire," Sir Clinton advised. "It was a .22 automatic that she bought, not a .32. Don't jump to conclusions too quickly."

"What could she want an automatic for?" Wendover ruminated aloud.

"To protect herself against the Castlefords, for all one can tell," Sir Clinton suggested. "They don't seem to love her much. And now, Squire, we proceed to the Chalet, where we shall find our energetic Inspector, a sergeant, probably Constable Gumley, and also some husky agricultural labourers with spades and other tools. I'm starting a Back-to-the-Land movement, and you mustn't miss the inaugural ceremony."

At the Chalet, the group he had described was waiting for him, and he led the way into the spinney where the dead cat had hung. There he marked out on the ground a rough circle of some six feet radius, with its centre under the string from which the tin can target had been suspended.

"I should dig up the soil inside that, first of all," said to the Inspector. "You've got these riddles I told you about? Good. See that every spadeful is put through the sieve. We must find these things, if they're here. If you don't find them in that circle, extend the digging a bit. And another thing, turn the sergeant and the constable on to hunt for empty cartridge-cases on the surface of the ground—anywhere within ten yards of this. I want every solitary specimen they can get. There must be plenty of them. That boy was shooting at both the can and the cat—probably at quite close range."

"I'll see to that, sir," Westerham assured him.

"Let me know this evening what luck you've had," the Chief Constable ordered.

He watched the digging operations for some time, but nothing seemed to come of them. Sergeant Ferryhill and P. C. Gumley meanwhile were searching among the grass and undergrowth with intermittent success. Each cartridge-case when found was submitted to Sir Clinton, who examined it cursorily and placed it in an envelope.

At last P. C. Gumley brought up his fourth find, and Sir Clinton inspected it like the others before putting it into storage. Wendover noticed that he paid particular attention to the base of the case.

"The things are there, right enough, Inspector," Sir Clinton said with a slight touch of elation, as he put the envelope back into his pocket. "Stick to it, and I can promise you that you'll find them, all right."

He glanced at his watch and then turned to Wendover. "It's getting near closing-time. I think we ought to be on the road again."

And with a final admonition to the Inspector, he led Wendover back to the car.

"Now for the Public Library again," he explained. "Things are going not so badly."

"What did you find in the spinney there?" Wendover demanded.

Sir Clinton put his hand in his pocket and passed the envelope across.

"Have a look at them, Squire."

Wendover examined the tiny cartridge-cases one by one. They were all, he judged, of .22 calibre. One of them differed slightly from the others in having a deep groove at the rim. Another had been slightly deformed, apparently by someone treading on it.

"I had a suspicion that some of them might be different from the rest," Sir Clinton commented. "Nice to find one's notions justified. By itself, unfortunately, it proves nothing."

"It proves somebody was using an automatic pistol in that spinney," said Wendover.

"Of course. But when? And she was killed with a .32 pistol and not a .22 automatic," Sir Clinton pointed out. "Well, we can only hope that friend Tenbury has not been labouring in vain."

In one sense, he certainly had not, for he met them with several sheets of typescript in his hand, when they were shown into his office.

"This is the list you asked for, Sir Clinton," he said, with obvious satisfaction at having got through his task so soon. "I've had several carbon copies made, in case you wanted them."

He handed over the ribbon copy of his list, and Sir Clinton, after thanking him, fell to studying it with attention. After a while, he put it down on the desk and turned to Tenbury.

"That's a very mixed bag," he observed. "But I suppose that's natural, since four people's tastes are included. H'm! It seems to be roughly made up of books on fine arts . . ."

"That's Mr. Castleford," Tenbury explained.

"Gardening and the countryside?"

"Miss Lindfield takes an interest in them."

"Travel?"

"Miss Castleford sometimes reads travel books."

"One or two books on spiritualism?"

"I think that's probably Mrs. Castleford. I've a sort of recollection that Miss Castleford took them out and laughed at them when I gave them to her. She didn't want me to think they were for herself, I think, and she mentioned Mrs. Castleford."

"Then there's fiction. Some fairly decent to begin with. Who read that, do you know?"

"Miss Lindfield and Miss Castleford. They've both got fairly good taste."

"Then I see some cheap sex novels and a few of the Sheik brand of thing."

"These would be for Mrs. Castleford, most likely. She seldom came for them herself. Miss Lindfield or Miss Castleford would ask me for 'some novel that would do for Mrs. Castleford,' and I gave them something of the sort, because I knew she liked it. She hardly ever asked for a book by name, unless it was being advertised as 'daring' or 'outspoken' or some tosh like that."

"Quite a lot of detective stories, I see."

"They were for Mr. Castleford."

Sir Clinton turned over a page in the list.

"Here's a peculiar group," he said. "I wonder if you remember anything about them: law-books, forensic medicine, workshop recipes, fireworks, and some volumes of *The Times*."

Tenbury glanced at the dates, which came all together, and shook his head.

"No, I'm afraid I don't remember anything about them. The fact is, I had a temporary assistant at that time—about two months ago—and he must have given out these books, for I certainly don't recall anything about them. He was a bad lot, that assistant. I had to sack him, because money and stamps were disappearing. I couldn't prove it, but when I sacked him without a character he made no great fuss."

"Where's he gone, do you know?"

"I never heard of him again. He drank a bit, too. I doubt if he'd get another job easily."

"That makes it a bit more difficult," Sir Clinton said, without making clear his exact meaning. "Now there's another matter. You see these dates—when these law-books were taken out. Can you give me any notion of what the weather was like, in that week?"

"I'll look up our records," said Tenbury obligingly.

"The sunshine and the maximum day-temperature will serve my purpose for the present," Sir Clinton explained.

In a few minutes, Tenbury returned with a slip of paper.

"It was a very hot week, that," he declared. "Here are the maximum temperatures: 72.2°, 84.9°, 85°, 73.4°, 79.2°, 80.9°, 74.8°. And now the sunshine record: 9.3 hours, 14.4, 13.4, 9.8, 12.5, 10.2, 12.8."

"Thanks, I'll keep that note of yours, if I may," said the Chief Constable. "And now these volumes of *The Times* for 1889-90 and 1910-11. Wendover, can you think of anything that happened in 1889?"

"The Crippen case was in 1910, if that's any help, but I can't think of anything in 1889, at the moment."

This suggestion seemed to jog Sir Clinton's memory.

"The Maybrick case was in 1889, of course," he recalled. "And after that, there was an action brought against an insurance company. Mrs. Maybrick's solicitor wanted to get his fees out of the proceeds of a policy on Maybrick's life, or something like that. H'm! That's the only thing I can remember which seems to fit."

Now that he had been reminded of it, Wendover recalled the outline of the Maybrick case; but as it was a matter of arsenic poisoning, he could not see its relevance here. Sir Clinton dropped the subject abruptly, picked up the list of books again, and ticked off some items in it, naming them as he went along:—

"Smith, *Forensic Medicine*; Hookham, *The Young Firework-Maker*; Shebbeare, *Administration of Estates Act*; *The Standard Physician*, in four volumes; Kenny, *Outlines of Criminal Law*; Henley's *Twentieth Century Home and Workshop Formulas*; Smith and Glaister, *Recent Advances in Forensic Medicine*; *The Scientific American Encyclopædia of Formulas*; and Jenks's *Book of English Law*. I'm afraid I'll have to impound these particular volumes, Mr. Tenbury. And would you mind writing your initials on the title-page of each of them, so that you'll have no difficulty in swearing to the particular copies, if need be?"

"When shall I get them back?" Tenbury demanded, his librarianship coming uppermost at the request.

"Never, most likely," Sir Clinton assured him cheerfully. "I'm going to have them treated with iodine or osmic acid; and I'm not sure they'll be pretty, after that. You won't lose by it. I'll see you get other books in their places, in any case. Would you get them for me now, please?"

Tenbury hurried off to the shelves and in a remarkably short time he was back, wheeling the collection along before him on a little waggon. Sir Clinton picked up the two volumes of recipes and hunted up a reference in each.

"H'm!" he commented, after reading the passages. "Borax, boric acid, and ammonium sulphate? I hardly think so. Alum's more likely."

He glanced casually over the remaining volumes on the waggon and then his interest seemed to kindle again. Four heavy red tomes attracted him and he picked up one of the set.

"*The Standard Physician*," he read, from the title-page, "*A New and Practical Encyclopædia . . . Especially Prepared for the Household*. Edited by Sir James Crichton-Browne, Sir William H. Broadbent, and a lot of other eminent men. You really must buy this for your library, Squire."

He turned over a page or two and then opened the book at the back.

"Hullo! Here's a cardboard mannikin, no less. Five copies of him, superimposed one on the other. No expense spared, evidently. One for blood-vessels, respiratory apparatus, etc.; another for the muscles; another for the skeleton; then the skeleton again, from the back; and finally one for organs, vessels, and nerves. Just look at this, Squire. It would be invaluable when you had a pain in the tummy and wanted to know if it was appendicitis or . . ."

He broke off abruptly. Wendover, who had been leaning over to look at the book, could see what had startled him. Clean through the cardboard mannikin, a pinhole had been drilled; and Wendover, recalling the Inspector's demonstration on his own back, saw at a glance that the pinhole corresponded exactly to the fatal wound in Mrs. Castleford's body.

". . . or merely stomach-ache," Sir Clinton concluded, making his pause seem merely rhetorical. "And now, Mr. Tenbury, when you've initialled these things, we must tear ourselves away."

Between them, they carried the books to the car and Sir Clinton again thanked the Librarian for his assistance.

"I'm just going to stop for a moment at the grocer's, if he's still open. You needn't come in, Squire."

When he came out of the shop, he seemed pleased with the result of his interview.

"What did you pick up there?" Wendover demanded.

"I merely inquired if anyone had bought alum, lately. Only one person did. Mrs. Castleford called there a couple of days before her death and asked for a couple of ounces."

Wendover was too exited about the previous discovery to pay much attention to this.

"What do you think of that pinhole?" he demanded. "Did you expect to find anything like that?"

"What a fine reputation I could get by a small lie or two," Sir Clinton said, chaffingly. "No, Squire, that was a gift from the gods, pure and simple. I'd hoped to find something in the anatomy section of that book; but the pinhole was far beyond my expectations. It clears things up remarkably and saves a lot of time barking up wrong trees."

22
NOT PROVEN

After his bustling weekend at Thunderbridge, Wendover found Talgarth Grange dull. As he came down to his solitary breakfast, a few mornings later, he was conscious of a certain dissatisfaction; and in his methodical way, he set about tracing this to its sources.

In the first place, Sir Clinton had disappointed him. He had expected to see the Castleford mystery cleared up, or, if not cleared up completely, then at least sufficiently clarified to let him see some path through the jungle of evidence. But nothing of the sort had happened. It was plain to him that Sir Clinton was still groping for crucial data and that the case was still unsolved.

Then, again, there had been a fresh atmosphere between the Chief Constable and himself in this case. In other affairs, Sir Clinton had treated him as a collaborator and had discussed the evidence as it turned up. This time, Wendover had felt himself a not-over-welcome intruder. The machine had functioned almost independently of him, and any intervention on his part had been frowned upon.

Finally, Wendover had to admit to himself that he had been disappointed in the Castlefords. He had gone to Thunderbridge in answer to the girl's call of distress, only to find on his arrival that he was apparently unwelcome. The complete Don Quixote, in fact, as Sir Clinton would say. Castleford himself had impressed Wendover unfavourably. Hilary had been entirely different from what he had expected. Even his natural chivalry had not been proof against the obvious fact that she had been something more than

255

merely disingenuous in her evidence. He was simple enough to expect candour from a young girl, and he had been shocked by the difference between his anticipations and the reality which had met him at Carron Hill.

He turned to the letters which lay beside his plate, and the sight of Sir Clinton's familiar handwriting aroused him from his rather painful researches in psychology. The first sentences of the letter served to clear away one of his grievances. As usual, Sir Clinton went straight to the point.

> My dear Squire,
>
> I may be wrong, but I got the impression that you felt rather hurt by the way in which I treated you at Thunderbridge. I could see that you had expected to come into the Castleford case on the same footing as in earlier affairs and that you resented my tacit refusal to discuss the thing with you as we went along. If you think over it, I think you will see my reasons. In other cases, you were an impartial on-looker with no axe to grind and no particular interest in the result. In the Castleford case you went into the affair with a watching brief for the Castlefords, which put you in an entirely different position. You would have given nothing away, of course; but your bias would have made frank discussions awkward to both of us, perhaps.

Wendover felt considerably relieved by this plain statement. He could see the force of it; and he recognised that there had been nothing personal in Sir Clinton's motives. The Chief Constable had kept him in the dark on grounds of pure policy.

> There seems no reason [the letter went on] why you should not have all the evidence. You can think it over; and when the case is settled up finally, we can go through it together and compare notes on

what each of us has made of it. Here, then, are the remaining points which you have not yet heard.

1. You remember the ash found in the grate of the Chalet? I submitted it to a man who specialises in micro-analysis, and he finds in it a much greater quantity of aluminium than should normally be present.

2. I submitted some of the fibres found in the wound to a microscopist who is an expert in that field. According to him, characteristic pine wood "pores" and some ribbony structure are visible in the specimens.

3. The .22 lead bullet found on the verandah had certain markings on its apex. These correspond to the pattern of the canvas facing on the old archery target which I took from Carron Hill. The weapon from which this bullet was fired had a right-hand twist in its rifling.

4. Westerham and his acolytes unearthed two nickel-covered .22 bullets in the ground where they were digging.

5. The leaden bullet fired through the Haddons' window had a rifling impress on it corresponding to left-hand rifling in the weapon.

6. The two .32 Colt automatics from Carron Hill have left-hand twists in their rifling. The rook-rifle has a right-hand twist in its rifling grooves.

7. Dr. Pendlebury's blood tests gave the following results: Philip Castleford, Group III; the blood from the coat-sleeve, Group IV; Hilary Castleford, Group III; the blood from Mrs. Castleford's blouse, Group I; Miss Lindfield's blood from my handkerchief, Group IV.

8. The examination of the books from the Public Library is not yet finished. I think my reference to the weather data probably showed you one of the

things I expect to find there; and the other thing is, I hope, in the text, though I am still busy with the matter.

9. I have looked into the Maybrick case, which seemed to be the interesting thing in the 1889-90 volumes of *The Times*. Maybrick took out an insurance policy which vested in himself and, on his death, in the trustees for behoof of his wife. After his death by poison, Mrs. Maybrick assigned the policy and her interest in it to her solicitor, to secure payment of his costs. The insurance company claimed that the policy was void; but Mrs. Maybrick and her solicitor claimed that the murder of Maybrick did not affect the interest of the assignee; whilst Maybrick's executors claimed that the murder did not affect the insurance company's liability, but only the person to whom the money was actually to be paid. The Court upheld the executors' view, on the general principle that a criminal may not profit by his crime and that therefore Mrs. Maybrick's beneficiary interest had lapsed on her conviction for the murder of her husband. Something similar turned up in the case of Crippen's estate.

You know the Scots verdict "Not Proven"? It generally means that the jury are *morally* sure that the accused committed the crime, but that *legally* the prosecution has not established its case up to the hilt. That seems to be the present position in this Carron Hill affair. You ought to be able to put your finger on the criminal; but it may be hard to prove the thing to the last dot. One jury might be satisfied; another one might not care to say: "Guilty." But both of them would be "morally certain" of the accused's guilt.

I hope to add just one further bit of evidence from the Library books, which will clinch the business;

and if you care to go down with me to Thunderbridge
in a day or two—I'll ring you up before then—you
may see the finale.

Yours

C. D.

Wendover, neglecting his breakfast, pondered for a time over
these fresh data. No. 1 suggested less to him than to Sir Clinton,
evidently. No. 2 recalled the fact that there were pines in the spinney about the Chalet. Nos. 3, 4, 5, and 6 were easy enough to
interpret. So was 7. No. 8 evidently referred to the hot spell which
Sit Clinton had found in the weather records; and a little thought
enabled Wendover to catch Sir Clinton's meaning. As to No. 9,
Wendover was at first rather puzzled by the somewhat intricate
situation, the more so as he had heard nothing of any insurance
question in connection with Mrs. Castleford. Then light dawned
on him and he began to see the case from a different standpoint.
As Sir Clinton said, it was a moral certainty, but that was a very
different thing from legal proof.

23
THE CASE AGAINST CASTLEFORD

Wendover, not altogether at his ease, glanced round the drawing room at Carron Hill. He could not forget that in the hall outside were the Inspector, Sergeant Ferryhill, and P. C. Gumley,
whom Sir Clinton had brought in his car. These people in the room
must know perfectly well that the Chief Constable had not fetched
his subordinates merely as a bodyguard. It was the number that
disquieted Wendover. Surely the Inspector alone would have
sufficed to arrest a criminal.

He glanced furtively round the group before him. Castleford,
evidently acutely nervous, was in a Chippendale armchair, his
hands gripping the arm-rests and his feet crossed and tucked under
the seat, as though he were unconsciously trying to contract himself into the smallest possible volume. His face was strained and
anxious, and he kept his eyes riveted on Sir Clinton almost as
though he expected a physical menace from that quarter. Hilary
Castleford, very white, seemed to concentrate her whole attention
on her father. From time to time she bit her under-lip to conquer a
betraying quiver at the corners of her mouth; and once or twice she
made a faint sound as though clearing her throat. Across the room,
Miss Lindfield sat in her favourite attitude, chin on hand, staring
sombrely before her. Beyond, Dr. Glencaple, apparently the least
concerned of all, leaned back in his chair and examined Castleford
with a kind of aloof curiosity faintly mingled with contempt.

"You may wonder why I have adopted this procedure," Sir
Clinton began in businesslike tones. "I admit it is quite unusual.

But not so long ago, public feelings were roused—rightly or wrongly—by some rumours about the manner in which people were questioned in private by officials. Suggestions were made that there was no unbiased person present to check the police reports of the interview. There may be very sound reasons, in this case, for forestalling any talk of that sort. I have asked Mr. Wendover, who is a Justice of the Peace, to be present as an unprejudiced witness; and to make matters still more open, I propose to put my questions in the presence of you ladies and gentlemen, so that there can be no allegations of a hole-and-corner affair in this case. I am going to call Inspector Westerham, who will take down in shorthand anything that we say."

Wendover, knowing the Chief Constable's peculiarities, might have regarded this statement as a piece of bluff, had it not been for a certain ring in Sir Clinton's tone which showed that he was in earnest. "Sound reasons in this case"? That slightly emphasised phrase set Wendover's mind to work.

"I wish to clear up certain points, one by one," Sir Clinton explained, when the Inspector had come in and seated himself at the escritoire. "In the first place, Dr. Glencaple, you believed at the moment of Mrs. Castleford's death that she had signed a will under which you, your brother, and Miss Lindfield stood to profit considerably?"

"That is so," Dr. Glencaple admitted, equably.

"On the other hand, Mr. Castleford knew that the will had not been signed, and that Mrs. Castleford, technically, was intestate at that moment?"

"Yes, I knew that," Castleford admitted in a breathless voice.

"And Miss Castleford also knew it?"

Hilary, at the sound of her name, gave a perceptible start.

"Yes," she admitted, recovering herself. "My father told me about it."

"Did he tell you what the exact state of affairs was: that if Mrs. Castleford died before making a new will, he would profit considerably, whereas under the new will he was to be worse off than before?"

Hilary threw a glance at her father, but he seemed too nervous to notice it.

"We talked over the whole affair," she confessed at last, in a reluctant tone.

"I believe, Miss Lindfield," Sir Clinton went on, "that you had first-hand information that Mrs. Castleford had not signed the new will?"

Miss Lindfield lifted her chin from her hand and nodded.

"Yes, she told me. Very stupidly, I urged her to take her time and consider carefully before she signed anything."

"With the result that you have lost the legacy which Mrs. Castleford intended that you should get?"

"Exactly," Miss Lindfield admitted, with some bitterness in her tone. "If I had let things take their course, I'd be in a different position."

"I'm going to put things bluntly," Sir Clinton said. "It comes to this. Dr. Glencaple had an apparent interest in Mrs. Castleford's death at any time in the future; Mr. Castleford had a real interest in Mrs. Castleford's dying before she had time to sign the new will; while Miss Lindfield had an interest in her half-sister's living until she signed the new will. That is what appears on the surface of the evidence."

Castleford made a slight sound like a suppressed hiccough, which still further alienated Wendover. The sight of a man in such a state of prostration was anything but pleasant.

"Take the next question," Sir Clinton pursued, paying no attention to Castleford. "Who knew that Mrs. Castleford would be at the Chalet that afternoon? Mr. Castleford certainly did, for he had arranged to walk part of the way with her. Miss Lindfield did, for she heard Mrs. Castleford speak about it at lunch that day. Miss Castleford, did you hear it referred to?"

"I don't remember hearing about it then," Hilary said, in a tone which convicted her of obvious fencing.

"But your father mentioned it to you? I thought so." Sir Clinton made no comment on this obvious disingenuousness.

"There was another person who certainly knew: Mr. Stevenage, who had arranged to meet Mrs. Castleford at the Chalet. There is also the possibility that the information was telephoned from here to an interested party outside the house."

"If you mean me," Dr. Glencaple protested politely, "I'm afraid you're barking up the wrong tree. I knew nothing about it."

"I'm merely taking possibilities into account," Sir Clinton assured him suavely. "I don't think your name was mentioned."

"Now we come to a fresh matter," he went on. "At lunch that day, Miss Lindfield arranged with Frank Glencaple to meet in the spinney beside the Chalet. That arrangement was overheard by Miss Castleford and possibly by you also, Mr. Castleford?"

"I don't remember," Castleford asserted, with a catch in his voice.

Sir Clinton did not follow the matter up.

"No definite time was fixed for that meeting. Frank Glencaple, I believe, was not a very obedient child. If he were kept waiting, he might get tired or bored, and leave his post."

"That's true," Laurence Glencaple confirmed. "Everyone would agree with that."

"The reports of the boy's rook-rifle obviously helped to cover the actual shot fired by the murderer," Sir Clinton suggested. "A single explosion would have attracted attention; but after the rook-rifle had been fired again and again in the spinney, no one would pay much attention to one shot more or less. As a matter of fact, what attracted Miss Lindfield's attention was a cry which she heard at the time the fatal shot was discharged."

Constance Lindfield gave a nod of corroboration, which Sir Clinton acknowledged.

"I thought so. And I take it that the boy's presence in the spinney that afternoon was known to Miss Lindfield, Miss Castleford, and possibly Mr. Castleford. Do you definitely deny that you knew he was to be there, Mr. Castleford?" he demanded sharply.

"No, I don't," Castleford said weakly. "I don't remember. I don't really remember."

"Obviously the boy's shooting in the spinney suggested something further to the murderer," Sir Clinton continued. "It made it possible to simulate an accident with the rook-rifle. That, in its turn, made it essential that Mrs. Castleford should be killed with a single shot—apparently a stray shot from the spinney. But that demanded that Mrs. Castleford should be sitting in a certain place. At the tea-table, she would have been sheltered from a dropping shot by the verandah roof. Her chair had to be dragged along the verandah into a better position. And, as Inspector Westerham found, she was actually occupying the chair while it was being shifted into its fresh position."

"How do you make that out?" Dr. Glencaple demanded.

"Inspector Westerham compared the scrape made by an empty chair with that made by Mrs. Castleford's chair, which was much more clearly marked on the concrete flooring," Sir Clinton explained. "One possible inference from that is that Mrs. Castleford may have been unconscious while her chair was shifted. And that brings me to the morphine question."

Dr. Glencaple glanced up at this, but made no remark.

"I haven't the slightest doubt that the dose of morphine administered to Mrs. Castleford came from Dr. Glencaple's supply. He was four tablets short when I inspected his books. Five people had a chance of access to that morphine when it was in Dr. Glencaple's bag which he brought here the night he was invited to dinner: the boy Frank, Miss Lindfield, Miss Castleford, Dr. Glencaple himself, and possibly Mr. Castleford."

"I never touched it. I never knew it was there, even," Castleford protested feebly.

"I think I'm correct in saying that your brother had no chance of taking it on that occasion," Sir Clinton said to the doctor, ignoring Castleford.

"Quite correct," Dr. Glencaple agreed. "My brother was never alone from the moment he entered the house until he left it with me."

"*I* didn't steal anything from Dr. Glencaple's bag," Hilary broke in heatedly. "I didn't even know that he had morphine with him that night."

Miss Lindfield threw a faintly cynical glance towards the Castlefords. Evidently she thought it unnecessary to add her own disclaimer to the chorus.

Sir Clinton seemed to attach little importance to the point.

"All I need say," he continued, "is that somebody came into possession of four morphine tables—say two grains of morphine hydrochloride. That's more than a fatal dose in some cases. In any case, it's enough to stupefy a person in ten minutes or so—in less than that if it's injected hypodermically. Now in the case of Mrs. Castleford, the major part of the morphine was found in her stomach, which points to oral administration. Morphine has a very bitter taste and the normal person would spot its presence in a drink as soon as the first sip was taken. But I understand that Mrs. Castleford had a habit of leaving her tea to go tepid and then swallowing the contents of her cup at one gulp—and in that case she might have swallowed the whole dose before she detected the full bitterness of the drug."

"That's quite correct," Dr. Glencaple confirmed. "She might easily have gulped down the lot, from what I've seen of her way of drinking."

"You have some saccharin tablets here, perhaps, Miss Lindfield?" Sir Clinton inquired. "I'd like to see them."

Miss Lindfield rose and from a drawer produced an unopened packet of saccharin which she handed to the Chief Constable. He extracted three tablets and laid them on a table beside him.

"And now, doctor, would you mind putting down three of the morphine tablets I asked you to bring?"

Dr. Glencaple did so, and Wendover examined the two sets. The morphine tablets were not exactly the same size as the saccharin ones; but the difference was so slight that either set might have been mistaken for the other unless they were placed side by side.

"Mr. Stevenage took three tablets from Mrs. Castleford's saccharin phial—the last three tablets in it—and dropped them into her tea-cup. That, I think, was the way in which the morphine was administered. There seems to be no alternative hypothesis. He did not observe any peculiar symptoms in Mrs. Castleford, for the simple reason that Mrs. Castleford did not drink her tea immediately, but left it to grow cold, according to her usual habit. But, curiously enough, when the residue in Mrs. Castleford's cup was examined, no morphine was found in it; and the analyst found traces of saccharin."

"You mean that the cup was washed after she had drunk from it, and that some saccharin was added to a few drops of fresh tea?" Dr. Glencaple asked.

"If you can suggest anything else that covers the ground?" Sir Clinton said encouragingly.

Dr. Glencaple shook his head.

"Then the murderer must have had access to saccharin," he pointed out.

"Anyone has access to saccharin at the nearest druggist's," Sir Clinton retorted. "As a clue, it's valueless."

He glanced at the tablets on the table.

"That suggestion of mine would account for three morphine tablets," he went on. "As four are missing, we have one to account for. That one was used in the hypodermic syringe which Mr. Castleford had for injecting his wife with insulin. It might be suggested that the syringe was filled in order to give a hypodermic injection of more morphine after Mrs. Castleford had been stupefied by the dose she swallowed in her tea."

"I never had any morphine. I never put it into the syringe. I deny that," Castleford ejaculated convulsively.

"I said it *might* be suggested," Sir Clinton pointed out, coldly. "I didn't accuse anyone in particular. And, if I may say so," he added in a stern voice, "I hope that you will be as ready to give information later on, when I have to put some direct questions."

Castleford shrank back in his chair at this. Evidently he saw a net closing round him. "That little beggar will be sick in a minute or two," Wendover commented to himself after a glance at Castleford's face. "He's just in the state for it." A feeling of disgust for his former protégé came over him. A dreadful exhibition for a man to make in front of his own daughter.

"That brings us up to the actual murder," Sir Clinton continued in a matter-of-fact tone, as though murder was an event like any other. Wendover could guess that it had been purposely assumed.

"The murderer's object was to suggest accidental shooting. Hence the shifting of Mrs. Castleford's chair after she had been drugged. But accidental shooting implies death by a single shot. Therefore the murderer had to be certain of killing with the first bullet. The obvious thing would be to shoot the victim in the head. And yet Mrs. Castleford was shot through the heart."

"I hadn't thought of that," Miss Lindfield said aloud, and then grew slightly confused as if she had blurted out what was meant to be a mental comment.

"There was a sound reason for it, I think," Sir Clinton explained. "A high-velocity bullet leaves an entrance-wound smaller than its own diameter—provided that the bullet strikes at a place where there is some 'give' in the tissues. There's no such 'give' in the skin of the head, which is stretched over the bones of the skull. The murderer's idea was to shoot with a .32 calibre bullet and yet leave the impression that the wound had been inflicted with a .22 bullet—the calibre of the rook-rifle. That determined the choice between the head and the heart, I believe."

Wendover, glancing inadvertently at Dr. Glencaple, was surprised at his expression. He seemed to be waiting for the Chief Constable to make a slip in the next step of his argument. At Sir Clinton's first words, his expression altered.

"It's not so easy to shoot a person through the heart," the Chief Constable went on. "Most people have very vague—and usually erroneous—ideas of the heart's position. A medical man"—he turned politely to the doctor—"is better equipped with knowledge. But even a medical man might find it difficult to shoot his victim through the heart at, say, ten yards. You're not a crack pistol-shot, I suppose, doctor?"

"Far from it," Dr. Glencaple confessed, brusquely.

"My point is that unless the murderer was a good shot, he must have fired at very close quarters so as not to miss the heart; and yet he had to suggest that the shot was fired from far off. He had to avoid powder-blackening on the skin and singeing of the fine hairs. That was managed rather neatly. A large sheet of paper, fire-proofed with alum, was held close to Mrs. Castleford's back; and the pistol was fired just far enough away to prevent the out-rushing gas from tearing the skin. The paper shielded the skin and fine hairs from the pistol-flame, and thus we get the simulation of a shot fired from a fair distance. Some of the paper-fibres were driven into the wound and have been identified by characteristic pine 'pores' which show that it was wood-pulp paper. After the murder, the paper was burned, probably with the help of paraffin, in the grate of the Chalet. The ashes had an abnormal amount of aluminium in them, evidently derived from the alum used in partial fire-proofing of the paper."

"Ingenious," Dr. Glencaple commented, drily.

"I think you'll admit that Inspector Westerham has worked up the case very well," Sir Clinton returned, with equal dryness. "Now there was another attempt to suggest accidental death. A bullet of .22 calibre was found on the verandah. Inspector Westerham identifies it as having been fired from the rook-rifle. The markings on it correspond. Further, on its point were certain impressions corresponding with the pattern of the canvas covering of an old target which the boy Frank used to shoot at in the harness room. Obviously that bullet must have been extracted from the straw of the target by the murderer and dropped on the verandah to reinforce the false idea that the fatal shot was from a .22 weapon. That hardly helps us much, except that such a bullet must have been procured by someone, or from someone, here at Carron Hill."

Wendover shot a swift glance round the group before him. Castleford had dropped his eyes and was staring at the carpet. Hilary was gazing at Sir Clinton as though he were some dangerous animal crouching for its spring. Miss Lindfield's attitude suggested a certain detachment from the whole scene, but under her brows Wendover could see a very alert pair of eyes watching the scene. Dr. Glencaple seemed to be following Sir Clinton's reasoning with the closest attention.

"Now I come to a rather peculiar incident," Sir Clinton continued. "About half-past four that afternoon, a telegram was delivered at the Chalet to Mrs. Castleford. It had been received through the post, having been dropped into the pillar-box nearest here. Owing to the initiative of Inspector Westerham and one of his subordinates, I am able to say that it was in a very simple code and it urged Mrs. Castleford to send Mr. Stevenage away immediately, as they were likely to be spied on by Mr. Castleford. On the face of it, this was a device to get Mr. Stevenage off the premises and to leave the field clear for the murderer. There is another possible explanation, but I need not go into that. The point is that this wire was worded in a very simple code; and Mr. Castleford has informed me that he and his wife, in earlier days, used a similar code for some of their communications."

"I know nothing about it. I never sent any wire, I never heard of it until this moment. I know nothing whatever about it," Castleford protested shrilly, his words tumbling over each other in his excitement.

"I never said that you did," Sir Clinton pointed out, coldly. "I don't even say that you destroyed that telegram—for destroyed it was, by somebody. That person must have had good reason for destroying it—perhaps to conceal the fact that it contained a simple code message. But you seem something of an agnostic, Mr. Castleford. You know nothing, it appears. There's one thing you do know, however. What were the contents of the anonymous letter you found waiting for you at the clubhouse?"

Castleford seemed to wilt under this.

"I don't remember exactly," he protested feebly.

"It sent you post-haste to the Chalet, whatever it was," Sir Clinton said in a tone which seemed to brook no denial.

"That's not true," Hilary interjected harshly. "My father was never near the Chalet that afternoon. I can prove that."

Sir Clinton eyed her with obvious disfavour.

"I advise you to wait till you've heard about something which Inspector Westerham unearthed. He found that someone had been on the verandah that afternoon and had tramped on a wet paint brush. A corresponding patch of paint was found on Mr. Castleford's shoe. Also, Mr. Castleford was seen going up to the Chalet and coming away from it, just about the time of the murder. We can bring witnesses in support of that. Do you still wish to prove what you said?"

Hilary leaned forward as though to answer, but Castleford made a sudden gesture which silenced her. "Don't say anything, Hilary," he cried. "It's no use, dear. You'd only harm yourself and do me no good."

"I'm glad to see you've taken my warning," said Sir Clinton to Castleford. "Neither of you can prove an alibi for the other, in the face of the evidence we have. And now I come to the final points. The murder was done with one of the .32 automatics from Carron Hill. That pistol is covered with finger prints, so that we can make nothing out of that evidence. Who had direct access to the weapon? Miss Lindfield, Miss Castleford, Mr. Castleford, and possibly the boy Frank. That's all we can say with regard to that."

"I never touched those pistols after I put them away," Castleford asserted, though his tone was rather hopeless.

"You protest too much, Mr. Castleford," Sir Clinton retorted sharply. "There's a final piece of evidence which Inspector Westerham brought to light. The sleeve of the jacket which you wore that afternoon has a bloodstain on it. It's human blood. You haven't offered any explanation of how it came there."

"I don't know," Castleford said wearily. "I can't think how it could have come there."

Sir Clinton nodded unsympathetically.

"I didn't expect that you could."

He glanced round the group.

"That would be the police case against Mr. Castleford. As you can see, it's well-constructed and holds together. The motive is plain enough; the opportunity is accounted for; the weapon and the method have been dealt with; and Mr. Castleford's alleged alibi has broken down. Would you care to make a clean breast of it, Mr. Castleford?"

24
IN RE MAYBRICK AND CRIPPEN

Wendover's hopes had been shrinking throughout Sir Clinton's exposition of the case, but they rose again suddenly at the conclusion. "The tragedy of Hamlet, with the character of the Prince of Denmark left out." The very things to which Sir Clinton had attached most importance during his investigation had been omitted from his survey; and Wendover knew him too well to suppose that mere inadvertence had dictated this course. Fingerprints, bloodstains, library lists, the peculiarities of the various riflings, and the Maybrick case, all had gone unmentioned. Plainly there was more to come. And, whatever this was, it could hardly be meant to tell against the Castlefords or Sir Clinton would have used it in its proper sequence.

Under the spur of Sir Clinton's blunt invitation, Castleford seemed to pull himself together with a certain energy of desperation.

"You've twisted the whole of that evidence," he broke out, "distorted it to fit your case and make it tell against me. Now I'll tell you the truth, for it can't make things worse for me. I'm sick of lying, and I haven't made much of a success of it, since nobody believes me. I did get a letter at the clubhouse, a vile thing that threw me off my balance. I went up by Ringford's Meadow; but instead of going on to the copse, I turned to the left and made for the Chalet. I'd no plans in my mind, I hadn't even considered what I'd do when I saw my wife. I was clean off my balance and couldn't think clearly at all. I simply wanted a final settling-up of things between us and an end to a state of affairs that had got beyond all

271

bearing. I knew about the will she was going to make, and I'd nothing to lose. I was worked up. I'd had years of that kind of thing—she was a standing disgrace to me—and I simply couldn't stand any more of it, now that there was nothing to gain by turning a blind eye on her doings."

"Had you a pistol with you?" Sir Clinton interjected, coolly.

"No, I hadn't a weapon of any sort, not even a stick. I came out from among the trees, and there on the verandah I saw my wife sleeping, as I thought, in a chair. I went up the steps, and I saw blood on the concrete. Then, when I came nearer, I saw she was dead. It staggered me. And then I lost my head altogether."

He paused and gulped painfully once or twice.

"You see, the day I got the first anonymous letter I'd been so shaken by it that I'd toyed with the idea of threatening her with a pistol, scaring her to death. I'd dwelt a bit on that in my imagination, and I'd seen myself shooting her. Of course I never meant to do it; it was just blowing off steam in my mind. And when I was faced with her dead body, suddenly I saw the rest of the thing—the arrest, the trial . . . I ought to have given the alarm, but instead of that my whole idea was to slink away unnoticed. Then, nobody could connect me with the business, you see? But if anyone found me there, I knew what people would think. I'd looked up the position in the *Encyclopædia* from curiosity. If by any chance she died intestate, then I came in, before anyone else. That would be enough to make people suspect me. I'd lost my head altogether; I really was hardly responsible for my actions at the moment. Finding her there, like that, was a terrific shock to me. Of course, it's easy enough to see now what a mistake I made. But suppose the pistol had been thrown down near at hand, who was to say I hadn't used it? Anyone would have seen I'd a motive for killing her. I simply made off. And as soon as I'd done that, of course there was no going back. I had to see the thing through, somehow, and stick to my story that I'd never been near the Chalet at all. I persuaded my daughter to back me up in my lies. There was nothing else for it, once the mistake had been made. And that's how it happened," he ended lamely.

If it was acting on Castleford's part, it was good enough to deceive Wendover. There had been a ring of hysteria in the confession; but after all, Castleford was a weak creature. And a weak creature might quite well have acted just in the way which he had described. He couldn't know that the pistol was missing; and if he had been found there, with a used firearm nearby, he would have been in a very awkward fix. Circumstantial evidence is a terror when there are no witnesses to rebut it.

And behind all this, Wendover saw a solution of another puzzle. Hilary, believing her father innocent, had sent out her S.O.S. for Sir Clinton. After all, the case against Mrs. Fleetwood in the Lynden Sands affair had seemed even more deadly than this one against Castleford. Then she had told her father what she had done; and he had taken fright and had infected her with his panic. Naturally she had regretted her move and had shown that plainly when Sir Clinton appeared on the scene.

Sir Clinton, to Wendover's surprise, made no comment on Castleford's statement.

"I said, a few minutes ago," he pointed out, "that the case I elaborated was a well-constructed one. It's too well-constructed, in fact, to be the result of mere accident. One can't help seeing the hand of an author in it. Or, better, perhaps, one can't help seeing the chess-player moving the pieces on the board to suit his game. The boy in the spinney, the arrival in the nick of time of that code telegram which takes Stevenage off the scene, the letter waiting at the clubhouse to drive Mr. Castleford to fury and bring him up to the Chalet, the shot that puts Mrs. Haddon on the alert, the other shot that startles Miss Lindfield: the whole series of events suggests a plan of campaign and not a jumble of accidents. I gave you what I called 'a well-constructed case'; but it was the murderer who constructed it, not I. It's a case within a case, intended to involve Mr. Castleford up to the neck. And, as usual, the murderer was a shade too clever. If the pistol had been left beside the body, things would have looked even blacker for Mr. Castleford, perhaps."

Wendover, glancing at the Castlefords, saw a sudden relaxation in their previous strain. Castleford was listening with an expression

273

which showed that he could hardly believe what he heard. Hilary, leaning back in her chair, seemed to have gone limp in her relief; and her big hazel eyes were fixed on Sir Clinton as though she were seeing him for the first time.

"I'll take some points in the evidence," Sir Clinton went on briskly. "First of all, the letter at the clubhouse. It was on different paper from the others, wasn't it, Mr. Castleford? Did you compare the writing with that of the other anonymous letters?"

Castleford shook his head.

"It was on white paper, I remember; but I didn't pay any heed to the writing. It was illiterate, like the other writing and looked much the same to me. I never thought of comparing it—I couldn't, in fact, because I'd burned the others. And I burned it, too."

"Did it mention a time when you could go to the Chalet with advantage?"

"Yes, it said that if I went there about a quarter past five . . ."

He stopped abruptly and Sir Clinton did not press him.

"You see? The hand of the chess-player moving the piece to suit the game," Sir Clinton observed. "And quite obviously that letter came from someone who knew more than the original anonymous writer could: Mr. Castleford's habit of going to the clubhouse once a week to read the papers, and also the fact that Mrs. Castleford and Stevenage would be at the Chalet that afternoon. As to the writing, any illiterate scrawl would do, in these circumstances. No expert forgery was needed.

"Then there's the code telegram. Mr. Castleford certainly didn't send that. It was the chess-player again, moving Mr. Stevenage out of the way. But if it wasn't Mr. Castleford, it must have been someone else who was deep in Mrs. Castleford's confidence; for she could read the code at once. The murderer knew that other people could read it also—hence the disappearance of the telegram from the verandah. That was another slip, I think.

"Take the morphine-saccharin business. That again points to someone perfectly familiar with the state of things at Carron Hill. And again, you have the slip—the loading of the dice against Mr. Castleford by putting morphine in the hypodermic syringe."

Wendover stole a glance round the group before him. The two Castlefords, now evidently completely reassured, were watching Sir Clinton with close attention. Dr. Glencaple's expression puzzled Wendover, with its faint show of suspicion mingling with scepticism. Miss Lindfield, with slightly lowered head, was regarding the Chief Constable under knitted brows, as though intent on following his argument.

"Mrs. Castleford bought the alum which was used to fireproof the sheet of paper used by the murderer. She also inquired at the post-office for some information which the murderer needed in order to synchronise events. That was most ingenious, making the poor creature collect the very things which were to be used against her and thus blocking the trail for a detective. But from what I have gathered about the relationships at Carron Hill, Mrs. Castleford did not run errands for Mr. Castleford or her stepdaughter. It was the other way about. If she did these errands, it must have been for someone who had influence with her, I think."

"She bought the alum for me," Miss Lindfield interrupted in a dispassionate tone. "She had a recipe for an alum eye-wash which she insisted on my trying. I let her get the alum for it, but I didn't think much of it."

"Thanks," Sir Clinton said. "And the post-office inquiries?"

Miss Lindfield shook her head.

"No, that had nothing to do with me."

Sir Clinton made a faint gesture, as though vexed with himself for having forgotten a point.

"Of course! I remember I asked you about the hours of collection from the nearest pillar-box, and you couldn't tell me. I was surprised at that, Miss Lindfield, for you've such a reputation for efficiency generally. You staggered the Inspector here by your minute legal knowledge about intestacy and its results. He hadn't expected it."

If Miss Lindfield suspected a side-thrust here, she did not show it. She gave the Inspector a friendly smile and then turned her eyes back to Sir Clinton.

"One picks up that kind of information by chance, and somehow it sticks in one's mind," she explained.

"Sometimes, of course, one has to refresh one's memory," Sir Clinton suggested. "I had to do that myself, lately, and I went to the Strickland Regis Public Library. And that reminds me that you people at Carron Hill seem to read a very peculiar selection of books."

Miss Lindfield glanced up sharply at this, but her features betrayed no sign of perturbation.

"I looked into Smith and Glaister's *Recent Advances in Forensic Medicine*, for instance," Sir Clinton went on in a casual tone, "and curiously enough, on page 13, I found the statement that a wound is smaller than the bullet which causes it, in some circumstances. The same thing is to be found on p. 166 of Smith's *Forensic Medicine*. And in both books there is a discussion of powdermarkings on the victim's skin. It's all in the way of business with me; but these books seemed peculiar reading for say, Miss Castleford or Miss Lindfield or Mr. Castleford. I don't think Mrs. Castleford was very likely to have looked into them."

Wendover saw Hilary glance suddenly towards Miss Lindfield and then look away again before she caught her eye. Castleford kept his eyes fixed on Sir Clinton, but seemed rather puzzled by the turn of the talk. Miss Lindfield was evidently following with keen attention.

"Another book on the Carron Hill list was less extraordinary," Sir Clinton continued. "It's a large work called *The Standard Physician*—a popular book on medical matters. At the end of the first volume there's one of these cardboard mannikins which open out and show the relative positions of the bones, nerves, muscles, and so on in the body. Curiously enough, there's a pinhole through that mannikin. And, more curious still, the pinhole almost exactly reproduces the track of the bullet through Mrs. Castleford's heart."

He turned to Dr. Glencaple.

"You're accustomed to auscultation and palpation in your practice, doctor. You know where the heart is, exactly, in the human body. Naturally you wouldn't need the help of a mannikin to tell you where to shoot. But what about a layman? Wouldn't he find the mannikin indispensable?"

"I expect he would," Dr. Glencaple agreed shortly.

"I know that I should, myself," Sir Clinton admitted. "It was my own ignorance that suggested the mannikin to me. Then I looked into some books of recipes to see if I could find anything about the fireproofing of paper. You can manage it, in a way, by soaking a sheet of paper in alum solution, according to one recipe."

"Oh, alum?" Dr. Glencaple interjected, with a curious look in Miss Lindfield's direction. "Yes?"

"Then there was a firework book," Sir Clinton proceeded. "That, of course, was in your young nephew's province. It gives some directions for making slow-match or touch-string. Did he make any of that, by the way?"

"Yes, I remember his showing us some, one night," Dr. Glencaple confirmed.

"I thought it likely," Sir Clinton said in a rather indifferent tone. "Then there were three legal books—again a curious choice in literature. I read through them myself, to see what I could find. There doesn't seem to be any doubt that they throw some light on Mrs. Castleford's death. Here's a quotation from Kenny's *Outlines of Criminal Law.*"

He drew a sheet of paper from his pocket and read:

"'As regards the effect of felonious homicide upon rights of property, it should be noted that both murder and manslaughter debar the killer from receiving any benefit under his victim's Will.' And it goes on to quote Crippen's case. Crippen tried to convey his rights in his dead wife's estate to someone else by making a will before he was executed. But it's a principle of English Law that a criminal may not profit by his crime, and the Court therefore decided that Crippen had no rights at all in the estate of his murdered wife. Something of the same sort turned up in the Maybrick litigation over an insurance policy.

"That principle of English Law lies at the root of what I called 'a case within a case.' The object of that well-planned manoeuvre was to get Mr. Castleford convicted of murder. Had that happened, Mr. Castleford would have lost all rights in his wife's estate. He could not have touched a penny of it, nor could he have disposed of any of his rights in it by will. It would have gone to the next-of-kin, whoever that may be.

"Now here again, the Carron Hill reading list covers the ground; for on it I found Shebbeare's *Administration of Estates Act*, which discusses that very question in detail. In the Appendix, there's a table showing the order of inheritance in the case of intestacy. There's a similar account in Jenks's *Book of English Law*, by the way; and it also is on the Carron Hill list. Here's the order as given in Shebbeare's book:

1. Spouse.
2. Spouse and Issue.
3. Spouse and any of the persons specified below except Issue.
4. Issue.
5. Parent.
6. Brothers and sisters of the whole blood.
7. Brothers and sisters of the half blood.
8. Grandparent.
9. Uncles and aunts of the whole blood.
10. Uncles and aunts of the half blood.
11. The Crown.

Mrs. Castleford had no issue, no grandparents alive, no surviving uncles and aunts.

"Thus in case of intestacy on Mrs. Castleford's part, her estate would pass to Mr. Castleford for life. But if he had been condemned for murder, he could not dispose of his interest in the estate in any way. The next heir would come in at once. Miss Lindfield was good enough to point out to me herself, at an earlier interview, that she was the next claimant."

Miss Lindfield's coolness did not forsake her even under this reminder.

"That is so," she said, briefly. "Naturally, I looked the thing up, just to see how we stood."

"After the murder?" Sir Clinton inquired suavely.

Miss Lindfield lost something of her equanimity. She thought for a moment or two, as though weighing something important.

"No, not after the murder," she admitted finally. "Before it, when the change in her will was mooted."

"So I suppose you were the person who borrowed Shebbeare's book and the other legal ones from the Library?"

"Yes," Miss Lindfield admitted, and immediately looked as if she could have bitten her tongue.

"And the volumes of *The Times* dealing with the lawsuits over the Crippen and Maybrick estates, too, perhaps?"

"No," Miss Lindfield contradicted coolly. "That must have been someone else. I didn't."

Sir Clinton's manner betrayed nothing of his thoughts on this reply. He dropped the subject and took up a fresh line of evidence.

"Inspector Westerham impounded the jacket which Mr. Castleford was wearing on the afternoon of the murder. There was a large stain of blood on one sleeve, which looked suspicious, especially as Mr. Castleford could give no explanation of it. This was another of these neat little touches which helped to build up the case within the case and implicate Mr. Castleford. Fortunately, it represents merely another slip on the murderer's part."

Castleford gave vent to a tittering laugh at this.

"Dr. Pendlebury tells me that there are four distinct types of blood. The blood on Mr. Castleford's sleeve belongs to Group IV. Mrs. Castleford had Group I. blood, so that obviously the stain was not her blood. Mr. Castleford and Miss Castleford both have Group III. blood, which shows that it was not either of them who made the stain. That stain was put on the coat while it hung in the wardrobe upstairs, with the object of strengthening the case against Mr. Castleford; and the person who put it there was someone with Group IV. blood. Such people aren't over common. Only one person in every twenty has Group IV. blood."

Despite himself, Wendover found his eye seeking Miss Lindfield. He saw her glance down at the bandaged hand in her lap. Then, with a feline movement, she braced herself like an animal at bay, and turned to face Sir Clinton. Wendover recalled the Shakespearean quotation which Sir Clinton had used, and now he could see the real interpretation of it. "I must be cruel, only to be kind." The cruelty was for Miss Lindfield, the kindness for the Castlefords. "Thus bad begins, and worse remains behind." It required very little imagination to see the meaning of that, now.

"I don't think there will be much difficulty in finding this person with Group IV. blood," Sir Clinton continued. "We can put that aside, at present, and come to another slip made by the murderer. The crime was actually committed with a .32 pistol; but the murderer purchased a .22 calibre Colt automatic, which played its part in the tragedy. The slip here was in forgetting that any gunsmith who sells a firearm must report the sale within forty-eight hours to the chief officer of police who issued a firearm certificate to the purchaser. Thus, although that .22 automatic was bought in an obscure gunsmith's in London, the police here had a report of the purchase inside a couple of days.

"You remember the vagueness in the appointment made with the boy in the spinney; and Miss Lindfield will recall that she was much later in reaching the spinney than the boy had expected. Naturally, being the kind of boy he was, he got tired of waiting and went away, taking his rook-rifle with him. That got him off the premises, quite naturally. But from the murderer's point of view, it was essential to suggest that he was still in the spinney at a much later period. This is where the .22 pistol became indispensable. The murderer removed the nickel-cased bullet from a .22 automatic cartridge and substituted for it one of the .22 rook-rifle bullets. Then a shot was fired through Mrs. Haddon's window to make it appear as if the boy were still firing in the spinney. But here the murderer made yet another slip. The rook-rifle's barrel has grooves with a right-hand twist, whereas the Colt automatics have a left-hand spiral in their rifling. The shot struck the window-curtain and was checked to some extent before it hit the wall of the room; and although it was deformed, the type of the rifling is easily distinguished. That shot was not fired from the rook-rifle at all, and is no proof that the boy was in the spinney at that time.

"Then there was the shot which went through Miss Lindfield's cardigan which she was carrying over her arm in the spinney. That also, I suspect, came from the .22 automatic.

"But this does not finish the work that .22 pistol had to do. It had to provide a perfect alibi for the murderer by going off—to represent the fatal shot—when the murderer was safely away from the Chalet after the real killing had been done under cover of earlier shots. Inspector Westerham found two strings tied to tree-branches in the spinney and one of these strings was charred at the end. We know that the boy Frank had been making fireworks, a slow-burning string amongst them. That inevitably suggests a use of touch-string to bring about the firing of the pistol. I don't profess to give you exact details, but I think it was done in this way, more or less. A long piece of twine was tied to the tree-branch. At the lower end, it had a slip-noose which enclosed the trigger and the back trigger-guard of the pistol. The twine was then looped up and tied with touch-string, so that the pistol now hung say three feet higher than before. When the touch-string burned down, the knot in it would be broken and the original twine would straighten out, allowing the pistol to drop to its original lower position. Naturally, as the jerk came at the end of the fall, the slip-noose would tighten round the trigger and trigger-guard; the trigger would be pulled back to explode the pistol. Of course the safety-grip in the butt of the pistol must have been tied down to put it out of action. And since there were two shots reported by Mrs. Haddon while she was at her cottage-door, I take it that the twine had been twice looped up, each loop being fitted with its own piece of touch-string—one short piece for the first shot, and a longer length for the second shot. I gave you that merely as a surmise just now. I'll come to the evidence immediately.

"You might reasonably ask: Why all this manoeuvring? It had a double object. The first was to provide a perfect alibi for the criminal; the second was to make the case against Mr. Castleford more deadly by suggesting a carefully-thought-out crime, a long-pondered murder and not merely a shooting done in sudden exasperation. A jury might pity a man driven momentarily beyond endurance; but they would have no mercy in the case of a murder thought out in cold blood. And the essential thing was to ensure the conviction of Mr. Castleford. That was the big gamble in the whole affair.

"Now I come to the evidence I mentioned. For whom did the .22 automatic provide an unassailable alibi? Obviously for the person who was talking to Mrs. Haddon when the shot was fired. Who heard a cry—from a drugged woman!—at the moment of the shot? Miss Lindfield, and no one else. Who had the best chance of removing and hiding the .22 pistol between the time of the murder and the arrival of the police? Miss Lindfield, since she was alone at the Chalet then. Finally, matches were needed to light the touch-string. Miss Lindfield does not smoke; and yet she had a box of matches in her cardigan pocket that afternoon. I suppose she took them out of it when she hung up her cardigan to shoot a hole in it."

He turned to Miss Lindfield, who had now thrown off her mask and was staring at him with an expression of rage and dismay.

"That's a very pretty story," she sneered. "You've supposed this and suggested that and hinted at something else. But it's all guess-work. It's all lies."

"I haven't told you everything," Sir Clinton returned, in an unruffled tone. "There was a spell of hot weather when you consulted these books in the Library, and your fingers were slightly moist. We had no difficulty in developing up fingerprints with osmic acid on all the crucial pages and they tally exactly with specimens of your fingerprints which I took the trouble to obtain."

Miss Lindfield shrugged her shoulders with an affectation of contempt.

"*That* kind of evidence wouldn't carry you far," she said.

For a second or two Sir Clinton looked her over speculatively, as though he were gauging something in his mind. Then, apparently, he decided to deliver the finishing stroke.

"One bit of evidence I did not mention," he said deliberately. "It's this. Inspector Westerham made a search in the spinney where the twine was hanging. Imbedded in the ground under the twine, he found the cases of two exploded .22 automatic cartridges. My 'guess-work' accounts for the presence of these things rather neatly. They correspond to the two shots fired while you were at Mrs. Haddon's cottage."

"That doesn't prove I had anything to do with them," Miss Lindfield pointed out.

"No, it doesn't. You're quite right," Sir Clinton admitted instantly. "But we can settle that question, one way or the other, without much difficulty. Each automatic leaves its own peculiar marks on an ejected cartridge-case: the mark of the extractor-hook, the impression of the striker-pin, and some smaller marks due to imperfections in the breech. I have the empty cases from the spinney in my pocket. If you'll be good enough to bring down your Colt automatic, we can fire a shot or two from it and make comparisons."

Miss Lindfield went suddenly white under her make-up. At this decisive moment, her mask of indifference slipped aside and Wendover glimpsed the real woman who had moved in such apparent detachment across the stage of the Carron Hill drama. Behind that unruffled screen had raged a turmoil of emotions: hate, envy, greed, malice, ruthlessness, fear; and now, in a flash of revelation, that sinister brotherhood stood unveiled. Fear was in her eyes, all the others were on her lips. But, though baffled, she kept her head high and looked Sir Clinton in the face. She seemed to be putting some unspoken question and seeking the answer in his eyes.

"I haven't brought any charge against you—yet," the Chief Constable said slowly, with the faintest accentuation of the last word.

Miss Lindfield nodded curtly, as though this answered her question. She glanced round the group, and when her eyes rested on Laurence Glencaple her lips twisted in a wry smile.

"I've made rather a mess of your affairs, Laurie. Sorry."

Then she turned, still with that crooked smile on her face, and left the room. Sir Clinton glanced at Westerham, who nodded reassuringly.

"It's quite all right, sir. I gave the orders. She can't get out of the house."

Sir Clinton made no reply. He leaned back in his chair, outwardly indifferent, but alert for a sound. Suddenly it came, the sharp crack of a small-bore pistol in an upper room. The Chief Constable was the only one of the group who did not start.

"Sometimes a jury of one is more effective than twelve men in a box," he said in a level tone. "And British juries have a rooted distaste for sending a woman to the drop if they can wriggle out of it with any decency. Will you go up with the Inspector, Dr. Glencaple? I had an idea we might need a medical man here."

Dr. Glencaple looked at him with a sudden suspicion, but apparently decided that the less said the better.

"Poor Connie," he said, with more feeling than Wendover expected. "In spite of it all, I'm sorry to see her end up like this."

"She was a devilish clever girl," Sir Clinton admitted soberly. "It's a pity she wasn't clever enough to see that a few thousands in the hand are better than £40,000 in the bush."

He turned to Castleford.

"I think I'd get Miss Castleford off the premises, if I were you. This isn't a nice business, and she's better out of it."

>>> If you've enjoyed this book and would like to discover more great vintage crime and thriller titles, as well as the most exciting crime and thriller authors writing today, visit: >>>

The Murder Room
Where Criminal Minds Meet

themurderroom.com